Jamie Costello lives in London and is the author of acclaimed YA thriller *Monochrome*. Under her own name, Laura Wilson, she is the author of six educational books on historical subjects for eight-to-twelve-year-olds, and thirteen critically acclaimed psychological thrillers, including the DI Stratton series. Her books have been shortlisted for many awards, including the Crime Writers' Association Gold Dagger, and she has won both the CWA Historical Mystery Award and the French Prix du Polar Européen. She was the Programming Chair for the Harrogate Crime Writing Festival in 2009, a co-programmer of the Killer Women Crime Writing Festival, and is also the *Guardian*'s crime fiction critic. *The Midnight Clock* is her second novel for young adults.

ALSO BY JAMIE COSTELLO

Monochrome

jamie costello

THE MIDNIGHT CLOCK

ATOM

First published in the United Kingdom in 2024 by Atom

1 3 5 7 9 10 8 6 4 2

A CIP catalogue record for this book
is available from the British Library.

ISBN: 978-0-3490-0392-4

Typeset in Dante by M Rules
Printed and bound in Great Britain by Clays Ltd, Elcograf S.p.A.

Papers used by Atom are from well-managed forests
and other responsible sources.

Atom
An imprint of
Little, Brown Book Group
Carmelite House
50 Victoria Embankment
London EC4Y 0DZ

An Hachette UK Company
www.hachette.co.uk

www.littlebrown.co.uk

To Paddy, with love

Author's Note

Some liberties have been taken with days of the week, which may not correspond to calendar dates for the relevant years.

Holloway Prison, on which the prison in this book is based, was the largest women's prison in the UK until its closure in 2016. Notable inmates included suffragettes Emmeline Pankhurst and Emily Wilding Davison; Irish Republicans Maude Gonne and Constance Markievicz; Diana Mosley, wife of fascist party leader Oswald Mosley; and Edith Thompson and Ruth Ellis, both of whom were convicted of murder and hanged in 1923 and 1955 respectively. Public unease over the execution of Ruth Ellis helped to pave the way for the abolition of the death penalty in the UK.

The case of Ruth Ellis was not the only one which led to calls for the abolition of the death penalty. Timothy Evans, hanged for the murder of his infant daughter in 1950, was later found to be innocent, and in 1953 Derek Bentley, aged only 19, was hanged after taking part in a robbery in which a policeman was shot dead by another teenager, Christopher Craig (who was too young to be executed, and served a prison sentence). All of these cases influenced the writing of *The Midnight Clock*, in particular the character of Annie Driscoll – both Evans and Bentley had special needs, although this is not how it would have been described in the 1950s. Both have been the subjects of feature films: *10 Rillington Place*, directed by Richard Fleischer and made in 1971, remains the best on-screen account of what happened to Timothy Evans, and *Let Him Have It* (1991, directed by Peter Medak) is the story of Derek Bentley. There is also a film about Ruth Ellis: *Dance with a Stranger* (1985, Mike Newell).

Chapter 1

'Seriously?' I hiss at Dad as Skye takes her bags through to his bedroom. 'She's *moving in*? Like, *now*?'

He closes the door and motions me over to the other side of the sitting room, which is still full of unpacked boxes, so we won't be overheard. '*Millie.*' That comes with the slightly crooked and patronising you'll-understand-when-you're-older smile I've seen a lot of recently.

'Stop looking at me like that.'

'Like what?'

'Like you're being so patient because I'm being immature for not just fitting in with what *you* want. I don't have to be "older" –' I do air quotes to irritate him – 'to know a dick move when I see one.' I fold my arms and glare at him.

'I didn't say that—'

'You don't need to. And I understand already – you're a self-ish twat.'

1

'*Millie.* I can't just change everything because your mum's decided to extend her holiday.'

'Right, so this is Mum's fault.'

'I didn't say that. But Skye's given up her place – I can't just tell her to find somewhere else until you can go home. And anyway,' he cranks the smile up a notch, 'this way you can get to know each other.'

'I don't want to get to know her.'

'*Millie.*'

'And stop saying my name like that! It's *really* annoying.' It's pointless carrying on this conversation, so I stomp off to my room.

So much for my first night at Dad's new flat. Aunt Saff was staying with me at our house the first week Mum was away, but then she decided to stay on in Greece for a while and Saff had to go back home to Cornwall. They were never going to let me stay in Dalston on my own, so Dad had to rush out and buy me a bed.

I guess Skye was always going to move in with him, only it wasn't meant to start while I was staying. I've met her a couple of times: massively awkward meals in restaurants with him doing this weird 'Jolly Dad' act because he's so nervous, and then telling me how the situation is 'far from ideal' – like it's some sort of natural disaster and not totally his fault.

Although . . . If Skye's here, maybe it'll stop Dad trying to *explain* it to me all the time. He does it like he's helping with a maths problem, not trying to justify leaving Mum for a woman twenty years younger who mostly talks in inspirational quotes. Last time he tried it I ended up calling him an old perv, so it wasn't exactly *my* finest hour, either. He looked so upset that I felt terrible, but kind of glad at the same time because of the way he treated Mum, so then of course I hated myself again.

The flip-flop emotions are real. I don't want to be angry all the time when there's nothing I can do about any of this. At least having to revise for exams will stop Dad trying to take me out for treats to try and make it up to me, as if I'm six, not sixteen. He's already given me £20 – guilt money, left on the pillow with a post-it note saying 'Love Dad xx' – like *that* makes up for anything. Having my own room is a relief, though, because it's not like this is a big flat and at the moment there isn't even a sofa I could sleep on.

It's OK for Mum. Her friend Cathy's got a villa with an actual private beach, which is where they're staying. I completely get it, though – even without the private beach – because Mum's been really unhappy, and I'm in favour of whatever makes her feel better.

My room has quite a high ceiling, but it's tiny: just enough space for the bed and the other thing Dad bought, which is this really horrible-looking Disney Princess chest of drawers. I've got no issue with sitting on the bed all the time, but there's nowhere to hang anything except a hook on the back of the door. This place used to be a prison before they converted it, so maybe this was one of the cells – except I think they knocked most of it down and started again. Mum said Dad had really lost it when I told her he'd bought a flat here, because ... well, creepy. Voices trapped in the walls. Guilt and fear and sadness, all of that. Not that it seems to bother Dad – he even kept the big old prison clock that was on the hall wall when he bought the flat.

With sunny rooms and no bars on the windows, you'd never know it used to be the biggest women's prison in the country. The only thing here that isn't new and shiny is that clock. I must have gone past this place hundreds of times on the bus coming home from school, but I never even thought about it. Dad said they've had loads of famous prisoners here, although I didn't recognise any of the names he mentioned.

It feels weird, knowing that. Most of my friends think it's cool, but they don't have to sleep here. It's good they think that, though, because it sort of makes up a bit for the five years when Dad was the constipated man in the Laxulite ads. I didn't even tell Yasmin, but of course someone had to recognise him so about thirty seconds later the entire school knew, and it was just really . . .

Urrgh, I can't even. *So* funny, right? Dad was an actor before he gave it up and started writing children's books. Mum's an illustrator, so she did the pictures – a whole series about a panda cub who lives in a village full of pandas who are farmers and have shops and things, and the little panda has very basic adventures where he's always home in time for tea. The books have been translated into about forty languages and made into cartoons, which is why Dad could afford this place. Actually, I think Laxulite maybe paid for some of it, as well – plus, we get a lifetime's supply of the stuff. This fancy box arrives once a year, at Christmas, with pictures of holly and reindeer and everything, which is just unbelievably *wrong*. Let's just hope he's remembered to tell them his new address, because if it's sent to our house Mum will probably find a way to feed him the whole lot when he finally comes over to collect the rest of his stuff.

I hope whatever new arrangement we have when Mum gets back isn't going to end up like I'm this piece of property and they're fighting over who gets to have it when. I was properly relieved, though, when Dad left, because the atmosphere at home had been horrible for ages. During lockdown it was just . . . No words. Not that it's been exactly great without him, because Mum's pretending to be cool with the whole thing when she really, obviously isn't – but it's better than having that hair-trigger feeling the whole time, just waiting for the next explosion. Plus, I couldn't bear to talk to anyone about it while the whole build-up to him leaving was going on. Yaz kept asking me what the matter was and I just felt like I couldn't go there because if I did then I couldn't carry on pretending everything was going to be OK. I don't blame her for being pissed off at me, though, because sad people aren't exactly fun. I know she's dying to see what it's like here. I feel like it'll be too awkward with Skye right now, so I'll give her a virtual tour, to try and make up for everything . . .

I bash the pillow – which helps a bit, so I do it some more. Why can't stuff just go back to the way it was before, when everything was OK with Mum and Dad? Or maybe not totally OK, but more OK than this, anyway. FML.

Dad knocked on the door about three hours ago to say dinner was ready, but I said I didn't want any. I'm too angry to be hungry, and I don't want to see either of them, but I am dying to pee, and it's been quiet for about the last twenty minutes, so I reckon they must've gone to bed . . .

I clean my teeth, then stand under the shower for ages, trying to get myself calm enough to sleep. On the way back to bed I stop to look at the prison clock. It's fixed to the wall, quite high up, and has a round face in a wooden frame, and Roman numbers. Dad's put up these two neon signs he got from a junk shop on either side of it. There's a blue one saying 'Casino', which is OK, and an orange one saying 'Massage Parlour' which I'm really hoping I can get him to take down, because *eww*.

Weird how he managed to get those but forgot to buy any furniture – I mean, priorities, much? I suppose they must switch off, but Dad's left them glowing eerily in the dark. I'm surprised how dull the clock looks in comparison, but when I look closer I realise it's because there's no glass, so the neon isn't reflecting. There's obviously supposed to be, because there's a sturdy wooden frame, but it must have got broken.

The clock face must have been white originally, but it's greyed with dirt and age, a kind of off-cream. The Roman numerals are painted on, and the hands are thin and black. The name of the clockmaker – SMITH & SONS – is in little letters above the centre, with something else just below that's so small I have to stand on tiptoe to read it:

Only Now

That *totally* sounds like something Skye would say – supposedly so significant but actually just really annoying because, if you think about it for more than a nanosecond, it doesn't mean anything at all.

6

Also, 'Only Now' is a pretty horrible idea for prisoners, because then you wouldn't want it to be 'only now' – you'd want it to be the future, when they let you out. Prison is even *called* 'doing time', like time itself is the punishment.

I reach up and touch the place in the centre where the hour hand and the minute hand are joined, so it's like the place where time begins. I don't know why I need to, I just do. I expect it to be cold and hard, because metal, but it's not. Instead, it's warm against my fingertip – and alive, like *another* fingertip, as if a hand were reaching through the clock to touch mine.

Chapter 2

Whoa! I am *so* not that sort of person. Being under the same roof as Skye must be getting to me already. Next thing, I'll be coming out with the sort of crap that sounds like it should be on Pinterest in front of a bad photo of a sunrise.

I go back to my room and get into bed.

Right. Lights out. I'm done with today.

I really, really want to go to sleep, but I bet I won't be able to, because now everything is unsettling, even the flat itself. These walls don't look like prison thickness, but they better be, because I am not up for listening to Dad and Skye getting it on.

Wish I hadn't thought of that.

Might try one of those mindfulness exercises that Mum does, except you're supposed to be relaxed and right now I feel like I'm made of barbed wire.

Still, though. Deep breaths. Don't think about prisons, or about Yaz pulling away from me, or about revision or about Dad and Skye . . .

In . . .

Out ...
In ...
Out ...

I'm five again, in an abandoned fairground. There are trees grow-ing through the rides, and towering above me, way, way too high, is a helter-skelter with the paint faded and flaking away. I've got to find Mum and Dad, otherwise – and I'm sure of this, even though I don't know how I know it – they're going to die. I run past the rusty Ferris wheel and the burnt-out dodgems and under the skeleton of the roller coaster, but I can't see them anywhere. If I don't find them, they'll die, and it'll be my fault ... But then the helter-skelter begins to sway, the curvy slide sidewinding like a thick yellow snake, and it's creaking and it's going to fall, and suddenly they're there, right next to it, and the creaking is getting louder and louder and—

Oh, God. That was *horrible*.

My heart's thumping like anything, and even though I know it was only a dream – and you wouldn't have to be a genius to work out what that one was really about – I can't shake off the feeling.

Or the creaking noise, which is still going on. Please don't let it be Dad and Skye because that would be *gross*.

Wait.

That's not creaking. It's something heavier, more mechanical-sounding.

Like an old clock.

Tick . . .

Tock . . .

Tick . . .

Tock . . .

What clock, though? There isn't one, except the big thing in the hall, which I got right up close to and it was really quiet. But now it's loud and insistent.

Tick . . .

Tock . . .

It's like it's trying to tell me something.

That's not possible, obvs, but it's still keeping me awake. And there *was* something weird about that clock. I know, because I felt it. Whatever it was.

No point in lying here getting annoyed; I'm going into the hall to have a look.

Chapter 3

No 'Casino' and 'Massage Parlour' glowing out of the darkness, even though I don't remember turning them off, just the faint outline of the clock. Tick ... tock ... tick ... tock ...

It's so loud I'm surprised it hasn't woken Dad or Skye, but maybe they're already used to it. Or maybe – I sniff – they aren't asleep, because I can definitely smell cigarette smoke. I really hope Dad hasn't started again, from the stress or whatever.

My eyes are adjusting to the dark, and I can see that the clock says midnight. The face looks whiter now, cleaner, and it's glinting ... because the glass has been replaced. I suppose Dad must have done it after I'd gone to bed, and I didn't hear it. That doesn't seem likely, but—

Wait.

The hall's starting to look different, somehow – longer, like it's being stretched out into a corridor, and there's a yellowish light, sort of foggy, at the end, which must be coming from the sitting room ...

Except the sitting room is at the other end. That end's supposed to be the wall.

'What the actual—?'

I say it aloud to the empty, glowing hallway. The kitchen door isn't there, either, or the bathroom door, or – when I turn to look – the door of my room, or Dad's. It's wall, all the way down, and it's changed colour from petrol blue all the way up to grey on the bottom half and cream on the top, plus you can make out the shapes of the bricks underneath. And there's a gritty feeling under my bare feet – not rugs on polished boards, but a stone floor.

It's like the whole building's been turned 180 degrees by a giant hand, because the doors are on the opposite side now. Three of them, spaced out, and then just bare wall down to the far end, where the sitting room used to be. They look like they're made of metal, not wood: a dirty greenish colour, sort of seasicky in the weird, foggy light.

I can still see the clock on the wall – exactly the same, but with a glass cover over the face. Its tick-tock is quieter now, and there's another sound, lighter and metallic, jangling. And footsteps, from where Dad's bedroom is supposed to be.

Skye? Better pretend I need the loo in case she thinks I'm doing something weird and gross like listening out for them . . .

Except, where is the loo?

And actually, why should I? I've got as much right to be here as she has – although 'here' doesn't seem to be *here* any more.

And it isn't Skye.

I cough so as not to startle the woman, but it's like she doesn't hear it. She's maybe fifty – face lined and hard-looking with the hair scraped back into a tight little knot – and sturdy in a dark-blue jacket-and-skirt uniform, military-looking with a belt and silver buttons, and black lace-up shoes. She's got a big bunch of keys on a chain.

Is she a security guard, looking after the flats? I could buy that if she was patrolling outside, but she doesn't even look at me, just walks past near enough to touch and stops outside the second door. It's slightly different from the others, with a small flat panel in the middle, the same dirty green metal, at head height.

Maybe she's embarrassed. All I'm wearing is Dad's Ramones T-shirt – I forgot to bring anything to sleep in – and a pair of knickers. Perhaps she thinks I'm drunk and she's hoping I'll just go away . . .

This better not turn into one of those dreams where you're suddenly naked in front of a bunch of people.

Except I'm not asleep, am I? Or maybe I've *been* sleepwalking, and I just woke up.

'Miss?' It sounds stupid, but I can't think what else to say. 'Can you help me, please?'

She doesn't even turn her head. Instead, she puts up her hand, flips the panel in the door downwards, and puts her face right up to it.

Must be a spyhole – but why? And what's she looking at?

Maybe she's deaf. 'Miss?' I say it louder this time, and she straightens her back and turns her head. 'I'm sorry to bother you, but I just . . . ' I falter as she steps away from the door and looks in my direction – and right through me.

It's not a pretending-not-to-notice type of looking-through, it's like I don't exist.

She picks out a key from the bunch on the chain and puts it in the lock.

Can't hear me, can't see me. Which means I'm not really here – or not for her, anyway. But I can feel my feet on the chilly, gritty floor, and when I put my hand out and brush my fingers against the wall, I can feel solid brick.

She's opening the door.

'Evening, Florey.'

I can't see who she's talking to, but if she can't see me, maybe I can get closer and the other person won't see me, either.

'Evening, Ray. Want to help me with the crossword? Annie's not keen.'

Ray is taking up a lot of the doorway, but I can see round her. It's a small room, painted the same as the corridor and lit by a bare bulb. There's a high, barred window, and the floor is covered in brown lino. The furniture consists of a little table with a bowl and jug on top, a wooden table and three chairs, a cupboard, and a narrow bed.

The woman sitting at the table must be Florey, because she's holding a pencil and has a newspaper spread out in front of her. There's an ashtray there, too, which accounts for the smell. She's also wearing a dark-blue uniform, but she's younger and softer-looking than Ray, with little curls escaping from her scraped-back ginger hair. If she can see me peeping out at her from behind her big friend, she's giving no sign of it.

It has to be a cell, which means Florey and Ray must be prison officers.

'Come on, Annie.' Ray's looking over at the bed, and her voice is fake-jolly. 'Take your mind off things. You'll wear that bed out, sitting on it.'

Annie – whoever she is – doesn't say anything, but just as Ray closes the door she stands up and I catch a glimpse of her.

I reckon she's only a couple of years older than I am, but she looks like a lost child. She's short and plump, with soft brown hair and cheeks that ought to be rosy – still pink, but the glow has gone – and she's wearing a shapeless grey cardigan over a dull blue dress. Big blue eyes, kind of hopeful and confused at the same time – make me think of photos I've seen of dogs in shelters, waiting for someone to take them home and give them love.

For a split second before the door clangs shut, she turns and looks in my direction. I freeze, but she isn't looking *at* me.

She's looking into infinity.

Chapter 4

'So . . . What are you planning to do today?'

Dad's grinning nervously over his coffee like he's willing me not to lose it, but to be honest I'm not really concentrating because I keep thinking about last night. It's funny, because I don't usually remember dreams well, but that was just so vivid. I even checked round the flat this morning, but of course everything's back to the way it was before I went to sleep. It's only me that feels different.

It's not exactly incredible that I should dream about a prison, but that girl's face was the first thing I thought of when I woke up. And I remembered her name immediately – Annie – and the two prison officers, Ray and Florey, and everything right up to the point of seeing her as she stood up, but nothing else. It's like a story that just stopped, halfway through, but I *knew* that something terrible was about to happen. Remembering it now is like a spike of fear, straight through me.

'Earth to Millie.' Dad's waving at me from across the table. I must have a weird look on my face because he asks if I'm OK. Behind him, Skye is busy playing house. Dad and I are still in our dressing gowns, but she's wearing an apron over her yoga stuff and has already *made* muffins – although I think that could be more to do with staking a claim on the kitchen than actually liking to cook.

'I'm fine. I've got revision, so I'll be in my room, OK?'

'OK.' Dad's relief that I'm not rehashing last night's conversation in front of Skye is evident. 'I'm off to the shops, so if there's anything you'd like foodwise, just let me know.'

'Can't think of anything.' Well, I probably can, but not right now. I get up to put my plate in the sink.

'That's OK!' Skye – big smile firmly in place – snatches it from me. OK, OK, OK – everything's OK. Except it isn't. 'Why don't you go and have a shower?'

Oh great, now she thinks she's my mum. 'I was *going* to.'

'Sorry. Just . . . your feet.'

'What about them?'

'They're sort of . . . filthy. Underneath.'

I lift one up to look, and she's right. I know they were clean when I went to bed because I'd just had a shower, but now the soles are grey with dirt.

The hall floor is clean enough, and so are the rugs. Maybe I *was* sleepwalking. I know people do sometimes open doors and things in their sleep – although, if I went out of the flat, is it possible I could have opened the front door *and* retraced all my steps without waking?

'No one's been doing any filming here, have they?'

Dad shakes his head. 'They'd have told us. Why?'

'Just wondered. You haven't started smoking again, have you?'

Skye gets there before he does – 'No he has *not*' – then looks at him like she's suddenly unsure. 'Have you?'

'You know I haven't.' Dad turns to me, exasperated. 'Stop it, Millie.'

'Stop what?'

'You know what.'

'I wasn't trying to make trouble, just . . . Look, it's not important.'

I can feel Dad and Skye exchanging glances as I leave the room. I check the front door on the way to the bathroom, but it's locked and the chain's on. And the clock is ticking, very, very quietly.

Dad marches out of the flat with a fistful of Bags for Life. He tells me – in a square-jawed sort of way, like he's the Protector of the Cave or something – to remember to lock up properly and take my keys if I decide to go out, because Skye has to go back to the house she used to share with her friends to collect the rest of her stuff (she works from home, doing PR for companies that make wellness kits and £100 scented candles). I don't intend to go out, though – or not yet, anyway.

The first thing I do once they've both gone is sit down in the middle of my bed with my laptop. I'll make a start on my revision in a minute, but first . . .

Sorry, Yaz, but I'm keeping this to myself until I've figured out what's going on: the whole dirty feet thing, and the cigarette smoke – I mean, you don't smell smoke in dreams unless your home has actually caught fire, so that *has* to be significant. If I really did go into the hall – which I must have done, because feet – that means I really did find it all different. I don't want Yaz to think I'm losing it, especially after what happened with Dad and Mum – not to mention Kieran, which is a whole other story.

I've never been that into the unexplained or mystical – like Dad, which is partly what baffles me about him and Skye.

Plus, I've never thought much about whether I believe in ghosts. But can you have a *ghost building*?

I go online and find some old black and white photos of the outside of the prison. The front gateway is like a castle, with towers and battlements. I'd definitely have noticed *that* when I was going past, so it must have been pulled down at some point before they demolished the rest of the place to build these flats.

The photos of the inside show galleries of cells on either side of a space with iron staircases in the middle, and netting strung across. They definitely look more how I imagine an old-school prison than the plain-looking corridor that I saw last night.

I find a few plans of the prison, too. They look pretty old, maybe Victorian, and sort of like the outline of a windmill with the two lowest sails missing. The bits that look like sails – sticking out in a fan shape – are the different wings, with rows of cells on each side, and then there are more wings, jutting out horizontally from lower down the main column, and lots of other buildings dotted about the grounds.

I start reading the prison's Wikipedia entry. It opened in the 1850s, so I was right about it being Victorian, but some of it was rebuilt in the 1970s, which was when they got rid of the castle-gateway thing. There's an aerial photo of the modern prison, in colour, and some details about how it closed down a few years ago, and how all the prisoners were sent to other places. The entry mentions the suffragettes and some of the other prisoners Dad told me about – and that executions took place here into the twentieth century.

Dad didn't mention that.

Chapter 5

Wasn't the death penalty abolished like a hundred years ago? I google and discover that it was ended for pretty much everything, including murder, in 1965. When I count the decades back, it suddenly feels very recent.

That's not cool, it's creepy.

I try and get into revising, but *Bonjour Tristesse* is basically a book about people being arseholes, even if they are all sophisticated and French and elegant, and it's depressing. I wander into the hall, but it feels like there's something lurking just out of range. I know it's only my imagination, and probably not unrelated to the horrible information about executions I've just discovered, but it's still weird and unsettling.

I go into the kitchen and open the fridge. Not sure why Dad was so set on going shopping, because Skye's already brought enough food to feed ten people. Maybe Dad told her Mum is usually too busy drawing pandas to remember stuff like that – although it's not like there's a law against men going into supermarkets – and she's trying to prove she's the opposite. Skye's food looks OK, but I don't really want any of it so I go downstairs for a walk.

It's really quiet. I try to imagine what the place must have looked like as a prison, but it's impossible – no atmosphere or anything. Even the sunshine is sort of flat, like it's determined to be as ordinary as possible.

I wander round the different buildings looking at things. Dad told me that the architect won a prize – which I reckon he or she must have got from some lame bunch of people who think that 'boring' equals 'subtle'. Dad's shown me the website, which has loads of guff about 'timeless elegance' and 'understated panache' – like that actually means anything except that the walls are pale-coloured and there are big windows and lots of space between the blocks. I don't mean to sound spoilt, because most people don't get to live in places half as nice, but it's sort of like those clothes that very rich women always wear. No details, and all cream and taupe. I suppose it's to show that even if they spill a bunch of whatever very rich women eat down their front, it doesn't matter because they can just buy a new sweater.

Mum doesn't do FaceTime, so I sit on a bench and ring her.

'Millie! Darling, what's happened?'

'Nothing. I just . . .' Just wanted to hear your voice. I don't say that, though, because I don't want to guilt-trip her for staying away longer.

'You never ring me!' She must be in a restaurant because I can hear people chatting and crockery and glasses clinking in the background. I'm getting a bad feeling about this. She's only ever called me darling twice before – I remember because both times she was drunk, which is *really* unusual.

'Oh, *sorry*. I felt like a chat, that's all.'

'That's lovely, darling. No, I'm fine – won't be a minute.'

'What?'

'Sorry, just some friends of Cathy's.'

'Look, I can call you another time if it's—'

'Don't be silly. Let me take you outside.' I hear a chair being scraped back and footsteps, giggles and a lot of excuse me's, and then it goes quiet. 'That's better.'

'Where are you?'

'On the beach. Hang on, I'll hold the phone up so you can hear the sea.'

Swooshy noises, like wind blowing, then a muffled 'Oh, shit,' followed by a thud.

'What was that? Did you just fall over?'

'I'm fine! Hang on, there's a rocky bit. It's glorious here. You must come the minute your term's finished—'

'Wait … You're staying until *July*? You said it was just for another week.'

'Cathy persuaded me, and honestly, I feel *so* much better. You will, too. It's the perfect—'

'Have you told Dad?'

'Not yet. But Cathy made me realise that I don't *need* to be back. I can work from anywhere, so why not?'

'So that means I have to stay at Dad's?'

'That's all right, isn't it?'

'I suppose so, but—'

There's a crash, then silence, then I hear Mum say, 'You talk to her,' and Cathy comes on the line. 'Millie? Sorry about that. Your mum's a bit upset at the moment.'

'Drunk, you mean.'

'Well, yeah, a little. Look, she's been having a pretty difficult time, and . . . well, it's a bit complicated . . . So, anyway, that's why I suggested she stay on for a while. I know things aren't easy right now, and you've got exams and everything, but—'

'When did you decide this?'

'A few days ago. We thought it was better to wait until we'd sorted out all the details before we told you – and you're very welcome to come and join us when you've finished your term. I'll get her to ring your dad later, and they can—'

'Right. Thanks for letting me know.' I end the call. So much for wanting to hear her voice: I'll have to spend the next five weeks here, minimum.

Mum sounds kind of out of control . . . But I guess she didn't expect me to call – and I know she's been trying really hard to keep it together in front of me for *ages*, and I get that she needs some time to herself. I just don't know where *I* am in all this.

Aaaargh. I clutch my phone hard so I don't hurl it against the nearest wall, and go back inside.

I go up to my room and stare at my screensaver for a bit. It's the three of us on holiday in Iceland a few years ago, when things were still OK – although not as OK as I'd thought they were, it turns out. It feels like even that picture is kind of a lie . . . but I don't remember any arguments, and Mum and Dad look properly happy so maybe they were, if only for that short time. I look quite a lot like Mum – wavy dark hair, pale skin and brown eyes – and we're both tall and sort of angular. Even though I'm only about twelve in the photo it's really noticeable, because we're wearing practically identical hiking stuff.

I want to get inside that picture and stay there – on the boat with the grey sea and the enormous chunks of pale blue ice – and for nothing to change.

Then Dad comes back, loaded down with shopping, and bangs on my door, whanging on about traffic jams and car parks like he's just had to slay a dragon or something.

'Yeah, you're a total hero.' I'm not saying anything about Mum's plan – she can tell him herself.

'Can you come and give Skye a hand? She's just been to fetch the rest of her stuff.'

The rest of Skye's stuff turns out to be an *unbelievable* amount of clothes, cosmetics and beauty products, crammed into an Uber. It's way too much for the size of car, and the driver, who's basically got aluminium make-up boxes piled round his *head*, is massively pissed off.

I make two journeys from the car park then go back to my room, where I wind up alternating between TikTok and Netflix. I can't concentrate, but anything is better than thinking about Mum and Dad because it'll just make me really angry, so what's the point? It's not like I can *change* anything.

When Skye knocks on the door with a soft 'Dinner's ready', I tell her I'm not hungry. About an hour later they go out to the cinema and when I go into the kitchen there's a tray waiting for me on the table, with a really fancy salad and a slice of cake. There's even a single flower in a little vase and a purple post-it: *In case you change your mind. S x*

It's nice of her – I get that. And actually I am hungry now, and the food looks great – and, looking round, I can see she's added a Gaggia coffee machine and an ice cream maker to Dad's very basic kitchen appliances, as well as a load of herbs in pots ... But it doesn't stop me wishing that she didn't exist – or anyway that I'd never met her because she'd never met Dad – and that none of this had happened.

I wash up afterwards, then go back to my room and lie on the bed staring at the ceiling. Everything, even my dream – if that's what it was – just feels so hopeless. I'm going to be stuck here, with *them*, and I'll just be getting angry and worrying about Mum, and then there's the whole Kieran thing ...

Tears leak out of my eyes and trickle down into my ears. As far as I'm concerned, the rest of today is cancelled.

Chapter 6

The clock wakes me.

    Tick

    Tock

    Tick

    Tock . . .

I'm in the hall again. The big clock face with its Roman numerals looms at me out of the sickly grey-yellow fog: midnight.

The space is elongating and the petrol blue walls are changing colour to half grey, half cream. Stone floor. Row of metal doors. Smell of cigarette smoke. All exactly the same as last night.

Jangle of keys. Footsteps echoing along the corridor. Someone's coming.

It's Florey – I recognise her from last night. There are three men walking behind her, two – one middle-aged, one younger – in old-fashioned suits and hats, and the third in overalls. The older suited one is taller and broader, with a weather-beaten face and pale blue eyes. There's something really focused about him, like he'd still carry on doing whatever he was doing, even if everything around him burst into flames – but the younger guy, who is carrying a big old leather case, has this deliberately blank expression. The man in overalls looks pale and sweaty.

Have they come to see Annie?

Florey stops outside her cell, and I think she's about to unlock the door, but instead she puts her finger on the small flat panel, uncovers the spyhole, and stands back. The older man puts his face close to it for a moment, then steps back, jots something down in a notebook, and shows it to Florey. 'Does that correspond with the records? Height and weight?'

'Yes, Mr Rutherford.'

'Good. Shall we inspect the chamber?'

Chamber? What is this, Harry Potter? And why aren't they going in to see Annie rather than just spying on her? Florey's face is expressionless, but I spot a flash of excitement in the younger guy's eyes as they move down the corridor to the cell on the right of Annie's. Florey must have caught it, too, because she suddenly glares at him. 'There may be a reprieve.'

'I'm aware it's irregular,' Mr Rutherford says, 'but as the apparatus hasn't been used for a while, it was thought best to make sure that everything is in good order.'

Reprieve? Apparatus?

Oh, no. *No.*

No, no, no.

What Ray said to Annie. *Take your mind off things.* That's what she wanted to take Annie's mind off – and that's why she and Florey were in there in the first place, because I'm betting prison officers don't usually hang around in the cells offering to help with crosswords.

They're going to kill her.

Florey unlocks the door of the next cell – which is narrow and totally empty except for two more doors on either side of it, facing each other. She unlocks the one on the right, then steps back to let the men go inside. I move forward to stand with Florey on the threshold. She clearly doesn't want to go in and, once I see what's there, I don't either.

The room is painted the same as the other one, like the corridor, but there's no furniture unless you count a stepladder, folded up and leaning against a wall. There's a staircase in the corner, going down, two big beams across the ceiling and bare boards on the floor with trapdoors in the centre, with a big lever sticking up at one side. Mr Rutherford gestures towards the leather case. 'Mr Finch, if you would . . . ' and the other man opens it and produces a rope.

Mr Rutherford positions the stepladder on the trapdoors and climbs up, and Florey and Mr Finch watch in silence as he fixes the rope to something on one of the beams. When he climbs down and Mr Finch moves the ladder away, I can see that the rope ends in a leather-covered noose, which hangs there, limp.

Mr Rutherford gives it a sharp downward tug. 'So far, so good. You've got sand, I take it?' He's asking the man in overalls, who I'm guessing must be a maintenance guy. He's been staring at the ground since they went in the room.

Sand?

'I'll make sure, Mr Rutherford.'

'Good.' Mr Rutherford walks round the trapdoor and shoves the lever forward, and the trapdoors fly open with a crash. Florey jumps, and I turn to look in the direction of Annie's cell, wondering if she can hear . . . and then I realise that the door on the other wall of the empty cell must be hidden by the cupboard on Annie's side. Does she know that there's only a piece of furniture and a tiny room between her and death? Do they move it out of the way when the time comes, and bring her through here to . . . ?

They *can't*. Please let there be a reprieve. I grab Florey's arm – it feels solid enough under my hand, but she doesn't even flinch. 'Please,' I shout. 'You can't do this! It's *wrong*!'

Nobody reacts. It's like before: they're not ignoring me, they just can't see or hear or – in Florey's case – feel me. It's pointless.

Mr Rutherford and Mr Finch lean forward to look through the big, square hole in the floor, their heads on either side of the noose. 'So far, so good. We'll test it a few more times to make sure.'

'Right you are.' The maintenance man's voice sounds faint, and I notice that he's begun to sidle away from the gallows, towards us. I don't blame him. Florey catches his eye and gives him a sympathetic half-smile. I know they're thinking the same as me: when Mr Rutherford pulls that lever Annie will plummet downwards and the rope will go taut and her neck will break.

Florey and the maintenance man stare down at their shoes as Mr Rutherford and Mr Finch go down the stairs. We can hear them moving about, murmuring – and then Mr Finch comes back up and they reset the trapdoor. They're quiet and efficient, like surgeons about to perform an operation. How can they be so *calm*?

I dash past Florey, grab the lever and give it a shove. The trap-doors fly open again – *bang!* This time, everyone jumps, and there's a yell from downstairs, and footsteps, moving fast. Mr Rutherford's head appears, halfway up the staircase. 'What the hell are you playing at?'

'Nothing.' Mr Finch is white as a sheet, backing into a corner. 'I didn't touch it.'

'Bloody hell!' The maintenance guy is staring at the hole like his eyes are about to pop out of his head. 'Sorry, ma'am,' he says to Florey, who's looking as if it's all she can do not to run out of the room.

Mr Rutherford looks thoughtful. 'Must be the mechanism. We'll need to report this to the governor.' He and Mr Finch bend over the lever. The maintenance guy is leaning against the wall, looking like he's about to be sick, and Florey's hands are shaking.

The last thing I see is the noose hanging in the centre of the room.

Chapter 7

I jerk out of sleep, sweaty and shaking, and, for a moment, I can't think where I am.

A knock on the door, and Dad's voice. 'Are you all right?'

'What? Why?'

'You were shouting.'

'Sorry. Just . . . bad dream.'

Dad puts his head round the door. 'Are you OK? What was it about?'

I sit up. 'Doesn't matter.'

'Well, you're awake now. You know it's after nine?'

'Obviously not. For some reason – possibly, I mean, just *possibly*, because all of this is fucking with my head – I forgot to set my alarm.'

Dad puts his hands up, like, *surrender*, and says, 'I can bring you some coffee from Skye's fancy machine.'

'Well, it has to be better than your coffee, so . . . OK. Thanks.'

'I can bring some toast as well, if you like.'

'Not hungry.'

'Sure?'

'Sure.' Right now, I don't feel like I'll ever want to eat anything again.

'Fair enough. We're going out after breakfast to choose a new sofa, so we'll leave you to it – unless you want to come with, of course? We can have lunch in town.'

Seriously? 'Er, hello? You know it's a school day, right? I can't just take it off to play *happy families*.'

'Oh, yes. Right. Sorry.'

He looks half disappointed, half relieved, like he's trying to make his face look a certain way but it's not cooperating. 'I'll be fine,' I tell him. Then, because frankly I'm grateful to have the flat to myself, 'Say thanks to Skye for the meal.'

'Right you are.'

He closes the door and I sit there with my head in my hands, feeling like everything's horrible. It's not just the whole Dad-and-Skye thing and Mum staying away – I don't reckon she's rung him yet, or he'd say something – but last night, that noose just hanging there. That was . . .

Urrgh. No, stop it. I swing my legs out of bed and immediately check my feet: filthy.

So, whatever happened the first time just happened again. And now it's worse, because Annie's going to be hanged. How could people *do* that?

Except . . . Florey mentioned a reprieve, didn't she? So that means Annie could be OK – or anyway, not dead. Even if she is some weird dream or ghost or whatever, all of this feels *way* too real.

I grab my phone and start googling, then switch to my laptop because someone's uploaded an actual plan of the place where they hanged people, and I need to see it bigger.

Whoa! This is so exactly like what I just saw that it's *unbelievable*.

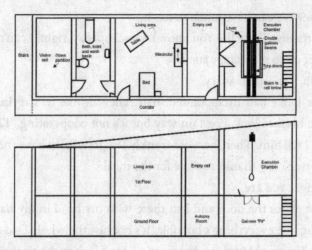

This flat is on the first floor, so there's one below it on the ground floor, and it all fits exactly with what I saw. The cell with the table and the bed . . . and there's the wardrobe, and that double-headed arrow must mean it moves, so it happens like I thought: Annie will walk through there to the gallows.

There's an explanation of how they used to get a sack of sand weighing the same as the person and hang it up a few days before to stretch the rope – which explains what Mr Rutherford said to the maintenance guy.

Dad knocks on the door, and I exit the page.

OK. I shakily open the blind and look out of the window. It's a beautiful day – sunshine, not spooky at all. Plus, this coffee is *really* good – way better than Dad's usual stuff.

But.

Take your mind off things.

Are you a ghost, Annie?

If she is a ghost, then so are all the rest of them. It wasn't like I got a sudden chill or anything, either time, and I wasn't *scared* scared, like terrified. It was more just . . . *strange*. But if this place is properly haunted, wouldn't Skye have picked up on it, seeing as she's always banging on about how she's such a 'spiritual person' and sensitive or whatever?

Or not.

Ha!

Thinking about it, though, it's a bit weird Skye hasn't been on Dad's case about this place having bad energy or whatever. I guess she didn't say anything because the relationship is new enough for them still to be at the stage of agreeing about everything and finding annoying things cute and a whole bunch of other stuff that doesn't happen for any length of time. I've had exactly one boyfriend, and even I know that.

There is definitely something going on, and neither of them have a clue about it. If Annie existed, maybe she got a reprieve. Maybe.

Those blank blue eyes.

No point even trying to revise now. Sounds like Dad and Skye should be on their way out any minute – noises in the hall – and then I'll have a shower and start investigating. But first . . .

I don't want to know, but I have to.

I go back to the Wikipedia entry for the prison, because I didn't read all of it yesterday. At the bottom, there's a list of the executions that took place in the twentieth century.

Six names on the list.

The last but one is Anne Driscoll, who was executed on 13 June 1955.

Anne Driscoll.

Is that Annie? *My* Annie?

Chapter 8

Today is 9 June. That reprieve Florey mentioned must have failed, because they're going to hang her in four days' time. They'll have to check the mechanism because of what I did, and perhaps that could buy a fraction of time, but it won't stop them.

Anne Driscoll has her own Wikipedia page. I click, and up it comes.

There's a photograph. It's black and white, but definitely the same person. She doesn't look crazy or evil or creepy, just young and round-faced and sad, like she doesn't have many friends. It's only her head and shoulders, but she's wearing a dress with fussy little flowers and short, puffy sleeves, and she kind of looks like she's got tangled up in the leaves and branches on the wallpaper behind her. I can't know, but I reckon she's standing in a bright, crowded room, watching everyone else have fun.

Annie Driscoll
Anne (Annie) Mavis Driscoll (20 March 1936–13 June 1955) was the penultimate woman to be hanged in

the UK, after being convicted of the murder of her sisters, Dorothy Walsh and Kathleen Driscoll, by poisoning. Aged 19 at the time of her death, Driscoll was the only teenage girl to be executed in Britain in the twentieth century.

Driscoll poisoned Dorothy and their youngest sister Kathleen with arsenic. Kathleen was aged 6 at the time of her death and Dorothy, 22. Dorothy had married Victor Walsh the previous year and was three months pregnant.

She was *nineteen* when they hanged her. Three years older than me. If Dorothy was pregnant, it was like she killed *three* people, or two and a potential one, anyway. Why would she *do* that? And who'd poison a six-year-old child?

I stare at the photo again, looking for clues, but there aren't any.

Early Life

Driscoll was born Anne Mavis Palmer and spent her early childhood in Dalston, London. Her father, Francis Palmer, was killed while on active service in the Second World War. Her mother Rose was subsequently remarried, to Charles Driscoll, and the family moved to Aylmer Terrace in nearby Islington in 1946. As well as her sister, Dorothy, born in 1933, Driscoll had a younger brother, Joe, born in 1938. Kathleen, her half-sister, was born in 1948.

Mum and I live in Dalston. Hope it wasn't our house, because it's certainly old enough ... except that the killings couldn't have happened there, because the family moved to Islington when Annie was ten.

> Driscoll struggled at school, and her education
> was further set back by periods of treatment for
> tuberculosis. She possessed low literacy skills and
> was prone to inventing stories about herself. After
> leaving school, she worked as a chambermaid at a
> local hotel. At the time of the murder, she was living
> at home, as were Joe and Kathleen. Dorothy and
> Victor lived nearby.

OK, so Annie wasn't great at school and she told a bunch of lies. Smart enough to work out how to poison somebody, but not smart enough to get away with it ... But wouldn't Dorothy and Kathleen have been, like, this food is rank?

I google arsenic and discover that it's tasteless and odourless, so no, they wouldn't. My search also tells me that, before companies started adding dye to rat poison – to make it less likely that you'd kill anyone by accident, I guess – it was a white powder that could easily be dissolved in water.

The symptoms of arsenic poisoning are vomiting, delirium, abdominal pain and watery diarrhoea that contains blood. Eww.

Plus, you die.

Chapter 9

Murder

On 10 March 1955, Driscoll helped prepare an
evening meal for Dorothy, Kathleen, Rose, and a
family friend but, due to a change in arrangements,
neither Rose nor the friend were present. The meal
consisted of sandwiches, scones, cake, and cups of
tea. Driscoll had made the cake herself the previous
day and the scones and sandwiches were made
by Rose before she left the house. When Driscoll's
brother Joe returned to work after a break between
shifts, she was in the house alone for a short time
before Dorothy and Kathleen arrived. Both her
sisters ate some of everything on the table, but
Driscoll ate only a scone. All three complained of
feeling unwell shortly after the meal, but Dorothy
and Kathleen's symptoms worsened, and, by the
time Victor arrived to collect Dorothy at 8 p.m., both
were experiencing severe cramps, vomiting and

diarrhoea. The family doctor blamed the symptoms
on 'gastric influenza' and gave them both a dose
of bicarbonate and water. In the early hours of the
morning, Kathleen collapsed. The doctor returned
and gave her morphine for the pain, but she died a
short time later. Dorothy, who had spent the night at
the Driscolls' house, was taken to the local hospital,
where she died the following day.

Both autopsies showed evidence of poisoning by
arsenic, and Driscoll's fingerprints were found on a tin
of rat poison in the garden shed. Driscoll claimed not
to know of its existence, and said that if she had given
poison to Dorothy and Kathleen, it was by mistake.

Sounds like Annie didn't really know what she was saying. The
fingerprints are the only mention of anything like forensics, so
I'm guessing they didn't have all that CSI-type stuff like now – and
I suppose everyone's fingerprints would have been all over the
house, because all the people involved either lived there, or they
were always visiting. The garden shed, not so much … Anyway,
doesn't poisonous stuff have a sign on it, like a skull and crossbones
or something?

Trial
Driscoll was tried before Mr Justice Houseman
at the Old Bailey in London, between 18 May and
20 May 1955. Eustace Matheson Landers led for

the prosecution and Driscoll was represented by
Claude Wetherby.

Driscoll denied that she was jealous because
Victor Walsh had transferred his affections from
herself to Dorothy (Walsh had earlier denied that
this was the case). She often appeared confused,
at one point telling Matheson Landers, 'If you say I
did it, then I must have.' Although there was some
controversy over whether or not she was mentally fit
to stand trial, Dr Pryce, a psychiatrist at the Maudsley
Hospital, stated that Driscoll did not qualify as a
'feeble-minded person' under the Mental Deficiency
Act (repealed in 1959 by the Mental Health Act). At
this time, English law did not recognise the concept
of diminished responsibility due to abnormal mental
function, and criminal insanity (where the accused is
unable to distinguish right from wrong) was the only
medical defence to murder.

The jury took 90 minutes to convict Driscoll,
who was sentenced to death and taken to the
condemned cell.

Which must be where I saw her.

Driscoll's appeal on 8 June was unsuccessful, and
her solicitor, Alexander Brighouse, petitioned Home
Secretary Gwilym Lloyd George for a reprieve.

Yesterday was 8 June – that's why Florey mentioned the chance of a reprieve. Guess she'll find out pretty soon that it didn't work.

> The Home Secretary decided that there were not
> sufficient grounds to justify advising Her Majesty
> Queen Elizabeth II to interfere with the due course
> of the law.

I google 'reprieve death sentence UK' and it says that the Home Secretary could basically tell the monarch that the person should get life instead, and they'd be like, fine. Then it says, 'If there was to be no reprieve, the Home Secretary would write "the law must take its course" on the file and the execution would then proceed.'

I imagine a man's hand with an old-school pen writing those words in black ink across a brown paper folder with Annie's name on it, and putting a big full stop at the end.

Day after day, waiting and hoping, while Florey and Ray tried to distract her with crosswords. And when whoever it was finally came to tell her, Annie must have known the minute she saw the person's face that they were going to kill her. Did she think she deserved it, because of Dorothy and Kathleen?

Two wrongs don't make a right, though.

Chapter 10

I google the hangman, Ronald Rutherford, and discover that he'd started executing people – just helping at first, like Mr Finch – in 1932, and by 1955 he'd done about 200 Nazi war criminals as well as a whole bunch of other people, so I guess he must have got pretty good at it. Plus, it ran in the family: his father and uncle were hangmen as well. Bet their Christmases were fun.

I feel sick, but it's like I can't stop reading.

> Driscoll's body was buried in an unmarked grave within the walls of the prison, as was customary. In 1971, during a rebuilding programme, the remains of all executed women were exhumed. Driscoll was reburied at Highgate Cemetery in North London.
>
> **Legacy**
> In the opinion of many contemporary commentators, Driscoll's intention had been to murder Dorothy

because she was jealous of her relationship with
Victor, and Kathleen's death was accidental.

Except, Victor said he'd never had a relationship with Annie –
although I suppose that wouldn't stop her falling in love with him.

Although there was public support for the
sentence – Dorothy's pregnancy and Kathleen's
age being major factors – Driscoll's hanging did
help to strengthen the growing distaste for the
death penalty, and there were protests outside
the prison on the day of the execution. These
were attended by Driscoll's younger brother, Joe,
who remained adamant throughout the police
investigation and subsequent trial that his sister was
completely innocent.

I stare out at the grass and trees for a bit and wonder what Annie
would have seen if they ever let her climb on a chair to look out of
that high window. A concrete yard, maybe? Or, if she looked up, a
little box of sky. I imagine it being bright blue with a tiny plane cut-
ting across one corner of it, taking people to a place she'd never go.

I have to get out of here. I go downstairs and sit on the same
bench where I phoned Mum yesterday. I think about that a bit, and
consider messaging Yaz, but I don't – she'll be all, like, WTF, and
want to FaceTime, and I feel like I need to be on my own right now.
Mostly, though, I think about Annie.

That photo: standing against the wall in her puffy-sleeved party dress, lonely in a room full of people. Although I don't actually *know* that. Perhaps she wasn't at a party at all.

Did she ever walk here? They must have let her out sometimes, for exercise.

Only nineteen, with blank blue eyes.

Dead in four days' time, sixty-eight years ago.

Chapter 11

I google frantically again to make sure there's nothing about how they made a mistake and she was innocent after all, but I don't find anything. Doesn't make what they did OK, though.

And why was Joe so sure she didn't do it? He can't have had any *evidence*, or not enough to make a difference, anyway. Maybe he just thought she was innocent because she was his sister and he loved her.

But – despite there being nothing online – what if he was *right*?

I feel like someone's punched all the breath out of me. It's just really hard to think about. I sit and look at the view for a bit, but I can't stop seeing Annie's face.

I go back inside and click on the last link in the Wikipedia article, which is something called 'Find A Grave', and up comes Francis Joseph 'Joe' Palmer. At first, I think it must be Joe's dad, but then I read the dates and realise they had the same first name. It says he was born and died in London and was buried in Highgate Cemetery, and gives the dates as 28 January 1938 and 15 (?) November (?) 1991.

Weird that they aren't sure about the date. He can't have been that old, either . . .

Fifty-three. The same age as Dad is now.

Poor guy.

Wait, though. Highgate Cemetery was where Annie ended up when the bodies of the executed women were moved in 1971. Did Joe organise that? If it's where the rest of the family were buried, then he must have wanted them all to be together – so he must have carried on believing she was innocent.

It's all so sad.

Underneath the dates on 'Find A Grave', it says: *Joe was the brother of Annie Driscoll, who was executed for murder in June 1955. Aged 17 at the time of her death, he always insisted that she was innocent.* Nothing new there, except that there's a photograph of him, and . . .

OMFG. He is *gorgeous*.

It looks like he was about the same age as me when the picture was taken. He's in a suit and his hair's slicked down, like really formal.

You'd never guess he was Annie's brother, because their faces are quite different. Joe has a sexy, angular face with high cheekbones, mischievous-looking dark eyes, and black hair. He's standing against the same wallpaper as Annie was in her photo, and someone's holding his hand. You can't see who because they're not in the picture, either because the photographer didn't want them there or because someone cut them off afterwards. Judging by the lacy frill that's just visible round the wrist, it's a girl, but – assuming it was taken on the same day as the other picture – not Annie, because her dress had shorter sleeves.

I google Francis Joseph Palmer. After a couple of misfires – Welsh boxer, American rapper – I get a photo. If it weren't for the caption, I'd never have guessed it was the same guy. This man looks totally different, and not just because he's older and his hair is thinning. It's the scruffy clothes and the stooped shoulders and the heavy, defeated face, like life drove over him in a tank . . .

Which I guess it sort of did. Poor Joe.

I find him in a few paragraphs from a newspaper article dated 2011, about loneliness in later life and how people become isolated.

> Sometimes the cause is easier to understand. An open verdict was recorded at a Westminster inquest in July 1992 on Francis Joseph Palmer, aged 53, whose body lay undiscovered for an estimated six months in his small third-floor flat in Euston.

Six months! No wonder they didn't know the exact date of his death.

> Palmer was the brother of Anne Driscoll, who was executed in June 1955 for poisoning their sisters Dorothy and Kathleen. Aged 17 at the time of her death, Palmer always maintained her innocence.
> The most likely cause of his death was suicide – an empty bottle of sleeping pills was found

near the body – but post-mortem evidence was inconclusive.

Palmer's struggle with depression was confirmed by his GP, Sheila Joffe. A neighbour, Omar Abadi, attested to Palmer's increasing paranoia in the last months of his life and described his flat as chaotic and dirty. Palmer had become convinced that people were trying to steal things from him, and wrote repeatedly to the then Home Secretary, Kenneth Baker. 'I don't know if it was about [his sister], or something else,' Abadi told the court. 'I had no idea about his past because he was mostly very private and reserved. I tried to be friendly because he didn't seem to have any family and nobody ever visited. To be honest, when I didn't see him for a while, I just assumed he'd moved without telling me … until I started to notice the smell. I reported it to the housing association in early March, as did other tenants, but it got blamed on poor rubbish disposal and no action was taken for several months.'

Palmer is thought to have died some time in November 1991. A partially burnt book and some papers were found in a wastepaper basket, which may have been an attempt to keep warm – Palmer was claiming unemployment benefit – or an accidental fire caused by a cigarette.

The most poignant detail was the rabbit cuddly

toy found lying by his side. Dr Joffe, who was aware
of Palmer's past, believed it might have been a gift
from his sister Anne. 'People fall through the cracks,'
she said. 'I wish I could have done more.'

The area near Euston Station is busy, but Joe would have been all alone, with just the haunted house of his mind for company. I imagine him sitting on an unmade bed in a filthy room, with the toy bunny, threadbare from stroking, beside him – and then lying dead while everybody rushed past the building to catch their trains, thinking about Christmas parties and presents and what they were going to do at New Year.

He must have been so lonely.

Chapter 12

I spend a bit more time on 'Find A Grave' and discover that Dorothy and Kathleen are also buried in Highgate Cemetery, although I don't find any mention of Rose, her second husband Charles Driscoll, or Victor Walsh.

I find a wedding photo, though. Victor looks maybe ten years older than Dorothy. He's tall, with a nice smile, and certainly looks handsome enough in his morning suit, but Dorothy is *stunning*. It's not just the white lacy dress, the veil, and the armful of roses, although they're all lovely, but she would be the best-looking person in pretty much any room anywhere. Anyone with her for a sister would have been jealous – but probably quite in awe as well, because she's so beautiful it would be kind of like having a unicorn in the family. There's a picture of Kathleen and Annie, too, as bridesmaids. Kathleen's skinny, with heavy black hair framing a pretty, cheeky face, and Annie's holding her hand and smiling down at her.

As an afterthought, I google Victor Walsh in case he's still alive, but don't find anything. I guess all that proves is that not everybody has an online presence.

I manage an hour of French after that, and then some German – hard to focus, but it's better than nothing. Dad and Skye get back about six, and something about the way he's being with her – kind of careful – makes me think that they might have had a row, and he was in the wrong. I hope it wasn't about the shopping, because Dad needs to buy quite a bit of new stuff for the flat, and if they argue over every single thing, that's going to be just *great*. She doesn't make a fuss when he suggests Deliveroo, though, and afterwards we put down the floor cushions they bought – the sofa they chose won't be here for another three weeks – and watch a film on Dad's big TV. I feel like I could eat something for the first time this whole stomach-churning day, and Dad ordered Korean which he knows I love. I feel an unexpected surge of gratitude towards them both.

If I'm honest, I'm starting to think Skye might be sort of OK – apart from all the Live, Love, Laugh stuff – just not as Dad's girlfriend. I think I need to be *with* people for a bit, even if it's them, and do ordinary things, in the here and now. By ten thirty, though, they're getting sloppy – probably because they've put away nearly two bottles of Skye's organic wine – so I decide to go to bed.

I can't decide if I'm scared or excited about going to sleep, but after about twenty minutes I'm just annoyed, because Dad and Skye are clomping about in the hall, giggling as they take plates back to the kitchen, and I put the pillow over my head.

*

Tick

Tock . . .

Tick . . .

Tock . . .

And I'm back in the hall again, and it's midnight.

Jangle of keys. Footsteps, echoing along the corridor. Someone's coming.

Ray appears around the corner first, her face expressionless. Even though I know she can't see me, she's only about a metre away and I stand absolutely still, barely daring to breathe.

This time, she stops at the first door and unlocks it. I remember the diagram of the cells: Annie must be expecting visitors.

More footsteps – several people, this time – and another prison officer appears from the same direction. Not Florey, but one I haven't seen before, with a beaky nose like a chicken and mean little eyes. After her comes a man who looks to be about Dad's age, wearing a suit and holding a trilby hat against his chest. He's large – tall and broad – with a fleshy face, dimples, and coarse skin. Hair almost too black, and shiny with product. Smell of cigarettes and something else, maybe the hair stuff.

The mean-eyed prison officer gestures towards the door Ray has just unlocked. 'This way please, Mr Driscoll,' she says.

So he must be Charles Driscoll, the stepfather.

Both of them look straight through me, and so does the woman behind, who has to be Annie's mother, Rose. She's wearing a two-piece suit and high heels, and even though her eyes are red and swollen and the sickly yellow light makes her look ill, I can see that she's beautiful.

Behind must be Joe, same suit as in the photo, head down.

They file past me as Ray steps back to let them into the cell. What I can see of Joe's face is so stiff and brave that I want to reach out and touch him, tell him I'm sorry.

I didn't realise I'd moved, but I must have done because he flicks a glance in my direction, conker-brown eyes narrowed like he's sensed something and – just for a second – his eyes widen.

My heart stops. Not only is he just as gorgeous as in the photo, but he's *seen* me.

Then he looks away and follows Rose into the cell.

Chapter 13

Somehow, I know that Joe isn't going to mention whatever it is he's just seen. I hesitate for a fraction of a second – Dad's T-shirt's not a *great* look, even though it's vintage, plus, bed hair – before curiosity gets the better of me. I slither into the visitors' cell behind Joe, just as Ray is closing the door.

It's a grim little room. There's one high, barred window, like in Annie's cell, and painted bricks like the corridor. Smoke swirls round the bare lightbulb because Charles Driscoll lights a cigarette as soon as they all sit down on the wooden chairs, like he can't wait another second. Rose sits down next to him, perched on her chair like it's a ledge on a high building and she's about to jump.

There's a partition down the middle of the room with a big window of reinforced glass. The beaky-nosed warder stands behind the family and I squeeze into a corner, trying to keep as far away from everyone as possible. For a moment, all I can see in the glass is the reflection of three bowed heads and the middle bit of the warder's tunic, but then a door opens on the other side of the partition and Ray appears. Annie's following her, moving slowly, like she's underwater.

As she sits down, Rose gasps and leans forward like she wants to hug her. Beaky Nose steps forward automatically to try and stop her, even though it's not like Rose can touch Annie through the glass.

Joe takes hold of Rose's hand. Annie's expression is still blank, like her brain hasn't caught up with what she's seeing.

Charles just carries on smoking. I can see from his reflection that he's uncomfortable, even embarrassed. He isn't looking at Annie, but somewhere off to the side.

Joe grins at Annie, big and sort of lopsided, and she gives him a smile, weak with effort.

'Hello Mum, hello Dad, hello Joe.' Automatically polite.

They stare at her. For a moment, it's like nobody knows what to do, then Joe says, 'How are you doing, Annie? They treating you all right?' He sounds fierce, like he'll fight them if she says they aren't.

Annie gives a shaky little laugh, trying to show him she's keeping it together. 'It's not so bad.'

The silence feels fragile, like glass. Joe shatters it. 'You shouldn't be in here.' Rose and Charles don't back him up and I can see from their reflections that neither of them is looking at Annie now. Charles is busy stubbing out the cigarette he smoked in about three drags and lighting another one, and Rose is staring down at her lap.

'I wish I could come home.' Annie's already given up trying to seem OK and her voice is small and pathetic. 'I'd be good.'

She's not looking at Joe when she says this, but he's the one who replies, sounding like there's something trapped in his throat. 'I'm sorry, Annie.'

Still, Rose and Charles don't speak, and Joe and Annie stare at each other, locking eyes. Suddenly, like someone's given her an electric shock, Rose starts gabbling. 'Mr Brighouse says there's every chance. He wouldn't have said that if he didn't believe it.'

Oh, God. She means the reprieve. They don't know yet.

The way she's speaking – fast and sort of flat – I can't tell if she believes what she's saying, or she's saying it to make Annie feel better, or just because she can't bear any more silence.

Charles clears his throat. 'I'm sure they'll do the right thing.' The way he says this makes me wonder what he thinks 'the right thing' is. I can see Joe's reflection giving him side-eye.

Annie says, 'So then I can come home?'

The hope in her voice is heart-breaking and there's silence afterwards. It's like the air in the room is so full of what's not being said that it could choke you.

'Well ...' Rose leans forward suddenly, like she wants to say something positive but can't think what, 'you've got to keep your chin up.'

It seems like a stupid thing to say, but what would be a smart thing?

'There's still hope,' Joe says, and I can tell he's having to try really hard to keep his voice from cracking. 'Mr Brighouse is doing everything he can, and Mr Partington from the dairy said he's going to start a petition.'

Charles clears his throat again. 'Well, we're not sure about that ...'

Rose says, 'All right, Charlie,' and puts out her hand like she wants to stop him saying anything else, but he jerks his arm away and she sort of shrinks back and looks down at her lap again. I suppose Charles means because of Dorothy and Kathleen, that if the family sign a petition for a reprieve it might seem like they don't care about them. Especially as I'm guessing that he, at least, thinks Annie is guilty.

Joe is openly glaring at Charles now, but I have no idea what Rose thinks. Even if she does believe that Annie's guilty, she surely can't want to lose her last daughter? And whatever she thinks, she still loves Annie. Under her careful outfit and pained smile, it's obvious.

'There's a cat here.' Annie leans forward, seeming pleased and bright in a way she hasn't before, even when she was trying to sound OK. 'A tabby one, like Tiger. She's the matron's cat and she doesn't usually like other people, but she always comes up to me when I go out for exercise . . .' She smiles at the memory. 'She lets me stroke her. She doesn't let the others –' she turns her head slightly towards Ray, who is standing with her back to the wall, hands behind her, staring straight ahead – 'only me.'

'That's nice.' It's Joe who speaks. Rose is staring down at her lap again, and Charles is still looking uncomfortable, like he can't wait to leave. 'What's her name?'

'Betsy. She's lovely,' Annie says, then frowns. 'Is Tiger all right?'

'Don't worry, I'm looking after her. She keeps leaving dead mice in my room.' Joe leans forward. 'Dad trod on one the other day. He didn't half swear.' Annie laughs, but there's more side-eye – both directions this time – between Joe and Charles.

'Will you stroke her for me, Joe?'

'Course I will.'

The silence stretches. Charles's smoke scratches at my throat and I want to cough. Would Joe hear me? He hasn't given any sign that he's aware of me standing behind him, but if I can see his reflection in the glass, he must be able to see mine . . .

If I have one. I can't see from here, because of the angle. I suddenly wonder if I could just melt through the wall, and press my hand against the bricks to see what happens. They feel solid, so I guess I can't. Perhaps those things only work if you're an actual ghost, rather than just having gone backwards through time, like I seem to be doing.

At least that thought distracts me from the cough, although I'm not sure how much longer I can hold it in . . .

Rose is talking fast again. 'Mrs Millichip sends her best. You know,' because Annie's looking blank, 'from next door. And Mr Bellamy from the grocer's.'

'They don't think you should be here, either.' As he says this, Joe shoots Charles a look that says *You're not the boss of me*, and Charles glares right back. I'm wondering whether Joe means those people think that Annie shouldn't be facing the death penalty or that she shouldn't be in prison at all, and I'm distracted and forget not to cough. Fortunately, it's not very loud – but I'm pretty sure Joe hears it because he turns his head very slightly for just a second, like he's seen something out of the corner of his eye. Then he says, 'Mrs Hewitt sends her best, too.'

I'm sure I'm not imagining that Rose is now giving him side-eye as well. I don't know what this Mrs Hewitt's got to do with it. Maybe nothing, but one thing is clear: the Driscolls are *not* a united family.

Rose asks Annie if she's remembering to pray – like that's going to do any good – and whether the prison chaplain has been to see her and a bunch of stuff like that. Before long, Beaky Nose is saying time's up and everyone's trying to smile again for the goodbyes and saying things like 'Cheerio' and 'God Bless'. Joe puts his palm flat against the glass of the partition. Annie does the same, opposite his, and they stay like that for a long moment, staring at each other. I can't see Joe's face because it's too near the glass for a reflection to show, but Annie's eyes are huge and solemn. I can't tell how she feels about Rose and Charles, but I can see how much she loves him.

Florey opens the door, and they all file through with Beaky Nose following and me slipping out behind her. They start down the corridor, back the way they came. Joe hangs back as the rest go around the corner, then turns to face me. For a second, we stare at each other.

Even though this is beyond weird, and it's the last thing I should be thinking of, I get this jolt in my chest and it's like I've forgotten how to breathe. Joe is looking at me like I'm some sort of specimen in a laboratory.

'Are you a ghost?'

'I don't think so.' The words come out in a squeaky whisper. 'I haven't been born yet.'

'So you're from the future?' He says this like it's a totally normal question.

'Yes.'

'Then you know.'

He says it flat, stating a fact, and I know my face has given him the answer already.

I can't look at him. 'I'm really sorry.'

I can feel Joe's eyes boring into me. 'Then . . .' He makes a noise like he's holding back a whole lifetime of pain. 'I need your help.'

'*Help?*' Now I'm staring at him.

'She's innocent.'

I look into his beautiful, desperate eyes, and even if I could think of something to say, I know I wouldn't be able to speak. Before Joe can say anything else, Charles comes back round the corner and grabs his arm. 'What are you playing at? Get moving.' As Charles yanks him towards the corner – roughly, like he's not bothered if it hurts – Joe looks back and mouths something. It takes me a moment to realise what he's saying.

'We. Need. Proof.'

Then he's gone, and I'm alone in the corridor.

Chapter 14

Seven a.m. Dad's T-shirt smells of Charles's cigarettes. So does my hair. Good job no one else is awake, so I can get into the shower before Skye and Dad get the wrong idea – especially after what I said about him starting smoking again.

The soles of my feet are filthy again, too. And it's the third time in a row. So that proves . . .

Proves what? I try to think about it all rationally as I wash my hair and the T-shirt in the shower.

The dirt and the cigarette smell really *are* from 1955, I guess. So: I can go back in time, but apparently only if I'm asleep. Which means that my dreams are real, or sort of, anyway. Joe wasn't scared, just matter-of-fact and accepting. I guess he doesn't feel he's got time to worry about whether he believes in ghosts or people from the future or whatever – all he cares about is if I can help Annie.

Can I? If so, how?

I want to figure out how this is happening, so I wrap my hair in a towel and google 'time travel'.

Shit. Turns out time travel is basically physics: the fourth dimension and general relativity, because how fast stuff moves depends on how fast other stuff is moving and which direction it's going. Plus, the curved space–time universe and wormholes and cosmic strings and whatever. And Albert Einstein – genius physicist with ultimate science boffin hair – said that the distinction between past, present and future is a total illusion, which I guess means that it's all happening at once anyway.

Except it isn't.

Is it?

I'm never going to understand any of this. Everything I've read is just abstract stuff, and I actually *did* it. Whether you understand it or not, I reckon that lived experience – even if you might not have been awake at the time – trumps theory, because real (dirt on feet and smell of cigarettes).

I think it must be something to do with the clock itself; linking the present and the past because it was originally here or somewhere nearby. What I felt when I touched it, that I thought was like someone's hand reaching out to touch mine, was *that* from another time?

We think time is just this thing that ticks away in the background, and it only goes in one direction – forwards – which must be true, actually, otherwise everything would happen at once. Unless it *does* all happen at once, but we don't know because we only exist in our own time . . . Also, time isn't the same for everyone. Or rather, we don't all experience it the same way. Like Dad saying it seems to speed up as you get older, or how it can drag if you're bored, or like it did in lockdown. Plus, there are different time zones round the world – why we say other countries are so many hours ahead of us or behind us . . .

Only Now.

Whose now, though?

If the clock tells the time in the past, or what *we* think of as the past, as well as the present – where I actually *am* – then maybe, just for that short time at midnight, it somehow connects the two.

I go into the hall to have a look at it. The front seems totally normal and I can't see the back because it's fixed too tightly against the wall. Our time obviously isn't an exact match with 1955, because their daytime is our night-time – but it must be in the same twenty-four hours because the dates fit. Backwards or forwards, though? Maybe there's air resistance, like with planes. Dad explained it to me once, how they fly: lift, weight, thrust and drag (the resistance bit). I just have to hope it's slightly earlier here than there, because otherwise there's even less time than I thought . . .

Although those clever-science-people websites *also* point out that to go back in time you'd have to move at more than the speed of light, and if you did that you'd burn up or explode anyway, so it couldn't happen . . .

Except that it just did happen. To me – and not once, but three times.

Maybe some things can't be explained, and you just have to accept them. Joe did. He was totally on board about me being from the future. Like he's so certain that Annie is innocent. He didn't even—

65

'Boo!'

I practically jump out of my skin. It's Dad, wearing a kimono that has to have been a gift from Skye, because if Mum saw him in anything covered with pink dragons she'd have pissed herself laughing.

'What's up?'

'Apart from *that*?'

'Very funny.'

'Actually, that.' I point at the 'Massage Parlour' sign. 'It makes you look like a creep, and you need to take it down. And I bet Skye doesn't like it, either.'

'She hasn't said anything.'

'No, well she wouldn't, would she? It's too soon and she still thinks you're great.'

Dad frowns like he's going to argue. Then he looks up at the sign and gets this weird expression on his face, as if he's seeing it properly for the first time. 'OK.'

'OK you'll think about it or OK you'll get rid of it?'

'Get rid. Let me get dressed first, though.' He pats me on the shoulder and goes into the kitchen.

I think about Joe as I dry my hair. Yes, he is gorgeous, and to be honest I keep wondering what he saw when he looked at me – if it was *actual* me or more ghostly (although that's not necessarily bad because being transparent would probably make you look thinner), but I'm also thinking about what he said.

I need your help.

To undo it. How, though? Once stuff's happened, that's that. You can't un-happen it, because it's already done. You can't change the past by what you do now, only the future.

Except . . .

My past – or not actually mine, but the time before I was born – *is* Annie's future, isn't it? Like, for all the people alive now, our future will be the past for the people who come after us. Or who we *think* come after us, but who may exist already if time doesn't actually work like we think it does. Which means that if I'm going to have children, they already exist, and so do their children, if they have any, and—

Whoa!

OK, so that's deep. But three days ago, I wouldn't have thought it was possible to travel through time, either. It's almost enough to make me wish I'd taken physics.

Chapter 15

We need proof.

That was the last thing Joe said.

Proof that Annie couldn't have done it, or that somebody else did? The best thing would be to have both. If I could find it, I might be able to save not only Annie but Joe as well. Now that I've actually met him, thinking about him turning into the sad old guy in that photo, who killed himself from despair, makes me want to cry.

I could stop that happening.

But surely, if Annie was – *is* – innocent, someone would have proved it already, and there'd be a podcast or a series or something? I googled 'miscarriages of justice' before, and her name didn't come up even once.

But – and forgetting Joe for a minute – what do *I* think?

Did she do it? I scowl at myself in the mirror – my hair is super thick, so drying it takes *for ever* – and try to figure it out. My instinct is . . .

I don't know. I desperately don't want her to have done it, which

I know is partly because she's a young woman and we're nearly the same age. I have no way of assessing how someone *should* behave if they were innocent or guilty, but I feel sure her kind-heartedness is genuine.

But ...

I don't always read people right. You'd think I'd have learned by now that how people behave isn't necessarily a great guide to what they're thinking. I mean, I had *no* idea Dad was cheating on Mum before it came out. Or that it wasn't the first time, or that Mum knew he'd done it before but hadn't said anything because she thought it would – her words to me – 'blow over'. I just knew there was something wrong.

Also, I like Joe, and that makes me kind of biased.

I carry on aiming the hairdryer with one hand and use the other one to pull my laptop towards me.

Surely it's right to give people the benefit of the doubt? I need to approach this with an open mind. That's what a good detective would do, whether or not they could time-travel. Plus, they'd find out as much as they could because knowledge is power.

It crosses my mind that if I meet Joe again, I might have to explain what the internet is and how I found out about his family, although it's not like I actually understand *how* we get the information – it's all just *here*. But will I want to tell Joe any of it? If there's no way of getting the proof he needs, it would just be pointless and cruel.

That's providing I keep on being able to get to 1955 to see him, of course. I've already got butterflies in my stomach, wondering if

I'll make it back there tonight – but it feels kind of *meant*, like it's what I should be doing, for him and for Annie.

Dad and Skye are in the kitchen, more all over each other than ever, and she keeps talking about the three of us having a spa evening right here in the flat. Turns out she trained as a beautician and nail technician before she went into promoting pebbles with healing vibes, which is why she's got so much kit.

I brought my breakfast back to my room, but I can still hear them. Skye's laughing like Dad's the funniest person ever. 'Oh, Dommie!'

There isn't a whole lot more stuff about the case online, but there are some scans of newspapers with headlines like JEALOUS SISTER SLAYS LOVE RIVAL and FAMILY'S GRIEF. As far as I can see – which is difficult, because the type gets pretty blurry when you try to enlarge it from totally minuscule – the Driscolls are always described as 'respectable'. One of the newspapers says Joe worked at King's Cross, cleaning engines, so he must have left school early. When I google that, I discover you could leave school at fifteen back then, and way fewer people than now went to university. He must have worked on steam trains like the *Hogwarts Express*, which is pretty cool.

There's a black and white photograph of the Driscolls' house at Aylmer Terrace with a policeman standing outside. It's at the end of a row of Victorian terraced houses, tall and thin, three storeys each with tiny front gardens and front doors set back in little porches. There's a number painted on the fanlight above the door, which I can just make out: 37. Those houses cost a fortune now, but Dad grew up in Islington and he told me that when he was born – which, OK, wasn't the 1950s but it wasn't *that* much later – the people there were poor. That makes sense because the buildings in the photo look sort of dirty, like nobody's got the time or money to look after them. A couple have boarded-up windows and there are no trees or cars at all, just metal dustbins all down the pavement.

Just my luck. When people time-travel in books and films, they always go back to somewhere beautiful or amazing – a palace or whatever. I get a prison and – assuming I ever get to see it – a street that's one step away from a slum.

A piece about Annie's trial mentions that Charles Driscoll gave evidence about her 'being fanciful' and 'making up stories' – what it said on Wikipedia – and that 'a family friend', Mrs Molly Hewitt, said she was meant to be going to the Driscolls' house for tea that day but was 'called away'.

Mrs Hewitt sends her best . . . Rose was not happy when Joe said that. Mrs Hewitt must have known the family a long time because the newspaper says she was from Dalston, which was where they lived before they moved to Islington. Could she have snuck into the house when they were all out and poisoned the cake, then found a reason not to stay for tea?

Questions buzz in my head like wasps, but none of the possible answers seem very likely. It's weird, though, that nobody seems to be a hundred per cent sure what Annie's motive was – unless she was a psychopath, of course, poisoning people for fun.

She certainly doesn't seem like one. I watched a programme

about them in lockdown – there were loads of things to look out for, like being clever and manipulative, and Annie seems to be the opposite of that. Plus, she was worried about the cat, and that was genuine.

Where do I even *start*?

Chapter 16

I feel like I need some inspiration. I also need to get out of this flat and away from Dad and Skye, and it's a lovely sunny day, so I decide to visit Highgate Cemetery. It's probably stupid, but I feel like being closer to Joe and Annie might help me with what to do next.

I tell Dad I have to go into school, and set off for the bus stop.

Even with the information from the website, it takes a while to find Joe. Highgate Cemetery is massive, and the grave is on the west side, which has all sorts of tombs and vaults and statues, mostly jumbled up and overgrown. Some bits are fenced off because they're too dangerous, but there are lots of paths lined with graves, some of them cracked or with headstones and crosses sticking up at odd angles, and lots of crazy Victorian stuff like the Egyptian Avenue. It's like a city-within-a-city where all the inhabitants are dead and it ought to be creepy, but I don't feel scared – or only enough that I can keep a lid on it – because it's peaceful and actually sort of romantic. Plus, there's loads of plant life going on: undergrowth, ivy everywhere, even some flowers, and everything looks dappled because of the sun coming through the canopy of trees.

I spot a fox scratching its ear next to a pedestal with a broken column on top of it. It sees me staring and gives me a look like, *whatever*, then trots down the path in front of me and into the bushes. The broken column means a life cut short – someone who died young. I've been here before, with Mum, and she explained the meanings of all the different stone symbols you see on the graves. My favourite is the clasped hands, sort of like a handshake, which means that the living and the dead will meet again – although I'd always thought it meant meet in heaven, not through some random time portal.

Joe's headstone is on one of the narrower paths and quite small, with no decoration, although it's surrounded by ferns and wild violets, which is lovely.

FRANCIS JOSEPH PALMER
28.01.1938 – 15.11.1991

That's all it says. I know from my research that the date of his death is an estimate, but I suppose whoever paid for his gravestone just went with the best guess.

I wonder why Joe changed his surname back to Palmer. If he was born in 1938 and his biological dad was killed in the Second World War, he can barely have remembered him. If it was because of Annie – people bullying him once they'd realised they were

related – that seems a bit odd, too, given he thought she was innocent and wanted to stand up for her.

I was hoping that I might get some sort of vibe from the grave.
Not a message – well, not really – but a feeling or an impression or
something, but there's nothing. I take a deep breath and close my
eyes and try to concentrate hard to sort of draw Joe towards me,
but nothing happens and there's no point pretending.

I want to put something on the grave to show that someone's
thinking about Joe, because that feels like the right thing to do. I've
got Dad's £20, but there wasn't a flower stall at the gate.

I look round and spot a stone cherub a few metres away, being
slowly strangled by ivy, so I tug some lengths free, plait them into
a wreath and fix all the ends together with my hair tie. I remember
Mum telling me that a wreath is a symbol of victory over death,
and, given what Joe was – or assuming that the past and the present do exist at the same time – *is* trying to do, that seems pretty
appropriate.

It's not brilliant, but when I prop it against Joe's stone it doesn't
look bad at all, so I take a photo. 'I want to help you, Joe,' I tell him.
'I'll do my best.'

On impulse, I lean forward and touch the carving on the stone.
As my fingertips stroke the 'J' of Joseph, I feel, through the stone,
the warmth and softness of something living, just as I did when I
touched the clock.

I suddenly realise that there's absolutely no sound. No leaves
rustling, nothing stirring in the trees or the undergrowth: like
everything's in freeze-frame, as if time itself is holding its breath.

I stare at a squirrel crossing the path ahead, its furry back and tail paused in mid-ripple, and I *know*, with blazing certainty, that Joe is right: Annie is innocent.

Then the trees and plants come back to life all around me. Everything is normal again, like nothing happened, and the stone is cold and slightly damp under my hand.

The problem is, though, that I don't know how to find any proof of Annie's innocence – if there even is any. I don't say this out loud, and I'll just have to hope that the dead or the alive-at-the-same-time-but-somewhere-else or whatever they are don't know what we're thinking. 'I'm going to find Annie now,' I say, and almost ask if I can take a message, only that would be completely ridiculous.

I've figured out that Annie's grave is over the other side of the West Cemetery, but the vegetation is far too dense for me to cut across the middle, so I go the long way round using the paths.

I stop to look at a huge stone angel. Most of the angels are upright, but this one is kneeling, slumped over the top of her monument with her face buried in her arms. I think it's meant to look like she's crying, but the effect, with the wings drooping down on either side, is more like she got bored and fell asleep. Hardly surprising, because she's been there a long time. She's covered in lichen and the inscription, for somebody who died in 1878, has been almost entirely worn away by years of rain and frost. I'm trying to figure out what the person's name was when I hear twigs snapping and catch a slight movement out of the corner of my eye.

I'm pretty sure whatever is making the noise is too big to be a fox, and when I turn I catch a glimpse of what I think is a dark-coloured coat, disappearing behind a bush. Security? A gardener? But they wouldn't hide from me, would they?

Silence. I decide I was mistaken and start walking again, but I've only taken a few steps when there are more twig-snapping noises, and a man steps out from behind a grave and onto the path.

My heart jolts in my chest. He's only about ten metres away so I can see him quite clearly: all in black, leather coat – even though it's summer – and aviator sunglasses, like a budget version of a character from *The Matrix*.

People come to cemeteries to do all sorts of strange shit. Perhaps he's a satanist or something. Maybe there are lots more like him, lurking in the bushes.

He's looking straight at me.

All the usual calculations – how far to safety, will anyone hear if I scream, and can I outrun him – flash through my brain at light-ning speed as I whirl round and back the way I've come. It's the opposite way to the main gate, where there might be someone who can help, but if I'm fast enough I can loop round. Heart pounding against my ribs as I run, I shove my hand in my pocket and thread my keys through my fingers, and all the time I'm thinking that if anything happens it'll be my fault because I'm not really supposed to be here and—

Shit!

I trip over a root and wind up flat on my face, palms stinging and ankle throbbing, sprawled across the narrow path.

Footsteps, coming up close. 'Keep back,' I shout. Then,

idiotically, 'Social distancing!' Like anyone does that any more, but I need to get up, get away—

'Millie?'

How does he know my name? 'Stay away from me,' I pant as I scramble to my feet and lurch away from him, trying to ignore the pain in my ankle.

'Millie, wait!'

Hang on ... that voice. It *can't* be.

I turn my head.

I barely recognise him, but it is.

Kieran.

What's *he* doing here?

Chapter 17

He never used to wear those clothes when he was still coming to school. Plus, he looks thinner. And ... well, like he came out by mistake because he usually spends all his time in a basement, trying to be scary online.

OK, so there's history. I haven't seen him for months, but he used to come to Climbing Club and we were dating, sort of. It was mostly just hanging out and messing around, but we did go and see films sometimes. He was properly clever as well as being cute and funny – in fact, he could probably explain all that Einsteiny time stuff – and it was all fine until he started getting weird and saying he didn't see the point of going to school, or doing anything, really. He'd had an accident climbing a couple of weeks earlier, falling off the wall at the leisure centre, but it wasn't a big deal. He went to hospital and got X-rayed and everything, and they said he was OK. I don't know if it was anything to do with that, and he certainly wasn't *physically* hurt, but ...

At first, the other boys teased him – he was being an edgelord or whatever – but once everyone figured out he wasn't trying to be cool, they kept asking me what was wrong with him, like I had any idea. He just kept getting more and more withdrawn and wouldn't talk to anyone, plus he was barely eating.

I didn't know what to do. We'd go and sit on a bench or something, and he'd just stare into space, or he'd try and give me things – expensive stuff like his laptop, and when I asked him why, he'd say he didn't need them any more. Obviously, I wasn't going to take them, but he'd keep on offering and it made me really uncomfortable, because I couldn't understand why he was doing it. I mean, if he'd wanted something from me, that would have been easier to cope with, because it would have made sense, but it was like he genuinely didn't think the stuff was any use to him, so it was just taking up space.

I feel bad that I didn't do more, but I'm not a doctor, and with everything going on at home with Mum and Dad, I really needed the other things in my life to be normal. That's not really an excuse, but ... I did *try*. I mean, I didn't just abandon him. I kept asking what was wrong, but he wouldn't tell me, except once when he said he was a zombie. I don't *think* he meant it literally, but by that point he was being so strange that I wondered if perhaps he actually *did* think he was one. That was when everyone started saying he must be really into drugs, especially because some people at our school do ketamine on Hampstead Heath or whatever, but I never saw him take anything, so ...

Then one day in December he didn't come into school and someone said he was being treated at the Adolescent Psychiatric Unit. I messaged him, but he never answered, so I don't know if it's true. But if it is, they must have let him out or he wouldn't be here. I never went to his house but I know he lives in Archway, so he wouldn't have had to come far.

OK, pretend it's normal. Take a breath. Say hello.

I'm giving myself all these instructions, but it's like I've forgotten how to open my mouth. It's better when he takes off his glasses, although his brown eyes look dull and his head is kind of skull-like because of the weight loss.

'Hi.' My voice comes out in a squeak.

'Visiting a friend?'

'Yes.' I grin at him, trying to be like *Nothing to see, it's all fine.* 'You?'

Kieran shrugs. 'I come here a lot.'

'Why?'

'It's just . . . comfortable.'

OK . . . just keep pretending this is normal. 'I come here a lot' sounds goth-weird, not stalky-weird, but . . . '*Comfortable?*'

He nods, like that's the most obvious thing in the world. 'I like what you did with the ivy.' So he *has* been watching me. 'Where are you going now?'

'To find another grave. Want to come with me?' Why did I say *that*? It's not what I want at all.

I stare at him, willing him to refuse.

'OK.'

Shit. I start walking, and Kieran falls into step with me. *Just pretend everything's normal, Millie.* Here we are together, and it's an ordinary day, and everything's fine in the past and the present and the future and we're all gonna have a good time, la la la.

I sneak a look at him as we go down the path. Apart from being too thin, he actually looks all right, now I've got over the shock.

'I thought you said you were visiting a friend.'

'Actually, friend was your word, but yes.'

'A guy who died before you were born.'

'It's complicated.'

I can feel Kieran's eyes boring into me, and I'm wondering what to do next when he says, 'Are you dead?'

I take a step away from him and almost lose my balance. 'Am I *what*?'

Forget pretending it's all normal. This would be strange even if Kieran were joking.

'Are you dead?' He's totally straight-faced.

'I don't look *that* bad, do I?' I laugh, like *that's* going to make everything all right.

'You know I don't mean that.' He sounds irritated.

'No, I *really* don't. You just asked me *if I'm dead*.'

'Yes.'

'Kieran, I'm here, walking around. Talking.'

'So am I.'

I stare at him. 'You're not dead, either.'

'But I am. That's why I'm here, Millie. I'm dead.'

Chapter 18

I stare at him, trying to work out if this is some weird joke after all.

'Dead.' Totally matter-of-fact. 'As in, no longer alive.'

'Yeah, right.' This is the most ridiculous conversation ever, and he's still looking totally serious. 'I don't understand.' I shake my head, like *huh?* 'Can we just . . .'

'Just what? You've got one dead friend –' Kieran points in the direction of Joe's gravestone – 'why not another one?'

'Because he actually *is* dead. As in, he's *under there.*'

'And I'm dead but up here.' Kieran sighs. 'I didn't really expect you to understand. No one does.'

'Er . . . You're *breathing.*'

Kieran shakes his head. 'I told you, it's why I'm here, in the cemetery. It's the logical place to be if I'm dead.'

'Why do you think you're dead?'

Kieran sighs, like he's given up trying to explain himself to stupid people. 'I don't think, I *know.*'

'All right . . .' I really don't need this, but it looks like I'll have to go along with it, 'but why?'

'I just do, OK?'

'Did you tell them that at the psych unit?'

'Yes. They gave me pills. They didn't work so I stopped taking them when I was discharged.'

'Do your parents know?' Kieran's parents are both professors with brains the size of planets, but I have a feeling they aren't exactly on point when it comes to nurturing.

'About the medication? No way.'

'Kieran, you need to tell them. Seriously.'

'They don't get it.'

'So . . .' There's no point arguing with him, so I decide I might as well go with the flow. I mean, today can't get any stranger than it is already. 'What does it feel like, being dead?'

'Like nothing.'

'You mean numb?'

'Numbness would be a feeling, because it's the feeling of knowing there isn't a feeling and there ought to be, right? This is like –' he screws up his face, thinking – 'the time goes past – one day, then another – but I don't exist in it. And there's no point behaving as if you're alive when you're not. Mum makes me clean my teeth and all that, but it's a waste of time. I just do it to avoid an argument. I thought you might get it, but . . .' He tails off, looking disappointed.

I feel really sorry for him, but I've got no idea what to say, because it just doesn't make sense. 'But . . . you know who you are and who I am, so that means you have consciousness, doesn't it?'

'You sound like my dad. Look: I know I don't exist, OK?'

'OK. So ... when did you die?' I can't believe I'm having this conversation.

Kieran frowns. 'I'm not sure. At first, I only felt like this sometimes, like I wasn't real, and then more and more often, and now it's most of the time. It took a while before I understood what was going on – that it's the only thing that makes sense.'

'But you can feel this, can't you?' I touch his elbow.

He jerks his arm away. 'Yes, but it's like it's not happening to me. I can't explain.'

'But I can talk to you. I mean, you can hear me. I don't have to ... I don't know, hold a séance.'

'I didn't say I *understood* it, Millie.' He shrugs. 'Just how it is.'

'So ... ' I look back at Joe's headstone. 'Could you talk to him?'

'Dead people can't talk.'

'You're talking.'

Kieran stares across the gravestones at something far in the distance. 'But it's not like I want to. People keep talking to me, but there's no connection. I think there's been a mistake.' He looks back at me and, for the first time, he smiles. 'They'll put it right when I start to rot. I mean, it's already happening, but they haven't noticed yet. They will soon, though – then they'll *have* to do something.'

I stare at him. 'You mean ... *bury* you?'

He nods. 'Then I can be here all the time.'

'Was that why you kept trying to give me stuff?'

'I don't need it any more, do I?' He shrugs, irritable. 'It's not like any of it matters. And anyway, you're the one with the imaginary friend.'

85

It occurs to me that, in some ways, what's happened – with Annie and Joe and everything – is no stranger than what's happened to Kieran, and that maybe if I tried to tell somebody about that I'd be put in hospital and medicated, too. But I could talk to Kieran about it, couldn't I? He's not going to say I'm crazy or go off on one, because it won't matter to him, will it?

So I tell him.

Chapter 19

'... and I want to help them,' I finish.

'It won't matter now,' Kieran says.

'But Joe shouldn't have died like he did. If Annie hadn't been hanged—'

'Even if she hadn't, Dorothy and Kathleen would still have been murdered.'

'I know. It's not like I'm trying to make everything perfect, because no one can do that, but at least Annie and Joe would have the rest of their lives.'

'Not necessarily. Joe might have committed suicide for another reason.'

Something occurs to me. 'You're not ... I mean, if nobody believes you, you won't ...?'

'Kill myself? Fuck's sake, Millie. How can I kill myself? I'm. Already. Dead.'

'Sorry, I wasn't thinking.' OMG. Change the subject, Millie, before your head explodes. 'I thought Rose's grave might be somewhere here, but I haven't found it.'

Kieran shrugs. 'Maybe she was cremated. That's sometimes a different part of the cemetery.'

'Don't families normally do the same thing for everybody?'

'Not always. Anyhow, the family wouldn't have had a choice about Annie, would they? And maybe she *did* do it. Even if she didn't, that's the thing about being dead. None of it matters.'

'It matters to Joe.'

Kieran shakes his head. 'Leave him alone.'

'But he wants my help – and it isn't fair, not on any of them. And I didn't ask to go back to the past . . . or whatever it is I do.'

'Just forget about it.'

I look back in the direction of Joe's headstone, trying to feel a connection with him, but right now, there's nothing. Yes, I feel sad for him because of how he died – that's why I made the wreath – but that's just *my* emotions. Like Kieran says: when you're dead, you're dead, and that's it.

Except that, whatever Kieran says, he *isn't* dead – and Joe wasn't dead when I talked to him, either.

I need your help.

Joe's beautiful, desperate eyes. Annie's face. The noose in the next room, hanging in the dark.

'You're wrong,' I tell Kieran. 'I can't explain it because I don't understand the physics or whatever, but I just know.'

'No, you don't. You were dreaming.' He kicks at a pebble and starts to walk away, hands in his pockets. He's not angry, it's more like he just doesn't see the point in talking to me.

I catch him up. 'That's the whole point – I wasn't! You don't bring back the smell of cigarettes from dreams.'

'You imagined it.'

This from the person who thinks he's a corpse. 'What about the dirt on my feet, then? I know Skye saw it, because she told me.'

'Who's Skye?'

'Dad's girlfriend.'

'Oh. Aren't your parents together any more?'

'No. I didn't tell you because . . . well, I thought you had enough to deal with, without me dumping on you. Anyway, what matters is that the dirt was real.'

'Yeah, from before.'

'No, because I'd had a shower – I told you that. Plus, the floor wasn't dirty.' I glare at him. 'I don't see why you should expect me to believe you when you don't believe me.'

To my surprise, Kieran doesn't meet my eye. Instead, he takes his head in his hands, as if he's in pain, and stays like that for such a long time that I start to think he's forgotten I'm there. 'It's not that I don't believe you,' he says eventually. 'Not exactly.' He sighs, and I can feel the enormous hopelessness of it, the confusion caused by something that cannot make sense, no matter how hard you try. 'I'm going to . . . ' He gestures vaguely in the direction of the overgrown graves away from the path.

'OK,' I say, 'but keep in touch, yeah?'

I watch him wander off, thinking how sad it is and wondering what on earth I can do to help. If this were a film, I'd be Kieran's saviour girlfriend, who only existed to teach him to embrace life – Manic Pixie Dream Girl, or whatever that character was called – but it isn't and I'm not, plus I've got my own shit going on. Also, if Kieran's parents and the health service can't help him, I don't see how I'm supposed to.

Although, he's not actually asking for help because, even though you'd think that believing yourself to be dead would not only be revolting – what with all the putrefaction – but also massively scary, he seems to be cool with it. Well, almost.

Anyway, right now it's Joe who needs the urgent help. It's weird, because you could say that they are opposites: a living person who believes he's dead and a dead person who believes he's alive – if that's what a ghost is.

Except that I don't think Joe is a ghost, any more than I am when I'm in his time.

FML. I really don't understand *any* of this.

When we were talking about ghosts at school once, Yaz said she'd seen one at her gran's, drifting about in a lane where a girl was murdered. I reckon it was because knowing where the murder took place made her suggestible, but I didn't say that because everyone else was totally into it. Me seeing Joe can't be because I'm suggestible, because I hadn't even *known* they used to hang people in the prison, never mind that Dad's flat is right beside the site of the execution chamber.

I eventually manage to find Annie's grave. The headstone is small and plain, like Joe's:

THE MIDNIGHT CLOCK

ANNE MAVIS DRISCOLL
1936 – 1955

It's stuck on the end of a row of big Victorian monuments, like an afterthought – but there's a bunch of pink roses on it, arranged in a metal vase. That's unusual – not many graves in the West Cemetery have flowers on them, mostly because they're way too old for living people to remember, and it's obvious from their freshness that these roses were put there quite recently.

Someone remembers Annie.

Chapter 20

I don't try to find Dorothy and Kathleen's graves – I'm not only creeped out by everything but suddenly really hungry and, because it's still early, I decide to get the bus back down to Holloway Road and see if I can find the Driscolls' house instead. I'm not sure how it'll help, but I need to do *something*.

Why did I get that warm feeling from Joe's headstone? Perhaps I'm the one being suggestible now, with being in a graveyard – but it felt so *real* . . . And thinking about it now makes the tips of my fingers tingle, like tiny electric shocks.

I walk back down Highgate Hill, picking up some lemonade and crisps on the way, and catch the bus, but I'm still quite hungry by the time I've walked to Number 37 Aylmer Terrace – or what I think must be Number 37, because you can't see the bottom half of the house at all. It's got hoardings with a construction company logo around it, so I guess the owners must be having building work done, although there doesn't seem to be anyone around at the moment.

Aylmer Terrace looks really nice. The front gardens may be

small – just strips outside the big bay windows – but there's way more space at the back. The street is rich-looking, with trees and lots of new paint, all shining in the spring sun like the whole place has been laminated. It's super quiet: I can see a lot of blinds down and wooden shutters across the windows, and not many cars parked, which makes me think that these are just people's London homes, and they've gone to their country cottages for a long weekend. I bet the people who own Number 37 will just stay in the Cotswolds or wherever until the work is finished. Even the hoarding looks posh – dark blue, with shiny health and safety signs about hi-vis and hard hats, and there's even a door with a keypad. I don't want it to seem like I'm loitering, though, because someone might look out of their window and get the wrong idea (or the right idea, which is that I'm planning how I can get over the hoarding), so I walk along a bit. All the houses are smart except the one next door to Number 37: peeling paint on the door and grey net curtains hanging in windows with rotting frames. It says '35' on the fanlight – big painted numbers, like in the photo I saw from 1955, and that makes me think that the owners might even be the same people. Well, not all of them, because anyone who was properly an adult in 1955 would be dead, but the same family. There must be ways of finding out who lives at a particular house, if they own it – a register or something.

Also ... Rose mentioned a next-door neighbour called Mrs Millichip to Annie, didn't she? *Mrs Millichip sends her best*. And there is only one next-door house, because 37 is at the end of the row, so she must have lived here. Perhaps she had a son or daughter.

Somebody who was, say, the same age as Joe in 1955 – seventeen – would be ... wait ... eighty-five now, so they might still be around, and I could ask—

And how's that going to work, exactly? 'Hey, I just met your ex-neighbour, who's been dead since 1991, and he told me ...'

OK, bad idea, but maybe I could ... I don't know ... write a letter? Except that would take too long, waiting for them to reply, because there's less than a week to go until the execution and I don't even know if time in the past moves at the same speed as it does in the present. Come to that, I don't know if I'll be able to go back to 1955 and see Joe again – I just have to trust that it'll happen.

I suddenly feel like somebody's watching me, and when I look up, I spot a woman at a second-floor window of Number 35. Just before she twitches the net curtain back in place, I see grey hair and a beige jumper, faded-looking like the house.

I go back round the corner into Ianthe Street where there are fewer people to see me. There's only the high wall of a garden directly opposite, and you'd have to really crane your neck to get a view from any of the houses at the end of Corinna Road, which is on the other side of the crossroads from Aylmer Terrace.

Stuff gets found when builders start pulling things down and turning up earth. Sometimes even bodies. Not that I think there'll be one here, but there may be something that no one else would think was significant ...

Can't hurt to have a look.

There's a tree by the side of the hoarding. Although the branches within my reach don't look that thick, I reckon there's one I could get to that might be OK for me to climb on and then get over the top of the boards next to it. I'll need to check that I can get back out, though . . .

Better scramble up and get a look into the garden first.

Chapter 21

'Excuse me!'

I almost fall out of the tree. I've managed to get hold of the branch and pull myself up, and when I get my balance back and wriggle round to look, the lady from Number 35 is standing watching me. She looks even more faded than she did through the window, like she might just bleach out and disappear at any moment.

I jump down, bouncing on the balls of my feet, and rub my hands together like dusting them off but in a jolly way, like *Hey, I'm just climbing a tree for fun!*

'What are you doing?' It's a London accent, old school. She's not carrying a shopping bag or anything, so I'm guessing I was right about her being suspicious. I grin at her. 'Sorry, just . . . you know, exercise.'

She frowns, and for a moment I think she's going to tell me off, and I wonder if I should just leg it, but then she says, 'Haven't you got any friends you can do things with?'

'I don't live round here.'

'Where do you live?'

My instinct is still telling me to run, but I reckon she might be able to help me – and I don't want her calling the police or anything. 'Dalston, usually. I'm staying with my dad for a bit. You live here, don't you? I thought I saw you just now.'

'That's right.'

I gesture at the hoarding. 'This must be . . . ' I search for the sort of word Mum would use. 'Disruptive.'

'You can say that again! They're extending it, although why they need more room, I don't know, when it's only the two of them.' She shakes her head, like disbelief. 'And the *noise*! Still, they told me they've got to wait for some supplies – held up at Dover or something – so at least we'll have a few days' peace and quiet.'

She's lonely, I think – why she asked about me having friends. I decide to go for it. 'I suppose this road's changed a lot over the years.'

'Oh, yes – completely different. I barely know anyone now. The couple here are nice enough, but I hardly ever see them.'

'Have you lived here a long time?'

'All my life, dear. Used to know all the neighbours, but it's different now. Different people – I'm the only one left who was born here.'

'Have the people at Number 37 been there long?'

She shakes her head. 'Six months or so. That one's changed hands quite a few times over the years.' She looks suddenly beady, as if she thinks I might be after something, so I deliberately keep my face neutral, like I haven't noticed. This seems to reassure her, because she says, 'I'm Shirley.'

'Millie.'

'Well, Millie, I'd best be getting back. Don't worry, I'm sure you'll see your friends again soon.'

'Yes,' I say, surprised. 'I'll wave at you next time I come by.'

'I'd like that.' Her whole face brightens when she smiles. 'Goodbye, then.'

She *is* lonely. I guess that means she lives by herself.

She looked suspicious when I asked about the people at Number 37. That could be because she'd thought I was trying to get into the place and steal something, or because she thought I'm some true-crime obsessive who wants to make a podcast . . . I don't think that's likely, though – judging by the lack of stuff online it seems like Annie and her family are pretty much forgotten.

Maybe, if I come back and wave to her, she might talk to me about it – although I'd better do any investigating at Number 37 *first*, before I go round the corner. I only managed to get a glimpse of the garden when I was up the tree, and it was bigger than I'd expected – only about ten metres across, but easily twenty-five metres long.

I climb back up, and as far as I can see the builders have already knocked down some of the back wall of the house, removed what I'm guessing must have been a patio – there are lots of paving stones piled up along the fence – and dug a deep hole. They've spread thick plastic sheets over the bits they've worked on and left a mini-digger and a bunch of tools on the remains of the lawn. I spot a tabby cat picking its way daintily across the mess, making me think of Tiger, who Annie asked Joe to stroke for her.

Do the people who own the house now know about the Driscolls? Maybe not, or maybe they do and they don't care because it's too long ago to matter to them.

I've been out a lot longer than I intended, and it's dark by the time I get back. The neon 'Massage Parlour' sign has gone from the hall, and Dad and Skye are both in the sitting room, working on their laptops. I wave at them, grab some weird energy drink I've never heard of from the fridge, and head for my room.

Shirley said she'd lived at Number 35 for all her life, so I reckon that means she might be the daughter of the Mrs Millichip Rose mentioned, and if she never got married ... I google Shirley Millichip, and up comes a load of stuff about some tree the council want to cut down and how a bunch of people are objecting, including 'Shirley Millichip, who lives at Aylmer Terrace'.

Maybe her parents bought the house and it passed to her when they died. I think about the hand holding Joe's in the photograph, with the lace frill round the wrist. Had Shirley been his girlfriend?

She wasn't always old and faded. When she'd smiled at me she'd looked quite pretty, and you could – sort of – see how she'd been before.

A sudden sharpness in my chest, almost like a stab, jolts me. Surely I can't feel jealous about something that happened years before I was born? And Joe isn't even alive – at least, not in *my* time. If he were, he'd be as old as Shirley – eighty or something – so if I'm jealous that's not only ridiculous but also just ... ewww. Except that in *our* time – meaning Joe's and mine, *where we met* – he's only a few months older than me, so go figure. Also, if they had been together, they'd obviously spilt up at some point because they hadn't got married, which is what you had to do back then if you wanted to live with somebody. Plus, back then women always changed their surnames to their husband's when they married, because patriarchy.

Maybe Annie had a boyfriend. There was nothing about that in what I read online, just stuff about her liking Victor Walsh and being jealous of Dorothy. But that didn't mean it was true, and maybe she was seeing someone in secret . . . But even if that were true, what did it have to do with poisoning Dorothy and Kathleen?

All questions, no answers.

'Aaaaaargh!'

'Are you all right in there?'

'Yeah. Sorry.'

Dad puts his head round the door. 'Dinner in an hour? Skye's making jackfruit shawarma.' He says this like he actually knows what it is. When I google jackfruit, I get a photo of a big lumpy thing with skin that looks like it's covered in little green spikes, and weird yellow lumps in the middle. I hope it tastes better than this energy drink, which is gross.

I sit and think about Annie and the rest of them, but I don't come to any conclusions. One thing, though: I'm sure of Annie's innocence now. It's a hard, bright feeling, like a diamond of certainty shining inside my chest – and I'm not going to give up, whatever Kieran says.

Chapter 22

The jackfruit shawarma is totally delicious. I can tell Dad's not sure at first because he's doing that whole performative tasting thing, like *What have we got here, then?*, but he drops the act after about two mouthfuls because it's *so* good. He and Skye talk about their day, which suits me fine because it's not like I want to answer a bunch of questions about what I've been doing. 'More Zoom meetings,' Dad moans. 'I had enough of them during lockdown. Urgh.' He closes his eyes and shakes his head violently, like a wet dog. 'All those emails saying the future was cancelled.'

'I know, darling.' Skye leans over and squeezes his hand. 'But at least lockdown was a chance to live in the here and now.'

I'm bracing myself for 'Today is a gift; that's why it's called the present' or some related piece of hashtaggy 'wisdom', when Dad says, 'Yeah – like a goldfish,' and Skye looks so totally WTF that I start laughing. 'Round and round the same bloody bowl. Except,' he adds, 'we knew were getting older each day, and they don't. Because that was the only thing that was changing, wasn't it?'

'Can you ever change the past?' I ask this partly because I want to stop Skye giving us a lecture about being positive, but also because I'm genuinely curious.

He frowns, and I wonder if he's thinking about Mum – which wasn't actually my intention – then shakes his head. 'We can only learn from it and try not to keep making the same mistakes.'

'But *if* you could.'

He gives me a searching look, like now he's *sure* this is going to be about Mum. I reckon Skye's thinking the same because she's suddenly got this laser-beam focus on her plate. Then he says, carefully, 'You can't, because you'd alter everything else as well.'

'How do you mean?'

'Well, like the grandfather paradox – if you went back in time and killed your grandfather, then you'd prevent yourself from existing.'

'But,' Skye looks up, 'you couldn't kill your grandfather because if you did then you wouldn't exist so you couldn't travel back in time and kill him, could you?'

There's silence while we all think about this and I get that feeling like in class sometimes, where one second I'm getting it and the next second it's *whoosh*, like straight over my head. Then Skye tells us about her actual grandfather, who walked all the way across Africa for Save the Children, and asks if we'd like yoghurt for pudding.

I'm finishing the washing up when I suddenly remember I promised Yaz that we'd FaceTime, because she's got summer flu – which is fine except she keeps going on about how fed up and ill she is. Then she tells me her big sister just had a baby, which is all her parents ever talk about – when they're not fussing over her brother, who's like the family golden boy – so she might as well not exist. I do my best to be sympathetic, and give her a virtual tour of the flat, although I think she's a bit disappointed that it's not more prison-y, like doors with bars on or whatever, but honestly, what did she expect? I think about telling her I saw Kieran – not in the cemetery, just that I bumped into him in the street or something – but I know she'll ask me how he is, and that seems way too much to explain, so I don't.

I message him after we've finished, to say I hope he's OK. It's a bit lame, but what *are* you supposed to say to someone who thinks they're dead? Rest in peace? Hope they bury you soon?

Bad taste, Millie. But seriously, WTF?

I start looking through my suitcase, pulling out things to wear. Dad's Ramones T-shirt is fine, but it's not like Joe is going to know who they are because I checked and they barely had rock 'n' roll in 1955, never mind anything else. Also, I ought to at least try to dress a bit more like people did in those days in case anyone else can see me and thinks I'm crazy or dangerous or something. Plus I won't feel so self-conscious and—

And actually, why am I trying to impress a ghost?

If that's what Joe is.

I dump a bunch of clothes on the bed and start looking through them. I know I'm doing this partly because of thinking Shirley might be Joe's girlfriend, which is sort of crazy like the way this whole thing is crazy, and also makes me not like myself a whole lot.

Still, though. I pick out the only dress I brought with me, a

103

vintage one with blue flowers on it, and put it on. I usually wear it with stompy boots, but I can hardly go to bed in those. The espadrilles I've been wearing round the house will have to do, so long as I don't kick them off in my sleep. I wonder about trying to keep hold of my phone, too, but there doesn't seem a lot of point because there wasn't any Wi-Fi in 1955 and surely it wouldn't be able to take photos if the camera technology didn't exist? Also, what if it got vaporised or burnt up or something on the way? I can't manage without it.

No. Bad idea.

Then I think about trying to stay awake – sitting on the bed watching a film until the clock strikes – but something tells me it's not going to work *unless* I go to sleep, and I don't want to risk it. Plus, I feel quite tired, so I probably wouldn't make it anyway. I brush my hair and put on mascara and lip salve – nothing else, because of smudging – then decide that'll have to be enough, and lie down and close my eyes.

Thinking about it, that was pretty smart of Skye to come up with the thing about the grandfather and it not being possible. It's a shame I can't go further into the past and stop Dorothy and Kathleen being poisoned, but I'm guessing the clock can only take me back to one particular time and place. Only here, and only now – whichever 'now' it is.

Chapter 23

I'm in the corridor, staring at the clock face through the yellow light that's penetrating the fog. The space around me is changing, like it did before, and, one by one, the metal doors appear.

All closed.

No jangling keys, and no footsteps: silence, except the ticking of the clock.

Am I too late? Surely—

A scraping noise, and the door of the visitors' cell opens. Florey comes out first, then Charles and Rose, and the three of them walk past me, round the corner and out of sight. Then Joe is standing in the doorway, staring straight at me, with Ray behind him, urging him forward because she wants to lock the door.

'I thought you weren't coming.' He whispers it as Ray turns her back on him and bends over, fumbling with her bunch of keys.

'I'm sorry. I can't control when it happens.'

'Can you come with me?'

'Outside? I don't know. I'll try.'

Ray straightens up and motions Joe to follow her. He stares at me for a second more, then reaches out and grabs my hand. His grip is warm and firm – a real human being – and a tiny jolt of electricity seems to run up my arm like a current, into my chest. He doesn't flinch when he touches my skin, so I guess I mustn't feel too weird to him, either.

I'm certain as I can be that Ray can't see me, because she turns away without changing her expression and leads the way down the corridor. We go round the corner and down some stairs. The weird indoor fog has lifted, leaving the sickly yellow from the overhead lights shining down on Rose and Charles who are about five metres ahead of us, walking behind Florey. Even from behind, I can see that Rose's whole body is taut, like she might snap at any moment. I can hear doors clanging in the distance and people shouting, although I can't tell what's being said.

I hold my breath, expecting that I'll bump into an invisible barrier any second and wake up back in my bed, but we just keep walking. Joe barely looks in my direction, but I can feel his determination as if it's flowing through his fingers. When we catch up with Rose and Charles, and Florey unlocks a heavy iron door to let us into a yard, he grips my hand so tightly that it starts to go numb.

The place is small and gloomy, cobblestones with buildings looming up on all four sides except for a gap in one corner. We cross to it and walk along a passageway between high brick walls which comes out at another, much larger, yard. Straight ahead is the castle gateway I saw online, bigger than it seemed in the photo.

Ray, Joe and I wait while Rose and Charles disappear into an office with Florey. When they come back out Rose's features are slack, as if she's in a dream, but Charles just looks slightly annoyed, like he went to a shop and they didn't have the thing he wanted.

A male officer escorts us all through the enormous oak door in the middle of the gateway, then hands over to another guy who unlocks another set of gates that open onto the street. The three of them stand in a huddle, with me clutching Joe's hand as tight as he is holding mine because I'm scared of what might happen if we let go of each other – that I'll suddenly find myself back in 2023, on the street in the middle of the night with no keys to get back inside and no phone.

Although it's daytime and summer, everything looks sort of murky. The buses have their headlights on, shining through the mist, and the traffic noise is muffled, like someone's thrown a giant blanket over it. I can see across the road, but not very clearly – houses and shops made of greyish-coloured bricks. I wonder if I'm having difficulty seeing and hearing because I don't properly exist in 1955, but when I brush my free hand against the wall of the prison gatehouse it feels totally solid and my fingertips come away black and sooty. A stream of people walks past us and I notice that nearly everyone, apart from Joe, has something on their head – trilbies or caps for the men and hats or headscarves tied under the chin for the women. They look formal: even the scruffier-looking men have jackets and ties, and the women are wearing skirts, with no trackie bottoms or even jeans anywhere. Pretty much everyone is thin, and the older people have sharp, pinched faces.

For a moment, none of Annie's family speaks, and I wonder if it's because they've had the terrible news about the reprieve, but then

Charles says something about getting more cigarettes and Rose says she'll go with him. Then she touches Joe's arm. 'You get off home. We shan't be long, and I'll get the lunch straight on so you won't have to wait.' She's saying it like she's placating him, which is odd because it's not like he's complained or even said anything about being hungry. I wonder if she's really saying it for Charles's benefit, even though he hasn't said anything about lunch, either. There's something about the way Rose looks at Charles, like, hyper-aware, which makes me think that, although she's prepared to stand up to him when it's for Annie – well, a bit – she's actually quite scared of him, and I wonder why.

'It's fine, Mum.' The way he says this – reassuring, smiling at her – tells me I'm right: Rose *is* afraid of Charles, and Joe knows it.

Chapter 24

I wait until they disappear round the corner. 'Don't let go of me, will you?'

Joe grins. Now we can't see Rose and Charles any more, he seems altogether more relaxed. 'Don't worry. What's your name, anyway?'

'Millie.'

'I'm Joe – but if you know about Annie, you probably know that, don't you? How did you get here?' He says it like it's the most normal thing in the world and I'm going to tell him I came on the bus.

When I tell him about the clock waking me, and what happened next, he nods like it's a perfectly rational explanation – and that reminds me of how he didn't seem that surprised to see me last time. 'Did you do something to the clock?'

'I touched it.' Joe looks awkward. 'In the middle, where the hands meet. I asked it for help. It sounds stupid now, but I suppose I thought . . . to stop time, or . . . I don't know why I did it, really.'

'It's OK. I touched it, too, and I don't know why I did it either.

That must be what ... connected us.' Thinking of the feeling I'd got from his gravestone, I correct myself. 'Connected me with your world, I mean.'

'I suppose,' Joe says, slowly. 'I ought to be surprised, but after everything that's happened, it's ...' He shrugs. 'But I'm glad you're here.' He looks at his wristwatch, then frowns. 'Your midnight must be our midday.'

'What's the date?'

'Ninth of June.' So they are twelve hours behind – which is something, I suppose. 'I'd have thought you'd know. I mean, they're letting you out today, aren't they?'

'Letting me out?'

'You're not wearing the uniform.'

'What?' As I say it, I realise he thinks I'm a *prisoner* from the future, and that Dad's Ramones T-shirt ... I almost laugh but manage to stop myself in time. 'It's not a prison any more. They turned it into flats.' How on earth did Joe think I was going to help him from prison, anyway? Maybe he thinks people from the future have special powers – in which case he's in for a disappointment.

'I thought you were a bit young. Don't think I'd like to live in there, though.' Joe grimaces. 'Are you warm enough? I mean, it's not cold, but it's not exactly hot, either, and you're not ...' He stops, looking uncomfortable.

'Wearing much?' I supply, looking down at my dress, bare legs, and the espadrilles, which have – incredibly – stayed on my feet. 'It's fine. I suppose it's because I'm here but not here, if you see what I mean.'

'Sort of. What year do you come from, anyway?'

'2023.'

Joe takes a step back, his mouth a perfect 'O' of surprise. 'So the world didn't get blown up by an atomic bomb, then?'

I shake my head. 'Not yet. There've been quite a lot of wars – since now, I mean – but no.'

'What's it like? Do people live on the moon?'

I can't help laughing this time, and his face sort of closes up like he thinks I'm mocking him, which I'm really not. 'Well, I don't know, do I? We keep being told it's the next step. That and robots.'

'People have been to the moon and walked about and stuff, and there are loads of satellites and things in space, but no one *lives* there. They haven't found any aliens, either. And there *are* quite a lot of robotic things in factories. There's way more electronic stuff, too.'

'Do you have pills instead of meals?'

'No! Cooking's a big thing, and so are restaurants. Food is much better than it used to be – according to my dad, anyway, although he wasn't born until 1970 – and there are way more things to choose from.'

Joe looks kind of disappointed at this, although I can't imagine why anyone would want to eat their meals in pill form, unless the food in 1955 is *really* disgusting. Then his face brightens again and he says, 'It's good about you not leaving the prison – sorry, flats – because it means we can still meet and you can help me.'

'About that, Joe . . . I want to help you – I mean, if I can – but I've got to ask: why are you so sure Annie's innocent?'

111

'Because I know she wouldn't do something like that,' says Joe, fiercely. 'When I came home, and Dr Sims was there, she was in floods of tears and she kept asking if they were going to get better. And when Dorothy said they were poisoned, she never said Annie did it. I swear it, Millie, Annie loved Kathleen, and she . . . well, she *worshipped* Dorothy. It wasn't true about her being jealous because of Victor.' He looks at me to see if I know about that, and when I nod, he says, 'She was a bit soppy with him, trying to sit on his lap and that, but it was just her fun.'

'That sounds more like something a little kid would do.'

'Well, in some ways she was a little kid. She didn't understand if something was . . . you know, the right way to behave or not.'

'Did she have a boyfriend?'

'*Annie?*' Joe looks astonished. 'You must be joking. Mum never said it to her face, but she worried that nobody would want to marry her.'

'Seriously? There are other options, you know.' But even as I'm saying this, I'm thinking that for someone like Annie, there might not have been options in 1955.

'She needed someone to look after her,' Joe says. 'And like I said, all that in the papers was nonsense. Even if she'd wanted to make a play for Victor, it would have been . . . well, ridiculous. And Dorothy loved Annie, too. When she had to go away, for tuberculosis—'

'I thought that was Annie.'

'Dorothy as well. It's infectious. It was when I was ten, and Dorothy sat me down and told me I had to look after Annie,

112

because even though she's older than me she's slow and doesn't always understand things. Annie would never have hurt her, or Kathleen—'

'So she wasn't jealous of Kathleen being the baby of the family, or anything like that?'

'Not at all! She loved Kathleen, and she was really excited about Dorothy's baby. And although she tells fibs, you *always* know when she's lying. What I mean is, it's not the same as a clever person doing it, thinking about whether something sounds true or not and how to make people believe it. Annie just says the first thing that comes into her head. And she doesn't know much . . . I mean, she'd know something if it was to do with her everyday life, but she wouldn't know how to poison anybody. I went to see her solicitor, Mr Brighouse, afterwards, at his office. He was nice about it, but he told me that although he can appeal against the death sentence, he can't do anything else unless there's new evidence. I haven't got any new evidence, but I *know* this isn't right. Come on – I'll explain more when we're home.' I hesitate, thinking I might wake up and find myself in the middle of a road or something, but when Joe gives my hand a little tug I decide I might as well go for it. We move off in the opposite direction from Rose and Charles, then over the zebra crossing and towards Caledonian Road. When I turn to look back at the prison, it's like some medieval fortress, with rows and rows of barred windows, towering over everything else.

Before long, we're retracing my steps from yesterday. The mist or fog or whatever isn't so bad here, and now that I can see better, I spot lots of things that are different. The cars, for one thing – way fewer, and they look small and kind of delicate in comparison with modern ones. There's a rag and bone man with a horse pulling a cart that's piled with junk, calling out something I can't understand, plus two women pushing enormous prams like boats on wheels. I can't see all that far because of the mist, but there don't seem to be any tower blocks, just Victorian terraces everywhere you look. Some are the same, only neglected and dirty, and some houses are missing entirely, like one out of a row of teeth, with just rubble and weeds in the space. There are no tags, or anything much that's brightly coloured.

The shops are kind of depressing, too. Some of them look like no one's been in to buy anything, ever. Even though Joe is tugging at my hand, I stop in front of one because I can't figure out what it's selling, and I'm curious. The front is *really* old-fashioned – two windows curving back to a door in the middle, with 'Smith & Sons' painted across the top. It's dingy inside, but when I look closely I can make out a big old grandfather clock, a glass case full of smaller clocks, and a wall of wooden cabinets stretching right up to the ceiling with a wooden counter in front of them that runs the whole length of the shop. There's a man in a brown dust coat, like shopkeepers wore in the olden days – so, *now* – standing behind it. He's so still he could be a waxwork – until he turns his head and, for a freaky second, I think he must actually be able to see me. Then I hear a cow moo and almost jump out of my skin. 'Wait, there's a *farm* here?'

'Cattle market.'

'*What?*'

Joe turns to look at me as if what he's just said is the most logical thing in the world. 'The cows come in by train.'

I stare at him. 'What, actual cows? Like, commuting?'

'Sort of. Except they don't go home again. They run them down the street to the market, and then . . . you know.'

'Er, no I don't.'

'The slaughterhouse.'

I stop dead. 'What, right here?'

'Otherwise they'd have to run them all the way to Smithfield, wouldn't they? Make a hell of a mess, and what with the traffic . . . ' Joe shakes his head, like, *what a stupid idea.*

'We're not going to bump into them, are we?' I imagine cows stampeding round the corner.

'They don't come down here. But that's why we live so close – Dad works there.'

'You mean he . . . ?'

Joe nods. 'He's a slaughterman. They gave him time off to see Annie.'

'That's horrible.'

'Someone has to kill them. I mean, you know where meat comes from, don't you? Or don't they have it in your time?'

'Yes, we do, but . . . ' But it's all far away and out of sight. Tidy little packages in a supermarket and no connection to living, breathing animals being murdered – because it's not like they *want* to die – just down the road.

I tell myself I'll think about this later, because I don't know how much time there is and we need to concentrate on Annie. But whatever Joe says – and it is absolutely true that if we're going to eat animals then somebody has to kill them first – I like Charles even less than I did before.

I turn my attention back to the shops. There are some adverts, but they're for brands I've never heard of, and I don't even know what some of them are: Lifebuoy, Quink, Toni, Passing Clouds . . . I think those must be cigarettes, because there's a drawing of a cavalier smoking one and looking really pleased with himself – although, historically speaking, that can't be right, can it?

'Why didn't your dad just go to one of these shops for his cigarettes?'

Joe rolls his eyes. 'He gets knock-offs. Got a friend who works for the Naafi and they're always nicking stuff.'

'What's the naffy?'

'Where they sell things to soldiers – there's a canteen and a shop. When they get big deliveries, things tend to fall off the backs of the lorries, especially when it's Mr Hewitt taking care of the unloading.'

'Mr Hewitt?'

'Mrs Hewitt's friends with Mum, from when we lived in Dalston, and Mr Hewitt's got a lock-up off Seven Sisters Road.' The second bit of that might be right, I think, but not the first, because I remember how Rose looked when Joe mentioned Mrs Hewitt's name. 'I think he gets rid of most of it in the market. For all I know, Dad helps him.'

'You don't really get on with him, do you?'

'Who?'

'Charles. You call him Dad, right?'

'Yes ...' Joe stares across the road, where a bunch of women with shopping baskets are clustered round a man who looks like he's selling something out of a suitcase. 'He's all right. Better than my real father, anyway.'

'How do you mean?'

He's still not looking at me. 'Works hard, brings his wages home and doesn't knock Mum about.'

'Oh, OK. That is really horrible. But ...' Remembering what it said on Wikipedia, I do a quick sum in my head. 'You can't actually remember that, can you? I mean, you'd have been really young when—'

'I hardly remembered him at all. Dorothy told me, and she said Mum was always having to borrow off Nana to buy food because he couldn't keep a job. How do you know about my real dad, anyway?'

'I was reading about the case.' Dorothy had been about five years older than Joe, so it made sense that she'd have been more aware of what was happening. But I have this weird, prickling feeling that there's something not quite right about all of this, only I can't think what. 'Is Charles a good dad?'

Joe shrugs again. 'He used to take us to see the trains sometimes, when we were little, and he made toys for Kathleen.'

'But he thinks Annie's guilty, right?'

'Honestly, I don't know. He won't talk about any of it because he doesn't want to upset Mum.'

'Your mum's scared of him, isn't she?'

'A bit, yeah.' Joe looks as if he wants to say something else but can't find the right words. 'But like I said, he's good to her, and he doesn't drink too much – or not very often, anyway. Come on.' He accelerates, so that he's almost running, pulling me along behind him.

Chapter 25

I don't *think* it's my imagination, but as we get nearer to Aylmer Terrace some of the people we pass turn to stare at Joe, and I catch a few faces at windows, too. One man puts down the wooden barrow of fruit and vegetables he's wheeling and comes over.

'All right, old boy?' The cigarette stuck to his lip waggles up and down as he speaks.

'Yes, thanks, Mr Hilliard.'

'That's the way.' Mr Hilliard claps him firmly on the shoulder. 'A bad business , . . ' I get the feeling he wants to say more but doesn't know how. He shakes his head, then picks out a red apple, polishes it on his jacket and hands it to Joe. 'There you are.'

'They're all right here, really,' Joe tells me once Mr Hilliard's trundled off down the road. 'Some people started avoiding us. They don't want to be associated with . . . ' He tails off. Or, I think, they're embarrassed, and they aren't all as brave as that guy. Can't really blame them, though. I mean, what are you supposed to say? And most of them probably think Annie's guilty, because why wouldn't they? The judge said so, and they've got no reason to believe otherwise. 'Mum's had some pretty horrible letters,' Joe adds. 'But none from round here – or we don't think so, anyway.'

I guess trolls didn't get invented with the internet, then. 'I'm sorry.'

Joe shrugs and holds up the apple. 'Not your fault, is it? Do you want some?'

'I'm OK, thanks.'

'Suit yourself.' He takes a bite. The tough-guy act is so far away from his desperation when he first saw me, or from how he was with Annie, but I don't blame him for it. You've got to have some sort of protection, or you'd be in bits the whole time, and that's not going to help anyone.

Aylmer Terrace looks *way* scruffier than it did yesterday. It's like the photo I saw online, with peeling paint, missing railings, and metal dustbins on the pavement instead of trees. All the houses have net curtains covering the lower part of the downstairs windows, and several of them are twitching like the people behind them are waiting for something to happen at Number 37 – which turns out to be the house I thought it was, at the end of the row.

There are a bunch of young kids playing a chasing game in the road, about halfway down. One of the girls spots Joe and nudges her friend, and suddenly all of them are silent and still, staring in our direction. There's a moment's silence, then a boy picks up a stone and throws it, missing Joe by about a centimetre.

'Hey! Lay off, will you?'

The boy says nothing, just stares at Joe as he puts his hand through the letter box and fishes out a key on a string.

'I thought you said people round here were all right.'

'Kathleen's friends,' Joe mutters. 'Can't blame them for being upset.'

'You just got that key right in front of everyone,' I say, once we're standing in the dark, narrow hallway. 'Aren't you worried about burglars?'

'What, here?' Joe rolls his eyes like I've said something ridiculous. 'Everyone does that – if they bother to lock up at all.'

It's only when he gestures at the key, which is hanging from its string on the inside of the front door beside the letter box, that I realise we are no longer touching. I do jazz hands. 'I'm still here, so I guess it must be OK.'

'Must be. Which is good, because if no one can see you . . .'

I think of the expression on the children's faces and the flying stone. 'I'm pretty sure those kids could.'

Joe's eyes widen in recognition. 'Alfie threw that stone.'

'Who?' Am I making a mistake, or is he blushing?

'He's Shirley's brother.'

'Shirley next door?' He's *definitely* blushing. My stomach plunges with disappointment, and I tell myself not to be ridiculous.

'Wait, how do you know Shirley lives next door? I never said.'

'Because she still does. I came here to have a look.'

'Blimey.' Joe sighs. 'That's complicated, too. Not her still living here, but . . . Well, it's *all* complicated – but none of it's as important as Annie.'

Which is true – and why I'm here, in this house. It has an odd smell, which I think is a mix of cigarettes and boiled vegetables. It doesn't look as if it's been cleaned recently, probably because poor Rose is so unhappy that she's given up on it – and I bet Charles wouldn't even *think* of offering to help.

The hallway is narrow and dingy – pinky-brown wallpaper with a design of little pots of flowers – and even though it's bright daylight outside, the stairs go up into semi-darkness. The only thing I can make out clearly is an old-school Bakelite phone on a little shelf that sticks out of the wall.

The kitchen is at the back of the house. It would probably be an OK room, because it's sunny, with nice pale green walls, but there are piles of washing up on the surfaces and a big frying pan on the stove full of something grey, greasy and solid that I think must be lard.

A tabby cat is crouching over a plate of leftovers on a big, messy dresser.

'Is that Tiger?'

'Yes. We've had her since we were kids.' Joe puts a gentle hand on the cat's head, and she rubs against him, obviously pleased by his affection. 'You're all right, aren't you, old girl?'

I reckon this room is where everybody eats – Annie must have tidied up a bit before everyone sat down to tea on the 10 March. I imagine the sandwiches, scones and cake arranged on the pretty plates from the vintage tea set displayed on the shelves of the dresser – except it wouldn't have been vintage then, but practically new. White china with blue roses, and everybody smiling, admiring the cake . . .

'You all right?' Joe's staring at me.

'Yeah – no – sorry . . . Just weird being here, that's all.'

The sitting room has the leaf-and-branch wallpaper I saw in the photos of Annie and Joe, but now I'm wondering if they were actually taken at a party because this place looks like no one had any fun in it, ever. Everything seems to be brown or a really dull green, and the sofa and two armchairs are clumpy dark wood with thin, hard-looking cushions. There are dirty cups and saucers on little wooden tables, and I count three ashtrays, all full to overflowing. The grate is full of ash, too, from the fire, and some of it has spilled out onto the rag rug in front of the hearth. The television is a massive wooden box with a tiny little screen inside, and the three china Shire horses standing on the top look as if nobody's dusted them for weeks.

Joe's standing in the doorway with this strange expression like he really wants to ask something but can't quite bring himself to say it, and then he blurts out, 'You know how you said Shirley still lived next door?'

'Mmm?' I don't like where this is going.

'What about me? Am I still in this house?'

'I don't think so.' Well, what am I supposed to say? 'No one's actually living here at the moment – I mean, at the moment in my time – because there's building work being done.' Joe obviously thinks I'm being cagey about something, because he's staring at me with this look on his face, like, horror.

'I didn't *marry* Shirley, did I?'

'We-e-e-ll . . .' I open my eyes wide, like, *revelation*, but he looks so dismayed that I change my mind about teasing him. 'Her surname's still Millichip, so I guess you're off the hook. Plus, she said she was the only one left who'd been born in the street, so everyone else must have moved away.' I say this like it's no big deal, but I'm thinking *Please, God, don't let him ask me anything else about himself.*

Whose body lay undiscovered for an estimated six months . . .

To change the subject – and OK, because I want to know – I say, 'Have you got a girlfriend?'

Joe shakes his head. 'Even if I did, she'd hardly have stayed around, would she? Not with all this.'

'I guess it would be difficult.'

'You?'

For a moment, I don't understand what he's asking. 'No. Or not any more.'

Joe looks at me, and for a moment – there and gone so quick I might have imagined it – there's a prickle, like a tiny electric charge in the air between us. Then there's an awkward silence as he turns away and I look round the room again, pretending to be interested.

Joe obviously thinks I'm admiring the television, because after a moment he says, 'Dad got the TV for the Coronation.'

'Coronation?'

'Queen Elizabeth the Second. Don't suppose she's still queen, though.'

'She died last year. It's King Charles now.'

'But she must have been . . .' Joe ticks off decades on his fingers and looks impressed. 'That was good going. We had half the street in here to watch her being crowned.'

If there were any family pictures on display in here, they've been put away, but there's a clock on the mantelpiece. Grandma Caro's got one like it; they're called Napoleon clocks because the wooden frame is the same shape as his hat.

I picture Rose and Charles on the morning of 13 June, sitting on the horrible three-piece suite and listening as the clock tick-tocked the last few minutes of Annie's life away.

But that hasn't happened yet.

Even if it were clean, this place wouldn't be exactly lovely, but right now, knowing what I know, it looks actually sinister. Even the doll's house, sitting on a table in front of the window, looks like it might have bodies buried in the garden – if it had one, and not just a sheet of newspaper underneath.

The doll's house is suburban-looking, with the front door in the middle and those criss-crossy leaded windows and wooden decoration on the pointy bit at the top that Mum calls 'Tudorbethan'. Nothing at all like this house.

'Dad made that for Kathleen. He's going to give it to one of the kids down the street.' I must be making a face because Joe adds, 'Bet your home is heaps better than this, isn't it?'

Shit, I've offended him. 'It's not that, it's just—'

'Bet you've got a robot to do all the cleaning and stuff.'

'I wish, but no one's invented those yet. There are vacuum cleaners that go around by themselves, but they cost a fortune. I reckon modern things are easier to keep clean, that's all.'

Joe gives me one of those looks like people do when they know you're being kind, and says, 'Dad and Mum'll be here soon, so we should make ourselves scarce. Come on, I'll show you the back.'

I follow him down the hall and into the garden. I notice he doesn't unlock that door but just turns the handle.

The garden is bigger now than it will be in the future, when people have eaten into it with extensions. Now, there's just a little bit of house, half the width of the building, that sticks out at the back – two small rooms, one on top of the other. Judging from the frosted side window, the ground floor one must be the bathroom.

'What's that?' I point at the concrete bunker next to it.

Joe looks like he can't believe his ears. 'That's for the coal. The fire, you know?'

'Oh. Right.' No wonder the air's so dirty.

On the other side of the back door there's a small wooden shed – I'm guessing that's where the tin of poison was kept – with a crate of what looks like bottled beer next to it. A brick wall runs down that side of the garden, separating it from Ianthe Street. I reckon it must be still there in 2023, only I couldn't see it because of the hoarding. The other side has a rickety-looking wooden fence separating it from the garden of Number 35, and between them is a scrubby lawn with a washing line stretched across it, and what looks like a vegetable patch. So far, nothing special – but, right at the end, half buried in the ground, is something that looks like a really low-rent hobbit house. The front is made of corrugated iron, with narrow double doors made of wood, and there's a hole lined with sandbags at the entrance, so you have to take a big step down to get inside. The semi-circular roof, which can't be much more than a metre from the ground, is covered in grass.

'What's *that*?'

Joe raises his eyebrows, like, *seriously*? 'Anderson shelter, of course.'

'Anderson . . . ?'

'You know, from the war.'

'I really don't.'

'Blimey. People slept in them if there was an air raid – it was safer than being indoors.'

'Sort of like camping.'

Joe stares at me. 'It wasn't a *holiday*.'

'Course not. Sorry.'

He rolls his eyes. 'Well, luckily I was evacuated. Hang on – I'll get us something to drink.'

Joe comes back into the garden a couple of minutes later with a bottle of lemonade. 'Come on.'

We climb down to the Anderson shelter, and when he opens the doors, I can see that the walls are pieces of corrugated iron that curve upwards to make the roof. The floor is covered in bits of plasterboard and there are wooden benches on either side. It smells a bit of damp, but I can see it could be quite cosy – or properly crowded if a whole family had to sleep inside it.

'Kathleen used to play in here,' Joe says. 'She'd invite me and Annie, and we'd pretend it was her house and we'd come for tea.' He pulls up a bit of plasterboard in one of the back corners. When he straightens up again, he's holding a battered tin box in his hand, with a picture of a young girl in a frilly pinafore, hugging a kitten, on the lid. 'Dad wanted to get rid of all her things, but I hid this.' When he pulls the lid off, I can see a doll's tea set, made from china: four cups with saucers, a teapot, a milk jug, and a sugar bowl.

'Noddy and Big Ears!'

'That's right.' Joe picks out two of the cups and huffs on them to get rid of any dust. 'I don't really know why I hid them.' He doesn't look at me as he says this, 'I suppose you think it's stupid.'

'Not *at all*.' I totally get it.

Joe pours lemonade into the two little cups, and hands one to me. 'To saving Annie,' he says solemnly, clinking his cup with mine.

'Saving Annie,' I murmur, trying to ignore the horrible sinking feeling in my stomach.

I reckoned I wouldn't be able to taste the lemonade, but it's delicious.

'I just wanted to keep *something*,' Joe says. 'They took everything else away – not that there was much in here, just empty tins and packets Kathleen got from Mum, for when she was pretending it was a shop. They took the things out of her and Annie's room, too.'

'Annie's stuff as well?'

Joe nods. 'Everything.'

'Did your mum want that?'

'I think she just did what Dad wanted. But I got this, as well.' He pulls an envelope out of his pocket and hands it to me. Inside is a folded-up piece of newspaper. It's a black and white photograph of three women in ballgowns walking down the middle of a fancy room full of smart ladies perched on chairs that look like they were borrowed from a Disney Princess's wedding. 'Dorothy's the one at the front.'

Although I've only seen one photo of her up to now, I'd recognise her anywhere, even with the snooty old-fashioned model expression: that long neck, those enormous dark eyes, the perfect profile.

'She was a mannequin, doing dress shows at the big department stores. Dad didn't like it – kept saying she was got up like a tart.'

'Is that where she met Victor?'

'And how!' Joe grins, remembering. 'At Danbury and Marsh – that's one of the big shops in the West End – and she *never* stopped talking about him. He's a commercial artist – posters and things. Reckon he couldn't believe his luck.'

'He must be heartbroken. Do you see much of him? I mean, since . . .'

Joe shakes his head, frowning. 'He had a row with Mum.'

'When was that?'

'A few days after it happened. I came home and they were in the front room. Victor was shouting. I heard Mum say something like "I'm telling you, they made a mistake" and Victor said, "They couldn't have". Then he started to say something about "what they found", but they must have heard me in the hall because they both shut up after that.'

'Do you think your mum meant the police had made a mistake about Annie?'

'I suppose so – although I can't believe Victor ever thought

129

Annie did it on purpose. He liked her. He told me once he was sorry for her.'

'Did he say why?'

'Because she was slow, I think.'

Joe sees me wince and gives me a funny look. I'm about to call him out, but then I remember it's the 1950s and people spoke differently, and he didn't mean to be unkind.

'Anyway,' he continues, 'when I went into the room that afternoon, I could see Victor was furious. Trying to hide it, but white and practically shaking with rage . . . and it was Mum he was angry with, not . . . you know, the whole business. I could see by the way he was looking at her.'

'Because she was saying the police got something wrong.'

'I suppose so. I asked Mum about it after he'd gone, but she just started crying, and then Dad came home and tore a strip off me for upsetting her.'

'What, he tore your clothes?'

Joe gapes at me, like *WTF*, then grins. 'It's just an expression, Millie. It means he told me off.'

'Oh. Right. Sorry . . . Did you ask Victor about the argument?'

'No. Dad told me I wasn't to bother him.' He's tense and still, not meeting my eye.

'Do you miss him?'

'Yeah. Victor's a good sort. But now . . .' He shrugs, so I turn back to the envelope. There's another picture in there, a little square photo, black and white again, of Dorothy and Annie at a picnic, sitting on a rug with Kathleen squeezed between them.

They're all laughing, as if just being side by side is enough to make them radiate happiness.

'That's lovely.'

Joe looks like he wants to say something but then he changes his mind – or doesn't trust himself not to cry – and just stares at me, so desperate, and I don't know what to say or how to comfort him. 'I'm so sorry, Joe, for everything.' And I do mean everything, including all the stuff that hasn't happened yet.

Anger flares in his eyes when he says, 'I just don't understand any of it! Why it happened, or why Mum and Dad are behaving as if it must be right because the judge said so and we have to accept it. It's *not* right, Millie. I know it's not.'

I put my hand on his arm, which seems to calm him. No wonder he's angry – what must it be like to be in that situation and feel so totally powerless? 'Joe . . . you said you'd explain the other reason you think Annie's innocent?'

Chapter 26

'Yeah . . . ' I pretend not to notice as Joe blinks and swipes his sleeve across his eyes. 'Because I was with her all the time she was making that cake, and I'd have noticed if she'd been messing about with tins of poison.'

'What about the fingerprints?'

Joe sighs. 'Annie'd helped Dad clean out the shed about a month before. They took everything out, so that's when she must have touched the tin.'

'So she *would* have known it was there.'

'It's not the sort of thing she'd have paid attention to, honestly. Dad might even have said, "Mind that, it's poison", but she wouldn't have remembered . . . She didn't even think to tell the police about helping Dad.'

'Did you?'

'Yes, but it was as if they'd already decided she was guilty. They weren't interested in anything that didn't fit in with their story. It was the same when Annie told them that she'd felt poorly. They said she'd lied to be the same as Dorothy and Kathleen – although . . . '

Joe frowns, 'I don't think Dr Sims believed her either, so maybe it wasn't true.'

'Well, you did say she told fibs.' I think of what it said on Wikipedia about Annie making up stories. If you've got a reputation for doing that, I guess nobody's going to believe you about anything.

'And how. The other chambermaids at her work said she told stories about how Dorothy was off to Hollywood to be in films and she was going with her, and how Victor was a millionaire, and how we were all going to live in a castle or something. A load of rubbish, anyway. I suppose she thought they'd be impressed, but of course nobody believed a word of it.' Joe shakes his head. 'She'd do it at home, too, say a big-shot American film star had come to the hotel, or something like that.'

'Why?'

'Just fanciful.' Joe suddenly looks surprised, as if it's the first time he's ever thought about this properly, then says, 'It's true, she was, but now I think about it, maybe she did it because she wanted attention. I used to take her to the pictures sometimes, and Dorothy was really good with her – although she didn't have so much time after she left home – and she and Kathleen rubbed along well, but Kath had her own gang, you know? Kids her own age – you saw them outside – and they didn't want Annie tagging along.'

'And your mum and dad? Did they pay attention to her?'

'Not really.' Joe sighs. 'They were busy. And she was just … well, just Annie. And I suppose … well, the more she made things up, the less we listened.'

And when somebody *did* pay attention to her, I think, it was to accuse her of murder. 'Do you think that was why she'd sit on Victor's lap?'

Joe frowns. 'Must have been.' He's starting to look despairing again, and I want to keep him on track. 'OK, so . . . was it a special occasion, with the cake and everything?'

'Sort of, for Mum – her birthday's at the end of February, and Dad was going to take her out somewhere, but she wasn't well so he said why didn't we have a nice tea instead.'

'But he wasn't there himself?'

Joe gives me an odd look, like, *why would he be?* 'No, he was out with Mr Hewitt.'

'What about her friends?'

Another odd look – which makes me think that Rose doesn't have many friends (apart from Mrs Hewitt, who she doesn't seem to like very much). 'Dad said to keep it small. I wasn't there because I had an extra shift at work.'

'Couldn't you have changed it?' Joe looks at me like I'm from another planet. 'OK, but you were here the day before watching Annie make the cake, right?'

'Yes, I went into the kitchen when I came home from work and she was there, so I made a cup of tea for both of us. She was really excited, because she loved anything like that.' His face brightens for a moment, remembering. 'I watched her take all the ingredients out of the cupboard, so if she'd added anything else, I'd have seen.'

'So that was late afternoon or early evening?'

Joe nods. 'Around six.'

'What sort of cake was it?'

'Victoria sandwich.' Joe sees my blank expression. 'Two bits of sponge cake with jam in the middle.'

'Oh, right. Where did the jam come from?'

'Mrs Hewitt gave it to Mum. It was in the sandwiches, too. Well, the ones that weren't meat paste or fish paste.'

'What's that?'

'If you don't know, you're lucky.' Joe makes a face. 'Meat paste is all right, I suppose, but fish paste is horrible. But the police tested everything they could find – even the tea and the sugar – and it was all normal.'

'So what they tested wasn't poisoned. But someone could have added something to the stuff that got eaten, couldn't they?'

'What, a slice of the cake or individual sandwiches or scones? How would the poisoner know who was going to eat what?'

'They might not have cared. If they were a psychopath or something.' Joe looks confused, and I suddenly wonder if psychopaths were a thing in the 1950s – I mean, they obviously were, but perhaps they weren't called that. 'I mean, somebody who doesn't have real emotions – who doesn't care about other people and who would do something like that just to see the results.'

Now he's looking really bewildered. 'But *who*? We don't know anyone like that.'

'No, OK. Stupid idea.'

Joe looks thoughtful. 'I suppose somebody could have got into the house and done it. I mean, Annie left the cake on the table to cool when she'd taken it out of the oven. We'd stayed in the kitchen up till then, and I'd helped Annie clear up the cooking things, but then we went next door to watch television.'

'You mean to Shirley's house? But—'

'Into the sitting room. Shirley came in.' Joe grimaces. 'She wanted to watch *The Grove Family*.'

'Did she leave the room at any time?'

'I can't remember. But why would Shirley want to kill any of us?'

'Well, it certainly doesn't sound like she'd want to kill *you*, but—' I see Joe's face turning pink and quickly look away. 'Fair point. Was anyone else in the house?'

'Mum was here, upstairs – she had a headache – and Dad came in later, after we'd gone to bed. I did tell the police all this, you know.'

'Sorry, I'm just trying to get it straight in my head. Did you put the cake away before you went to bed?'

'Annie put it in a tin last thing. I didn't see where it went after that, but she said she put it in one of the dresser drawers.'

'So someone could have tampered with it during the night?'

'I suppose so. It wasn't being *guarded*. I'm at the top, so I wouldn't necessarily hear someone moving around if they were being really quiet – but apart from me and Annie, it was just Mum, Dad and Kathleen, as usual.'

'Did the cake stay in the dresser until teatime the following day?'

'So far as I know. Annie said she took it out of the dresser to put on the table, and hers were the only fingerprints found on the cake tin.'

'That doesn't prove anything though – if somebody'd taken the tin out of the drawer to tamper with the cake, they'd have wiped it afterwards, wouldn't they? Or used gloves. Who was in the house on the day of the party?'

'Just Mum, for most of the time. Mrs Hewitt came by in the afternoon – she was in the kitchen with Mum when I got back from work—'

'Between shifts, right?'

'Yeah. Normally, I wouldn't have gone home, but I thought I'd get some flowers for Mum, just so it would be a bit more special.'

'That was nice of you,' I say, because Joe's looking a bit embarrassed.

'Yeah, well. Even before I opened the front door I could hear they were arguing – a real ding-dong – so I took the flowers upstairs with me.'

'OK . . . Do you know what it was about?'

Joe shrugs. 'The never-never. Or that's what it sounded like.'

'The *what*?'

'Hire purchase. You know, when you pay for something by instalments because you can't afford all the money at once . . . Unless everyone's so rich in your time that you don't need it.'

'You're joking! People have *loads* of debt. Were they arguing while your mum was making the scones and sandwiches?'

'That's right. The kitchen door was open – you can see in from the stairs. I couldn't see Mum but she called out hello or some-thing – reckon she thought I was Annie because she was due back from work about that time – but I saw Mrs Hewitt standing by the table and there were bowls with flour and whatnot. I remember

137

thinking Mrs H couldn't have been there long, because she was still wearing her coat, and I was wondering what the hell had happened, but I wasn't going to get involved, so . . .'

'Was Annie back?'

'No. I heard the door bang about ten minutes later, and she came upstairs to her room.'

'But you didn't see her?'

'Not till I judged the coast was clear and came down again. Mum had just put the flowers in a vase when Mrs Millichip came round and said Shirley'd had an accident at work.'

'Was that the "change in arrangements" I read about?'

'Must have been. Mrs Millichip had to go to the hospital, and she was really worried so Mum went with her.'

'What about Shirley's dad?'

'Mr Millichip's got a gammy leg. He was in the fire service in the war and a wall fell on it, so he's in and out of hospital himself. Mum said he'd had to go back in that morning – reckon that was why Mrs M was in such a state, if she thought something awful had happened to Shirley as well. Can't really blame her.'

'And Mrs Hewitt went along too? Did she know Mrs Millichip?'

'Well, they'd met quite a few times because of Mum, so . . .' Joe shrugs. 'Moral support? I suppose they made up after the row.'

'Was Shirley all right?'

'Bruised and concussed, but she was fine in the end. No bones broken. But she'd fallen off a ladder at work, so it could have been serious.'

'A *ladder*? Is she a window cleaner or something?'

Joe gives me another WTF look, like I'd asked if Shirley was a Martian. 'She works in a shoe shop – you know, those tall shelves where they keep all the boxes. Dad was angry with Mum for going off with Mrs Millichip, but like Mum said, how was she supposed to know it wasn't serious?'

'Did she say that to your dad?'

'Yeah . . . ' Joe blinks, like he's surprised by the memory of Rose confronting Charles. 'She did.'

'So . . . the scones and sandwiches were in the kitchen with nobody there?'

'Well, Annie was in the house. I went back to work.'

'You said you'd come back for something to eat, so you must have gone into the kitchen, surely?'

'Of course. But I wasn't that hungry, so it was only a couple of sandwiches. They were cut into triangles – quarter of a slice – and Mum made a lot and saved some on plates in the pantry for Dad and me . . . Actually, I think she might have put some away for her and Mrs Hewitt, too, because they didn't know how long they'd be at the hospital.' He grins suddenly. 'I remember Annie tried to pinch some. She can be really greedy sometimes, and she'll steal food and eat enough to make herself sick. She got sulky when I told her off and said she wasn't to have anything until Dorothy arrived, or I'd be sure to find out and tell Mum and then she'd be in big trouble . . . Wish I hadn't done that now.'

'That was before you went back to work, right? So she was by herself for a bit . . . Where was Kathleen?'

'Out with her gang.'

We stare at each other, and I'm suddenly out of ideas. I don't want Joe to think I'm accusing him of anything – I'm not – and, although I'm sure there are more questions to ask about all this, because something definitely isn't right, I don't know what they are. There are things that seem off about the Driscolls, too, but they don't really add up to murder . . . Trying to think like a detective, I say, 'Can I have a look at Annie and Kathleen's room?'

'I don't see what good it'll do.'

'A fresh pair of eyes?'

Joe shrugs and stands up. 'If you like.'

There's a shout as we clamber out past the sandbags, and a girl's head and shoulders appear over the wooden fence. 'You coming over?'

This *has* to be Shirley – sixty-eight years younger than when I last saw her, and far more brightly coloured. Red hair in two bunches, and a scattering of freckles across a snub nose – pretty, if her smile hadn't turned to a sulk because she's just spotted me behind Joe. She's not looking surprised, though, which means that little brother Alfie must have said something.

'Mum saved some cake. It's a chocolate one this week, and we made cheese straws.' She flicks me a glance which says: *Beat that, bitch.* I give her a look that says, *Seriously?* but then I remember how Grandma Caro told me there was rationing after the war, when she was growing up, so perhaps this *is* still quite a big deal. Also, in the circumstances – people not knowing what to say and everything – it's nice that Shirley and her family are trying to include Joe in some normal stuff.

Joe looks at me, then Shirley, then me again, clearly embarrassed. 'Maybe later?'

I can tell Shirley is disappointed, but she hides it well. 'We'll keep some for you. As long as you're all right . . .'

'I'm doing OK.' Joe almost sounds like he's apologising.

Her eyes linger on Joe as he moves towards the house. I decide to leave it a few seconds to see if she's going to engage with me, and, sure enough, she waits until I'm close enough and mutters, 'Made yourself right at home, haven't you?'

'What?'

'Brought your slippers.'

Confused, I stare at my feet. 'They're espadrilles.'

'Oh, *espadrilles*, are they?' She elongates the word sarcastically, then narrows her eyes and hisses, 'Your precious friend Dorothy wasn't all that. I know because I heard Mum talking about how they hushed it up. I bet you're the same – and he won't be so keen on you when he finds out, so I wouldn't bother making eyes at him.'

Chapter 27

It's so unexpected that I just stare at her.

Then Joe, who's by the back door, waves and shouts 'See you later!' Shirley gives me one last bit of side-eye before she waves back and disappears behind the fence.

I run to catch up with Joe, annoyed with myself for being shaken by what she said (although at least it seems like she's improved with age). What did she mean about Dorothy, though? And why does she think we were friends?

Once we're safely in the kitchen, I say, 'Shirley, right?'

Joe nods, looking gloomy. 'She's just so . . .' he screws up his face, searching for a word, '*persistent*. Every time I go into the garden, up she pops like a Punch and Judy show. I mean, I know she's trying to be kind, because of . . . you know . . . But it's just . . .' He tails off, shaking his head. 'Look, whatever she said to you, I'm sorry, OK?'

'She seems to think I was friends with Dorothy.'

Joe looks surprised for a second, then says, 'I suppose because you're tall, and . . .' Am I imagining it, or is he starting to look uncomfortable and slightly pink? 'nice-looking, and your dress and everything . . . She must think you're one of the mannequins.'

'Did any of them come here?'

'One did. Helene – Helen really, but she told us the modelling agency made her change it to be more French and sophisticated. She lives near here, and she helped make the bridesmaids' dresses when Dorothy got married.'

'So they were good friends?'

Joe nods. 'They used to go to the pictures together all the time. Did Shirley say anything else?'

When I repeat the stuff about Dorothy not being 'all that' and things being hushed up – although not the bit about me making eyes at him – Joe turns actually red. 'She didn't *have* to marry Victor, if that's what Shirley was getting at.'

'Sorry, "Have to . . ."?'

'You know.' Joe looks even more uncomfortable. 'If she was having a baby.'

'But even if she was . . . ' Again, I realise how much I'm looking at all of this through modern eyes. There were *way* fewer choices in 1955, especially for women.

'She wasn't! If Shirley's been putting that about, it's slander. And if she's written it in her stupid diary, it's libel. If I find she's said anything, I'll . . . I'll . . . ' He doesn't say what he'll do, but he looks furious.

I think back to what I've read online, but can't recall any mention of a wedding date, only that Dorothy was three months pregnant when she died. 'She probably meant something else.'

'What, though?'

'Well, if Shirley thought Dorothy had stolen something, maybe.' Remembering a conversation from PSHE about changing attitudes, I add, 'Or that she was gay?'

Joe looks totally bewildered. 'Why wouldn't she be? She was excited about the baby.'

I remember that it's not only attitudes that have changed, but language as well. 'Sorry. I mean that she was a lesbian.'

'Oh.' He looks surprised, then frowns. 'Are people allowed to be, er, *like that* in 2023?'

'Yeah, totally.'

Joe looks as if he's considering this. 'Fair enough. Takes all sorts. But Dorothy wasn't.' He goes quiet again and I start to think he might be wondering if she *had* been but hadn't told him, but then he says, 'Also, I'm pretty sure that Shirley's mum doesn't even know that women can like other women that way. It's obviously different in your time, but no one ever talks about those things – or no one I know, at any rate. And Dorothy certainly wasn't a thief, so that's out.'

'OK, so could Shirley's mum just have been mean about Dorothy for having lots of boyfriends – before Victor, I mean? She was so gorgeous that I bet lots of men wanted to date her.'

'That's true.' Joe grins. 'And she did go out with them sometimes. One fellow was so crazy about her that he'd leave flowers on the doorstep all the time – great big bouquets of flowers. It used to drive Dad up the wall.'

'How did he know where she lived?' I'm thinking stalker.

Joe looks at me like it's a stupid question. 'Because he'd drive her home, wouldn't he? After dinner or the pictures. She wasn't half as gone on him as he was on her, though. When she got engaged to Victor, she told me she'd never fallen in love with anyone before and he was the one for her. I told her she was soppy. Wish I hadn't said that now, either.'

'I'm sure she didn't mind. Were you close? I mean, did she often talk to you about boyfriends?'

'Not really. But – even though I said that about her being soppy – the reason I asked her about Victor was . . . well, I wanted her to be happy. I mean –' he looks suddenly awkward – 'I didn't have a particular reason to think that she wasn't, but I wanted to be sure.'

'OK. I know you just said she was in love with Victor, and you obviously think he's a good guy, but . . . it couldn't have been him, could it?'

Joe shakes his head vigorously. 'I haven't seen him since he had that row with Mum, but he's in pieces, Millie. Really devastated. He adored Dorothy, and he was so pleased about the baby – also, he'd been visiting some relatives in Ireland, and he only got back the evening of the party, so he wouldn't have had the chance.'

'OK – just thought I'd check. What was Dorothy like? As a person, I mean.'

'Kind,' Joe says immediately. 'She was always helping people, and she looked after Annie and Kathleen. There was none of that "Oh, I'm too grown up to bother with you", like some older sisters. She used to let them try on her clothes and everything. And she always sat with Mum when she was bad with her nerves.'

'Nerves? What do you mean?'

'If Mum had a turn ... She's bad with her nerves sometimes, scared of her own shadow, and when that happens she has to stay in her room. Me and Annie would help with housework and that, and Dorothy did, too, but she was best at looking after Mum. She always put her first – she'd tell her boyfriends, "I can't come out with you because my mum needs me."'

'Has Rose always had ... turns?'

'I don't remember it happening when I was at infant school, but maybe I was just too young to understand. The first time I *remember* it happening was a few years after we came here.'

After she married Charles, then – unless Rose had always had mental health issues but Joe just didn't know about them.

'Did Dorothy ever mention it? If it happened before you moved, I mean.'

Joe frowns. 'I don't think so.'

Maybe it was post-natal depression. Mum told me Aunt Saff had it when my cousin Jack was born, and it sounds horrible. 'Was it after she had Kathleen?'

'Maybe. I can certainly remember Dorothy and Annie taking Kathleen out in the pram so the house would be quiet.'

But, I think, even if it was that, would it have gone on for such a long time? It didn't sound like Rose ever got any treatment for it, but still ...

Joe's still frowning, as if he's puzzled by something – or maybe just trying to organise his memories – and I wonder if there's something he has an instinct about, something that was off that he can't put into words. Again, I get the weird, prickly feeling of something not right – but it's like when there's a thing you can just about see at the corner of your eye, but you can't focus on it. 'Do you think that might be what Shirley meant about something being hushed up?'

'I shouldn't think so. For a start, it's about Mum, not Dorothy – and anyway, Shirley's mum cooks us meals sometimes if Mum isn't well and Annie's at work. Mrs Hewitt does, too, so both of them know if something's up.'

'You won't say anything to Shirley, will you?'

'I'll pretend you didn't tell me. I want to know what she overheard, though.'

'I know, but—'

'I'll be careful. But we've got to do *something* ...' Joe looks around the kitchen as if the answer might be hiding behind the pots and pans. 'And I haven't a clue where to start.'

'Can you get in touch with Helene?'

'What would be the point of that?'

'I'm wondering if Dorothy might have confided in her about ... well, anything that might help us make sense of this, really.' Joe looks at me doubtfully. 'Look, if Annie didn't kill her and Kathleen, then someone else *did*. There must be a reason for that, and we need to find out what it is. Girls tell each other things, Joe – stuff they don't want their families to find out. I'm not saying Dorothy was ... *bad*, or anything, but she probably had secrets from her family because ... well, because most people do, even if it's just stuff they're worried might happen.'

'Helene told Mum the police never questioned her because she was on holiday when it happened. But if Dorothy told her to keep something secret and she hasn't already told the police, then she's not going to tell me, is she?'

'Maybe she didn't tell the police because she didn't think it was relevant. It's not impossible.'

'I suppose ... I know Dorothy used to call her sometimes, so they'll be in the telephone directory.' Joe disappears through the door and returns a moment later with a big book with paper covers. 'Hang on ...' He flicks through the pages. 'Bicknell ... Bloxham ... Blunt ... Bolting ... Here we are – Bone.'

'That's her surname?'

'Yup. Only a few of them, thank goodness ... And there's one with an address in Landor Street, which is only a few roads away, so I reckon that must be her dad. Are you sure it's going to help?'

'No, but we've got to start somewhere. Also ... and I realise this might be more difficult, because of what Charles said and because he might not want to talk to you, but can you speak to Victor? Ask him what the argument was about?' Joe's looking like he *really* doesn't want to do that, and I decide there's no point pressing it. 'Look, we don't know how long I've got here – it's been way longer than last time already, and I might find myself back in 2023 any minute – so maybe you should think about that after we've looked at Annie and Kathleen's room?'

Chapter 28

We pass a closed door on the first, small landing – the room above the bathroom – and go up more steps to where Annie and Kathleen's room is. 'I'm by myself at the top,' Joe says, with a nod in the direction of the other staircase. 'Well, me and Dad's wood-work. That's Mum and Dad's room ...' He points to the room at the front. The door's open, and I can see part of a dressing table. 'And Annie and Kathleen were in here.'

As soon as he opens the door on our right, I can see that the room is almost completely empty; just dusty floorboards, with no hidey-holes that I can spot. The wallpaper – small pink roses on a cream background – looks scuffed, with scratches and gouges below waist-height, like someone removed a bunch of furniture without taking much care. The only thing left – or possibly added afterwards – is a small table with an old-school typewriter on it. There's a piece of paper sticking out of it, and more paper in a box by the side.

'What's that for?'

'Something Dad's cooked up with Mr Hewitt.' Joe sighs. 'Best not to ask.'

'For the things that fall off the backs of lorries?'

'Yeah. Paperwork to make it look legitimate. Mrs Hewitt types it for them.'

I wonder if Kathleen died in here but can't bring myself to ask. Instead, I say, 'That was Dorothy's room we passed on the landing, right?'

'Yup.'

'Why didn't Annie move into it when Dorothy got married?'

Joe frowns. 'Wanted to stay in here with Kathleen, I guess. I used to hear them singing, or Annie telling Kathleen stories.'

'That way round?'

'Always. All about us lot having adventures.' I can't see Joe's expression because he's staring out of the window.

'Like the stuff about film stars and castles?'

He turns back to me, looking thoughtful. 'No – or not that I ever heard. It was more just . . . Well, stuff someone might actually do, like going to the seaside and eating ice cream with Mum and Dad.'

'Did you?'

'Did we what?'

'Do that stuff.'

'Not really.'

Annie's perfect life, I think: to be properly part of a family who did do that stuff. I reckon Joe is thinking the same, because he looks really troubled. He doesn't reply, though, so I figure it's best to pretend I haven't noticed. 'This is a pretty small room. With two beds, there'd hardly be room for anything else.'

After a pause, Joe says, 'That didn't bother them. Annie

wasn't really interested in clothes and all that, not the way Dorothy was.'

'So what happened to Dorothy's room?'

Joe shrugs. 'Just bits and pieces in there.'

'Can I see?'

He gives me an odd look. 'If you like.'

Dorothy's room is smaller than Annie and Kathleen's. More dusty dark floorboards, but with some wooden shelves, a single bed – just a mattress on an old-fashioned iron frame – and three big trunks piled one on top of the other.

The top trunk is tin, with initials painted in white on one end of it: 'FJP'.

'Stands for Francis John Palmer,' Joe says, seeing where I'm looking. 'My real dad. Everyone called him Frank.'

'He died in the war,' I say, remembering Wikipedia.

'Fall of Tobruk,' Joe says. 'June 1942. He was in the Eighth Army – North Africa Campaign.' I must be looking blank because he adds crossly, 'Don't you learn *anything* about the war at school?'

'Yes, but not every single detail.' I feel defensive – because it's not like a bunch of other stuff hasn't happened since the Second World War, is it? But at the same time, I can see that for people in 1955 it was the big event that overshadowed their whole lives. 'I'm sorry. It must have been really hard.'

Joe shrugs – tough guy again. 'These things happen.' I remember what he'd said about his biological dad not treating Rose well and wonder if maybe they were secretly relieved he didn't come back.

The tin trunk is completely empty inside, and so are the two trunks underneath it. I stack them up again and turn to look at the shelves. There's not much there: a little wooden box with a few sewing things; a china brooch in the shape of a flower, and a few ribbons in a paper bag.

'I think Dorothy left those behind when she got married.'

'What about these?' I point to a row of books on the bottom shelf.

'Those, too.'

I examine the books with no real idea of what I'm looking for. They're all novels, hardbacks with paper jackets, like the kind of books you see in second-hand shops, that people collect. I haven't heard of any of the authors except for Agatha Christie. I flick through the pages – in books, things are always hidden in books – but there's nothing there. The last one is *The Robe*, by somebody called Lloyd C. Douglas. It's got 'One Man's Quest for Faith and Truth' written in big letters across the front, and a picture which makes me think it must be about Jesus and the Romans. There's a handwritten message on the first page:

To dear Dorothy, with love from Muriel Carr
Chase Farm, Yorkshire
September 1948

I turn the book towards Joe. 'Who's Muriel Carr?'

He shakes his head. 'A nurse, maybe?'

'Why a nurse?'

'Or another patient. Chase Farm must be the sanatorium.'

'You mean when Dorothy had tuberculosis.'

'The date's right – she was there for about six months – and it says "Yorkshire". I never visited,' he explains. 'Only Mum did. Children aren't allowed.'

'Perhaps this Muriel person was just visiting because she lived locally, and Chase Farm is her address.'

'I don't think so. They hardly let anyone visit those places in case they catch it. And if Muriel Whatsit was a relative, I'd know.'

'Family friend?'

'Doubt it. All the people Mum and Dad know are here. And we were evacuated to Wales – Mum came too because I was a baby – not Yorkshire.'

'Evac— Oh, you mean in the war. What about holidays?'

'We always go to Southend or Margate or somewhere like that, not right up there.'

'OK . . .' I'm racking my brains for another idea when the sound of the front door opening makes us both jump.

'They're back,' Joe whispers. Coming out of the room, we can see Rose standing in the hall, taking off her hat, Charles behind her.

Rose looks up at us and – although I'm positive she can't see me – she freezes, her eyes wide with terror.

Chapter 29

I'm awake. The blinds are edged with daylight, my phone reads 7.15 and Dad is banging on the door and asking if I want breakfast.

'Coming!'

For a second, I can't remember why I'm in bed fully clothed, but then it all clicks into place: Joe's fury and desperation; Shirley giving me side-eye over the garden fence; Rose at the bottom of the stairs, her face full of fear – and something else that flickers across the surface of my brain, there and gone before I can catch it.

Later.

My skin feels sort of grimy, and my dress looks a bit grubby, too, which, remembering how dirty the wall of the prison gatehouse was, I reckon is because of the air quality back in 1955. I grab the Ramones T-shirt – I *so* want to tell Dad how Joe thought it was prison uniform, but that's not going to happen – and shoot down the hall to have a shower before anybody sees me.

I grab a cup of tea and a bowl of chia pudding with berries – whatever I think about Skye being Dad's girlfriend, I have to admit that she's acing the whole domestic goddess thing – and head back to my bedroom. I'm just arranging myself with the laptop on my bed when I realise my espadrilles must have come off in the night and migrated to the bottom – where, sure enough, they are ... But there's something else, too, flat with sharp corners, underneath the duvet.

The Robe, by Lloyd C. Douglas. The book that had the inscription in it, looking dirty and battered – hardly surprising, since it's sixty-eight years older than it was a few hours ago, poor thing. I must have still been holding it when I came back.

OMG. That is *amazing*.

When I open the book to remind myself what's written inside, I spot that both the paper cover and the cloth and board underneath it are blackened in one corner, as if somebody's tried to burn it. I think of the websites with stuff about time travel that said that anything moving at more than the speed of light would burn up ...

Although 'burn up' is not the same as 'get a little bit charred'. The book is not even warm. Also, why would *it* get burnt, and not *me*?

So ... I reckon this book would still exist somewhere in the present day even if it hadn't just arrived with me – which I suppose is why it *could* arrive with me – and that somebody tried to burn it at some point between 1955 and now.

Some random accident, or deliberate? And if it was deliberate, why didn't whoever set fire to it finish the job?

Mystery. Let's start with the stuff in the message: Muriel Carr, Chase Farm, Yorkshire.

I type Chase Farm into the search engine ... What would it be?

Chase Farm Sanatorium, I guess. Nothing comes up, but there is a Chase Farm Hospital.

Except that it's in Enfield, which is just outside London, so not even close to Yorkshire. Unless there was a special tuberculosis unit up there because the air was better? I skim the hospital's history on Wikipedia, but there's no mention of anything like that, so I try Muriel's exact words: Chase Farm, Yorkshire. Up comes a website about holiday cottages with lovely photos of converted barns, green fields, and stone walls. 'A peaceful and romantic haven on the edge of the Yorkshire Dales National Park'. It says the farm has been in the Carr family – so it's obviously the right place – for generations. Might Dorothy have stayed there *after* she'd been in the sanatorium? Five green blobs on TripAdvisor – 'Didn't want to come home!', 'Delightful place', 'Martha made us very welcome'.

Martha could be Muriel's daughter or granddaughter. I can't just contact them and ask, though. *I'm not interested in renting a cottage, just in getting some personal details about your family . . .* Yeah, like that would work.

I'm staring at *The Robe* and thinking about all this when a detail from the newspaper report about Joe's death comes back to me: the partially burnt objects found in the wastepaper bin in his room. The result of a fire, maybe trying to keep warm – but also maybe because he didn't want them to be found.

I pick up the book again and start thumbing through it slowly, to make sure I don't miss anything. Please not a code, because I'm useless at stuff like that.

Nobody's written anything inside it, but there's a piece of folded paper fixed to the middle pages with Sellotape so old it's gone yellow and brittle. The paper's wrapped around a small black and white photograph of a very handsome man in army uniform. He looks *a lot* like Joe, so, even though there's nothing written on the back of it, no prizes for guessing who it is: 'Hello, Francis Palmer.'

I remember how you couldn't really see up the stairs at Aylmer Terrace and I picture Rose standing in the hall, looking terrified. Had she thought she'd seen a ghost rather than Joe?

The paper has a list of what must be different amounts of money, before decimal currency, because there are three columns, marked '£', 's.', and 'd'. None of the amounts are more than £5, but there are a lot of them, in neat handwriting, with dates from June 1946 to June 1960 written next to them down the left of the page, which is about three-quarters full . . .

And there's something else – a scrap that I don't spot until it flutters down to the floor. Most of it is burnt away, leaving only a strip with a blackened edge underneath, and the end of a sentence:

ask you to forgive me

Chapter 30

Who is 'you'? And who are they being asked to forgive?

Forgive . . .

Oh, no. Please no.

What if it's Joe's suicide note?

But then, why burn it? Maybe that really was an accident, or he wrote it then changed his mind but it was too late because he'd already taken the pills.

The thought of showing it to him makes me feel cold all over.

This – so much this – is why we're not meant to know the future.

I can't bear to think about it any more, so I turn back to the list of amounts of money. I have to google again to find out how to add it all up – 12 pennies in a shilling and 20 shillings in a pound, how mad is that? I get there eventually: sixty-five pounds. Old people are always going on about how they bought an entire house in the middle of London for 50p or whatever, and I know that money was worth a lot more then than it is now. I check, and it turns out that in 1955, £65 was worth about £1,621.10 today, so that's some Big Inflation Energy right there. But who was paying who, and why?

I take photos of everything, then lie back and stare at the ceiling for a few minutes, feeling defeated. Then I decide that it makes a lot more sense to get on with trying to find out stuff from what I know, rather than speculating about things I can't possibly work out right now.

So, back to Muriel Carr – which, when I add the word 'Yorkshire', brings me to a photograph of white roses in the *Yorkshire Post*, with a death notice underneath:

CARR
Muriel Jane
(*née* Millichip)

Millichip! I skim the rest:

Passed away peacefully at home on the 10 April
2018, aged 90. Beloved wife of the late Howard of
Chase Farm near Kirkby Stephen, mother to Martha,
John and Angela, grandmother to Marcia and Aiden.

OK, so could Muriel have been Shirley's cousin?

I google Millichip and discover it's a pretty unusual name. So really, what are the chances? I reckon they must be related.

Except, wouldn't Joe have known about it? Even if Shirley hadn't mentioned having a relative called Muriel, wouldn't one of the grown-ups have said something? Although I guess you don't take that much notice, unless someone talks a lot about a particular person. I mean, I know some of Yaz's cousins because they go to our school, but she's got loads of others, and I don't even know their names.

There'd hardly be a big secret about the next-door neighbour's cousin sending care packages to a young girl in a sanatorium. But Joe was only ten, and there's no reason why he'd remember.

I heard Mum talking about how they hushed it up. Perhaps Shirley *had* meant that Dorothy was pregnant before she got married, and Joe just didn't know it.

Wikipedia says Dorothy was three months pregnant at the time of her death – 11 March 1955 – and that she and Victor got married the year before . . . I click on a few links and discover that the marriage took place 'in the summer' of 1954. No actual date is mentioned, but – counting backwards – January, or the end of December, is definitely not summer, so it seems like whatever 'they' were hushing up wasn't *that*.

What other things do I know?

That Charles insisted on clearing out all Annie and Kathleen's stuff. Joe managed to save the doll's tea set and two pictures – but somebody must have kept other photos, otherwise they wouldn't be online. Victor, probably. And what was the mistake that somebody made that he and Rose were arguing about?

So many questions . . .

I really hope Joe does try and talk to Victor, and the model who lived nearby. Helene Bone, that was it. I couldn't find Victor, but maybe I can find *her*. If she was the same age as Dorothy and she's still alive, she'd be about ninety now. But even if she didn't get famous from modelling, perhaps she's got a Facebook page or something . . .

OMG, she has. Not Facebook, but an actual website:

BONE & HOLLICK
Fabric – Wallpaper – Find a Retailer – Contact Us
High quality modern fabrics, using traditional
methods such as block and screen printing, inspired
by nature . . .

And from the look of them, definitely not cheap.

Founded in 1959 by former model Helene Bone and
her husband, graphic designer George Hollick, and
now overseen by their son, Joe, Bone & Hollick's
design philosophy has always been . . .

Yada yada yada. There's an address at the bottom of the home-page – Highgate, so really close – and a link to a magazine article from last year, with a photograph of the three of them. Helene looks like the most stunningly beautiful great-grandmother ever, with a puffball of platinum hair and perfect bone structure. But how do I get in touch? Ask if I can interview her for a school project? I could do an interview on Zoom. I'll need to prepare some questions to ask, though, about designing stuff . . .

After half an hour trying to make notes and not getting very far, I decide to give myself a break by googling tuberculosis (not fun, especially as it turns out you can get it in your spine, kidneys and even your *brain*) and then I remember the television programme Joe mentioned. The Green Family? Grant Family? *Grove* Family. Maybe there's something on YouTube.

Well, that's twenty minutes of my life I'll never get back. Turns out *The Grove Family* is the first ever British soap opera. I'm guessing the bar was set pretty low back then, but even so, it is *unbelievably boring*. The first episode – or as much as I managed to watch without actually falling asleep – is about how this guy comes round to advise Mr Grove on home security (he says not to hang a key on a string inside your letter box, but I guess nobody in Aylmer Terrace saw that bit). It's funny, though, how the Groves' sitting room looks almost identical to the one in Joe's house, only tidier, with the same clock on the mantelpiece . . .

Wait, what?

I *knew* there was something – it was right before I got sidetracked by the cows mooing.

Clocks.

I jump off the bed and go out into the hall. Sure enough, the name on the clock face is Smith & Sons, the same as the name of the weird old shop Joe and I passed, where I thought the guy behind the counter could see me.

If he *could*, he's the only actual adult in 1955 who's been able to, so far. Even Annie, who is nineteen and kind of childlike, doesn't seem to know I'm there. As Joe is seventeen, and Shirley must be about the same, I'm guessing there's a cut-off point.

I suddenly realise that the wall looks different. Skye has hung a framed poster in the place where the neon 'Massage Parlour' sign used to be. Against a background of wildflowers and butter-flies, it reads:

> The past cannot be changed;
> the future is yet in your power.

What, she's getting into my *thoughts* now?

Although actually – and much as I hate inspirational quotes, especially against a background of nature because that's almost enough to make you hate wildflowers and butterflies *as well* – I've got to admit that this one has a point.

But what happens if the future is also the past? Do they some-how cancel each other out – and if they do, does that mean that I *can't* make a change, or that I *can*?

I have to believe it's the second one. Otherwise, Annie Driscoll has only four days left to live.

Chapter 31

Could Smith & Sons still exist?

I go back into my bedroom and google them. The company was founded in 1850, but it turns out the shop *is* still there. I might go and have a look – and I'm thinking I might go back to Highgate Cemetery and find Dorothy and Kathleen's graves, too, just in case there's something there.

According to the website, they're on the other side to Annie and Joe.

I need to sort out that email to Helene Bone first, though. Although . . . if Bone & Hollick have an office or a shop in Highgate, maybe Helene still lives somewhere round here?

Worth a try, anyway. I go and consult Dad, saying it's something I need for school, and he tells me to look up the company on the government site for Companies House, because if Helene Bone is still a director of Bone & Hollick, she'll be there. He and Skye are still in the kitchen, chatting over the breakfast stuff, so I make more coffee and promise to hoover later on to keep him onside in case I need any more help. When I come back to my room and get

164

stuck in, I find Helene immediately. Her home address isn't Landor Street, like in Joe's old-school directory, but a square in the *really* posh bit of Highgate, just up the hill from the cemetery.

I can hardly go and just knock on her door, though – and even if I could, what would I say? Trying to work that out is even more difficult than writing an email – guess I'll just have to hope for some inspiration when I get there.

None of this feels like much of a plan, but it's all I've got right now.

I grab a banana and a Diet Coke – Dad went and got some after breakfast because I'd complained about Skye's weird energy drinks, which was nice of him – and set off for the cemetery. The east side is laid out more like a conventional graveyard, with rows of headstones and hardly any trees or bushes, but I still get hopelessly lost. I do spot the grave of Douglas Adams, who is one of Dad's favourite authors, and take a photo – but then I remember I can't show him because a) I'm still pissed off with him, in spite of the Diet Coke, and b) awkward questions about what I'm doing here.

After what seems like an hour, I come across a double grave:

DOROTHY	KATHLEEN
HELEN WALSH	MARGARET DRISCOLL
1933–1955	1948–1955

"UNITED IN ETERNITY"

It's plain, like Annie's, and there are fresh pink roses in a metal vase in front of the stone. I take a picture of that as well.

'United in Eternity' seems like an odd message – more the kind of thing you'd read on the grave of a couple. And the style of the writing is different, like maybe it was added later.

By Victor, perhaps? I wander up and down looking for his grave, but don't find it. Maybe he remarried and, if he's dead, his remains are now lying alongside somebody else, or his ashes got scattered on a moor or something.

The message probably just means that Dorothy and Kathleen are united with God in eternity. That's the problem with this stuff – you start overthinking. Some things just are what they are; it's not like everything has to be *significant*.

Who left the flowers, though? They're identical to the ones on Annie's grave *and* – I pull out my phone to double-check – so is the metal vase. It has to be the same person, and, judging by the freshness of the roses, on the same visit.

Someone cares, but who?

I think about this as I make my way back to the road, but don't come up with any answers. I've half been wondering if I might see Kieran again, but I'm guessing he prefers the other side of the cemetery because it's messier, more Gothic, and generally *deader*, if that's a thing.

It's hot and sunny, and by the time I've got to the top of Highgate Hill I'm definitely ready for the banana and Diet Coke. I wander off the main road and sit down on the grass in the middle of a lovely big square that's all trees and Victorian lamp posts and smart old houses. There's a pub, too, with seats outside. It's like being in a village on a postcard, and I'll bet you have to be properly minted to even think of living here.

Which Helene Bone clearly is, because when I check out her address on my phone, I realise I can see it from where I'm sitting. A huge house with loads of windows and a pretty garden in the front with a lawn . . . And a woman on a bench in the middle of the grass with a stick resting by her side, leaning back and gazing at the bright blue sky. She's slim, in a lovely flowing dress, with platinum hair and amazing cheekbones – that has *got* to be her.

Chapter 32

OMG. Before I can stop and think what I'm doing or what to say, I jump up and rush across the road.

'Hello!' I grin over the hedge like an idiot, but she raises a hand and waves as if we've known each other all our lives.

'Hello there! Who are you?'

'Millie.' Might as well go for it – after all, nothing about this is normal. 'Are you Helene Bone?'

She stares at me intently for a moment. I cross my fingers that she can hear OK.

'Do I know you?'

'No. Or . . . ' I take a deep breath, then gabble, 'not yet, anyway. Please may I ask you something?'

Honestly, I sound like I'm about six, and for a moment I think I've blown it – I mean, you can't just go up to random strangers and ask them stuff. But after another moment, Helene's face relaxes into a smile, and I swear it's like what my hippie granddad's druid friend says about being winked at by God. Kevin's a stoner and what comes out of his mouth is mostly word salad, but I totally get that part now: it's something that happens right when you need it to, a perfect cosmic coincidence.

Right, Millie. Do not mess this up.

'If you like ... Millie, is it?'

'Yes. It's about ...' Suddenly, my tongue feels like it's glued to the roof of my mouth by Dorothy's name.

Helene's still smiling. 'You'll have to be quicker than that – I've not got much time left.'

'I'm sorry ...'

'Don't be. I'm not. I've been very fortunate. It's just that I probably shan't be around for a great deal longer, so I probably won't get the chance for many more conversations with ... Well, I was going to say strangers, but what you said was better: people I don't know "yet".' She looks at me beadily. 'Now, what is it you want to know?'

I think of what Kieran said about how nothing matters when you're dead. Maybe this, with Helene, will be the ... the *good* version of that, meaning she'll be OK with telling me something because stuff stops being so important when it can't hurt anybody any more.

'I wanted to know about ...' I squeeze my eyes shut for a second, then open them. 'Dorothy Walsh.'

Helene's eyes open wide. 'That was very sad. But it's all online, isn't it?'

'Not everything. I don't think Annie Driscoll killed her, and I reckon there were a bunch of things that never came out at the trial.'

169

Helene stares at me, head on one side, while she considers this. Eventually she says, 'You might well be right. But why are you interested, when it was such a long time ago? Are you a relative?'

I shake my head. 'I know her brother.'

'Joe. I met him a couple of times. *Very* handsome boy.' She's looking beady again and I cross my fingers. 'One doesn't forget a face like that. Dorothy was beautiful too, of course. But also – and this was the outstanding thing about her – she was *kind*.'

'Joe said that, too.'

'Well, he was right. People took advantage of it.'

'Do you mean Annie?'

Helene shakes her head impatiently. 'Annie didn't have the brains to take advantage of anyone.'

Harsh. 'Was there something wrong with Annie? Mentally, I mean.'

Helene looks as if she's considering this. 'She certainly had a low IQ. I think it would be described as "having learning difficulties" nowadays. In the 1950s, they would have said "educationally subnormal".'

'That sounds horrible.'

Helene nods. 'People weren't . . . well, I was going to say they were unkind, but I don't think they meant to be. It was more that they were thoughtless. People got put into boxes, really. Somebody would get labelled as . . . well, limited, if you like. Even "mentally defective", sometimes. Annie was fortunate in that she was able to hold down a job, but she got overlooked at home. I'm not saying that was right, but I can see how it happened: first Dorothy came

170

along – this beautiful, sweet girl – then Joe, so handsome and smart, and a *boy*, of course – and then Annie.'

'Who needed *more* attention!' I burst out. 'Not less.'

'Yes, she did. If Annie had been violent or aggressive, it would have been a different story – but she wasn't, so . . .' Helene shrugs. 'I don't mean to dismiss it, Millie, I'm just trying to explain how a lot of people thought back then. And their mother had her own problems.'

'It's really unfair.' I think of what Joe said about Annie's behaviour and feel angry for her – and a prickle of unease that I can't quite place. Puzzling over this, I miss what Dorothy is saying.

' . . . a good man.'

'Sorry, who?'

'Victor.' Helene frowns at me. 'Dorothy's husband. I think they'd have been happy.'

'Is he dead?'

'Well, he was quite a few years older than Dorothy, so if he *is* still alive he's even older than I am, which is saying something. George knew him a bit – mainly through work, really – but they lost touch after he emigrated.'

'Where did he go?'

'Australia. He was what they used to call a Ten Pound Pom – that was the cost of the fare. I'd probably have done the same in his shoes. But for what it's worth, I never thought for a moment that Annie killed anybody – or not on purpose, anyway. There was something very wrong in that family. A lot of secrets, and Dorothy's mother always looked scared of her own shadow.'

'You said she had problems . . . ' I have a sudden image of Rose standing in the hall, looking terrified. 'Do you think that was because of Dorothy's stepfather?'

'Don't know, never met him. But Mrs Driscoll always seemed . . . ' Helene frowns, remembering, 'haunted. Not by an actual ghost, more a sort of permanent anxiety, as if something might go wrong at any moment. Which it did, of course, but I'm talking about before that. She was someone who couldn't relax.'

'Bad with her nerves,' I say, remembering what Joe told me.

'Haven't heard that expression for a long time. I used to have a friend who reminded me of Mrs Driscoll. Her husband was an alcoholic, and she was tense all the time, waiting for what he'd do next.'

'But Charles wasn't—'

Helene cuts me off, impatient. 'I'm not saying he was. It's the state of mind I'm talking about . . . Hypervigilance, that's it. Always on the lookout for threats. That was Mrs Driscoll to a tee. She didn't last long after Annie . . . ' Helene shakes her head at the awfulness of it all. 'Poor, poor woman.'

I think of how I'd felt when Mum and Dad were still together, like I was always on red alert for the next row. Totally exhausting – and that was just a few months, not my entire life. 'When did she die?'

Helene raises her eyebrows, like, *aren't you nosy*, and I realise I must sound way too interested in someone else's tragedy.

'Sorry. I'm not being, like, a *ghoul*, I'm just interested. Because of Joe.'

'Because of Joe,' Helene repeats, and stares up at the sky again.

'Beautiful Joe . . .' She closes her eyes for a moment, then lowers her head and looks at me. 'It was about five years later. Same week as the execution, I remember that.'

'So, June 1960?'

'Sounds about right.'

The last sum of money on that sheet was dated June 1960. Coincidence, or something else?

'It might sound fanciful,' Helene says, 'but I wondered if she hadn't wished herself away . . . Although there wasn't so much they could do for cancer back then, not like now.'

'Is that what she had?'

Helene nods. 'All the smoking – and of course the stress of what happened would have made her smoke even more. And sadness, of course, and blaming herself—'

'Why?'

'Women always blame themselves.' Helene's voice is brisk, like she's stating a fact. 'For all kinds of things. Society encourages it – makes it easier for men to get away with murder.'

'*Literally?*'

'Maybe. As you said, it's possible that Annie didn't kill Dorothy and Kathleen, but I simply don't know.' Helene stares at me for a moment, then says, 'But for Mrs Driscoll, the loneliness must have been the worst thing of all.'

I open my mouth to say that at least she still had Joe – I wasn't going to mention Charles – but Helene holds up a finger to silence me. 'I'm not just talking about losing Dorothy, Kathleen and Annie, although God knows . . .' Helene closes her eyes and shakes her head. 'I'm guessing you're too young to know this, and I hope you'll be lucky enough in your life never to find out, but being in a relationship with a person you can't talk to is a thousand times lonelier than being by yourself. And for Mrs Driscoll, it must have been a thousand times worse even than that . . . I think,' she adds, quietly, 'she must have been glad to go.'

I can feel Helene's eyes on me as I think about this.

ask you to forgive me

If Rose had blamed herself, had she written that to somebody before she died? The list of money is all figures except for the dates, which are written in capitals, so I can't tell if the handwriting is the same . . . And in any case, Rose might not have written the list of figures.

Now Helene is giving me a *very* beady look. 'Joe obviously didn't tell you.'

'No, he didn't. I think,' I add, truthfully, 'there's a lot he can't talk about.'

'I'm sure there is.'

She puts her head on one side and smiles. It's starting to feel like she's humouring me, so I figure I might as well carry on asking questions: 'You don't know what happened to Charles, do you?'

'No idea.'

'And the secrets – do you know what they were?'

Helene's eyes narrow, and I fully expect her to tell me to mind my own business, but instead she looks thoughtful. 'Only one of them. Dorothy was absolutely terrified of anyone finding out, especially Victor.' She shakes her head, a wondering look on her face. 'I'm amazed she told *me*, really. I think she'd buried it so far down inside that she could almost convince herself it hadn't happened.'

'What hadn't?'

'She had a child when she was fifteen.'

Chapter 33

I gasp, Shirley's spiteful hiss in my head: *I heard Mum talking about how they hushed it up.* 'Joe told me she was sent to a sanatorium for tuberculosis when she was fifteen.'

Helene nods, satisfied. 'Makes sense. A good reason for her to be away for a few months, and then the parents could say she was cured and bring her home – without the baby, of course. And everyone would act as if it never happened and expect poor Dorothy to do the same.'

'What about Dorothy's school, though?'

'Easy enough to tell them she had TB. People didn't expect you to show certificates and letters and so on for everything back then. In any case, she'd have been leaving at the end of the year, so . . .' Helene shrugs.

It *could* have happened. I picture Muriel's message inside the copy of *The Robe*, with the date: 1948, the year Kathleen was born.

'Except . . . I think Dorothy might have come back *with* a baby. Everyone said that Kathleen was her sister, but—'

'But Mrs Driscoll pretended the baby was hers. That sort of

thing happened a *lot* more than anybody let on. It's hard for someone your age to imagine, but things were very different back then. Women were a lot more dependent on men, because the law and society made it that way. The choice for a girl in Dorothy's position was either to have a backstreet abortion, which might well kill you, or – unless you were very lucky indeed – to be disowned by your family and wind up in some terrible home for unmarried mothers where you were treated like dirt. What the Driscolls did was the best thing, because it gave Dorothy a chance to have a life, and it stopped Kathleen being sent away God-knows-where for adoption or called a bastard.'

'Why would anyone call her that?'

Helene sighs – and I recognise it as the same sound I make when I even think about explaining stuff from now to Joe. 'You think it just means someone's horrible, but the original meaning is a person whose parents weren't married, and it was a serious insult. People used to look down on illegitimate children, Millie, and they could be very cruel. It was a different world, and people were vile in all sorts of ways it's probably impossible for you to imagine.'

'OK . . .' It's not like things are perfect now, but Helene's right. It *is* hard to imagine a world where people are mean about that, because it's just so stupid. 'Who was the father?'

'She wouldn't tell me.'

'But she must have had to tell Rose and Charles.'

'That's what I thought, but apparently not. They must have tried to get it out of her, but she told me she was determined never to say. If Dorothy was fifteen at the time, her parents wouldn't have been able to arrange what they used to call a "shotgun wedding" – which of course they might not have been able to do anyway, if the guy was already married . . . Of course, what happened was rape, because of Dorothy being underage, but back then most families were more concerned with reputation than justice – because that would involve washing their dirty linen in public – so the men usually got away with it.'

'That's totally unfair.'

'Yes, it is. Mind you, we don't *know* that she didn't want sex, even though it wasn't legal. And if *he* was underage too then they'd both have committed the same criminal offence, although I believe the police rarely get involved in cases like that. But I do remember thinking that if she'd been in love with the father – or what one *imagines* "in love" means when one is fifteen –' Helene rolls her eyes – 'then surely she'd have told someone his name. Especially if he was the same age. Although . . .' Helene pauses to look up at the sky again, 'that's purely conjecture.'

'Do you think Kathleen knew Dorothy was her mother?'

'Absolutely not. There was *so* much going on below the surface back then, Millie. People kept secrets for their entire lives – things that your generation would tell the world without a second thought.'

'Do you think that's why Rose was like she was? Worried someone would find out?'

'Maybe . . .' Helene takes hold of her stick and leans on it as she stands up. Her fingers look old and twisted, but she holds her head high, like a ballerina, and her back is straight. 'I doubt it's the whole story, but who knows? I hope I've been of some help. I was very fond of Dorothy, you know.'

'Did you leave the roses on her grave?'

'That wasn't me.' She walks towards the house, then stops and half turns on the porch. 'This *has* been interesting. Goodbye, Millie, and good luck.' The front door must be ajar, because it opens when she prods it with the end of her stick.

I've got more questions, but it's like there's a knot of thoughts in my head and I can't untangle them fast enough to say anything that makes sense. Before I can even ask her to wait, Helene says, casually, like it's an afterthought, 'If you see Joe – who died before you were born, by the way – give him my regards, won't you?' Then she raises her stick in a 'goodbye' gesture and disappears into the house.

Chapter 34

Well, *that* happened.

It takes me about a minute just staring at the house before I get myself together enough to head back into the square and plonk myself down on the grass again. Helene didn't say it like, mic drop, just really matter-of-fact: Joe died before you were born but, yeah, you might see him. Like she knew what I was saying couldn't be true, but she also knew I wasn't lying.

Maybe Helene sees ghosts too, but she doesn't think it's a big deal. She certainly doesn't seem to think death is a big deal – which I guess is just as well, really.

Poor Rose, though. She can't have been that old when she died ... forty-five, perhaps? Not much more, anyway.

I'm not going to tell Joe.

I lie back on the grass and stare up at the cloudless sky, going over the conversation. Judging from what I've seen, I reckon Helene's right about Rose being on the alert all the time. I have a sudden image of her lying in bed beside Charles, staring into the darkness while he slept, so lonely ...

That was what I'd thought about Joe, at the end of his life. Couldn't he and Rose have talked to each other, at least? Unless . . .

Helene said Rose blamed herself because women always do. Plus, I reckon any parent in this situation would feel guilty because they'd think they should have done something to stop it or they must have brought their kids up badly or whatever – but what if there was something *else*? Karma: not necessarily because Rose was the killer, but that she'd let a man get away with murder?

More questions. Urrgh.

That wasn't me. What Helene said when I asked if she'd left the roses on Dorothy and Kathleen's grave – like she knew about them, so I guess she visits sometimes . . . Turns out I wasn't overthinking the message on the grave, though: 'United in Eternity' could easily mean that they can be mother and daughter in the afterlife as they weren't allowed to be in this one.

That's a point – the whole secrecy thing. That list of different amounts of money couldn't be payments to a *blackmailer*, could it? I check the photo on my phone – but the first payment was made in 1946, two years before Kathleen was born, so, unless Dorothy had an elephant-length pregnancy, then no, it couldn't.

But, if the payments stopped around the time Rose died, was she paying someone for some reason? Unless somebody was paying *her*, of course . . .

But why?

Trying to work it all out is like trying to fit a jigsaw together when half the pieces are missing, and after about ten minutes

I'm ready to give up and go home. I'm just sitting up when I hear my ringtone.

Kieran.

Freaky, although I guess I messaged him yesterday, so maybe not – but . . . an actual *phone call*?

'I see your point.'

'Hello to you, too. What point?'

'About why should I expect you to believe me when I don't believe you.'

Wow, practically an apology. 'Thanks. Are you OK?'

He makes an impatient huffing noise. 'Let's say I do believe you.'

'You do? Like, properly?'

'For the purposes of this conversation, I do. So . . . I just wanted to say be careful, OK?'

'In what way?'

'You've heard of the butterfly effect, right? A minor change you make to the past may cause a major change in the future.'

'What's that got to do with butterflies?'

'That's just the example that gets used: one butterfly flapping its wings in China might cause a hurricane in the Caribbean. Which – in your case – means: if you insist on interfering with something that's already happened, it may have unintended consequences.'

'I suppose,' I say, thinking of what Skye said about going back in time and killing your grandfather. 'But not *that* major. I mean, Annie not being hanged for something she didn't do isn't likely to . . . I don't know, start a war, is it?'

'No, but it might cause something else you don't want to happen.'

'Like what?'

'I don't know.' Kieran's starting to sound impatient. 'Just something.'

'OK – although, to be honest, I don't really see how I can possibly make things *worse*. But I thought you didn't care about any of this?'

'I don't. You might, though. So . . .' He sighs, like it's a massive effort to go on talking. 'That's all, really.'

'Well, thanks.'

'Right then . . . Bye.' He ends the call.

I roll my eyes at the phone. *Great help, Dead Boy. Really outstanding.*

It's only 4 p.m. when I get back to the flat, so I decide I might as well take a detour down the Cally Road before I go in, to see if I can find Smith & Sons.

The shop is still there: faded, flaking paint, and grilles that look like old-school lift cages over the windows and door. There's a sign hanging on the inside of the door saying 'Closed'. It looks like it might be shut for ever, but when I peer through the window I can see that the ceiling-high wooden cabinets and the long counter are still there.

Walking away, I have the weirdest feeling of being watched, but when I turn there's nobody at any of the windows, either in the shop or the upstairs flat.

When I get home, Dad is on a Zoom call with his publisher about what the pandas are going to do next. Skye's in the kitchen, making bread. 'Hope that's not sourdough,' I tell her. 'Dad said it was like eating a mattress when Mum made it in lockdown, and she's really good at baking.'

I don't know why I said it, really – just the sight of her standing at the table with all the bowls and everything, like she owns the place. Any prickles of warmth I've felt towards Skye lately disappear as I hear Dad talking about the work he and Mum used to do *together*. I can't believe I haven't thought of it before, but how are they going to keep working on those books? I think about someone other than Mum drawing the pandas because they can't stand to be in the same room or Zoom together, and a wave of pain sweeps over me. Compared with everything I've been thinking about recently, it seems bizarre to be so upset by this, but I can't help it.

I disappear before Skye has a chance to reply.

At least Dad's Zoom gives me an excuse to put off the hoovering for a bit, so I go to my room and google post-mortems instead. I know – Wednesday Addams – but I'm thinking about what Helene told me and the argument Joe said Victor had with Rose.

All the stuff about determining the cause of death makes me wonder what Kieran thinks he died of, because I never thought to ask him that. In fact, apart from feeling sorry for him (and rolling my eyes a bit, tbh), I didn't really engage with it, and I'm beginning to feel . . . not exactly guilty, because – same as before – it's not like he asked me for something and I didn't give it, but that I ought to be paying more attention.

I push my laptop away and lie on my bed. I feel exhausted by all this – not only Kieran and Mum and Dad, but Annie and Joe as well. Plus, I've got to get some revision done, but there's no point starting on any of that now, with all of this going round and round in my head. I have a go at one of Mum's mindfulness exercises, but I just wind up lying on the bed feeling incredibly anxious and totally powerless at the same time, which is just the worst possible combination.

After about five minutes of staring at the ceiling, I go and hover at the sitting room door while Dad finishes his Zoom call. I'm not really sure why. I just feel like I want to reach out to him – for things to be like they were before, I suppose, even though I know that's not realistic.

He ends the call and looks up. 'Hello there.'

'What's going to happen about the pandas?'

'How do you mean?'

'You and Mum. Are you still going to do the books together, or will it be somebody else?'

'The stories are hers as much as mine, Millie.'

'So she'll carry on drawing them?'

'Of course!'

'And she's OK with that?'

Dad looks puzzled. 'She hasn't said otherwise.'

'Don't you think you should check?'

'Sure, but . . . has she said something to you?'

'No. I just . . . I don't want anyone else to draw them.'

'Nor do I. Honestly, Millie, she'd have said. It'll be all right.' Dad gives me the lopsided smile I've seen so much of recently, only this time it looks relieved, not patronising. 'Have you had a nice day?'

'OK,' I say automatically. Then, because I want us to carry on talking, 'Have you ever heard of an illness where somebody thinks they're dead?'

'Oh, now . . . ' He puffs out his cheeks, thinking. 'Actually, I have. When I was still acting. You won't remember, because you were only about five, but I had a few episodes in one of those hospital drama things that run for ever, and there was a storyline about a man who had that.' He grins. 'If this is for school, they don't half teach you some weird stuff nowadays.'

'So . . . did it have a name?'

'Must have done. Hang on . . . Begins with "C", I know that. Compo . . . Coppard . . . No, wait . . . Cotard, that's it! Cotard's Delusion. Also known as Walking Corpse Syndrome.' Dad looks pleased with himself. 'I remember them talking about it on the set, because it's very unusual. I think the bloke in the series – the character – got it from a bang on the head. Some sort of accident, anyway.'

'Did he get better?'

'Yeah. I don't know if people always do, but they have medical advisors on those shows to make sure it's accurate, so that must mean they *can*. I shouldn't think there's very much data.' He frowns at me. 'You don't *know* someone who's got it, do you?'

I'm about to deny this, because TMI, when Skye saves me by calling out that the food's ready, so I just tell him I'm pleased about the pandas.

Dinner is really nice. I'm really pleased it's veggie again – aubergine parmigiana – after what Joe said about those cows. The bread *is* sourdough, but it's lovely – no one's ever going to hear me say this, but Skye is a *lot* better at cooking than Mum. After that, though, the evening seems to drag on for ever. Dad and Skye start watching a documentary on the big TV about some leathery old rock band, which has to be *his* idea because she's way too young to remember them. Anyway, they're getting all loved up on the floor cushions – *ick* – so I go to my room and FaceTime Yaz. Liv's there as well. She went over to cheer Yaz up, but all she's doing is moaning about how Mia, her girlfriend, has gone off to her parents' cottage in Norfolk – they're minted – to revise for her A levels. I feel bad for both of them but, compared to Annie and Joe's problems . . .

Most people's lives – including mine – are pretty OK if you compare them to the Driscoll family.

I feel so *useless*. I scroll for a bit, then decide to watch a film, but it's impossible – I try about ten different things but each time I barely get five minutes in because I'm too restless to concentrate.

Skye puts her head round the door at about ten thirty and asks if I need anything, which I reckon is code for 'Shouldn't you be in bed by now?'

The part of me that's still about six wants to tell her she's not my mum, but the grown-up bit knows that she's reaching out. Plus, I know, rationally, that not all of this is her fault, even if I want it to be, because it's not like she put a spell on Dad. 'I'm fine, thanks.'

'Are you sure?'

Oh, great, now she wants a heart-to-heart. I nod, hoping she'll get the message and go, but she says, 'You know, Millie, everything happens for a reason.'

Urgh. I am so not listening if she's going to start whanging on about her and Dad. I mean, how insensitive can she *be*? 'Does it?'

'It might not seem like it at the time, but yes. We—'

'You know he used to be the face of a laxative, right?' I have no idea why I say this, other than her whole superior I-understand-everything-in-the-universe holistic crap is really infuriating. 'You're having an affair with a guy who is married to somebody else – and you're doing it because *you want to*, so don't make out it's for some *cosmic* reason.'

OK, so I know she hasn't actually said that, but still.

'I wasn't going to.'

'Well, good, because—'

'Millie, I'm not trying to take anything away from you. Believe me, I understand. My dad was … Well, let's just say he wasn't the best—'

'Yeah, but we're talking about *my* dad, and he's a cheating arsehole.' Dad's old-man-getting-up-off-the-floor noise from next door makes me rethink, because I really don't want to get into this with both of them, especially after the chat I had with Dad before dinner, so I backtrack. 'OK, let's examine this. Everything happens for a reason could mean two totally different things.' Skye's looking kind of bewildered now, but I'm going to run with it. 'One, that there's a cause for everything, like, you got hit by a car because you stepped on the road without looking first; and two, that there's a purpose behind everything, like it's God or the universe doing it for your benefit or to teach you something or whatever … So, I get the first one, but doesn't the second one depend on how you look at it? I mean, you might think something that happens is great for a while, but then it might turn out to be shit. Like . . . you win fifty million pounds on the lottery – great, so God loves you and you're special. But then you lose all your friends because they're jealous or they feel you ought to be helping them out more or whatever, so you're all lonely in your beautiful mansion and you wind up surrounded by toxic freeloaders who sell you drugs, and you get addicted and mess up your life and make your family sad. So actually, God hates you and the only reason you're special is that you got given this massive chance and you totally blew it.'

'She's got you there, hun.' Dad comes up behind Skye and puts his arms round her waist.

Hun?

No. Just *no*. He might mean it just as a general sort of endearment – ick – but my mother's name actually *is* Honey. OK, so that isn't Dad's doing – Grandma and Granddad are hippies who live off-grid in Cornwall, so it's Honey Dharma, which she never mentions because cultural appropriation – but *seriously*? He used to call her 'hun' all the time. I glare at him.

'Darling . . . ' Skye, who's now looking very relieved, twists slightly to plant a kiss on his cheek before turning back to me. 'I see what you're saying, Millie, but it's about being *positive*.'

About not giving the pair of you a hard time, you mean. As I turn my head away so I don't have to see them slobbering over each other, I remember Dad telling me, about six months ago, that the world is full of random shit and that coping with it is what makes you an adult. He was a bit drunk and probably trying, in a really clumsy way, to prepare me for when stuff got real over his affair with Skye. Looking at the two of them, I can't help thinking that in his case there's been quite a lot of *self-generated* random shit, because no one put a gun to his head and *made* him have affairs with Skye or any of the women before her (does she even know about them?). But really, both ways of looking at it – the random shit and the things being for a reason because God or some cosmic force set them up – seem to me like a way of letting yourself off the hook. I guess that's easier for Dad than facing the truth – what he's done to Mum – and, for a second, I almost tell Skye that he'll do it to her, too, so she'd better watch out. Instead, I say, 'At least with the second one – God singling you out – it's like you're important, rather than just being, I don't know, an ant, and somebody trod on you without even knowing it.' I slide off the bed. 'I'm going to clean my teeth.'

As I'm brushing, I think about how maybe we just say stuff is 'meant' when it's what we wanted all along, or we're trying to make something good from a bad situation. Then I remember what Kieran said about unintended consequences. Why does everyone have to be so *cryptic*, anyway?

And I certainly can't see how an innocent person being hanged is 'for a reason'. Not a *good* reason, anyway. I feel like going to ask Skye how that's meant to fit into her Little Miss Positive world picture.

I don't, of course. I just spit, rinse, and head back to my room. I'm about to close the door when Dad appears and sits down on the bed.

'Go easy on Skye, darling. She's doing her best.'

'Whatever.'

'She's on your side.'

'Oh? And how does that work, exactly, *hun*?' I hate how bitchy my voice sounds, but right now I hate Dad more.

Dad winces. 'Did I say that?'

'Yeah, you did.'

'Well, if it's any consolation, Skye's been telling me off.' Dad looks rueful.

'For calling her hun?'

'No.' To my surprise, he looks sheepish.

'I was a bit upset when Honey rang yesterday and said she's staying in Greece for a while.'

'You mean you were furious – her staying away means I'll be around for longer, spoiling your love nest.'

'Because it's difficult, Millie. She didn't give me a whole lot of choice.'

'Why should she? You caused all this. And by the way, she didn't give *me* a whole lot of choice, either.'

'OK, I asked for that. But . . . ' He sighs. 'How long am I going to be in the wrong?' Now he looks, and sounds, pathetic, and that makes me even more angry.

I shrug. 'Can you leave, please? I want to go to bed.'

Dad sighs. 'Fair enough. But I do love you, you know.'

'Shut the door on your way out.' I turn my back on him and start picking out clothes for waking up in 1955.

Chapter 35

I'm in the corridor again: fog, yellow light, and the clock face. One by one, the metal doors appear . . .

All closed. No sound except the clock

Like last time. If I wait . . .

I look down at myself to make sure everything is in order. I didn't feel the cold last time, but I decided to go for practical anyway. So: jeans, a really nice Vogue sweatshirt I nicked from Mum, and Converse (I haven't forgotten what Shirley said about my espadrilles, plus I cleaned them all over with wet wipes so the sheets wouldn't get dirty). I didn't think there was any point trying to bring my phone, but I did shove the actual book, with the two pieces of paper and the photo inside, in my sweatshirt, but that's not there, either. Wait, it's on the floor – but now it looks much newer and it's not burnt any more.

I pick it up and shake it . . . nothing. The papers and photo have gone.

So: an object can travel back to 1955 provided it was already in existence at that time.

The photo of the man I'm 99 per cent sure is Francis Palmer must have been taken during the war but only put in the book afterwards, which is why it isn't here now, and the 'ask you to forgive me' message might have been written either before or after 1955 . . . So: great deduction, Sherlock, but no help *at all*.

Tick, tock, tick, tock . . . The minute hand inches forward as I wait. No other sound or movement.

Am I too early? Too late? Perhaps the family aren't allowed to come every day. I step across the corridor and very quietly pull down the flap to expose the spyhole in the door of Annie's cell.

The first thing I see is Florey, sitting at the small table with her back to me. Next to her is a jowly man. He's wearing a black suit and a vicar's collar, so I guess he must be the chaplain. There was something about that on Wikipedia, how he'd pray with the condemned prisoners.

Annie's sitting opposite him, looking like she's in a dream. The chaplain's obviously been saying something to her because he's leaning forward like he expects a response. Eventually, as if it's a huge effort to concentrate long enough to get the words out, she says, 'I still don't understand. If they say I did wrong, then I must have, but I don't see how I could.'

The chaplain frowns, then pats her hand and says, gently, like he's talking to a child, 'God sees you, Annie.'

Annie looks round the cell like she's expecting Him to be in the corner or something. For a second, I think she must see my eye in the spyhole and wonder if that's God, but she never saw me the other times, so I figure it's OK.

'He sees you, and He will forgive. God's mercy is infinite.'

'But ...' Annie looks bewildered. She shakes her head, like it's too much to explain, then bows her head, like the chaplain's defeated her. I want to bang on the door and scream that she hasn't done anything to be forgiven *for* and why isn't he actually *listening* to what she's saying instead of parroting some rubbish he learnt in vicar school, but of course there's no point.

There's no point standing here being angry, either; I need to do something useful. It's doesn't look like there'll be visitors any time soon, but there's nothing to stop me doing some snooping by myself.

As long as I can slip through the gates here – and they must open sometimes, because the officers need to move around – I can get to Aylmer Terrace. And I woke up in my own bed after last time, so getting back to the present won't be a problem. Also, even if children in 1955 can see me, adults can't, so it's not like anyone's going to call the police or anything. Plus, good wardrobe choice if I need to get over a wall or whatever. The book will be a nuisance, though. Perhaps if I leave it at the dark end of the corridor, where the gallows room is, nobody will notice, and it'll be waiting for me in our hallway when I get back?

I move to the right – I don't know if it's my imagination, but it seems like it's colder here – and stand the book flat against the end wall.

OK. I've got this. I retrace my steps, then go round the corner and down the stairs, then wait by the locked door for someone to come. After about five minutes, although it seems like a lot longer, someone does: a distinguished-looking grey-haired woman wearing a smart checked jacket and skirt. She's accompanied by an officer who is practically bowing while she opens the door, so I'm guessing she's someone important.

I wait until they're both through, then slither past them quickly and run down to the yard, where I wait beside the big iron door for someone to let me out.

Fortunately, a prison officer wants to come this way, and I manage to slide past her when she opens the door. I then run down the passageway between the brick walls and across the big open space at the front of the prison under the giant arch of the castle gateway, next to the huge oak door.

It doesn't take long before a bunch of people are escorted in – I'm guessing staff or visitors because there are no handcuffs in sight – and I jee-ust manage to slip out into the street before the officer locks the door behind them.

Curiosity makes me stop in front of Smith & Sons, even though the sign hanging inside the glass door reads 'Closed'. I lean forward to peer past it into the dimness of the shop, then practically jump out of my skin.

There's a man standing right next to the sign, staring at me through the glass, like he appeared by magic. He's wearing a brown dust coat, same as the guy I saw before. If it is him, then close up he's even more like a waxwork, still as a statue in the half-light, with glistening grey-beige skin—

Until he opens his mouth in a horrific snaggle-toothed yellow grin.

I jump back, gasping, then dig my nails into my palms and will myself not to turn and make a run for it. As he opens the door, something jangles loudly.

'I wondered if you'd be back a third time.' His voice sounds creaky, like it doesn't get used very often.

'Third ...?' I've only been here once in 1955, when I came past with Joe.

'Come in, then.'

The door is wide open now, but I hang back. With his eyes half hidden in shadow, the guy looks basically demonic. Even if there were people in the street, all they'd see is a man opening a door, and they wouldn't hear me if I screamed, either. But ...

I don't reckon he could kill me because I haven't been born yet. Plus, Annie.

There is no choice. I step forward into the gloom.

Chapter 36

The man holds out his hand. 'Smith. Great-grandson, in case you were wondering.'

'Millie.' I'd thought his skin might feel ... I don't know, slimy or something, but his hand is warm and dry. 'How come you can see me?'

'Because I'm the same as you.'

'You mean you're still alive in my time? But you must be ...'

'A hundred years old. And very, very tired.' When Mr Smith closes the door, I can see there's a small brass bell attached to it, which must be what the jangling noise was. Knowing this makes me feel a tiny bit better, like, at least I understand *something*.

He reaches up and pulls on a little chain hanging down from the ceiling light fitting. As the room becomes brighter, he starts to look a whole lot less frightening – an ordinary guy who could use a visit to the dentist, really. 'Bet you've never seen a gas lamp before, have you? We shan't convert to electricity for another couple of years ... I saw you looking in yesterday.'

'I thought somebody was watching me. Where were you?'

'In my room, upstairs. Ageing almost seventy years in one night is not a pastime I can recommend, although, thank God, I have largely retained my good eyesight. I am visible to others here and now, in 1955, because I was alive – but, as you see, not a matinee idol even then. That's not the same for you, I think, although that boy . . . ?' He raises an eyebrow.

'He can see me. I think it's anybody who's under eighteen – and you, of course.'

Mr Smith nods slowly, like he's thinking. 'That makes sense. I am so very glad to see you, my dear. I'd almost given up hope of meeting another traveller. How did you come to touch the other clock?'

'*Other* clock?'

'I made two of them, do you see?'

'Not really, no.'

'Why don't you come and sit down?' I look round the shop, but there doesn't seem to be anywhere *to* sit. 'I think it might help if I explain a few things, and then you can tell me your story.' Mr Smith's voice is gentle. 'We keep a couple of stools hidden over there.'

We go behind the counter and he takes two wooden stools with red velvet tops from a hidey-hole underneath the massive old cash register. As well as rows of cabinets all the way up the wall, there are shelves underneath the counter filled with strange-looking metal tools that I can't identify, all jumbled together with bits from the insides of clocks and watches. Mr Smith produces a battered tin Thermos flask and two tin mugs from the middle of it all. 'We repair timepieces as well as making them. I like to think that we're the custodians of time, although there aren't so many of us left now ... In *your* time, I mean.'

'It's your time, too.'

'Not really. I'm just waiting it out.' He gives me a smile, like, *grin and bear it*. 'Hope you don't mind tea with sugar.'

'It's fine.' I say this to be polite, but actually the red-brown liquid he pours doesn't taste that bad. 'When you saw me before in 1955, with Joe, did you know then?'

'Joe, is it?' He raises an eyebrow. 'When I saw you then, I thought you looked ... well, *different*, which is why I remembered you. But it wasn't until you came by again in the present that I put two and two together.'

'OK.' I decide to ignore the knowing way Mr Smith just said Joe's name. 'So ... the clocks you made?'

'I've always been fascinated by time, Millie. It's free, but it's priceless. We can measure it down to the last septillionth of a second – yes, really – but it's the one thing we have absolutely no control over, and, no matter how powerful we are, it defeats us all in the end.' I'm obviously looking at him with a glazed expression – I get that it must be a relief for him to be able to say all this to someone, but I'm not sure I need to hear it right now – and he says, 'I'm sorry, I'll get to the point. In the early fifties, I'd been looking at ways to develop quartz clocks for the consumer market. Quartz is a mineral which is used to create a signal with a very precise frequency – meaning that quartz clocks are more accurate than mechanical clocks. They've been the most widely used timekeepers since the 1980s, but now, in the 1950s, they are still in their infancy. I was always fascinated by developments in horology—'

'Horo what?'

'Sorry. Horology is the study and measurement of time. I'd read everything about quartz that I could lay my hands on, and I'd been doing a few experiments of my own in the workshop at the back. It was such a joyful time, Millie. My wife and I were very much in love, and our son Robbie, who was seven, was our pride and joy. Jean had just discovered she was expecting again, after hoping for so long, and we were delighted. I'd got through the war without a scratch on me – which was pretty remarkable, given that I went through the Battle of France and the D-Day landings – and I thought I must be one of the luckiest men alive.

'My efforts in the workshop were clumsy, but in the end I managed to produce two clocks using quartz. I finished them both on the 5 June 1955 – and seven days later, on 12 June, a bus went out of control on the Holloway Road, and Robbie and Jean, and our unborn child, were killed.'

Chapter 37

I had no idea where he was going with that, but it definitely wasn't *there*. 'I'm *so* sorry.'

12 June: the day before Annie's execution.

'It was ...' Mr Smith's face is twisted in pain. '*Terrible*. What happened was nobody's fault. The bus driver was a young man, apparently in the best of health. Nobody had any idea there was something wrong with his heart, but the attack could have happened at any time ... Unfortunately, it happened while he was at the wheel, and the bus mounted the pavement and crashed through a shop window. Jean and Robbie weren't the only ones who lost their lives.' He shakes his head. 'People talk about time being a healer, but that's not quite how it works. You simply get used to missing people, that's all. Or – in my case – I would have done if it hadn't been for the clock.'

'I don't understand.'

'As I said, quartz is a mineral. Here.' He produces a black and white photograph of a chunk of clear crystal from underneath the counter and hands it to me. 'When it's subject to mechanical stress different electrical charges are formed at each end, creating vibrations. That's why it's used in oscillators – devices that swing back and forth in a regular rhythm – within timepieces.' He ducks down again and picks out something from the clutter on the shelves under the counter. 'You could almost say . . . ' He's staring at me so intently now that it's starting to feel uncomfortable, 'that this oscillator –' he holds up a small, brass-coloured cylinder – 'is able to contain time itself. From as far back as Atlantis, every civilisation has believed in the power of quartz and used it for healing, meditating, protecting, and channelling energy.'

Despite his old-fashioned way of talking, he's starting to sound quite a lot like Skye. I must be looking sceptical because he says, 'This isn't just mythology, Millie. The ability of quartz to focus, amplify, store and transform energy is the reason it's also used in radio transmitters, electronic circuitry, and memory chips in computers. And it's why you're here. You know this.'

'Do I?'

'What did you feel when you touched the clock?'

'The glass had gone,' I tell him. 'You know, that usually covers the face. What I was touching was metal, not quartz – the place in the centre where the two hands are joined – but yes, I did feel something. Warmth and life, like I'd pressed my fingertip against somebody else's.'

'Yes! A channel.'

'But I still don't understand. You just said that loads of clocks are quartz now – I mean, in my time – so if it's, like, an *energy portal* or something, then you'd just be able to touch any clock in the way

I did and you'd find you'd woken up in a different century. And if that was true, time travel would be a thing – even if you weren't doing it yourself, you'd be bumping into people from the future all the time – and it's not.'

'You're right. I've often wondered, over the years, about what makes these two clocks special. In fact, I wasn't even sure that the second clock *was* special until you came along. But the piece of quartz I used was purchased by my great-grandfather, Amos Smith, when he was a young man. It came from the Ouachita Mountains in America. Quartz had been mined there for years by the Native Americans, who used it for arrowheads and in rituals. Whether the piece of crystal Amos bought was mined by them I don't know, because by the 1850s, when he obtained it, white prospectors had got in on the act, but there's no doubt that it's unusual.

'Amos had leased this building a few years earlier, to start what would become the family business. He lived to be ninety-five, and when I was a child we used to sit together, and he'd tell me stories. He told me how a man had come into the shop, offering to sell him the piece of quartz. He said the fellow told him it would bring him good fortune, and he almost laughed because this chap looked as if he'd never had a day's luck in his life – thin as a skeleton and dressed in clothes that were hardly more than rags. But he felt sorry for the man, and even pretended he had no change in order to give him a little more money than he'd asked.

'Amos and his wife, Clara, kept the crystal in the flat upstairs, as an ornament. And Amos *did* have good luck – not fame or untold riches, but in the things that truly matter: a long and happy marriage, healthy children and grandchildren, and a thriving business. Eventually, he handed over the reins to his eldest son Charles – my grandfather – who, in due course, passed it on to my father, Archie, who then passed it on to me.

'Amos told me something else about the crystal. I don't know if he'd ever told Charles or Archie, but somehow I don't think he did, because I'm sure one of them would have mentioned it. What do you know about the Carrington Event?'

'Nothing. I've never heard of it.'

'It took place in September 1859 – the most intense geomagnetic storm in recorded history. It's thought that a release of matter and magnetic field from the outer layer of the sun's atmosphere collided with the earth's magnetosphere to cause a solar flare so bright that people thought morning had come in the middle of the night. There were reports of auroras – streamers of light in the sky, in every colour you can imagine – from every corner of the world. People said it was the most beautiful thing they'd ever seen. If an event like this occurred in the twenty-first century it would cause a devastating universal power cut, but back in 1859, there was very little to disrupt.

'Amos told me that he and Clara were so entranced by the beauty of the storm that they could barely take their eyes off it – but when Amos turned away for a moment he saw that the crystal was glowing, too, radiating different-coloured lights as if it were sending an answering signal up to the sky. As he got closer, he saw that it was vibrating with energy and humming as though it were alive.

'By morning, it was back to normal, but something had

definitely happened. Amos couldn't explain it. He scoured newspapers and scientific journals for accounts of similar occurrences, but found nothing. He said Clara was always afraid of the crystal after that, and begged Amos to lock it away in a cupboard in his workshop. He did as she asked, and that was the end of it.

'We've had several clear-outs over the years, and I'd always assumed that the crystal had been got rid of at some point. But a few years after the war I was tidying the workshop and I found it at the back of a drawer of odds and ends, wrapped in a length of black silk. When I unwrapped it, it seemed to me that I felt a faint tingling sensation on my skin. I didn't tell anyone about that, but it gave me the idea of trying to make a quartz clock, and after a few more years and a lot of experimenting, I'd completed two, each containing a small amount of the crystal. One of them is still in this building, and you must have – or have had – contact with the second one.'

'It's in my dad's new flat. You know the ones they built on the site of the prison?'

Mr Smith nods, satisfied. 'That makes sense. It was sold a week before Jean and Robbie died. Our clerk told me it had been bought by the prison governor. I assumed it must have been for her own office, because items for use in the prison itself would have been government purchases.'

I think of the smart woman I'd seen with the guard. Was she the governor? 'Well, it ended up outside the condemned cell.'

'How strange. Perhaps she decided she didn't like it after all. Anyway, I wanted to keep the other clock, so I took it up to the flat.'

He jerks his head towards the ceiling. 'The three of us used to live up there, and I stayed on after Jean and Robbie died. My brother-in-law had taken charge of the business for me, and he helped to fix the clock on the wall.'

'Did you put "Only Now" on that clock, too?'

'Yes.' Mr Smith looks slightly embarrassed. 'I'd wanted my happiness – the way I was feeling as I made the two clocks – to last for ever. It sounds foolish now, but I suppose I thought if only I could capture that, and keep it . . .'

I want to say it doesn't sound foolish at all, but it's all so sad that I can't get the words out, so instead I lean over and squeeze his hand to show I understand.

'Thank you, my dear.' He stares down at my hand for a long moment, then clears his throat. 'Five years later, my sister and brother-in-law were helping me move some furniture when the glass on the face got broken. I was setting it right and – just like you – I felt the warmth and life from the place where the two hands met. That night, I'd had rather too much to drink and fell asleep, fully clothed, in the armchair by the fire – something which used to happen fairly often in those days, I'm afraid. I was woken at midnight by the ticking of the clock, but it was no longer on the wall. I couldn't understand it: I was alone, and even though I'd had a skinful, I was pretty sure that robbers couldn't have got in and out of the place without waking me. Just in case, I picked up a frying pan, reckoning I could use it as a weapon, and I went downstairs – and there was the clock in my workshop, with the glass intact. I was wondering how my brother-in-law could have succeeded in repairing it without my noticing, when Jean appeared in the doorway. She said she'd been calling me to come up for lunch.'

'But . . . wouldn't there have been two of you? The 1955 one and the one from the future?'

'Don't think I haven't wondered about that, too. I can only conclude that because there *is* only one of me at any given time, I can't exist in one place twice, and somehow, the older me merges with the younger one. Certainly, I appeared the same to Jean. She laughed and asked me what on earth I was doing with the frying pan, then told me I must have gone soft in the head when I took her in my arms and kissed her.

'That was the first time it happened – and the following morning I woke up back in 1960. The next night was a repeat of the previous one, only I was back in 1955 for a longer time. I ate lunch with Jean and Robbie, and even walked him back to school afterwards, which he thought was very odd because it was only round the corner and he usually went with his pals. It happened the next night, too, and by then I was determined to find a way to undo what I knew was going to happen on the twelfth. The school finished early that day – there'd been a problem with the roof, and workmen had to come and make it safe. That was how come Jean and Robbie were walking down the road when the driver lost control of the bus. They were on their way to the cinema.'

'The Odeon?'

Mr Smith shakes his head. 'That was bombed in the war, and it didn't reopen until 1958. They'd gone down to the Rex in Islington to see *20,000 Leagues Under the Sea*. Jean had stopped to buy yarn from Pell's, the wool shop, just down the road here. She was friendly with Mrs Pell, who told me afterwards that she felt terrible, because if Jean hadn't stayed chatting with her for that crucial five minutes, she and Robbie would have been safely on their way to the cinema when the accident happened.

'I knew that, even if I carried on leaving 1960 every night, I shouldn't assume that I'd arrive in 1955 at the same time or stay for the same length of time – which meant I couldn't be sure of being there in time to stop Jean and Robbie being hit by the bus. So, I looked in Jean's workbasket, worked out what type of yarn she was about to run out of, and went round to Pell's to replace it.'

I can't keep quiet any more. 'Did it work?'

Chapter 38

When Mr Smith sighs, it sounds like all the sadness in the world in a single breath. 'When I retired to bed on the night of the twelfth in 1960, I was quite sure that I'd solved the problem. When I arrived in 1955 the following day, the clerk told me that Jean and Robbie had left about twenty minutes earlier for the cinema. I was confident that Jean would have no need to go into the wool shop, but I wanted to be absolutely sure, so I walked to Holloway Road.

'I'd only gone a few hundred yards past the corner when I heard the screech of brakes and then a colossal bang. The bus was slewed across the pavement and its front end had gone through the window of the dress shop next door to Pell's. I hadn't seen the accident before, and it was dreadful, but I still felt sure that Jean and Robbie would be safely on their way to the cinema. Policemen had stopped the traffic and were directing people to walk past on the road, so I followed, thinking I might wipe the impression from my mind by joining the two of them to watch the film.

'Then I saw, on the other side of the bus ...' Mr Smith stops, swallowing hard. When he speaks again, his voice is a whisper. 'There was a policeman, bending down over a body pinned underneath one of the wheels. I could see blood trickling out in streams around his feet, like lacework, and then ... then I saw ...

'Jean had a favourite hat, a red beret with a velvet bow, and it was lying by the side of the bus. When the policeman took a step back, I could see a small foot with a grey school sock fallen down round the ankle.' Mr Smith buries his face in his hands.

'I'm sorry.' I slither off my stool and give him a hug. 'I'm so, so sorry.'

After a while, I ask, 'So ... Jean went to the wool shop anyway?'

When Mr Smith raises his head, his face is as bleak and exhausted as if he were experiencing the grief for the first time. 'Yes. What I hadn't reckoned on was that the pattern she was using required an entirely different yarn for stitching the pieces together. The shock of it was like losing them both all over again.' He shakes his head in defeat. 'I come back just for this week, every single year, but whatever I do, I can never save them. Believe me, I've tried everything, but there is *always* a reason why Jean and Robbie are outside Pell's when that bus mounts the pavement.

'I've tried making my peace with it, accepting that I am unable to save them and trying to make the last week of their lives as happy as possible, but it hasn't been easy.'

'Do you only ever come back for this week?'

'Yes. The rest of my life is quite normal – or it would be if I didn't lose my wife and son afresh every year. I've never been able to

210

make progress, emotionally speaking. When I tried to remove the clock from the shop, I found myself in agony the moment I crossed the threshold. The pain was so great that I fainted. The same thing happened when I tried to smash it to pieces with a hammer, as soon as I landed the first blow. Taking it apart piece by piece only meant the pain built up more slowly. When I asked my brother-in-law to do it, the same thing happened, so that I begged him to stop. It made him wonder if I might be going mad, so I took care never to mention it again.' Mr Smith gives me a sad smile. 'I am so very sorry to burden you with this, my dear, but you are the only person I've ever been able to tell.'

I feel sick. Is that what'll happen to me – having to repeat this week over and over again, never succeeding in changing anything? Before I can speak, the shop bell jangles again, which is so unexpected that I nearly fall off my stool. It's a woman in a smart suit, pointy-toe court shoes ... and a red beret with a velvet bow on the side.

Jean. And beside her must be seven-year-old Robbie, smart in a blazer and shorts. Perhaps they've been to church.

'You're not *still* working, are you?' Jean pulls off her gloves, finger by finger, then leans across the counter to kiss Mr Smith on the cheek.

Robbie, next to her, grabs the edge of the counter and bounces up and down. 'Who's that girl, Mummy?'

'Don't be silly, dear. And stop doing that.'

For a moment, I think Robbie's going to argue, but he just says, 'All right,' like he's going along with what she wants even though she's the one who's silly. He puts his head on one side and gives me a long look, then wanders away.

Jean rolls her eyes at Mr Smith. She has a lovely smile and a glow of happiness that makes her really attractive. 'Lunch will be ready in quarter of an hour.'

'Yes, dear.' The way Mr Smith looks at her is so lovely – like he's seeing her with his whole heart – that I want to cry. 'Just finishing up now.'

I blink furiously as her heels click-clack across the floor and away up the stairs. Robbie takes a last look at me, gives a dramatic sigh, and zooms after her, pretending to be an aeroplane.

Mr Smith pours the rest of the tea into my mug. 'What about you, my dear?'

When I start to explain about Annie, he nods in recognition, then puts his head on one side and looks at me beadily, just like Robbie did, and says, 'So you think Annie Driscoll's not guilty, do you? Not that I agree with capital punishment, even if she was,' he adds, 'although I have to admit I thought differently in those days. When one looks back, there are so many things one simply *accepted*, that seem barbaric now.'

I tell him about Annie and Joe, and what I've found out so far.

Mr Smith looks thoughtful. 'None of it's conclusive, of course, but I can see why you might have doubts. I'm sorry I got you into this, my dear – although I do wonder . . . ' He breaks off again, and frowns for a moment before shaking his head, as though he's just had a quick argument with himself.

'What?'

He shakes his head again, but this time it's slower and less certain.

'Please, Mr Smith. If you can tell me anything that would help, that'd be great.'

'Well, I was thinking that the clock connected me to the past because, despite the pain, I *wanted* it to, even though it turns out I can't change what happened. But for you, there was no connection, unless . . . You aren't related to the Driscoll family, are you?'

'I hadn't thought of that. I'm sure I'm not, though, unless it's so far back in the past that it doesn't really count. But Joe told me he touched the clock. In 1955, I mean. I think that might have connected us – although, why didn't he come to our time?'

'Good question,' says Mr Smith. 'Maybe it only works one way – although you and I on our own aren't enough to prove that, of course. The other reason might be the energy. Do you know if Joe is still alive in the present?'

'He died in 1991. But he could travel through time as a ghost, surely? I mean, I don't exist in 1955, but here I am.'

'Yes, but you're . . . how can I put this? You're a *possibility*. In the present, Joe is a spent force. That's what I mean about the energy – it's different. In Joe's case, enough to make a connection, but not enough to travel.'

'I suppose.'

'There are so very many things we don't understand, my dear.' Mr Smith turns his head to stare at the wall of cabinets on the other side of the room before he continues. 'I think you got to 1955 rather by accident, but you've kept coming back because you *care*. I can see how much you want to help Annie.' He turns to face me once more. 'And handsome young Joe, if I'm not mistaken.'

My face suddenly feels hot and I can't look at him, so I stare at the floor instead. 'As much as anything else, Millie, this is about love. Mine for Jean and Robbie, Joe's for his sister, yours because you love justice and care about your fellow human beings . . .' He's silent for so long that I look up – and he's giving me this really quizzical stare. 'There's something I've been wondering about, my dear.' He says this like he hasn't noticed that my face is basically *on fire*. 'You very sensibly asked why there aren't two of me here now, didn't you? Well, it appears that my real self – the frail, hundred-year-old-man – is able to merge with my former self, the man I was in 1955. When I realised I was unable to change what happened to Jean and Robbie, I began to ask myself why I couldn't. I came to the conclusion that it was because I was here when the accident originally happened, which meant that the *ingredients* of the tragedy, as it were, did not change when I came back. But you are an *additional* factor, and I think you may be able to make a difference. And perhaps – although I make no promises – I may be able to help you.'

'I hope so.' Now I *can* look at him, and there's no embarrassment there, just this invisible bond between us. 'Thanks, Mr Smith.' For a moment, there's silence, then the sound of Robbie's feet as he thunders down the stairs.

'Lunch, Daddy!'

Mr Smith stands up. 'On my way.'

Robbie shoots his toy racing car along the counter so that it falls off the end, then stares at me. 'Is *she* coming?'

'"She" is the cat's mother, young man,' Mr Smith tells him – one way of dealing with it, I guess. 'Go and tell *your* mother that I'll be right up.'

Robbie shrugs and picks up his car. 'OK.' He frowns at me for a moment, then shouts 'Goodbye!' and runs back upstairs.

The bell jangles as Mr Smith opens the shop door. 'Good luck, my dear. If there is anything I can do to help, just ask. And . . . be careful, won't you?'

Chapter 39

I run all the way to Aylmer Terrace. There aren't any children about – I reckon they're all inside having lunch, like the Smiths – but there's a van parked right opposite the front door, which is open. I can hear voices from inside – Charles and another man, not Joe – and when I go up to the porch I can see cardboard boxes piled up in the narrow hallway.

There's the sound of plates clattering from the back of the house, and I can smell gravy as well as cigarette smoke and boiled vegetables, so I reckon the family just finished eating.

A man – shorter than Charles, with oiled hair and a suit so shiny with wear that he seems greasy all over – comes out of the kitchen. He opens the door of the understairs cupboard, then picks up the boxes one by one and shoves them inside.

I skirt around him and plaster myself against the open kitchen door. It looks like they had roast beef and Yorkshire pudding followed by something with custard, but there are only three placemats on the table so I'm guessing that neither the man in the hall, nor the woman leaning against the drainer, came for lunch.

She's a bit older than Rose, with scarlet lipstick bleeding into the lines around her mouth, and mahogany hair so obviously dyed that she might as well have used paint.

Charles is still at the table, leaning back in his chair and talking loudly about football to the man moving the boxes. Rose is standing at the sink with an apron on, washing up. She's got her shoulders hunched and her elbows pressed close to her sides – really stiff, like she's angry or just doesn't want to be there. When the woman next to her leans in to say something, she shrinks away as if she doesn't want any contact, even by accident.

There's something *really* odd about the whole atmosphere. Given the circumstances, it wouldn't be surprising if it were strained or sad, but it's just weird. Charles is being sort of aggressively jovial, like he's making a point that's got nothing to do with how Arsenal are playing. The woman next to Rose seems relaxed enough, but Rose keeps giving her side-eye and muttering in reply. I can't follow what the two of them are saying. Every time I catch a few words the rest gets drowned out by one of the men, but at one point the woman says, 'Pots and kettles, dear,' so it must be something domestic.

The back door opens and Joe appears. He looks like he'd rather be anywhere else and is carrying two bottles of beer, which I'm guessing are from the crate by the shed. He nearly drops them when he sees me, and Charles, who's facing him, shouts, 'Watch out!'

'Sorry, Dad.'

'Dozy idiot! Give those here, or they'll end up on the floor.'

Charles picks up a bottle opener and calls out to the man in the hall. 'You'll stay for a drink, won't you?'

Joe's face is expressionless as he crosses the room to Rose. 'Thanks for lunch,' he says, so quietly I almost miss it.

Her body relaxes a little as she turns and gives him a resigned half-smile. 'You hardly ate anything, love. At least take an apple.'

'All right, Mum.' He puts his hand on her arm and there's something about the little gesture that's so supportive and tender that it brings a lump to my throat. Then he picks up an apple from a bowl on the dresser, holds it up so Rose can see, and heads for the stairs without looking at me.

I follow him to his room at the top of the house. It's big but basic, with a few flimsy-looking bits of furniture arranged around the walls and a large threadbare rug covering the floorboards in the middle.

The room is incredibly tidy, mainly because there isn't much in it. No posters on the walls, only a calendar – but even that doesn't have a picture, just rows of blocky red numbers.

There's an old wooden school desk under the window, next to shelves with model aeroplanes on them. They're old biplanes, so delicate – thin wood with sewing thread to represent the struts between the parallel wings – that they seem more like insects than war machines. 'Those are beautiful. Did you make them?'

'Yeah.' Joe shuts the door. 'I thought you weren't coming. Want an apple?'

'Thanks.' It's lovely, and I'm quite pleased to find I can eat *and* drink in 1955.

'Keep it. Lost my appetite.' He says it like it's no big deal, but the despair in his eyes gives him away and I just want to hug him.

Instead, I press the apple back into his hand. 'I know, but you've got to eat *something*. Go on.'

'OK.' Joe takes a few bites and I notice his teeth properly for the first time – white and cutely irregular, with wolfy little canines.

'I thought you'd be at the prison.'

'They said we couldn't visit today. Mum only told me this morning.'

'I'm sorry you didn't get to see Annie.'

'Well . . .' Joe sighs. 'At least you're here now.'

'And I found out some stuff.' I glance around to see if there's a sample of his handwriting anywhere. There's a row of books at the back of his desk, spines facing out from the wall. I pick the one that looks oldest: *The Schoolboys' Annual, 1950*, with an illustration of a rosy-cheeked boy in cricket whites on the front, and inside:

Joe Driscoll

37 Aylmer Terrace

London N

England

Great Britain

Planet Earth

The Galaxy

The Universe

I let out the breath I've only just realised I'm holding. It's not the same as the writing on the burnt paper – and although it's a bit like the list of amounts of money, I know it's not the same, because Joe crosses his sevens. I put the book back beside the others.

'I don't know why you're grinning.' Joe sits down on the bed. 'I tried to see Victor this morning, but he wouldn't even let me into the flat, let alone talk to me. He's still so angry, Millie. And they're all downstairs, acting like nothing's happening! It's just ... ' He hunches over, head in hands.

'What was that about, anyway? Those boxes?'

'Stuff from the Naafi.'

'That was the Hewitts?'

'Yeah – and what he's nicked. Mum hates it being in the house.'

'She hates Mrs Hewitt being in the house, too. The body language was *really* telling.'

Joe tilts his head and squints at me. 'The *what*?'

'Body language. How people communicate without talking. Your mum doesn't like Mrs Hewitt *at all*.'

He looks up, shrugging. 'Like I said, they had an argument.'

'I remember.' The day of the tea party, something about debt, although that was three months ago, so it must have been serious ... No point thinking about it now, though. 'I've got some information.' I sit down next to Joe on the bed. The mattress is saggy, and I lurch against him. 'Sorry.' I move away, feeling awkward and hoping he hasn't noticed, and perch at the pillow end. There's something sticking out from under the sheet – pale blue, knitted, stuffed. When I pull it out I can see it's a plump toy rabbit

220

with button eyes, a cute nose, a powder-puff tail and a white ribbon tied in a bow around its fat little neck.

'Annie made it for me when we were kids. I think Mum must have helped her quite a bit.'

They found it next to his body.

Joe must mistake the expression on my face for shock, because he says, 'I wouldn't have it on my bed, but ...' He looks away, embarrassed.

'I understand.' I can barely get the words past the lump in my throat. I turn away from him to put the rabbit on the pillow, taking time over smoothing the bed linen so I don't have to look at him.

'I have to hide it, though. If Dad saw, he'd make me throw it away.'

'Well, I think it's lovely that you have it on your bed.'

Joe shrugs. 'Doesn't do anything to help her, though. What did you find out?'

I start telling him everything – or most of it, because I don't think I'm ready to talk about Mr Smith yet, and I leave out the stuff about the book being burnt – and Joe stares at me with eyes like saucers. 'How did you manage to find out all that in such a short time?'

There's still no way I'm even *trying* to explain about going online, so I just say, 'It's easier to do that kind of stuff in my time. You use a computer – lots of people have them at home.'

Joe looks disbelieving, and I remember, too late, a photo I'd seen of the really basic computers from the Second World War, that took up entire rooms. 'Look, all that's changed a lot since ...

since now, and it would take way too long to explain so you'll just have to take my word for it.'

He shrugs. 'Fair enough.' This sounds a bit too much like Kieran's 'Let's say I believe you' for my liking, but I guess there'd be a bunch of stuff I wouldn't believe if a person from the 2080s told me, so . . .

'I never heard anyone next door mention someone called Muriel,' he says, thoughtfully. 'But that doesn't mean you're wrong, of course.'

'The thing is,' I have to get this out before I lose my nerve, 'I don't think Dorothy had TB, and I don't think she was ever in a sanatorium.'

'What?'

'It might not be relevant to what we're trying to find out, but I think I know why Shirley next door was talking about hushing things up. You're not going to like this, Joe, so please don't get up in my face—'

Joe's whole body is rigid with tension. '*What?*'

'Dorothy went away to have a baby.'

Chapter 40

It's as if I've dropped a bomb in the room – air quivering in the dead silence between us.

'No.' Joe says it flatly, like *End of*. He doesn't even look at me.

'Look.' I try to sound as calm and unemotional as possible. 'You said Dorothy told you she'd never been in love with anybody before Victor, but that doesn't mean she didn't *fancy* someone.'

'She didn't.'

'You mean she didn't tell you about it.'

'No, she *didn't*. Dad wouldn't have let her.'

'You can't stop people liking each other.'

'You know what I mean.'

'Lots of people's parents are strict, but it doesn't stop them enjoying themselves. They just find a way round it.'

'It's not possible.'

'It *is* possible, and you know that.'

More silence, and then, very slowly, Joe turns to me, his face drained of colour. 'But . . . how?'

I almost laugh. 'Seriously? Please tell me you know how babies are made.'

Joe's face is crimson. 'I don't think it's a stork and a gooseberry bush, if that's what you mean.'

'I literally have *no* idea what you're talking about.'

'What I mean is yes, I do know.'

'Right. So you know girls and women don't get pregnant *by themselves*.'

'Yes.' Joe's huffy now. 'I know that. But I don't see ... I mean, it was Mum who was ... ' He indicates a pregnant stomach with his hands.

'Ever heard of cushions? A pillow? Helene said it used to happen—'

'Wait. Helene?'

'Yes. I found Helene Bone.'

Joe's eyes widen. 'She's still alive? You're a much better detective than me. When I went round to Landor Street, the woman said the family'd moved and she didn't know the new address.'

'She lives in Highgate now. We had a long talk, and one of the things she told me was that, back in the ... well, *now*, a mother would pretend to be pregnant so that no one would know that it was her unmarried – and in this case, underage – daughter.'

Joe shakes his head. 'Except ... if she'd done that – the cushion thing – then Dad would have known, wouldn't he?'

'I'd guess so.'

'Was she quite sure? I mean, Helene might have been like ... *that*, but Dorothy wasn't.'

'Like what?'

'You know.'

'No, I don't. And I'm going to pretend you didn't just say that, because I really need to concentrate on telling you about this. So, I got lucky with Helene's address, and she was at home.' I tell him about our chat, although not the bit about Rose, or Helene's last words, because I *really* don't want to have either of those conversations with him.

When I finish, Joe puts his head in his hands again, and stays quiet for such a long time that I think he must be in shock. When he looks up, his face is even paler than before – which I shouldn't have thought possible, but it is. 'What else did you find out?'

I tell him about Dorothy and Kathleen's graves, and how I'm sure somebody added the words 'United in Eternity' later on. 'Someone had left flowers, too.'

'That's good. Whoever it was, I mean. I know you said Helene said Victor went to Australia, and that Dorothy was terrified about him finding out about Kathleen, but perhaps she did tell him, and he came back to get the words added – or asked somebody else to do it.'

'I don't think she told him.' As I say this, something occurs to me. 'But I reckon he found out.'

'*How?*'

'The post-mortem. He had a row with your mum, didn't he?'

'Yes, but—'

'No, listen! You said Rose said something about "they made a mistake" and Victor said they couldn't have and then something

225

about what they found, and you thought it was your mum he was angry with – like, specifically – rather than the whole situation. That's right, isn't it?'

Joe nods.

'So . . . I don't think that "they" meant the police – something they found – but the forensic pathologist.'

'Who's that?'

'The person who does the post-mortem. Because you can tell when a woman's had a baby.'

'Well, she was going to, wasn't she?' Joe sounds irritated.

'No, when a woman's actually given birth. It changes your body. Whoever did the post-mortem would have seen that, and it would have been in their report. And if the argument between Victor and your mum was about that, it makes sense of Charles not wanting you to ask her about it afterwards, too. Also, I discovered that tuberculosis leaves scars on your lungs, which I bet you'd see during a post-mortem – provided they were actually there. My guess is that because Annie'd had it as a kid – all that school she missed—'

'You knew about that before. How?'

'I read it in an old newspaper.' Well, it's sort of true. 'Anyway, I reckon that Annie having it gave your parents the idea of saying that Dorothy'd got it as well.'

'So why didn't anybody say anything in court – not about that, but the . . . other thing?'

'OK, so I'm not really sure about this, but I'm guessing because it wasn't important to the case. If they thought Annie did it, and she didn't even know that Kathleen was her niece and not her sister . . . She couldn't have known, could she?'

'Absolutely not.'

'Well then, why would it matter to the prosecution or the defence? It would have been different if they thought Victor'd done it. Then they could have said that he was angry with Dorothy for not telling him she'd already had a baby. But it wouldn't be a reason for Annie to kill her, would it?'

'You mean,' Joe's face hardens, 'it wasn't in their interest to say that Dorothy was a slut.'

I jump off the bed and stand in the middle of the room, staring at him in disbelief. 'She was *fifteen*. Which, unless the law is massively different in 1955, means she was under the age of consent, which means – as far as police and lawyers and people like that are concerned – that she was *raped*. OK, so they might not have known *when* she had the baby, but even if they didn't, why would you automatically assume she was a slut? What about the guy who got her pregnant? Is *he* a slut? Where's the law that says boys and men aren't responsible for their actions? And anyway, who forces a fifteen-year-old girl to give birth and then makes her pretend it never happened? What is *wrong* with all of you?' I'm really shouting now.

'OK, OK.' Joe looks up at me, totally stunned, like I'd just slapped him. 'Calm down. I'm not saying it was *all* her fault.'

'You just called her a slut, Joe. On the basis of no evidence whatsoever. You're basically blaming the victim – next thing you'll be telling me is she deserved to get murdered.'

'Of course she didn't! Please stop looking at me like that, Millie.

I'm sorry.' Joe's staring at me with this total WTF look on his face – and actually, I sort of get it. I've just rocked his world. I can hear Helene's voice in my mind: *It's just what society was like – people didn't know any better.* And what Mr Smith said to me, in the shop: *When one looks back, there are so many things one simply accepted, that seem barbaric now.* Also, it's not like there isn't plenty of victim-blaming still going on in the twenty-first century, even though I'm being like, oh, we're *so* much better.

I guess the thing is that we're all influenced by the ideas around us – why wouldn't we be? It's really hard to break away from groupthink. I suddenly wonder what people will think of *our* ideas in seventy or so years' time – like, all the stuff we're wrong about – and it makes me feel off-balance, like I'd gone down a step I hadn't known was there.

'I understand what you're saying, really I do,' Joe says. 'It's just so . . . It's not . . . '

'OK. Whatever. I shouldn't have yelled at you. Let's park it for now, yeah?' Joe looks confused, but relieved. 'There's something else we need to do. You know that list I told you about? I know it wasn't you, but it could be Rose or Charles. If you can show me some of *their* writing, I reckon I'll be able to remember well enough to tell if it was one of them.'

Joe looks round. 'Don't think there's anything up here.' He stands up. 'Let's try their room.'

When he opens the door we can hear laughter from down-stairs – Charles and Mr Hewitt – plus a female voice, which sounds too braying and nasal to be Rose. I follow Joe down to Rose and Charles's room, which is directly below his. The furniture is bigger and much more solid-looking – oak, I think – and the bed has a shiny eiderdown, the colour of tinned salmon.

The dressing table I saw through the half-open door last time has a sheet of glass over the top, with a crocheted mat, a hand mirror and a hairbrush, powder in a fancy glass container . . . and a scrap of light brown paper with writing on it.

Gay Donald 33/1
Halloween 7/2
Four Ten 3/1 F

'What does *that* mean?'

'Horses. Looks like a betting slip.' When Joe picks the paper up and turns it over, I spot WILLIAM HILL in big letters across the top. 'That's Charles's writing.'

I take it from him and have another look. 'Pretty sure *he* didn't write our list. Anything with Rose's writing?' I spot a piece of paper on one of the bedside cabinets, next to a jewellery box in the shape of a miniature chest of drawers. Guessing that's her side of the bed, then. 'What's that?'

Joe walks round the bed to look. 'Shopping list. Here you are.'

Lard
Veg
Jam
Bacon
Cotton wool

Instant relief: Rose obviously didn't write what was on the burnt paper.

But I'm 99 per cent sure she wrote the list of money.

Chapter 41

So if what's on that paper *is* a suicide note, it's not from Joe. Or Charles, although of course I don't know what happened to him, other than that he must be dead by now – *actual* now, that is – or he'd be the oldest man in Britain.

Of course, it might not be a suicide note at all, but just somebody apologising for something . . . Anyway, it means I can tell Joe.

'Millie?'

'Oh, sorry. Yes, it's the same as the list of money. It couldn't be that never-never thing, could it? What you said your mum and Mrs Hewitt were arguing about on the day of the party?'

Joe shakes his head. 'You pay the same amount each time – and anyway, Dad doesn't like buying things on hire purchase because you end up paying over the odds.'

Not a mortgage, either, because I'm pretty sure that's the same time each month . . . 'Could it be your savings?'

'How much is it?'

When I tell him, he whistles. 'In my dreams. Doesn't sound like it's household stuff, either.'

'Still a mystery, then. But there's something else, too.' I tell him about the burnt paper.

'Ask you to forgive me,' Joe quotes. 'Was it in proper handwriting?'

'Yes.'

'Not Annie, then. Her writing was all capital letters. Do you think it might be Kathleen?'

I shake my head. 'No way was that written by a six-year-old.'

'So—' Joe opens his mouth, then closes it again.

'So?'

'What about Dorothy?'

Something in his face makes me wonder if he'd meant to say something else, but decided not to – but I'm not 100 per cent sure, so I don't call him on it. 'Could be. Or it might have been given to her. We ought to rule her out, though. When your dad made you get rid of all the stuff, you didn't manage to keep anything with her writing on it, did you?'

'There may be a card or something somewhere, but . . . ' Joe tails off, looking doubtful.

'What about in there?' I point to Rose's bedside cabinet.

'I doubt it, but . . . ' Joe makes a 'go ahead' gesture, and I crouch down to have a look. There are two shelves in the little cupboard, crammed with odd bits of make-up, sewing things, and a lot of bottles of tablets. At the very back, there are twenty or so envelopes containing letters.

'All the same handwriting, and all addressed here . . . ' I pull one out. 'Somebody called Minnie?'

'Mum's friend from school. She lives in Scotland. That's no good, then.'

I think about what I'd do if I wanted to hide a piece of paper. 'Wait a minute.'

I sit down on the rug beside the bed. While I'm checking the envelopes, Joe goes to listen at the door – more gales of laughter from downstairs and a shriek of 'Des, you're terrible!' which has to be Mrs Hewitt – and comes back a minute later saying, 'Found anything?'

'Not yet, but there are a few more to go ... Wait, what's this?'

I pull out a black-and-white photograph of a man in army uniform. Not only am I sure it's Frank Palmer, but it's the same photo as was sellotaped into the back of *The Robe*. 'That's your dad, isn't it?'

Joe freezes, and when I hold the picture up for him to see better, he actually backs away from it. 'I didn't know Mum had kept any pictures.'

'I found this in the book, in my time. Maybe your mum missed him, even if he was ... you know ...' *Maybe later on you wanted the connection too*, I think, *given how much you'd lost*.

Joe gives me a really loaded look. I have no idea what it means, so I say, 'These things can be complicated.' Which, judging by how I currently feel about Dad, has to be the world's biggest understatement.

Joe just jams his hands in his pockets and stares at the floor, so I go back to looking through the envelopes, and after a minute or two ...

'Yes!' This comes out really loud and makes Joe jump, and then we both freeze, listening for footsteps up the stairs, before we remember that no one except him can hear me.

'What?' Joe sits on the bed and looks over my shoulder at the letter.

'It's from Dorothy. She seems to be on holiday with a school friend. Butlin's in Clacton, by the sound of it. I read a passage out:

> We go swimming every day and there is a fairground and crazy golf. Yesterday we saw 'Jassy' with Patricia Roc and Margaret Lockwood, and—

'What about the handwriting? Does it match?'

'No. The other writing was more slanted, and these g's are different. Sorry, I just want to finish reading this ... Right, OK, so there's a bunch of stuff about what they've been up to and how much fun it is and then, at the end ...'

> I am sorry you were so upset, Mum, but don't worry. You could not have known, and I will never tell a soul.

'What does *that* mean?'

'The baby, of course. She's saying that Mum couldn't have known that she – Dorothy, I mean – was ... you know ... and that they can keep it secret—'

'But wouldn't Rose be reassuring Dorothy instead of the other way round? Also, when's Kathleen's birthday?'

'September ninth.'

'In 1948, right?' I push the letter under his nose and point to the date at the top: August 15th 1947

Joe obviously knows enough about the facts of life to understand, and I can practically hear his thoughts screeching to a stop.

'There's another secret,' I tell him.

Chapter 42

'Very dramatic.' I stare down at the letter. '"I will never tell a soul."
OK, so she was fourteen – but the way it reads makes it sound like
it was something Rose found out that made her really upset. Yet
her words make it sound like she is forgiving *Rose*, not the other
way around.'

Joe looks bewildered. 'If Dorothy had upset Mum, she'd apol-
ogise properly.'

'OK, so it's not something Dorothy did, but something to do
with Rose herself. Can you remember anything . . . I don't know,
unusual happening around that time?'

Joe screws up his face, thinking, then shrugs and shakes his
head. 'Not really. It was our first summer in this house and I was
too busy mucking about with my new friends all day to notice. I
was only nine,' he adds, defensively.

'No, OK . . . Do you think this might be something to do with
that list of money?'

'I thought you said that started in 1946.'

'Yes, in June. So I'm wondering if it might be something that

Rose *already* knew, and Dorothy found out later on.' Am I imagining this, or does Joe look uncomfortable?

'Do you mean . . . *blackmail*?'

'Well, maybe? It wasn't you, was it?'

'I was *eight* in 1946, Millie.' After a moment, he adds, 'But I wonder if it *was* me – me in the future, I mean – who sellotaped the things in the book. I must have discovered why it was significant, so I kept it . . . Maybe Mum told me. And that list with the money . . . What was the date of the last amount?'

'June 1960.'

Rose's death. Please let's not go there.

'Was that the bottom of the page? I mean, might there have been another page with more amounts?'

This is the point where I should start lying, but I just can't. Too much might depend on it. 'There was more room on the paper.'

'So, if you're right about blackmail, that means whoever it was either stopped asking for money – or if it was Mum receiving it, that stopped too – at that point. But she would never blackmail anybody.' I'm deliberately not looking at him, but something must give me away because it's suddenly like there's a change in air pressure and the silence has an edge and when I *do* look at him, he's staring at me so intensely that it's hard to breathe. Joe narrows his eyes. 'Tell me.'

I swallow, trying to work saliva into my mouth. 'I'm really sorry, but your mum . . . Well, sometime in 1960 – I'm not sure of the exact date, but . . . she died.'

Joe stares straight ahead. 'I'll bet it was the anniversary of Dorothy and Kathleen's deaths,' he says. 'Or Annie's.'

'She was ill, Joe. It wasn't . . . suicide.'

His brown eyes are muddy pools of misery and the words sound like they're breaking his voice. 'It didn't have to be. Poor Mum. What happened to the girls was enough to kill anyone.' He turns to look at me. 'At least we have a chance to save Annie. But the worst thing is, when you just said that, I wasn't even surprised. It's almost as if I knew what you were going to say.'

'We're going to stop it,' I say, firmly.

'But *how?*'

My heart breaks for him as he hunches over, lost and forlorn. I scramble up on the bed and hold him in my arms and we stay there, in silence, for a long, long time.

Chapter 43

I'm in bed. My bed. But . . .

There's something. A memory. No, not a memory. More an impression.

Joe's fingers touching my cheek. His lips on mine. Warmth, softness.

My skin is tingling. And . . .

Urrgh. The jeans, sweatshirt and Converse, which I'm still wearing, have made me all sweaty and clammy. I sit up quickly and throw off the duvet. The stuff I tried on and discarded yesterday evening is all over the floor, and the things I found in the book are on the end of the bed.

Joe kissed me.

Did he? The other times, I've remembered exactly what happened, but *this* . . .

So, I was comforting him, because of Rose. I had my arms round him, and we sat on Charles's and Rose's bed for the longest time without saying anything. I definitely remember that.

Was there some sort of lead-up? Did one of us say something or was there an awkward moment, or . . .

Why can't I remember? And what about next time I see him? Joe, I have a memory that we kissed but I don't know if it was an actual thing because I think I started time travelling half-way through?

It would probably be OK to say that in the circumstances. I mean, it's not like we got drunk at a party or whatever – but still . . .

OK. Can't sit here staring into space for ever. I'm just about to head to the bathroom for a shower when Mum rings.

'I'm really sorry about when you phoned, Millie. I was . . . well, let's just say it wasn't a good day.'

'Mmm.' I'm still thinking about Joe and the kiss.

'Millie?'

'Sorry. Yeah, Cathy said. Honestly, it's OK.'

'Is it? I just wanted to make sure you're all right. Dad said you were upset.'

This gets me straight back to the present. 'Dad said *I* was upset? Judging from what he said, he was pretty pissed off with you for spoiling his fun.'

'Why? I'm not spoiling anything.'

'No, but I am. Third wheel, you know?' I hadn't meant to mention anything relating to the fact that Skye's here – although Mum must have guessed, even if Dad didn't actually tell her – and I regret saying it the moment it's out of my mouth.

Mum sighs. 'I'm sure he doesn't think that. He's doing his best, you know.'

'You're joking, right? If this is his best, I'd hate to think what his worst—'

'No, really. He's not all bad, you know. He's got your interests at heart, and it's not as if our marriage was . . . I don't know, perfect or anything.'

'So you're saying that what he did was OK?'

'Of course not, just that it's more complicated than you think.'

'Cathy said *that*, too.'

'Well, she's right.'

'So, what? You've forgiven him and I'm the only one who's angry? And if you tell me I'll understand better when I'm older, I'm ending this call.'

'I wasn't going to.'

'You *were*. I can tell by the way you said it.'

'Sorry, Millie.' There's a pause before she says, 'I really am. About all of this.'

'It's not your fault.'

'Some of it is. I'm still figuring it out.'

'Well, let me know when you've got an answer, won't you? Then I can adjust my feelings accordingly.'

I'm about to end the call when she says, 'We both love you, you know,' and then asks me about school, which takes me by surprise, although I'm not sure why. We chat about how I'm doing with my A level subjects for a bit – and actually I'm quite glad, because being this angry and confused all the time gets pretty exhausting, and it's sort of soothing to have a regular, boring type of conversation for once.

*

As I'm cleaning my teeth I think about what Helene Bone said about a bad relationship, and that Mum must have been lonely with Dad for a while before everything imploded. Even though they were talking to – well, shouting at – each other, it wasn't actual communication, and she must have lain in bed and stared into the darkness and felt totally alone, too.

When I go into the kitchen after my shower, Dad and Skye are in matching kimonos – *double ick*. I *knew* the one I'd seen him wearing had to be a gift from her. Urgh, PDA over the scrambled eggs. *Shoot me now.*

Of course, Skye's scrambled eggs can't be just ordinary ones, they have to contain miso and sesame seeds, but actually they do look really nice. Despite what Mum just said, I don't feel ready to engage with either of them at the moment, so I'm about to take some breakfast back to my room when Dad says, 'Hang on,' and bends down to pick something off the floor.

It's *The Robe*: still burnt at the edge, but now soaking wet as well. 'You know, it's much easier to read in the bath.' It's so not what I expected that I just stare at him. 'It's yours, isn't it?'

'Where did you find it?'

'In the shower. I'm afraid I didn't see it till after I'd turned on the water.'

I'd forgotten about leaving the book at the far end of the prison corridor – the shower makes sense, because the bathroom must be on the same spot. Guess that means that Florey or Ray or whoever didn't have a reason to go down there yesterday, otherwise they'd have found it.

'Millie?' Dad's waving the book at me now. 'I said, it doesn't look like your kind of thing.'

'It isn't. Someone lent it to me.'

'Looks like you set fire to it.' He turns the book around, inspecting it. 'Or buried it and then set fire to it.'

'It was like that when I got it.'

'Pot, kettle.' Skye plucks the book out of Dad's hand. 'You're always breaking spines and turning down pages.'

'At least I don't leave books in the shower. That's what bookshelves are for, in case you hadn't—'

'What did you say?'

'Bookshelves. The clue's in the name.'

'No, what Skye said. The pot thing.'

Skye looks blank for a moment, then says, 'The pot calling the kettle black. It means you're accusing somebody of having a fault when you have it yourself. My nana used to say it.'

'Because people used to cook on open fires,' Dad adds. 'The saucepans and things would get covered in soot, so they'd all be as dirty as each other.'

So Mrs Hewitt hadn't been talking about domestic stuff, but something quite different. What, though?

Skye's voice breaks into my thoughts. 'I can dry this for you, if you like. The pages might not straighten out completely, but I'll do my best.'

'Thanks.'

That was nice of her – and at least neither of them asked for an explanation for why I'd apparently taken a book into the shower.

I'm eating the scrambled eggs – which are delicious, even cold – sitting on my bed, when it strikes me that Joe didn't say anything at all about who the father of Dorothy's baby might be. OK, he was in shock, but he didn't really even mention it, just acted like, of course she didn't have any boyfriends. But she was gorgeous-looking, and he'd confirmed she was popular – which must have started before she became a model, surely?

I get that he didn't want to think about it, and also that Dorothy not telling him was hurtful, kind of a betrayal, but all the same . . .

And I can't stop thinking about that kiss. I know it's not a good idea to start obsessing about it – I mean, it might not even have happened, although the feeling was *so* real.

Concentrate on what we've discovered, instead.

So much to think about – and Annie has only two days to live, and I've got no idea what to do next.

It seems like a lot of people at Number 37 were hiding things, whether it was secrets, or actual, physical stuff like Rose with Dorothy's letters, and Joe with the little tea set in the back garden. Maybe he hid other things there, too. Dad just said the book looked like it had been buried before it got burnt, didn't he? And Joe must have lived in – or at least visited – the house at Aylmer Terrace for at least five years after 1955.

I need to investigate that garden – and this is the perfect time, because Shirley said the builders won't be back for a few days. There wasn't a skip outside the house, so maybe they'd just filled one and were waiting for a replacement when things got held up.

Anything they've already found and chucked away is gone for good, of course, but there might be more . . .

Maybe I could talk to Shirley again, too. When I said I'd wave at her next time I came by, she'd seemed pleased, so perhaps she'd like a chat. Not necessarily one about the murders next door, of course, but it's still worth a try.

Think I ought to have someone with me, though. For a lookout – and in case I fall out of the tree or get stuck in the garden.

I don't want to do this, but . . .

Apart from Mr Smith – and I can hardly ask a hundred-year-old man to come with me – Kieran is the only person who knows. I think it's OK because he did contact me, and it's not being a user because a) someone's life is at stake, and b) I'm pretty sure undead people don't do emotions and sex and whatever unless they're characters in books about vampires.

OK, take the plunge: an actual call. I pick up my phone. Also, Kieran's at least pretending to believe me, and I don't reckon Yaz or Liv would do that. Plus, it would take *way* too long to explain.

I'm so surprised when he answers immediately that for a moment I can't think what say. 'It's Millie. Look, I get what you said yesterday and I'm not going to do anything crazy, but I need some information, OK? And I'll need some help getting it, so . . .'

Kieran's sort of grunty and not that keen – guessing I woke him up – but he agrees to meet me at the corner of Aylmer Road and Ianthe Street in two hours' time. He wanted to wait till after dark because there's less chance of us being seen, but I pointed out that it would also make it impossible for me to find anything.

Also – although I didn't mention this – Shirley might go to bed early, and if she woke up and saw someone creeping around next door's garden with a torch, she'd call the police.

Actually, though, why would Kieran care about being seen? OK, so being seen might get us into trouble, but why would that matter if you're dead? I mean, what could they do to you? Maybe he's just worried for me – but I hope it's both of us, because surely that would mean that he's starting to feel less dead than before?

As I get dressed, I think about what I could ask Shirley without sounding weird and mad. I have to try very hard not to think about Joe, and it sort of works – except that by trying not to think about him I actually *am* thinking about him because I'm thinking about not thinking about him. Which means it sort of doesn't work, as well. But that kiss . . .

STOP IT. Places to go, people to see, discoveries to make – I hope.

Chapter 44

Kieran's still wearing the *Matrix* clothes, so he's not exactly inconspicuous, but it's better than no lookout at all. He still looks ill – although, when he takes his dark glasses off, there is actually a sort of sexy vampire vibe. Even if there's still a massive disconnect, it somehow feels like he's engaging with me more, despite what he said on the phone about how he's only here because he's given up on everything else, plus I asked for help. I wonder if helping me – and Joe and Annie – might help him. Maybe it won't – I mean, I'd be pretty conceited if I thought I could do anything the doctors at the psych unit can't – but it seems like the whole being dead thing might be pretty lonely, so I guess I can maybe help with that.

'You know you might not find anything, right?' he says now.

'But it's worth a try. I really appreciate that you're here, by the way.' We're standing by the tree in Ianthe Street. There's no sign of the builders, or the supplies Shirley mentioned. A skip has been delivered, but there's nothing in it yet.

Kieran doesn't look at me – he hasn't once, not properly – just glances up and down the empty road. 'Better go now, before someone comes.'

'Right.' I swing myself up – it's an easy climb, which is just as well because I don't want to make an idiot of myself in front of Kieran. Fortunately, when I get over the top of the hoarding, sit on the brick wall and swing my legs over, I discover that there's a wisteria plant growing just below my feet, so climbing down into the garden is easy.

I can't see anything unusual where they've started digging out the foundations at the back of the house. When I peer behind the paving stones stacked along the new-looking fence that separates Number 37 from Number 35 and look underneath the plastic sheets laid over what used to be the lawn, there's nothing there, either. After about ten minutes of crawling around getting muddy, I start to wonder if Kieran was right and it's a waste of time.

I walk down the line of wooden boards to the end of the garden where the Anderson shelter used to be. That must have been removed years ago, the sandbags taken away and the big hole it was dug into filled up with earth. Judging by what's here now – the plastic sheets don't come this far, so it's easier to see – this area has never been paved over or even made into a flowerbed. I reckon it was just grass, with some trees and bushes – there are some holes where they've dug them out, and a big pile of roots and branches.

Holes first. Three of them are just earth, but the fourth has something small sticking out of one side. I almost miss it, and have to kneel down before I can make out what it is: a teeny tiny doll hand. I suddenly remember – probably because of the muddy holes and the sandbags – this film they showed us at school about the First World War, with a photo of a trench. The voiceover said that sometimes the hands of dead soldiers stuck through the trench walls, and the men passing by would shake them for luck. I don't see how shaking a dead man's hand could bring luck – especially if the chance that you were about to die the same way he did was so massive – and I don't see how this little hand can bring *me* luck, either . . .

But perhaps it can tell me something.

I lean over and touch it, and it feels cold and hard. Not plastic – metal, I think, with the shapes of the tiny fingers sort of pressed into it. I'm guessing it was painted, but the colour's worn off. I hadn't looked closely enough at Kathleen's doll's house to see if there was a family inside, but maybe there had been.

I need something to use for digging. When I go over the pile of branches and twigs to pick out a stick that's sturdy enough, I spot a length of wood, about 30 centimetres, that's splintered to a point at the end, too smooth to have come off a tree . . . and there are flakes of red paint sticking to it.

Part of the dolls' house roof? The way the end is splintered makes me think that someone held this piece of wood over their knee and broke it.

I use the pointy end of the stick to clear the soil away from around the tiny metal hand. It's attached to a miniature schoolgirl, dressed like on the cover of Mum's old Enid Blyton Malory Towers books, with her hair in two plaits.

It seems like someone had been so furious that they'd smashed the house to smithereens and buried the remains in the garden. Something tugs at a corner of my mind, and, for a moment, there's an eerie stillness, like I'm the only person in the whole world left alive, and even the air has stopped moving. It's like what I felt when I was beside Annie's grave, only this isn't a confirmation, but something creepy and malevolent that makes me shiver, even though it's a warm day.

I really, desperately, want to get out of the garden, but this may be the only chance I get to look around properly in my time, so I force myself to stay. I scrape about some more in the nearby earth, but don't find anything else, so I go back to look at the pile of garden stuff. I spot a scrap of muddy plush fur with a googly eye that looks like the remains of a glove puppet, but I reckon that's a lot more recent than 1955. When I burrow into the pile a bit – quite difficult because stuff keeps snagging in my hair – I find a chunk of wood that must have been from the front of the dolls' house, because it's got rusty hinges on one side and the edge of a window frame on the other. It looks like somebody stamped on it.

Who, though?

I must have dislodged quite a few branches when I was pulling the things out, because something slides down from the top of the pile and lands by my feet. It's a tin square: filthy, but when I spit on it and rub some of the dirt away with my fingers, I can just make out the girl in the pinafore with the kitten.

The lid of Joe's biscuit box.

I can't see the bottom part, and I'm sure that the little tea set with Noddy and Big Ears must be broken by now, or even ground into powder – but there's something fixed onto the underside …

I turn it over and find an old-fashioned school exercise book, with a crest on the front, that seems to have been glued there. It's dirty, and damp at the corners so the pages are clumped together – but I'm positive it wasn't in there when Joe and I drank lemonade in the Anderson shelter, or I'd have seen it.

When I peel it off the lid and blow the remaining earth off the cover, I can just spot, in neat but faded handwriting:

Shirley Millichip
Form V
Miss Bateman

Once I've managed to peel the pages away from each other, I can see squared paper. The first few pages are full of algebra – looks like Shirley was pretty good at it – then nothing. Maybe she left it at Number 37, thought she'd lost it, and had to ask Miss Bateman for another one.

But then why would Joe – assuming he was the person who'd glued it to the lid of the biscuit tin – keep it? Unless he'd wanted to write in it himself, of course.

A bit of the back cover is still stuck to the tin, but all the pages at the end are intact. The first couple are blank, but then …

Sat 15th May 1954 – Went to see Doctor in the House. Dirk Bogarde is dreamy but not as much as J!

Same handwriting: not Joe's diary, then, but Shirley's. I whip out my phone and, as I start taking photos of all the pages with writing on, I catch sight of Dorothy's name, and Rose's, as well as a lot of Js, which *have* to be for Joe.

We were chatting in the street when Dorothy came along and spoilt it. She thinks she's so special and she can't bear it if the attention isn't on her, even if it's just someone talking to her own brother . . .

And, two days later,

I could tell J wanted to stay and talk to me, but Mrs Driscoll called him to come in . . .

Poor Shirley. I imagine Joe racing past Number 35 so as not to get caught.

Dorothy makes eyes at anyone in trousers and Mrs D's no better than she should be, either.

She's really got it in for Dorothy. I reckon it must be jealousy, but it's so *judgy* . . . And actually, what does that last bit even *mean*? Is it like, Rose *ought* to be bad? Plus, she sounds more like some eighty-year-old woman than a teenager.

Mum's seen her with her fancy man, I heard her telling Mrs Hutchinson about it. I was too young to understand what she meant when she said it, but now I do.

Wait, what? Rose was having an *affair*?

Chapter 45

I almost drop my phone. Is that possible? I can't think of anything else that 'fancy man' would mean, but it seems like Rose would be too afraid of Charles to see anyone behind his back . . . Unless that's the *reason* she was afraid of him, of course – that he'd find out – and *that* was the cause of all the nerves and whatever.

My mind is throwing up questions at warp speed as I take pictures of the rest of the pages. Had Shirley found out who the man was?

What was it Dorothy had written from Butlins in 1947? Something about how she's sorry Rose is upset and she won't tell anyone . . . And how Rose 'couldn't have known' – that Shirley's mum had seen the two of them, maybe? Odd that Dorothy seems to think it's OK, though – or least there's no suggestion that she doesn't.

I don't reckon Mrs Millichip is the blackmailer – if there actually *is* one – because the way this diary reads makes it sound like she's gossiping about Rose, and surely the whole point about blackmail is that you get money for keeping quiet?

Of course, we only have Rose's word for it that there were no visitors who came into the house on the day of the poisoning, other than Mrs Hewitt. What if her lover had come? Just because none of the neighbours saw him ... I remember something I once heard on a true crime programme: *absence of evidence is not evidence of absence*.

But, but, *but* ... While I can see why whoever-it-was might want to poison Charles, there'd be no reason for him to want to kill Dorothy or Kathleen, would there? Unless—

'Hey!'

I whirl round and see Shirley – or rather, Shirley's head and shoulders – over the fence: a fuzzy halo of white hair and, in spite of the hot weather, a beige quilted jacket. 'You're trespassing!'

It crosses my mind to pretend I'm from the building firm, but there's no point because she's obviously recognised me. 'You were trying to get over the wall the other day, weren't you? What are you after?' I stare at her, heart hammering, clutching the exercise book, mind blank. 'You better tell me, or I'll call the police.'

I suddenly feel icy calm, and my mind is sharp and clear. If Shirley were afraid, she'd have called the police before she confronted me. Judging by her body language, though, she seems more curious than scared.

I remember how I'd thought she was lonely, and decide to go for it. 'I've got your diary.'

'What?'

'Your diary, from 1954.' I approach the fence, although not near enough for her to snatch, and hold up the diary. 'Shirley Millichip, Form Five. Miss Bateman. You *really* liked Joe, didn't you?'

For a second, she looks confused. 'Joe Driscoll,' I prompt. 'The boy who lived here.'

Her expression stiffens from bewildered to indignant. 'That's mine, and it's private. You can't just get into people's gardens and dig things up.'

'So you knew it was here? Why didn't you bury it in your own garden?'

'Give it to me.'

'If you answer my question.'

'I lost it.' Shirley holds her hand out. 'Come on.'

'You really didn't like Rose and Dorothy much, did you?'

'What? You've no business reading it. Give it here.' She clicks her fingers impatiently and I take a step back.

'You're pretty unkind about people.'

Shirley shakes her head, but now she seems more flustered than angry. 'You can't just accuse me of things – I told you, I'll call the police.'

'See, I don't think you will.' I can hardly believe I'm saying any of this – it's almost like it's not me at all, but a character in a film. 'If you were going to call the police you'd have already done it. And I haven't actually accused you of anything – I'm just interested, is all. It says here,' I thumb through the pages of the exercise book, 'that your mum saw Rose Driscoll with her fancy man.'

'What do you know about Rose Driscoll?'

'I know she was Annie Driscoll's mother, and I know what happened.'

'How do you know?'

'Er, the internet?'

'Yes, well. What went on in that family was nobody's business . . .' Shirley makes a dismissive noise.

'Until two people got killed, and then it was everybody's business.'

'You have no idea what it was like, living next door. Men from the newspapers all up and down . . . It was a nightmare.'

'Not as much as it was for Joe and Rose, though.'

'Obviously not.' Shirley says it crossly, as if I'm trying to take something away from her. 'But none of it was *our* fault.'

'It wasn't theirs, either.'

'Don't you believe it.' Now she's got a righteous expression on her face. 'The way Rose behaved, it's no wonder Dorothy turned out like she did. That Victor didn't know what he was in for – and Annie was no better.'

'How do you mean, no better?'

'Carrying on . . . It was embarrassing, the way she behaved. Pushing herself on men. You have no idea.'

'The man your mum saw with Rose – do you know why she thought he was her lover?'

'Because it was obvious. I asked Mum about it years later, and she said she saw him hold Rose's hand and kiss her.'

'That doesn't prove anything.'

'Don't you believe it. People behaved differently back then – none of this sex in public like there is now.'

Yeah, right. I mean, you see *that* all the time. 'Did she recognise the man?'

Shirley frowns, like she's really concentrating, then says, 'I don't think so. I just remember her saying he was handsome.'

'So it wasn't Mr Hewitt?'

'Who?'

'Charles Driscoll's friend.'

'That bloke who used to come by all the time with the van?' Shirley shook her head. 'Uh-uh. My dad reckoned he was a crook – up to something with Mr Driscoll. His wife was a piece of work, too. Mum never understood what Rose saw in her. How do you know about all this, anyway?'

'Google.' I figure Shirley either doesn't have Wi-Fi or doesn't know enough about going online to be able to check if I'm telling the truth. 'Why were you so horrible about Dorothy? It wasn't her fault that Joe didn't like you.'

Given what Shirley's already said, I'm expecting her to come back with something sharp, so I'm surprised when she doesn't meet my eye. 'It's true about Joe, I suppose. I always wished he'd look my way, but . . . ' She really *was* in love with him, I think. It's years and years ago, but she's never forgotten. I wonder if perhaps she never married because she never got over him, and feel sorry for her.

'Do you know what happened to him?'

'He moved away after Rose died.' Shirley flinches, as if the thought of Rose's death is painful, and I think back to what Helene Bone told me. 'I know what I said about her behaviour, but nobody deserves even a quarter of what that poor woman went through.

All of it, eating away at her – the cancer was just the physical part.'
She shakes her head slowly, lips pursed. 'Terrible. Mr Driscoll
married again a few years later, and they moved down to the West
Country, which was where his wife's family came from, I think. I
know she was a widow with a couple of children, but that's about
all. Don't think Mum and Dad ever heard from him again. Well,
you'd want to forget, wouldn't you? And poor Joe . . . I don't suppose he ever got over it. If he's still alive, that is.'

So she doesn't know. I don't think the internet was a thing
in 1991, so it would be easy to miss the information unless you
happened to see it in a newspaper, and I suppose there was no
one around who knew both of them and could tell her. 'In those
days . . . ' Shirley looks past me, into the middle distance, and I
wonder what she's seeing, because I'm sure it isn't the plastic-
sheeted garden. 'Well, let's just say there were things you didn't
talk about.'

Figuring that two murders in a family would be just as hard to
talk about now as it was then, I reckon she's thinking of something
else. 'Do you mean Dorothy getting pregnant as a teenager?'

Shirley looks surprised. 'Oh, you know about that, do you?'

I nod. 'Online.'

'Privacy's a dirty word these days.' Shirley looks disgusted and I
feel bad for lying, even though I can hardly tell her the truth. 'That
was certainly one of the things we didn't talk about. I suppose
everyone did their best in the circumstances, but . . . ' She tails off,
shaking her head.

'Do you know who the baby's father was?'

Shirley sighs. 'Let's just say my mother had her suspicions.'

'And . . . ?'

Shirley's eyes snap wide open, as if I'd disturbed her out of a daydream. 'And you mind your own business! Like I said, it was nothing to do with us. You need to stop poking about and leave those poor girls in peace.'

So now they are 'poor girls', not the badly behaved daughters of a badly behaved mother. It's like Shirley's really conflicted – and I reckon she's sorry for at least some of what she thought back then, so she's being defensive about it, like old people get when you call them on stuff. 'Do you think Annie really did kill Dorothy and Kathleen?'

'Oh, for goodness' sake! She was found guilty, wasn't she? I'm not listening to any more – you just hand over my property and go back the way you came.' She makes an angry gesture at the wall behind me.

I pass the exercise book across the fence and she snatches it and clutches it to her chest. I can tell she's surprised that I'm giving it to her without a fuss – but then she doesn't know I've already got all the pages in my phone.

'Thank you.' She turns to go into her house.

'Wait! Please . . . Look, I'm sorry if I was rude, but can you just tell me one thing?'

'What now?' Her arms are folded across her chest and she's got a not-giving-anything-away look on her face. 'I've warned you . . . '

'I know, but can you just tell me – is it you that leaves the flowers on the graves?'

I'm half expecting her to tell me to mind my own business again, but her face softens. 'Dorothy and Kathleen, you mean?'

'And Annie.'

Shirley has a strange expression on her face – sort of confused and exasperated all at once. 'I go up there for Mum and Dad sometimes, so I have a look, and I always put flowers on Dorothy and Kathleen's grave. Annie's grave wasn't always in there, because they used to bury them in the prison grounds . . .' She looks to see if I know about this, and when I nod, she says, 'I only found it by chance, walking around. There were flowers on it for a while, like there were on Dorothy and Kathleen's, but then I stopped seeing them. I always reckoned it must have been Joe – and maybe it was, sometimes – but once when I was there I saw that solicitor fellow.'

'Mr Brighouse?'

'Oh, you know *all* about it, don't you? Well, he was putting flowers on Annie's grave.'

'How did you know it was him?'

'Introduced himself, didn't he? He must have been nearly as old I am now. Didn't say much, but I reckon he thought he'd failed her.'

'Because she was innocent?'

Again, Shirley gets that disorientated, slightly annoyed look – which I'm guessing is because she doesn't want to come right out and tell me she doesn't want to go there. 'I wouldn't know about that. I meant because of the sentence. Anyway, then the flowers stopped, so I reckoned he must have died, but I thought *someone* ought to remember, so . . .' She tails off with a look that says: *There it is, think what you like.*

I wonder if maybe Mr Brighouse paid for Joe's grave. 'That's really kind of you. Do you know where Rose is buried?'

'Under your feet.'

I jump back. '*Here?*'

'Well, in the garden, anyway. She was cremated, and Mr Driscoll told Mum that's where he'd put the ashes. It wasn't sentimental, because Rose never spent much time out here and any gardening was done by him – more like she was a dog, or that's what Mum said, although the poor man must have had it up to here with deaths and burials, so you can't really blame him. He gave her a proper funeral, of course,' Shirley adds quickly. 'And it's not against the law.' She screws up her face, as if she's looking at something very far away, then says, 'It's for God to judge, in the end,' in a way that makes me think she's talking about something more than Rose's ashes. 'Now, if you'll excuse me . . .' She turns away, then stops suddenly, as if I'd called her back, and looks round. 'It wasn't all better back then, I'm not saying that. There was a lot I didn't understand about what happened here. And the adults should have spoken up, but they didn't, because it wasn't done – and because people make mistakes. You young people think you've got everything right, but you'll make mistakes, too. You'll get things wrong, because everybody does, and when your children and grandchildren ask you questions, your answers won't be good enough. One day, you'll find that out.'

Chapter 46

I watch Shirley make her way round the clumps of brambles. The back of her house looks as run-down as the front – dead ivy still clinging to the bricks, and a bunch of window frames that look like they're rotting away. She doesn't stop to wave, or even look in my direction, just goes inside and closes the door after her.

I should have told her about Joe's grave.

When I scramble back across the top of the wall and jump down, Kieran is sitting on the pavement with his back to the brickwork, staring into space. For a moment, I don't think he's even registered that I almost landed on his head, but then he says, 'All done?'

'Yeah. Some lookout you are.'

'Nobody came past. Were you talking to someone?'

'The woman next door. Thanks for coming to my rescue.'

'What could I have done?'

I'm about to suggest Kieran could have climbed the wall and stuck his head over and pretended we'd lost a ball or something, but then I take another look at him. Sunken eyes, greyish-white skin stretched like cling film over his cheekbones, and he doesn't seem like he's even got the energy to stand. Also, my conversation with Shirley was useful – if kind of unsettling. 'Are you all right?'

'I'll be OK.'

'It's almost lunchtime. If I buy you some food, will you eat it?'

Kieran shrugs. I take this as a 'yes' and put out a hand to help him up. For a second, he just stares at it, but then he says, wearily, 'Go on, then,' and takes hold. His fingers are so cold that I can't help thinking of the graves in Highgate Cemetery, and what he said about starting to rot. 'Come on.'

Kieran says he's still vegan, so we go to a café on Holloway Road that I heard Skye talking about (although I'll eat my own feet if she ever manages to get Dad through the door) and buy him the all-day breakfast. He chooses a matcha latte, so I get one, too, and it's really nice. Not cheap, though – it took all of Dad's £20 with only just enough left for a tip.

'We're going to sit here till you eat all that,' I tell him when the food arrives.

Kieran turns the plate around slowly, eyeing the sourdough toast and avocado salad from different angles. 'Who are you, my mother?'

'For the purpose of this exercise,' I say, taking a paper napkin from the holder and presenting it to him with a flourish, 'consider me *in loco parentis*.'

He gives me a look that's sort of halfway to a smile, then picks up his fork and begins prodding at the salad, which I guess is a start. 'Thanks.'

'That's OK.'

'I meant for not being scared of me.'

'I was a bit, in the cemetery – but more worried, really. When you said you were dead and everything.'

Kieran sighs. 'I am dead. But you said you're already friends with one dead person, so what's the problem?'

'When you put it like that ... But my dead friend eats and drinks. I've seen him.'

'You *think* you have.'

'No, I *actually* have. Which means that dead people can eat and drink, so *go on*.'

I stare at Kieran until he prongs a bit of cucumber and puts it in his mouth.

'See? Not difficult. Now you have to chew, remember.'

He does, looking martyred, then swallows.

'Again.'

'It doesn't taste of anything.'

'You haven't given it a chance – and anyway, cucumber doesn't taste of much. Here –' I slice one piece of toast into quarters – 'try that.'

To my surprise, he obeys. After a couple of bites – small ones, but still – he looks up and says, 'So ...?'

'So ...?'

'What happened in the garden?'

'Oh, you're interested now?'

'Not really, but you want to tell me.'

He's right, I do want to tell him. I reckon it's better than trying to talk to him about how he's feeling, because he'll just shut me down. This way, there's a chance he might get interested in something outside himself. Plus, talking to him might help me figure things out, and I can show him the pages from Shirley's diary. I'm dying to read them properly – and maybe I can actually get Kieran to believe me. I start with everything that's happened in the last few days, so he gets a complete picture, and try not to leave anything out in case there's something important and I haven't realised.

'So, Shirley *seemed* to be saying,' I finish, 'that because Annie "pushed herself" on men, she must have killed Dorothy and Kathleen, which makes no sense *at all*. And she was *definitely* saying that her own parents knew something bad was happening in the Driscoll family but they didn't tell anyone about it. Was it only Rose having an affair and Dorothy's teenage pregnancy? I mean, you'd think those things would be enough for any family – but now I'm wondering if there was something else going on as well. And what about Shirley's mum's suspicions about the man who got Dorothy pregnant? She shut me down *so* fast when I asked about that. Oh, and I found this –' I produce the tiny schoolgirl doll from my pocket and prop it up against the salt cellar – 'as well as the diary. I think it came from the doll's house.'

Kieran's been looking quite interested – for him, anyway – during the ten minutes or so that it's taken me to explain everything. Plus, he's eaten half a slice of toast with avocado on it, so I'm counting that as a win – although maybe that's just because his mum found out he'd stopped his meds and made him start taking them again. 'Did you take photos of the diary?'

I slide my chair round the table so we can look at my phone together. After a few minutes' silent reading, Kieran says, 'I see what you mean about being bitchy, but what's the deal with this shoe shop? You said this is an exercise book she's writing in, but she never even mentions school.'

'I think that's because she's left and the shoe shop is a full-time job. You could leave school at fifteen back then, and loads of people didn't bother with A levels because you didn't need qualifications for everything.' Bit off-point, but it's nice knowing something Kieran doesn't, for once.

I tell him about how it was Shirley falling off the shop's ladder that caused Rose and Mrs Hewitt to leave the tea party, and he nods his head slowly. 'OK . . . '

Several pages have 'Shirley Driscoll' and 'Mrs J. Driscoll' written down the side. I imagine Shirley practising the signature, daydreaming about marrying Joe, and wonder if she's looking at them now, remembering how it felt to be that hopeful teenage romantic . . . And then I think about me and Joe and have to pretend to be looking for something in my bag because I can feel my face going red.

Went to see 'The Runaway Bus' at the Rex with J. I thought it would be just the two of us, but Annie insisted on coming, which spoilt everything . . .

'What's the girl equivalent of a cockblock?' Kieran's not exactly laughing his head off, but he is actually smiling.

'Ha, ha. Bet Joe *asked* Annie to come.'

'Shirley really likes the cinema, doesn't she? That's ten films she's been to in . . . what? Six weeks?'

'That's because the TV was rubbish.' I tell him about *The Grove Family*. 'Plus, no streaming.'

'I knew *that* . . . Bet it was cheaper, too.'

'*Everything* was cheaper.'

Shirley didn't write every day. After the first few weeks, the entries started to get shorter and more and more spaced out timewise, so that sometimes she'd miss whole months. The diary confirms what Joe said about her dad having health problems from what happened in the war, which I'm guessing rules *him* out as Kathleen's father – although, as Kieran points out, he was capable of it, because Shirley's little brother Alfie must have been born after the war ended (unless Rose wasn't the only one with a lover, of course).

Had Shirley started the diary thinking it would be the story of a romance with Joe, but that never happened so she got fed up with writing it? After a lot of entries that were hardly more than a note of whatever film she'd seen, or if she'd gone to a friend's birthday party or visited the dentist, the final entry, dated 1 March 1955 – nine days before the poisoning – was really long. This time, it wasn't Shirley who'd gone to the cinema, but her mum and dad, and she was home babysitting Alfie, who was sulking and refusing to eat his dinner:

*I sent A to bed so I could carry on reading my book in peace,
but when I went out to feed Rosie and Thumper, the back door*

was banging at No. 37. Mrs D was in the garden and looked like she was crying, and Mr D came out and pulled her back inside. Then they both started shouting. Mr D said something about it being her fault and she should have thought less of herself and looked after her children better. I couldn't hear very much of what Mrs D said, but once it was 'How could you?' and that she'd done something for Dorothy, not him. After about five minutes, I heard Mr D go into the hall, and then he left the house & slammed their front door really hard. I've never heard them shouting before. It must be because of Mrs D's fancy man, like Mum told Mrs Hutchinson.

I hadn't shut the hutch properly so Thumper got out and I had to chase him all over the garden. I caught him eventually but not before Alfie had come downstairs & got upset over his precious rabbit and in the end there wasn't enough time to finish my book and now I'll have to wait until Thursday because it's Rangers tomorrow.

Kieran looks up. 'What's Rangers? Doesn't sound like it's the team.'

I google it. After scrolling past a load of guff about football, I discover that it's a sort of extension of Girl Guides. 'At least Shirley didn't spend *all* her free time hanging around hoping Joe would notice her,' I tell him. 'Sounds like Charles found out about Rose's lover, doesn't it?'

'Maybe. But why would *Rose* say "How could you?"? Surely *he* would be saying it to *her*?'

'Perhaps he tracked the guy down and beat him up,' I offer. 'He looks as if he could be violent, and he kills for a living, so—'

'He does *what*?'

I explain about the abattoir. Even though Kieran's vegan, I kind of expect him to say something about how we all die in the end, so what's the difference, but he doesn't, just looks a bit sick – which I guess means that, despite what he says about not having feelings, he does care about some things. Then, to my surprise, he leans forward, sounding almost excited. 'You've heard of Occam's Razor, right?'

'What?'

'It's a problem-solving principle, attributed to a thirteenth-century monk called William of Occam. Entities should not be multiplied beyond necessity – or, to put it another way, the simplest explanation is most likely to be the right one. It's like they say in medicine: when you hear hoofbeats, think horses not zebras.'

'Do they?' We're back to *him* explaining shit to *me*. Of course we are.

'They do.' Kieran looks pleased with himself.

'Unless you're in Africa.'

Now it's his turn to look confused. 'What?'

'Well, if you were in, say, the Kruger National Park, and you heard hoofbeats, it *would* be zebras, wouldn't it? What I mean is that the simplest explanation depends on where you are and who's around. It doesn't have to be geographically, but just . . . well, generally. Because I don't think that Annie killing her sisters *is* the simplest solution.' Also, I want to tell him, you're the living – or

OK, possibly dead – proof that the medical think-of-horses thing isn't always right, because Cotard's Delusion is probably about as common as finding a zebra in Holloway Road.

'The police thought it was.'

'Yes, because Annie didn't have an alibi and the tin of poison had her fingerprints on it – so it was the simplest explanation for *them* because it was the *easiest*, right? So basically, it was kind of lazy, because they just didn't bother trying to get any more information. And just by the way, I don't see what razors have to do with it, unless that Occam guy cut himself shaving or something.'

Kieran looks like he's trying not to be impressed, then says, 'Actually, I don't see, either – about the razor, I mean.' He stares at the spider plant on the shelf opposite for so long that I reckon he's gone into a trance, but finally, he says, slowly, 'The principle still applies, though. *And*,' now he's looking so superior that I want to hit him, 'correlation is not causation.' He taps my phone to bring back the photo of Shirley's diary entry with the description of the row between Rose and Charles. 'He said she should have looked after the children better and not thought about herself so much, and then she said, "How could you?", right? I don't think they were arguing about her having an affair at all – you just conflated the two things. What Shirley said about Rose having a fancy man was new information to you, so that was your biggest takeaway from the conversation. But she said other things too, didn't she?'

'Of course. I told you.'

'Tell me again.'

'Well, she said that what went on in that house was nobody's business and that none of it was their fault – meaning her family's – and that Rose had a lover and was a bad example to Dorothy and Annie about men, and that her mum had had her suspicions about who Dorothy's baby's father was, and . . . ' I stop to think.

'And after that,' said Kieran, 'she said they were "poor girls" – like, victims, didn't she? What does that tell you?'

'That she can't make her mind up?'

'Definitely that, but there was something else, too – and I reckon that's what Rose and Charles's argument was about. There are things you've said – stuff you learnt from Joe about Dorothy and Annie – that back it up.'

'Back *what* up?'

'"How could you?"' Kieran quotes. 'That's what Rose said. And I think she said it because she'd discovered that Charles was Kathleen's father.'

Chapter 47

I almost drop my matcha latte. 'Seriously? He's a bit ... I don't know, kind of a bully, but Joe seems to think he's all right.'

'Who says Joe's such a great judge of character? You've met the guy what, twice?'

'Three times.'

'OK, three times – but it's not like you *know* him.'

'I ...' I'm about to argue when something occurs to me. 'You said that like you actually believe me.' Also, pipes up a little bat squeak in the back of my mind, you said it like you're jealous. 'Actually, I think that's more because he thinks Charles is better than his biological dad. But ... really? His stepdaughter?'

'Don't be naive, Millie. It happens – and it wasn't like Dorothy could have called a helpline or got a DNA test. Show me the diary page again.'

I bring it up on my phone, and Kieran reads aloud. '*I couldn't hear very much of what Mrs D said, but once it was "How could you?" and that she'd done something for Dorothy, not him.*' His energy is completely different now, like he's enjoying himself. Almost like the old

Kieran, in fact. 'She *had* done something for Dorothy – pretended to be pregnant – and she's just found out that she was covering for *him*, too. That's what she's talking about!'

'But . . .' I stare at him, trying to process this. 'Wait, though . . .' I find the photo of Annie and Kathleen as bridesmaids at Dorothy's wedding. 'She's the one on the left.'

'OK, so . . . does she look like Charles?'

'Well, she's tall for her age, and Charles must be at least six-two – but Dorothy can't have been short because she was a model, and Joe's pretty tall, so that could be in her genes without Charles being involved.' I study the photo. 'She's got black hair like Charles. I've only seen black and white pictures of Dorothy, but it looks as if she's fair, and so are Annie and Rose – although Joe has black hair so that's not conclusive – but . . .' I spot something, and enlarge the photo as much as I can without the bit I'm focusing on turning into a grey smudge. 'Dimples.'

'And?'

'Charles has dimples, too. Dorothy doesn't, and neither do Joe, Annie, or Rose, but his are really noticeable . . .'

'I'm guessing,' Kieran says, sounding actually excited now, 'that the resemblance got more obvious as Kathleen got older. Usually, when someone says a person looks like their dad, it's not a big deal, because why wouldn't you? But if people kept on saying it about Kathleen . . .'

'And one person too many said it in front of Rose, and she got suspicious . . .'

'And the penny finally dropped . . .'

'And she asked Dorothy. What must *that* conversation have been like?'

Kieran looks suddenly sceptical. 'If they ever had it.'

I remember Helene's words: *People kept secrets for their entire lives.* And Shirley, saying that there were things you didn't talk about, and about how cancer was only the physical part of what was eating away at Rose – and how she'd closed right down when I tried to ask about Kathleen's father.

My stomach lurches. Everything about this makes horrible, horrible sense. The more I think about it, the more strange it seems that Charles, who was obviously a pretty forceful guy, wouldn't have made it his business to discover who the father of Dorothy's child was. Helene had told me Dorothy was determined never to say – but of course Charles wouldn't have needed to find out if he already knew the answer, would he?

Rose must have been pretty sure to call Charles out like that, but had she and Dorothy *ever* talked about it? Both Joe and Helene had said how kind Dorothy was: if she hadn't wanted to upset Rose further, and if Charles had gaslighted her into thinking it was somehow her fault – which I bet he had – then I reckon it would be one more secret to add to the pile.

'I really hope you're wrong about this, but ... And you're right that there'd be way less support back then.' Poor, poor Dorothy. I want to fly back in time right now and just ... 'Aaargh.' I curl my hands into tight fists and count to ten. Getting angry won't help. I need to concentrate.

'I suppose,' Kieran says, 'that she might have told Rose herself.'

275

'I don't think so. She wouldn't have wanted to rock the boat.' And it was certainly another reason why Dorothy had been so desperate for Victor not to find out about the baby – because of course the first thing he'd ask was who the father was – and why she'd asked Joe to look after Annie while she was away, supposedly for tuberculosis, in case Charles started on her ...

Which might be the reason Annie didn't want to move into Dorothy's room when she left – being alone would make her more vulnerable. But on the other hand, perhaps the reason why Annie had been, in Joe's words, 'soppy' with Victor was because she thought it was a way to get the 'attention' she was missing. Perhaps she'd glimpsed Dorothy through a half-closed door, forced to sit on Charles's lap, or noticed the way he looked at her. Little things that had stuck in her mind, and, not understanding what they meant, she wanted them for herself.

Oh, Annie.

The whole thing is just so wrong and so sad.

Joe couldn't have put two and two together because he didn't have enough information. Annie must have done the same with Charles as she had with Victor, and possibly even Mr Hewitt, and no one – not even Dorothy, because no one who really understood would *want* that sort of attention – had realised its significance.

I feel sick.

And – *OMG* – Shirley had said that Charles's second wife was a widow with a couple of children, hadn't she? If one or both of them were girls, had he done the same thing all over again, and got away with it?

'But either way,' Kieran says, thoughtfully, 'Rose couldn't go to the police because she'd basically colluded by pretending Kathleen was hers. There was no way of proving that she hadn't known – or that Kathleen was Charles's child – so it would just be her word against his.'

'And Dorothy's.'

'Yes, but only if Dorothy was willing to tell them – and she'd be worried about Kathleen, wouldn't she, as well as Victor? I mean, imagine finding out *that* about yourself.'

'I wonder if with Rose, it was like when you have a kind of background thing going on where you know that something's wrong but not what it is. I had that for a few years before Mum and Dad split up. Kind of like a premonition, only about something that's happening right now – and you can sort of make yourself think you're imagining it, but not quite.'

'Elephant in the room, you mean.'

'More like, you're scared to open the door in case there's an elephant on the other side.'

Kieran's looking hurt, which surprises me. 'I wish you'd told me.'

'You weren't well, and it didn't seem . . . I don't know . . . and I was scared.'

'Seems like you were right to be.'

'Well, yeah. Saying it would have made it real.'

'Feelings . . . ' Kieran shakes his head suddenly, like, that's just Living People Shit.

I want to say, *You have feelings, too*, but I don't. I wonder if that's a pose, Kieran saying that, or was it like he really didn't think he could feel anything any more but then he suddenly did? Because Kieran certainly just looked like he had, even if it was only for about thirty seconds.

Now he's staring at the spider plant again, looking puzzled. 'I suppose someone could have blackmailed Charles about Dorothy – I mean, if it started from 1946, when he and Rose got married—'

'But how would they have found out? If Dorothy didn't tell Rose or Joe, she was hardly going to say anything to anyone else, was she? And the list was in *Rose's* handwriting.'

'Perhaps Charles told her that the money was for ... I don't know, some scheme with his sketchy friend.'

'Mr Hewitt? I suppose ... *Oof*. My head's spinning.' And it really is – I'm starting to feel actually dizzy as well as confused. 'But I'm really grateful that you came with me, and ... all this. Even if you did keep talking about razors and zebras.'

'You did, too.'

'Yeah, but you started it.'

'Do you want the rest of this?' Kieran pushes his plate towards me. 'Sorry. I know it wasn't exactly cheap.'

'No, you're all right.' I really *am* starting to feel weird now; queasy and headachy and clammy. I wonder if I'm in shock – and Kieran is definitely looking tired. 'Come on, Sherlock. I'll walk you to the bus stop.'

Although Kieran was – compared to last time I saw him – pretty upbeat in the café, he shuts down again as we walk up the road. I'm feeling worse by the minute, and I know that trying to restart the conversation would be pointless, so we stand in silence until a

Number 43 arrives. When I thank him again and say goodbye, he doesn't answer, just touches my shoulder so lightly that I barely feel it, and gets on board.

I lean against the side of the shelter and watch as the bus moves out of sight.

I know we don't have any proof, but the more I think about it, the more I'm sure that Kieran is right ... and that I'll have to tell Joe.

Chapter 48

It's not like I've managed to help Joe much so far: all I've done is found out – or guessed, although I'm sure as I can be that Kieran is right about Charles – a bunch of horrible stuff about his family.

Joe said the birthday party was Charles's idea, and he definitely knew the poison was in the shed because he'd cleaned it out a month before. And if it was him who mainly looked after the garden, then I suppose he would have bought the stuff. Perhaps he'd tried to poison Rose – if he thought she was going to go to the police – but somehow Dorothy and Kathleen ended up eating . . .

What? Nothing was found in any of the food the police tested.

It's no use – I can't think about this any more. Can't think about anything. Just need to get home.

By the time I get to the corner of Dad's road, my headache is almost blinding. I know I'm going to throw up, and I really, really want to get back to the flat before that happens.

Why is this happening? It can't be the matcha latte – oat milk wouldn't make you ill, would it? I haven't eaten anything since breakfast, and that was *ages* ago, so—

I don't make it. Instead, I puke on the grass outside the block. Someone is shouting – at me, I think – but I'm too ill to pay attention. Normally, being sick makes you feel better almost straight away, but not this time. Instead, the headache gets worse – I'm squinting so much it takes an age to press the right combination of numbers into the keypad, and I stagger up the stairs to the first floor and then puke again, this time on the landing.

I'm shivering as I fumble with the door key, waves of nausea still coming up into my throat even though there can't be anything left in my stomach. I can't make the door unlock, but I can hear noises from inside, so someone must be home. I feel like slithering down to the ground and staying there, but I beat on the wood and croak, 'Let me in,' and after what seems like an hour, during which I puke for a third time, Dad appears.

'Millie! What the—?'

I take one step forward and the world somersaults. The next things I see are the little air holes on the fronts of his Reeboks, right beside my head.

His voice, coming from somewhere above me. 'What's happened to you? You didn't tell us you were going out. I've been calling and messaging all day.'

'Didn't hear.' Too much effort to tell him it's because I forgot to turn the volume back up.

'Never mind that, Dom, she's ill!' Skye's voice, from further away. OMG, now it hurts just to move my head. What's happening to me?

I can just see her feet – sunshine yellow toenail polish – in the middle of a bunch of random stuff on the hall floor: pieces of wood, cogs, bits of metal . . .

The clock. Oh, God, the clock.

Mr Smith tried to take his clock out of the shop and fainted from the pain.

'What have you been doing?' Skye kneels down beside me and strokes my hair. 'Your fingernails are *filthy*. Come on, let's get you to bed.'

'No,' I gasp. 'Put it back.'

'Put . . .?'

'The clock.'

'I'm afraid it got broken.' Dad's voice. 'Skye thought it would be better somewhere else in the flat. She got the idea when we were taking down the "Massage Parlour" sign.'

Oh, *great*. Well done me.

'She said the energy's bad there, so it's not the right place for a clock, and we were taking it off the wall when—'

'Not *now*, Dom.' Skye's voice is sharp. 'Millie, why don't you come and lie down, and then we can—'

'No!' My head is splitting and even keeping my eyes open is an effort. But I've spotted something on the floor – the small, brass-coloured cylinder that Mr Smith said was called an oss . . . something. The thing that contains the quartz. His voice in my head: *You could almost say that this is able to contain time itself.*

Time.

Time.

TIME.

The word reverberates in my head, louder and louder. No chance of standing upright or even crawling, so I try to pull myself forward. The pain is so enormous now that it's taken me over, like the only thing in the world. It's almost unbearable but I've got to keep trying . . .

Getting closer . . .

Closer . . .

In the background I can hear somebody talking, urgent gabble but not words, and the hall seems to shake and blur in front of me as I stretch out my hand, past the clock face, now with a hole in its centre, the two hands broken apart, and pieces of mechanism, and open my fingers to grasp—

Chapter 49

Where am I?

The pain has gone, but it's dark, and someone is sobbing.

As my eyes adjust, I can make out the clock – on the wall in front of me, in one piece. Half past four: but of course it's early morning, not afternoon.

The sound is louder now, more howling than crying.

Annie, behind the cell door. Ray or Florey saying, 'Ssh now, come on, that's enough.'

They must have told her there won't be a reprieve. I picture that smart, important-looking woman I saw in the corridor coming into the cell to tell her, holding up the letter from the Home Secretary.

As I tiptoe towards the door of Annie's cell, I can just make out her words through the sobs. 'I'm frightened.'

'I know, dear, I know.'

'Does it hurt?'

She sounds like a child asking about an operation.

'No, dear. It's very quick.'

Poor, poor Annie. As I inch up the cover of the peephole with my finger, I feel like my heart is breaking for her, and for Joe. Now I can see her, staring round the cell like she can't believe no one's there to save her, tears running down her face. 'I want Dorothy. Where's Dorothy?'

'Come on, now ...' Ray is sitting beside Annie on the bed, rubbing her back.

Annie squirms away from her. 'Dorothy!'

How can they *do* this?

Ray goes over to the table and picks up something small. 'Why don't we have another one of these?'

Annie just stares at her. She's wearing a cream-coloured night-gown made of cotton almost as thick and rough as canvas.

'Come on.' Ray stands over her. 'Open your mouth.'

They're drugging her so she'll shut up.

Ray hands her a glass of water. 'That's it. Now you'll feel better.'

Better?

As Ray turns away from Annie to put the glass back on the table, I see that she has tears in her eyes, too, and wonder, for the first time, what all this is doing to her and Florey. No one should have to do this job.

She sits down again and carries on rubbing Annie's back as Annie carries on sobbing, her face in her hands. 'God will forgive you, Annie.'

That's what the chaplain said. I suppose Ray can't think of any-thing else – but I want to thump the door and shout that she's talking about the god who let Dorothy be abused and did nothing to stop it. Instead, I slump down, back to the wall and eyes full of angry tears.

What am I going to do?

Eventually, Annie goes quiet. When I get to my feet and look through the peephole again, I see that she's curled up on the bed, covered with a blanket. Ray is sitting at the table, watching her, face blank with exhaustion.

Less than ten paces away, in the execution chamber, there must be a bag of sand that weighs the same as Annie, hanging in the darkness.

I reach for a tissue to wipe my eyes. There should be a little packet in the pocket of my hoodie, but it isn't there. Instead, there's a small, hard cylinder. When I pull it out, I realise it's the oss ... thing. *Oscillator*, that's it, with the quartz inside. It must have brought me here.

Bit sticky, though – I must have had a loose sweet or chocolate wrapper or something in my pocket. But ... how can it be inside the clock and in my hand at the same time? Mr Smith said he thought that his older self merged with his younger self because he couldn't exist in the same place twice, so how come this thing can?

Is it because the clock in my time is broken and this one is whole and working? Before, the future clock was just older – like Mr Smith – but now it's in a different state: not a clock any more, just a bunch of bits and pieces. Is that it?

Whether it is or not, I'd better make sure this little cylinder stays in my pocket, because if I'm not here, I can't save Annie. Plus, if I go back to the present I'll be in agony. I don't know what would have happened if I hadn't got hold of the quartz, but I know it wouldn't have been good, because no one could stand that level of pain without . . .

I don't know what. But I can't think about that now.

I need to get to Aylmer Terrace.

It takes a long time to get to the front of the prison because it's really quiet this early in the morning, and I have to wait ages for someone to come along and unlock the doors so that I can slip through. It's only when I reach the big main gate that I realise I might have to wait another hour, or even more, before people start coming in and out. I've been standing in the courtyard for about ten minutes, wondering if there's *any* way I can get over one of the walls without breaking my neck, when I hear a clanging noise – metal on metal – coming from somewhere on my right.

When I investigate – there's an alleyway between two of the buildings at that side of courtyard – I find a bunch of guys in flat caps carrying metal dustbins like the ones I saw in Aylmer Terrace on their shoulders. They're all filing out of a side gate, and I run towards them and just manage to slip through the doorway and onto the pavement before the officers lock up again.

I run past their lorry and round the corner, then cross over the main road and head for Aylmer Terrace. It's getting light, but there's hardly anyone about, so I guess the dustmen must go to the prison before the rest of their round.

The distance between the start of Ianthe Street and where Aylmer Terrace joins it isn't that much, and as I come round the corner, I spot Tiger jump down from the side wall of Number 37's back garden and shoot across into Corinna Road. She's out of sight in a flash – a tabby streak with her ears flattened against her head, which makes me think something must have scared her.

The next second, a trilby hat appears over the same bit of wall. Charles? What's he doing?

Except it isn't Charles.

'Joe?'

I start running towards him, calling his name, but it's like he can't hear me.

'Joe!'

He's pulling himself up onto the top of the wall . . .

Now I'm only about twenty metres away, and I can see him from the waist up, I realise it isn't Joe, but someone bulkier – not much, but enough – and, once I move close enough to see his face more clearly, obviously older.

I stop dead as he drops to the ground with a grunt, then straightens up, brushing dirt off his clothes with his hands. He's wearing a trench coat, like in those old black and white noir films Dad watches, with a turned-up collar.

He looks straight through me, then up and down the road – kind of furtive, like he's checking nobody's watching.

Just like Joe, if Joe were older.

That black and white photo, stuck inside the book: a handsome man in army uniform.

No, that's impossible.

It can't be, but it is: Frank Palmer.

Chapter 50

A ghost?

Might be why the cat ran away.

But why would a ghost be climbing over a wall? Also, I heard his feet on the pavement, and he grunted, which isn't exactly otherworldly.

And he definitely doesn't know I'm here.

He stops to light a cigarette, then tosses the match into the gutter and walks off in the same direction as the cat ... Joe had said they'd had Tiger since they were kids, so maybe she'd fled because she remembered what a bastard Frank was. If he'd hit his wife, he wasn't going to think twice about kicking a defence-less animal.

Oh, Rose. You certainly know how to pick them.

But how could it be Frank? He'd died in the Second World War. It said so on Wikipedia, and Joe had confirmed it. Something about the fall of somewhere in Africa in 1942.

The match is still in the gutter, where he dropped it – and when I touch the burnt end, it's very slightly warm.

Should I follow him? I cross Ianthe Street and when I look down Corinna Road, I spot him, head down and walking fast. Then he turns down a side road – but I reckon I'll find out more by going to Number 37, so I turn back.

The house looks as if everyone inside is asleep – curtains drawn, silent. Very gently, I put my hand through the letter box and grope for the string with the key on it – even if *I* can't be seen or heard, anything from 1955 that makes a noise because of me surely will be.

Got it! I hold my breath as I put the key in the lock, turn it, and push the door . . . Just as I step inside, Joe's head appears round the kitchen doorway.

His eyes widen when he sees me. He points to his watch, holds up one hand for 'five minutes', then ducks back inside the room again.

'It's OK, Mum – no one there.'

As I edge down the hall, I can hear the sound of muffled sobbing.

Rose is sitting at the table, wrapped in a shawl with her face buried in a handkerchief and Joe standing behind her, one hand on her shoulder. No Charles, just the two of them – and, judging by the wide-open window, the full ashtray and the three glasses on the table – they've been up all night and they've just had a secret meeting with Frank.

'Why don't you go upstairs and try to get some sleep?'

Rose nods without looking round, then reaches for her handbag, which is on the chair next to her.

'Here you are.' Joe undoes the clasp and hands it over, and Rose gropes inside with shaking hands and pulls out a small pill bottle.

'Are those the new tablets?'

Rose nods again, too broken to speak. She pushes back her chair and stands up, hunched with grief and moving stiffly, like a woman twice her age. It's so pitiful that I almost can't bear to look.

'I'm sure they'll do the trick, Mum. Come on ...' Joe puts an arm around her and steers her across the room.

He turns as they reach the doorway and points to one of the chairs: wait.

Another woman being drugged. I'm not going to tell Joe how I heard Annie screaming for Dorothy.

I feel like I ought to do something, so I empty the ashtray into the bin and wash it up with the glasses and a whole bunch of other stuff that's piled in the sink, then put it all away in the dresser.

Rose's handbag is still on the table. It's vintage – except it isn't *now*, because it's still quite new – and made of stiff black patent leather, with a short handle at the top and a clasp. Its metal mouth is gaping open like a big baby bird, so I look inside. There's a purse, a powder compact, a lipstick, and a small notepad with a leather cover and little pencil attached to the side, as well as hairpins and a bunch of used envelopes and scraps of paper with shopping lists written on them, as well as another page, cream coloured and folded in half.

JAMIE COSTELLO

James Marshall
Court Hotel, 42 Seven Sisters Road

I don't need to have the burnt scrap of paper with me to know
it's the same handwriting as the 'ask you to forgive me' letter.

Chapter 51

Joe comes back about five minutes later and sits down opposite me without speaking. He looks exhausted, dark circles under his eyes and the rest of his face blueish white in the light of the unshaded bulb hanging above the table.

'How's Rose?'

'How do you think?'

'Will she sleep?'

'I hope so. This is just . . .'

Joe leans his elbows on the table and massages his temples. 'I can't believe this is happening.'

'Where's Charles, Joe?'

'With Mr Hewitt. He said he'd be back tomorrow.'

'Does he know that the execution is going ahead?'

'He knows.' Joe's voice is quiet, and oddly expressionless. 'So much for Mr Partington's petition. Mr Brighouse came yesterday evening and told us. Dad went out about an hour later. Said he had some business to attend to, and that I should look after Mum . . .

Mr Brighouse said it would be ... would happen ... tomorrow morning. Is that ...?'

'It's what I read, yes – but there's still *time*, Joe. And I need to know about Frank.'

The second I say this, it's like the air between me and Joe is taut enough to snap. He stares at me, eyes wide with shock. 'I saw him climb over the garden wall. It is him, isn't it? Calling himself James Marshall. I saw the piece of paper in your mum's bag.'

As I'm saying this, the niggling feeling in a corner of my mind, that something was off, resolves itself as sharply as a picture snapping into focus. 'When you brought me here from the prison and I was asking you about Frank, you said, "I hardly *remembered* him" ... which doesn't make sense unless you've seen him *since* you were a little kid. And,' I add, when Joe still doesn't speak, 'it's why your mum looked so frightened when we'd been in Dorothy's room and she came back and looked up the stairs. She couldn't have seen me, so it must have been *you* that scared her – the light's bad up there, and she thought you were Frank.' And, I think but don't say, she was so frightened over Frank, and so full of her own guilt, that she wasn't paying attention to what was happening with Charles and Dorothy.

The silence in the room seems to get thicker and thicker, until it's like an actual barrier between us. Joe stares at the note on the table. 'That piece of paper – *ask you to forgive me*. You knew it wasn't going to be a match with Dorothy's writing, didn't you?'

I'd been so relieved that it wasn't a suicide note from Joe that I hadn't paid enough attention to his reaction.

'I didn't absolutely know, but ...' Still, he doesn't look up. 'It's the kind of thing he writes to Mum. Sentimental. I thought she must have burnt the rest of it – that's what she usually does – and somehow it got missed.'

'Why didn't you tell me?'

He jerks his head back with sort of a gasp, like someone who's been underwater. 'Because if anyone found out, Mum would go to prison! And Annie would still be ...' He clamps his mouth shut, like he can't bear to say the words, and shakes his head. 'I can't bear to lose Mum as well.'

'I understand, Joe.' And I do. Rose is all he has left. 'But—'

'But nothing! And don't start saying I ought to tell some-body, because there's no point. It has nothing to do with any of this, and—'

'Are you sure about that?'

'How could it have?'

'I don't know, but it's not impossible. We still don't know why Dorothy and Kathleen were poisoned, so for all you know this *might* have something to do with it.' My brain's gone into overdrive. That's why Rose was, as Helene Bone and Joe had both said, 'scared of her own shadow': not because Charles would find out about some random boyfriend, but about *Frank*. Who was yet another reason why Rose was too preoccupied to pay attention to Annie – and who, I'm guessing, was the 'fancy man' that Shirley's mum had talked about. She wouldn't have recognised Frank, because she'd never met him: Rose had only come to live in Aylmer Terrace when she and Charles were married.

'Look, I'm not saying you have to tell the police or Mr Brighouse or whoever, but why don't you tell me about it? I can hardly go and blab to a bunch of people who can't even *see* me, can I? And right now . . . Well, what difference can it make?'

Joe stares at me for a long moment, as if he's not sure who I am or even where he is. 'OK. I suppose I didn't tell you because I was so scared of talking about it to *anyone*, in case . . . Well, what I said. I found out when I turned sixteen. Mum told me he wanted to see me. She'd never have said anything if he hadn't. He doesn't live round here, just gets in touch if he comes to London.'

'Dorothy knew though, didn't she? That letter when she said she'd "never tell a soul".'

'Yes.' Joe sighs. 'You probably won't believe this, but at first I didn't put two and two together when you read that out – about it referring to Frank, I mean. We'd been talking about Dorothy and going away to have a baby and everything, and it was such a shock. I just . . . I don't know. It's a lot to take in.' He's talking as though he's in a trance, staring through the open window at the soft colours of the early morning garden as if I'm not even there. 'You can't absorb it all at once, somehow. When Mum told me about Frank, Dorothy was there. We were sitting in here, and we were the only ones in the house because Dad was at work and Annie'd taken Kathleen to the park. I said she should never have married Dad if she had any idea that Frank was still alive, and what did she think she was playing at. I was pretty angry about the whole thing, but Dorothy was . . . Well, I'd never seen her like that. Normally, she just wanted everyone to get along, and she'd hardly ever raise her voice, but she was shouting at me, really furious, saying I had no idea what Mum had been through because I was just a kid. She said it was bad enough when Frank was around, but then Mum never got a pension because he was only listed missing and not killed. We'd come back to London, and she was working all the hours in a factory but there was never enough money for the four of us, and with Nana dead—'

'When did that happen?'

'The end of 1944 – her house was hit by a V-2.'

'Sorry, a *what*?'

'It's a bomb. They were the biggest – the Germans had them at the end of the war, and they could take out a whole street. It wasn't as if Nana had much money to leave us, and it meant that Dorothy had to look after me and Annie while Mum was out working—'

'But she was only about . . . ' I stop and think.

'Eleven,' Joe says. 'One of the neighbours came in sometimes, but it was mainly Dorothy doing the cooking and stuff.'

I think of how Annie called out for Dorothy – the person who'd been like a second mother to her – and duck my head and blink quickly to stop the tears coming. When I feel I've got it under control, I look up to see that Joe's staring out of the window again, looking dazed.

'I'm not surprised Dorothy was cross with you,' I say. 'Sounds like she had a tough time, too.' And she took Rose's side despite what Charles had done to her. I remember Helene Bone's words: '. . . she'd buried it so far down inside that she could almost convince herself it hadn't happened.' Like, gaslighting yourself because you kind of have to.

Joe's eyes snap back to me. 'Yeah, she did. Then, after the war, Mum lost her job, but she wasn't trained for anything and even if she had been she wouldn't have earned as much as a man, so . . . It was like Dorothy said, either Dad – I mean, Frank – really *was* dead and the army didn't know about it, or he'd just left us to fend for ourselves, so what was Mum supposed to do? When I got angry with Mum, after I found out, she just sat there and . . . took it. Dorothy was the one who told me to shut up; Mum just sat there looking sad. I felt terrible afterwards because Dorothy'd made me see it from Mum's point of view, and when I got off my high horse and thought about it properly, I could remember how she was always so tired and worried about money. She just said, "I couldn't see a future for any of us. I wasn't strong enough."'

What had Helene said? *Women were a lot more dependent on men, because the law and society made it that way.* 'But when she married Charles, wasn't there paperwork? I mean, didn't she have to prove she was a widow?'

'She told them she'd lost her papers when Nana's house was destroyed. That sort of thing happened a lot back then, with all the bombing. It wasn't always easy to get a replacement letter or certificate or whatever it was, because army places and record offices got bombed as well, so . . . ' Joe shrugs.

Of course, no online backup. If the paper records were destroyed, that was that.

'She had to sign a declaration. And it wasn't *exactly* lying – I mean, she didn't know Frank was dead, but she didn't know he wasn't, either.'

'But then he came back.'

'Then he came back.'

'When was that?'

'I think . . . about six months later.'

'So, 1946.'

'Yes.'

'Right. So . . . you know what I'm going to say next, don't you?'

Chapter 52

Joe looks at me with empty eyes. 'Why don't I make us a cup of tea?'

'OK.' I get why Joe wants to do something normal – when the worst imaginable thing has happened, a small comfort is better than no comfort at all. Plus, that thing of doing something while you're having a difficult conversation – like all the ones I had with either Mum or Dad when we were going somewhere in the car, so they were focusing on the road and we didn't have to look at each other. And actually, a cup of tea would be great right now, because I really need to keep it together.

Watching Joe fill the kettle and strike a match to light the gas makes me think of before the party – Annie getting everything ready, happy and excited – but when he opens the pantry door to refill the sugar bowl, I feel suddenly uneasy, as if I've forgotten something important.

What, though? Joe takes a large china pot with the word 'Sugar' painted on it from a row of similar containers. Something to do with ingredients? I spot 'Flour', 'Currants', 'Sultanas', 'Rice' and 'Tapioca' – whatever *that* is – but none of them seem significant in any way, and nor does the big tin bread bin or the cans of condensed milk, Spam, and golden syrup.

No. Whatever it is will just have to wait. 'Rose was paying someone to keep quiet about Frank, wasn't she?' Joe has his back to me, but the way his shoulders stiffen tells me I'm right. 'The list of payments I found in the book.'

'Yes. And before you ask, I don't know who it was.'

'Honestly?'

Joe turns, leaning against the sink. 'Honestly. And Dorothy didn't know, either. Mum won't say – she reckons I'll only go and have it out with them. But ever since I started earning I've given her money. Dorothy did, too.'

'Where does she get the rest? And you two weren't always earning, so . . . ?'

'The housekeeping. It's a running joke, how bad she is with money – Dad saying she ought to take lessons off Mrs Hewitt, that sort of thing.'

'Doesn't Charles ever ask her to . . . you know . . . *account* for it?'

Joe shakes his head. 'He gets fed up with her sometimes, but so long as there's a decent meal on the table and he's got enough to put on the horses, he just puts up with it, like when she's bad with her nerves. He gets good wages, and there's what he does on the side, as well.'

'With Mr Hewitt, you mean?'

'Uh-huh.'

'And you have *no* idea who it is?'

'Could be a few people. I can't go round asking, can I? "Please sir, are you blackmailing my mum because she's a bigamist?" Dorothy and I did try following her to see if she was meeting anyone to give them money, or sending it in a letter, but she was careful to do anything like that when we weren't around. And now it's just me. But you know something, Millie? After what you told me about that list – once I'd figured out what it was – and about Mum dying, well . . . I'm going to find out who it is if it's the last thing I do, because I reckon it was their fault just as much as any illness. And when I do—'

'Joe, I get it.'

He stares at me, eyes wide and jaw clenched.

'I totally understand how you feel, and we'll find out who it is, OK? Maybe we can even get some of the money back – but right now, we have to save Annie. So count to ten, OK?' Joe blinks, surprised. 'Just, like, in your head or whatever. And take deep breaths. We *have* to do this one thing at a time, right?'

He nods and holds up his hand, like, *Give me a minute.*

'OK?'

'OK.'

'So . . . Does Frank know about the blackmail?'

'No. Mum's just as adamant about that.'

'Because he's violent?'

'Because he's all over the place! One minute it's "I love you" and "I'm sorry", and "forgive me", and the next he's talking about going to the police if she stops seeing him. Then he'll disappear for months on end and turn up again like a bad penny. He was always planning some great scheme that was going to make him rich and we could go and live with him in a big house and all the rest of it, but none of it came to anything.' Joe rolls his eyes. 'Where Annie got all her pie in the sky from, I suppose.' Rose has still got a soft spot for Frank despite everything, I think – that photo hidden in her bedside cabinet. 'I asked him once, why he was such a . . . why he was like that, and he said it was the effect of the war. And it's true it could make people a bit –' Joe taps his forehead – 'but he was no bloody good before – sorry for the language, Millie, but it's the truth – so I reckon that was just an excuse.'

'Does he want Rose to leave Charles and go back to him?'

'Doesn't seem like it. He wants to see us, though. Well, her and me and Dorothy, anyway. He's never been interested in Annie.'

Her name seems to echo round the room, silent but impossibly loud. Then Joe buries his face in his hands. *'Annie.'*

I jump up and hug him. Even when I'd told him about Rose, he hadn't cried, but now it's like a dam has burst – not just tears but deep, shuddering sobs, coming from somewhere right down inside.

'Sorry,' he gasps. 'I'm so sorry.'

'Stop it.' I rub his back. 'Nothing to be sorry about.'

We stand there by the sink for so long that I wonder if he's crying every tear he's held back since childhood. Perhaps he didn't even cry when Dorothy and Kathleen died, because it wasn't manly or something, and he's been not crying for so long that he's forgotten how, because this is almost like choking.

'You're OK,' I tell him. I don't want to say, 'it's OK', like people usually do, because it – as in, this situation – is not OK at all, plus there's worse to come. 'I'll do my best to help you.'

Eventually, he disengages himself and turns away from me

to pull a handkerchief out of his pocket and blow his nose. He's muttering angrily under his breath – guessing he's telling himself off for crying – and I feel like I shouldn't say anything, so I just stand there while he blows his nose two more times and shoves his handkerchief away again.

Eventually, he turns round, but he can't look at me. 'I'm sorry, Millie. That was ... That ... .'

'That was a perfectly normal thing to do,' I finish. 'Everyone's allowed to cry, Joe.'

He looks at me like, *yeah, right*, then turns his back on me again and starts spooning loose tea into the big brown teapot.

'I mean it. Being upset doesn't make you ... I don't know, less of a man or something.'

'It's silly.' He thumps the lid back on the caddy with unnecessary force.

'No, it *isn't*.'

He turns back to me and it's like he's about to argue, but something stops him. Instead, we just stare at each other and it's weird because, despite everything, I have this really strong feeling that he wants to kiss me. My memory of our first kiss – or what I *think* was our first kiss – is like a kind of electric charge in the air, and I can't tell if he's feeling it, or if it's just me. He makes a small move towards me, and I can feel his breath on my face—

And then a weird shrieking sound from behind him makes me jump back.

Joe makes a spluttering almost-laugh noise. 'Don't you have these?' He takes the kettle off the gas and the shrieking stops.

I can't tell if he's relieved or disappointed, but it's kind of awkward, so I reckon we better get back to the subject of what's going on in his family. 'So,' I say, 'Frank knows about ... all of this, right?'

'Mum couldn't tell him anything because she hardly ever knows where he is, but he reads the paper. He carried on like anything when he heard about Dorothy and Kathleen – his beautiful daughter and all the rest of it. To hear him talk, you'd think he'd brought Dorothy up single-handed. But that's him all over, making a drama out of everything with him in the main part – and always the victim. Mum was in bits, but oh no, nobody in the world could suffer as much as him. Selfish bastard.' Joe picks up the kettle and pours water into the teapot. 'Sorry, Millie.'

'What for?'

'Swearing.'

'Oh, right. That's OK. What about when you told him about Annie this morning?'

'Even *he* knew he couldn't make that all about him. He was just ... really quiet. Hardly ever seen him like that before.'

I sit down at the table again. I'm not surprised Frank went quiet – it's like it's too terrible to think about. And poor Rose, upstairs ... 'Does your mum ever talk about her own childhood?'

'Not really.' Joe has his back to me, stirring the pot. 'She once said that Granddad was violent. You know – street angel, house devil. She told us she was relieved when he died because it meant she and Nana could get some peace, but then,' he looks round, grimacing, 'she met Frank, didn't she?'

I've never heard 'street angel, house devil', before, but I know immediately what it means. 'And he was the same,' I say.

'Worse, because Granddad was a foreman in a factory, so at least he got good money.'

I wait until Joe puts two cups of tea on the table and sits down opposite me. 'You don't think, if Charles found out about Frank, he might have tried to kill your mum, but it went wrong?'

'He's not the type to use poison. And if he found out, I reckon he'd track Frank down and bash the living daylights out of him before he did anything else.'

'OK. What about the other way round?'

'How do you mean?'

'If Frank found out that Charles had done something terrible?'

Joe looks bewildered. 'I know the stuff he does with Mr Hewitt is . . . ' he taps the side of his nose with one finger, 'but I bet Frank's done worse.'

'It's not about pinching things from the army place, Joe. And Frank might not know anything about it . . . But there's something I need to tell you.'

Chapter 53

By the time I've finished explaining about what I found in the garden, what Shirley said, and my conversation with Kieran afterwards, Joe is white with fury.

'You're sure?'

'I wouldn't have told you otherwise. Joe, I'm really—'

'I'll kill him.'

Before I can stop him, he snatches one of the cups off its saucer and hurls it against the wall, then jumps up so fast that his chair clatters to the floor behind him. He's glaring at me, like he doesn't know what to do next but it's going to be violent.

'Stop!' I run round the table. When I grab hold of his arms, I can feel a current of rage pulsing under his skin. 'Joe, please. Wait. Calm down.'

I put my arms round him again, this time as tight as I can, to stop him damaging himself or anything else. With my face against his chest, I can feel the tightness of his jaw through the top of my head. For a few moments, the only sound is his ragged breathing and a series of drips as tea from the cup he threw trickles off the edge of the dresser top onto the floor. I can see, out of the corner of my eye, that the rest of it has run down the pale green wall.

'That . . .' The next word comes out as a growl.

'I know, Joe.' I'm clutching him so hard that it's making my shoulders hurt. 'He's a pervert and he's vile. But getting angry will just make things worse, and it won't help Annie. We need to work out what happened, and then we can make him pay for it.'

Joe jerks backwards out of my grip. 'Do you think he did it to Annie as well?'

'No, I don't. I think Annie wanted—'

'No!' Joe's right in my face, yelling, so I can feel spit land on my cheek. 'That's disgusting! Annie's totally innocent about sex. You can't say—'

'Please, Joe. *Listen*. You said yourself that Annie wanted attention. She didn't know that the attention Dorothy was getting from Charles was sex, because – like you said – she's innocent. When you said about her being soppy and sitting in Victor's lap, it did seem a bit strange, but now it makes sense. I'm guessing she did it with your dad, as well.'

'Yes. Yes, she did.' Joe stares into space for a moment, his face expressionless. 'I should have protected her, Millie.' He clenches his fists. 'Her and Dorothy. I should have—'

'How? You were a *child*, Joe. None of this is your fault.'

Joe shakes his head furiously, then turns to me, eyes blazing. 'Do you think he killed Dorothy and Kathleen as well?'

'I don't know – although I don't think he's the type, either. Like you said.'

We stare at each other. Joe's eyes are wild, and he looks as stiff and tense as a dog about to attack.

'Keep calm, OK?' I tell him. 'Let's sit back down and try to—'

Footsteps, then voices. Someone's opening the front door.

'Oopsy daisy!'

Charles's voice, sounding tipsy, if not actually drunk. I grab Joe's hand and, muttering 'Remember what I said', into his ear, pull him out into the garden. Then I remember the handbag with the address in it, charge back inside, and just manage to grab it off the table and close the door behind me before Charles and Mr and Mrs Hewitt come into the kitchen. Joe slides down underneath the windowsill, looking furious, and I kneel up – not comfortable on concrete – so I can see what's happening.

The men seem sort of dishevelled, so I guess Charles has been trying to forget about the reprieve failing, and Mr Hewitt's been helping. Both the Hewitts plonk themselves down at the table, and Charles heads – *shi-i-i-t* – for the back door.

'Hide,' I hiss at Joe, and shove Rose's handbag at him. For a moment, I think he's going to argue, but then he scoots sideways and hunkers down between the coal bunker and the bathroom wall, out of sight, just as the door swings open and Charles appears. He's a bit unsteady, with that weird pinpointy concentration that drunk people get when they're trying to focus, but he manages to collect three bottles of beer from the crate by the garden shed.

'Let's have some tea as well, shall we?' Mrs Hewitt's voice. At least someone's being sensible. I turn back to the window as Charles fumbles, one-handed, with the door.

Mr Hewitt's still sitting at the table with his back to me, but Mrs Hewitt's got up and is standing in front of the sink – and therefore right in front of me, on the other side of the window frame – holding the teapot. 'Still warm.'

'I suppose Rose couldn't sleep.'

'Poor dear.' Mrs Hewitt's expression, as she says this, is so totally opposite to the sympathetic tone in her voice that it makes me feel as cold as if I'd been suddenly drenched in icy water. Her eyes are beady and mean – and of course she has no idea that anyone can see her. A crunching sound behind her makes her turn. 'Someone must have dropped a cup. I'll get the dustpan and brush.'

'Leave it.' Charles lurches as he kicks a piece of the broken cup out of the way. 'Here you go.' He's slurring, clumsy as he thumps the bottles down on the table. 'We don't need tea, Moll – just get us some glasses.'

'If you're sure.' Mrs Hewitt removes the rest of the tea things and takes two glasses from the dresser. 'In that case, I might just nip upstairs and make sure Rose is all right.'

'Good girl.' Mr Hewitt leans over and pats her on the bottom.

That look. Mrs Hewitt may be acting the kind, concerned friend now, but my spidey senses are telling me that something is *wrong*.

'I'm going after her,' I tell Joe. 'You stay here.'

Chapter 54

Joe glares at me and makes a move to stand up in the cramped space. 'I *mean* it. This is not the moment to lose your shit.'

The glare turns to shock. OMG, now he's pearl-clutching because of a tiny swear. What is *wrong* with these people? 'Look, do *not* go back into the house, OK? Whatever happens, stay *here*.'

He looks furious, but nods, then raises his eyebrows and jerks his head at the window.

'Guess so.' I lever myself onto the flat top of the coal bunker, then put one foot on the windowsill and scramble sideways, so that half of me is inside the room. It's a good job they opened the window wide to let all the smoke out, and that I put away all the stuff I washed up earlier, because I have to clamber right over the draining board before I let myself down onto the floor.

I tiptoe up the stairs and edge myself noiselessly round the door of Rose and Charles's bedroom, which is ajar.

The curtains are drawn, but the lamp on Rose's bedside table is on, casting a pinkish light over the pillow. Rose looks to be asleep, and Mrs Hewitt is standing by the bed, looking down at her.

'Just come up to see how you're doing, dear.'

Rose murmurs something. Those new tablets may be strong, but my guess is that Rose has been taking sleeping pills for so long that they wouldn't have as much effect as they should.

Mrs Hewitt perches on the side of the bed, her back to me. 'I'm ever so sorry about Annie, dear. I know you all did your best, but ... what can't be cured must be endured, as they say.' She reaches out a hand to stroke Rose's hair. 'Poor dear.'

Rose makes a small sound.

'There, there.' Mrs Hewitt moves her hand away and sits so still for such a long time that I start to wonder if I've made a mistake. Telling Rose she has to endure the situation isn't exactly helpful – I mean, what does Mrs Hewitt think she's been doing for the past few months? – but I guess it must be one of those things people come out with when a terrible thing has happened and they feel they have to say *something*.

'At least you're comfortable, dear. Can I get you anything?'

Another murmur from Rose.

'You're all right, dear? That's good.' After a moment, she adds, 'And have you got something for me, dear?'

Wait, what? I inch forward until I'm about a metre away from where Mrs Hewitt is sitting. Rose opens her eyes very slightly for a moment, and slurs something.

'Where, dear?' Mrs Hewitt leans over so that her ear is by Rose's mouth.

Rose must have said something I couldn't hear because a moment later Mrs Hewitt straightens up and turns to the bedside table.

'In here, dear?' She pulls the miniature chest of drawers jewellery box towards her and starts opening the drawers.

I inch closer, but all I can see are bits of jewellery – until she opens the bottom drawer and, after a bit of scrabbling, pulls something out . . .

Pots and kettles. Mrs Hewitt's sly way of reminding Rose about what she knew. Folded paper, green swirls on a white background, the number one in a geometric design. It's money. Mrs Hewitt holds it up between her fingers. A one-pound note in 1955 is worth a *hell* of a lot more than our pound coins are.

'Much obliged, dear. Now, are you sure I can't get you anything?'

You total and utter bitch, I think, as Rose makes a slight movement with her head.

Mrs Hewitt blackmailed Rose for years, and – I think of the dates on the list of payments – had carried on getting money out of her even when she was dying. How vile can you *be*?

'Ta-ta, then.'

I feel like snatching the money right out of her greedy, evil hand, but I don't. Instead, with a jolt of pure adrenaline that powers through my body like electricity, I have a brainwave. While she's getting her purse out of her bag to put the note away, I dash out, open the door to what was Annie and Kathleen's room, and start banging away on the old typewriter. I can't see a return key, but that doesn't matter because what I have to say will fit on one line. It's *really* noisy: *chik chak chik chak chik chak—*

'Des?'

The typewriter table is facing the doorway, so she can't miss it – and when I glance over my shoulder, she's coming out of Rose and Charles's room, just in time to see the keys going up and down all by themselves – *chik chak chik chak chik chak* – and—

'Oh, my God!'

Now she's staring at the typewriter, mouth wide open. There's a smear of lipstick on her yellow teeth. Just a couple more words . . .

Chik chak chik chak chik chak chik chak

I jump as her scream cuts through the air like a knife, but I keep typing.

Chik chak chik chak

Shouts from the kitchen, feet on the stairs. Just two more letters to go . . .

Chik chak

And a full stop.

Chik!

Mrs Hewitt comes past me as I bolt out of the room. She's brave, I'll give her that, going in for a closer look . . . She's shaking as she rips the paper out of the typewriter rollers, scrunches it up and stuffs it into her coat pocket. I get halfway up the stairs that lead to Joe's room, just before Mr Hewitt appears round the corner from the lower landing with Charles behind him, leaning against the wall to keep upright.

'What's up?'

Mrs Hewitt's eyes are like saucers, and she's still quivering with fright, but she says, 'Sorry. I just gave myself a scare, that's all.'

'Sounded like a bit more than that.'

'Really, it's nothing. Just me being silly.'

'You sure?' Mr Hewitt looks through the door into Annie and Kathleen's room. 'Funny. Could have sworn I heard someone typing just now – wondered what you were doing up here.'

I almost see the cogs in Mrs Hewitt's mind whirring as she tries to come up with an explanation, but she doesn't have to because the next second Rose appears and leans against the bedroom doorway, pale and groggy in her slip, blinking as though she's in a dream. 'What's happening?' Her voice is thin and scared.

'Nothing, dear. It's all right.' Mrs Hewitt takes Rose's arm. 'Let me help you back to bed. I'll be down in a minute,' she tells Mr Hewitt, who's looking doubtful, then practically yanks Rose back towards the bed.

'Brandy,' says Charles. 'Need some brandy. All need brandy.'

'All right, Charlie. Let's go and find some, shall we?'

Charles starts going back down the stairs and bumps into Joe, who's on the way up. Charles staggers backwards – caught by Mr Hewitt on the stair above – and blinks at him. 'Where you come from?'

I cross my fingers. *Please don't lose it, please . . . please . . .*

Joe, who is still carrying Rose's handbag, glares at him. My heart sinks, but he just says, 'The sitting room. I must have fallen asleep.'

'Poor old boy.' Joe's eyes narrow. Charles reaches out to pat him on the shoulder, pitching forward when Joe sidesteps and almost falling down the stairs. 'Don't be like tha', old boy . . .'

'Come on.' Mr Hewitt takes charge, steering Charles with a hand on his shoulder. 'You best go up to bed, son,' he tells

Joe. 'I'm so sorry. Try and get some rest if you can.' His voice is quiet and kind.

'Nigh' nigh', old boy,' says Charles, as they stumble back down to the kitchen. 'Nigh' nigh'.'

I motion to Joe to stay where he is on the landing until Mrs Hewitt reappears. She looks furtive and shaken, and when she sees Joe, she gasps. 'You gave me a fright, son.'

'Another one?' Joe's got his back to me so I can't see his expression, but his voice is steely and suspicious. 'You scare easy.'

'Yes.' Now Mrs Hewitt looks even more flustered. 'Like I said, dear. Just me being silly. I won't disturb you any further.'

Once Mrs Hewitt is safely back in the kitchen – we can hear cupboard doors banging downstairs, which I'm guessing means the search for brandy is underway – I put up one finger for Joe to wait, and go back into Rose and Charles's room. Rose is curled in the foetal position, fast asleep, and she doesn't stir when I slide open the bottom drawer of the miniature furniture chest.

The pound note has been returned.

Mrs Hewitt got my message, all right:

Give the money back, bitch.
Leave Rose alone.

Chapter 55

'No wonder your mum didn't like her. And of course she knew Rose before she married Charles, didn't she? So she must have spotted Frank and – unlike Shirley's mum – she knew exactly who he was. And Rose couldn't retaliate by dobbing in the Hewitts for stealing from the army because that would have got Charles into trouble, too . . . Like one of those films where all the people end up in a circle, pointing guns at each other. But,' I add quickly, because Joe is pacing up and down the room like a tiger and obviously about to go off on one, 'it's one problem solved, isn't it? I'll bet she never asks Rose for money again. She won't be able to convince herself she imagined what happened, because she stuffed that paper in her pocket.'

'I'd like to wring her neck.' Joe stops in front of the bed, where I'm sitting. 'Thanks, Millie. I knew you must have done something, because she *really* screamed. God, I could—'

'I know, but this isn't the time.'

'Do you think Mr Hewitt knows?'

'Well, she took my little note out of the typewriter quick enough—'

'Because she didn't want Charles to see. Not that he's in a condition to read anything at the moment.'

'Or to take in much of what anyone's saying – but she kept it together enough to tell Mr Hewitt that it was nothing, even though she was properly terrified. And when Rose came out of the bedroom, just before you appeared, she hustled her back in there really fast so he wouldn't ask any more questions. Also, didn't you say that Charles and Mr Hewitt had a joke about how Mrs Hewitt was good with money and Rose wasn't?'

'Yeah, although that's more Dad. Mr Hewitt never says it. Also ...' Joe breaks off, and sits down beside me, looking thoughtful.

'What?'

'Well, the first time you said Mum didn't really like Mrs Hewitt, I thought about it afterwards, and it's true. I supposed I'd assumed they couldn't be proper friends because Mum's a lot better-looking than Mrs Hewitt, and girls and women can be really jealous and catty ... Dorothy definitely had that problem, and you must, too ...' He glances at me, then looks away, which is just as well because I'm *so* not going there. 'But anyway, the odd thing is that, despite Mum hating having the nicked stuff under the stairs, she actually *likes* Mr Hewitt. And he likes her – I don't mean like *that*, although I suppose he might.' I bet he does, I think, and I bet Mrs Hewitt knows it. 'But I've often seen them having a laugh together, and she's relaxed, you know? And yes, Mr Hewitt pinches stuff from the Naafi, but that's the army, not a person. Charles and Rose are his friends, so ... honour among thieves, and all that.'

I've never heard the expression before, but I can see what he means. Then something occurs to me. 'Joe, you know you said that Rose and Mrs Hewitt were having an argument when you came home on the day of the party? When one of them said something about the never-never? Well, supposing they didn't mean actual . . . what's it called . . . '

'Hire purchase.'

'Right. What if it wasn't that they were talking about, but the blackmail money? Because that really *would* be the never-never, wouldn't it? I mean, if you bought a car or something, you'd pay it off in the end, wouldn't you? But with blackmail, you'd never finish paying. Or . . . ' I take a deep breath and then, with a plunging feeling, like if you were in a lift and the cable was cut, I say, 'Not until one of you died.'

'Mum *did* die. You told me.'

'Before that, I mean. What if . . . '

Silence. The air seems to be pressing in on me as I stare down at the threadbare rug. Beside me, Joe is completely still. After what seems like an age, he says, very quietly, 'What do you mean?'

My mouth is so dry I almost can't get the words out. 'Rose was making the scones and sandwiches, right? Well – and I know you won't want to hear this – what if she'd decided to poison Mrs Hewitt? Or . . . ' now I've started, I reckon I might as well go for it, 'if she'd found out about Dorothy – the argument that Shirley overheard and wrote about in her diary – and decided to kill Charles?'

Joe opens his mouth to answer, but I hold up a hand to stop him, because it's like somebody suddenly lit a fire in my brain. 'When people are in a corner – like, totally trapped – they get desperate, right? You said she'd kept some sandwiches back – for you and Charles, only you said you don't like fish paste, so as long as she didn't put any poison in the jam ones or the other ones . . . '

Joe is staring at me, appalled. 'That's my mother you're talking about.'

'Yes, I know, and I'm sorry, but—'

'She'd never let Annie take the blame – not in a million years. No mother would do that, unless they were that thing you said – a psy . . . something.'

'Psychopath.'

'Well, she isn't. She loves us.'

'I'm not saying she doesn't! Just that she's been under a lot of pressure for a very long time, and people get broken, that's all.'

'It can't have been her. Look, we don't actually know that Dorothy didn't tell Mum about what Charles did. I mean, she might have worked it out and then confronted Dorothy and got her to admit it. And if Mum had said that to Charles, then perhaps he was afraid that one of them could have told somebody else, and—'

'I thought you said he wasn't the type to use poison? And when did he get the chance, anyway?'

'I don't know, but . . . ' Joe shakes his head miserably.

'Also, if Rose had even the slightest suspicion that he'd killed them, wouldn't she have gone to the police? I mean, knowing what he'd already done to Dorothy, it would have been a bit late to worry about what the neighbours thought, or caring if anyone else would find out about Frank, surely?'

320

'I don't *know!*'

'Keep your voice down,' I hiss.

Joe slumps sideways on the bed, hands over his face. 'It's like a nightmare.' His voice is tight, as if he's trying not to cry. Instinctively, I reach over to stroke his arm, and he grabs my hand and holds it tight.

We stay like that for a couple of minutes, Joe in a tight ball of misery, and me wishing I could just wave a wand and make everything right.

'Come on.' I rub his back with my other hand. 'Let's try and think about this from the beginning.'

When I start to run through what I know about what happened on the day of the party, it occurs to me that I never asked Joe anything about what happened *after* the meal.

'I know you must have gone over all this with the police, Joe, but we've already found some stuff out, so—'

'No, it's fine. I mean,' Joe adds, bitterly, 'what have I got to lose?'

'OK. What time did you get home?'

'About eleven.'

'Did you eat the rest of your sandwiches?'

Joe shakes his head. 'When I saw how upset Mum was, that was the last thing on my mind. It was pretty chaotic. Victor was here, and Mrs Millichip and Shirley, and nobody seemed to know what to do – and then the doctor came . . .'

'Mrs Millichip and Shirley? Why were they here?'

'Mum invited them in when they all came back from the hospital.'

'But—'

'She didn't know anything was wrong, did she? Mrs Millichip's always helping, and Mum wanted to return the favour. But by that time, Dorothy and Kathleen had started to feel ill, so she sent them upstairs to lie down.'

'What about Mrs Hewitt?'

'She wasn't here. I think she must have gone straight home from the hospital once they'd realised Shirley was going to be OK.'

'And Charles?'

'He came in soon after me. I remember Mrs Millichip making tea for everyone, and people coming in and out, but not where everyone was, or—'

'What sort of state was the kitchen in?'

'How do you mean?'

'Well, was the party food still on the table?'

'No. Mum and Mrs Hewitt had cleared up when they got back.' Joe narrows his eyes, imagining the scene. 'That's right – no cloth or anything. All that was left on the table was the flowers I got for Mum.'

'So all the plates were washed and put away?'

'Everything.' He doesn't even stop to think. I guess I must look surprised because he says. 'Mum's quite particular about that – or she was *before*. It was one of the ways we'd know if she was OK, because the house would be clean and tidy. When her nerves got bad, she'd stop doing that stuff. We learnt to look for the signs.'

'I get it. What about the leftover food?'

'Some of it must have gone in the bin – if it was half-eaten or something – but there was at least one scone left, because the police tested it, and they definitely kept the rest of the cake because that got tested, too. Dad – Charles – put the dustbins out when he got back. But at that time, nobody – not even Dr Sims – was talking about poisoning, so it wouldn't have occurred to anyone to keep the stuff . . . Actually, I think Mum did throw away the sandwiches on the table – or Mrs Millichip did – because the police asked about them later. But I know they tested the ones from the pantry, because they talked about that in court. But I didn't actually look in the pantry when I came in, and I'm pretty sure that Da— that Charles didn't, either.'

'Right. But some of the evidence could have been taken away by the dustmen?'

'Yes, because they were due in the morning – why the bins were out. Kathleen was taken bad at about four a.m., so Mum called Dr Sims and he came back and gave her an injection, and while he was here Dorothy got worse, so he called an ambulance. He didn't want to move Kathleen because she was too ill.' Joe's face creases in distress, and I can imagine what he's remembering – the half-lit house, air stiff with anxiety; nobody daring to put their fears into words in case they scared the others, but offering to make tea instead; then hushed conversations, trying to work out what the doctor wasn't saying; the neighbours twitching their bedroom curtains as the ambulance arrived before dawn . . . 'Nobody knew what to do, even Dr Sims. Mum kept asking him if they'd be all right, and it was obvious he didn't know what to tell her – up till then, he hadn't even mentioned food poisoning, let alone . . .' Joe shakes his head. 'And when they took Kathleen's body away, and

323

then Victor rang to say that Dorothy had died, nobody would tell us anything. We were just … Oh, Millie, it was *awful*. But the police didn't come till the day after.'

'You're doing really well.' I lean over and squeeze his hand. 'So … *somebody* had over twenty-four hours to remove the tin of poison from the house if they'd wanted to.'

'And Annie didn't! In the court they were making out that she'd planned all this as if she were some sort of criminal mastermind, and she's just not capable of it. I mean, the first thing you'd do is get rid of the evidence—'

'But no one else did, either. Which means that either they meant to incriminate Annie, or they couldn't get back to the house for some reason … Who was here on that day?'

'Well, the four of us. The Hewitts came over at some point, I remember that, and Mrs Millichip, but no one else.'

For a moment it's like when you run out of charge in the middle of something and the screen goes blank – then I have this really clear picture of myself staring at those big china pots in the Driscolls' pantry, thinking I'd forgotten something important …
'When you came in that night, what was Shirley doing?'

'What's *that* got to do with anything?' Joe looks irritated.

'Try and remember, OK?'

'Helping her mum make tea, I think. She was in the kitchen, anyway.'

I look over at Joe's alarm clock. It's one of those old-school round ones on little legs, that look as though they're wearing earmuffs, and it says 8.15.

'What time does Shirley go to work?'

'About now, I think … Don't worry,' he adds sardonically, 'I've got today off, and tomorrow. It's all arranged. Nice of them, wasn't it?'

'Listen, Joe, I'll be back, OK?'

Chapter 56

I charge down the stairs – I can hear Charles and the Hewitts talking quietly in the kitchen – and let myself out of the front door as quietly as possible, leaving it ajar behind me.

The street's the busiest I've ever seen it: people going off to work or the shops, kids on their way to school, and an old man walking a dog. No Shirley, but from where I'm standing in the tiny front garden of Number 37, I can see movement in one of the upstairs rooms, so I don't reckon she's left yet.

I'm right. Thirty seconds later the front door opens and out she comes. She jumps when she sees me. 'What you lurking there for?'

'Waiting for you.'

She looks me up and down. 'To take me to a fancy-dress party?'

'Ha, ha. Shirley, can you help me?'

'Why should I?'

'So I can help Joe. Annie's reprieve was turned down.'

'Oh.' She stops, one hand on the gate. She's not looking at me now, and there's a hard flush on her cheeks. 'I ought to tell Mum, so she can . . . ' She looks past me to Number 37.

'Of course, but in a minute. Can you just tell me something?'

Shirley's eyes flit from the house to me and back again. 'All right, if it's quick.'

'It's quick. I know your mum's a really good neighbour, and that you were both there on the night of the tea party – after, I mean.'

'Mum said I had to come in because I was concussed, and she didn't want to leave me alone.'

'Sure – I mean, that's really sensible. Did you help your mother in the kitchen?'

'Yes. She made tea, and I was starting to feel better, so—'

'Did you go into the pantry?'

'Mmmm . . .' Shirley screws up her face, thinking. 'Yes, I did. Why?'

'Were there any sandwiches?'

'Yes, on a plate.'

'Just one?'

'Yes. I remember that. Someone had put a cloth over it. Fish paste.'

'You're sure? All fish paste?'

'Yes. I checked because I'd missed my dinner and I was hungry, but I don't like fish paste. So? I didn't do anything wrong.'

'Of course not, it's fine. Just . . . Joe was confused about something, that's all. He'll be really grateful,' I gabble, backing towards the front door. 'Thank you so much. Have a lovely day.' I can feel Shirley's eyes on me as I push the door open and go back inside, and for a moment I think she might try to follow me . . .

Then I hear the click-clack of her heels on the path as she goes back into Number 35 to find her mum.

When I get back up to Joe's room, he's leaning over his desk looking down at the street. 'What was that about?'

'I've just told Shirley you're going to be *really* grateful to her.' I roll my eyes.

'Thanks *a lot*. And . . . ?'

I explain about the plate of sandwiches left in the pantry. 'But you said Rose left them on plates, right? Plates *plural* – not just one.'

'Definitely. I saw her do it.'

'I'm kind of surprised they didn't mention that in court – like, where did the other sandwiches go?'

Joe shakes his head. 'I told you – they'd already decided Annie was guilty. And every time Mr Wetherby tried to make a point about anything like that, the judge said it wasn't relevant and basically told him to shut up. And Mum was in such a state – not sleeping, not eating – that she got confused when she was in the witness box and Matheson Landers kept bullying her, so she got in even more of a muddle and it looked like she was either lying or . . . ' He taps his forehead. 'She fainted afterwards – right outside the courtroom, so Mr Brighouse paid for me to take her home in a taxi. He was furious with old Landers, but there was nothing he could do. Honestly, Millie, the whole thing was a *disaster*.'

'I can imagine. Sorry – didn't mean to sidetrack you. But, missing sandwiches . . . '

Joe sits quite still for a long time, eyes narrowed. He's obviously thinking about something, and I'm starting to worry that he's still dwelling on what happened in the court when he says, 'Thing is, Dorothy wasn't a big eater, and nor was Kathleen – well, not sandwiches, anyway. But Annie . . . Remember I told you how I'd said not to eat anything until the others arrived, or I'd find out and tell Mum? Well, she must have waited until I'd gone, and then I reckon she'd have stared at all that food until she couldn't resist. She couldn't cut a slice of cake – too obvious – or have a scone, because Mum only made a few so that might be noticed, too, but the sandwiches . . . There were lots of those, and she wouldn't have been able to stop at one, or even two or three.'

'So then she'd have to get the other sandwiches from the pantry to fill the gaps on the plates. But why not tell the police that?'

'Because of what I'd said! She'd have been scared when the police were questioning her. I mean, she knew that Dorothy and Kathleen were dead, so it was serious – but in her mind, getting into trouble with Mum was serious, too, and she wouldn't necessarily have made a distinction between the two. If Annie'd been so full of sandwiches that she hadn't wanted any more when they sat down to eat properly, then it would make sense that she'd have a scone – because Mum wasn't there, and Dorothy wasn't the type to make a fuss about eating things in the right order. So of course that's what she'd say – because she'd think anything else would get her into trouble . . . Oh, God. This is all my fault.' Joe jumps up and – before I can stop him – slams his head against the wall, hard.

'Don't!' I grab hold of him and, after a tussle, manage to shove him back down on the bed. 'Please, just wait. We might be getting somewhere, and hurting yourself isn't the answer.' Joe looks a bit dazed, which isn't surprising, and, after a long moment, he nods, but I stay standing in front of him, just in case.

'OK, so everything I know about police procedure comes from crime dramas, so half of it probably isn't right, but what about her solicitor?'

Joe squints at me. 'She didn't have one then, only later.'

'Oh, OK. I think the rules might be different in my time. Anyway, if that's the reason why there was only one plate of sandwiches in the pantry by the time Shirley and her mum arrived, the ones that got replaced must have been meat paste and jam, because she just told me that the ones left were all fish paste.'

'So . . . ' Joe speaks slowly, thinking aloud, 'if Annie wasn't poisoned by the sandwiches on the table, that means it must have been only the *replacement* ones that were poisoned. And if they were jam and meat paste, not fish paste, that must mean they were intended for Mum or me.'

Joe stares at me, face white, eyes burning. He looks so intense that I'm afraid he's going try and do more damage to himself, so I hold my hands up for calm. 'Because?'

'Neither of us like fish paste. No one does except Charles. And Mrs Hewitt. I know she does, because we talked about it once.'

OK, so *that* was unexpected. It's like, everything I do causes Joe more pain.

I've let him down. I've been like, I'm from the future and we've got the internet and we know better about everything and I can help you, but I've just made it all worse. I can feel Joe's eyes burning into me, and I have no idea what to say.

I can't look at him. I get up and walk over to the window. I can hear Shirley's voice in my head – from my time, standing by the fence in her back garden – *You'll get things wrong, because everybody does . . . your answers won't be good enough.*

It's true.

I did one good thing: Mrs Hewitt won't cause any more problems. But the rest . . .

Annie has less than twenty-four hours to live. At 9 a.m. tomorrow, Ronald Rutherford will pull the lever and the trapdoor will open beneath her feet. As her body plummets downwards, her neck will break.

In Aylmer Terrace, everything will look the same, but it won't be.

And even if Rose isn't being hounded by a blackmailer, she'll still have Frank to contend with on top of everything else, and—

'Sorry, Joe. Say that again.'

'I don't know why anyone would want to kill me. It doesn't make sense – and I can't see why anyone would want to kill Mum, either. I know . . . all the stuff we've talked about . . . but . . . ' He shakes his head. 'To be honest, right now I wouldn't mind if somebody did want to kill me. Or even if they actually did kill me.' He's still staring at me, but now his pale face is set, as if he's come to a decision. 'If I ask you something, do you promise to answer honestly?'

There's a terrible stillness in the room. Time is waiting, like the noose above the trapdoor.

I know what he's going to ask.

Chapter 57

It's an effort to breathe because my rib cage suddenly feels two sizes too small. 'I might not know the answer.'

'I think you do. I'm asking in case it helps Annie.'

'I don't see how it can. Really, Joe, I—'

'I told you about Frank. You need to tell me what's going to happen to me.'

'I honestly don't think it'll help.'

'Can I be the judge of that?' Joe's voice is calm, almost gentle. 'It is me we're talking about, after all – and now I'm sure you know.'

'OK . . .Well, I know what's going to happen to you if . . . if this happens . . . but we've already stopped the blackmail, haven't we? So that's got to have changed something. And if we can save Annie, too, then your future will probably be totally different, and—'

'Just tell me.'

'Are you sure?'

'Yes!'

My rib cage seems to have shrunk even more as I come over to sit down next to him on the bed. 'This just feels so wrong, but . . .

look, I only know, like, really basic stuff about what happened – happens – to you, OK?'

'OK. Everything you know.' Joe's not looking at me now, which is a relief, but staring down at his shoes.

'Right. So, somewhere along the line you change your name from Driscoll to Palmer. I'm guessing because Rose tells you what Charles did, maybe at the same time as she gives you that paper with the list of all the blackmail money. I'm guessing it's you who smashes up the doll's house Charles made – maybe after your mum dies – and that you add the words to Dorothy and Kathleen's gravestone at some point, but I suppose we'll never know any of that for sure . . . When you're in your early fifties you live in a flat in Euston, so it looks like you never move very far . . . unless you go away and come back, of course.' I can hear myself gabbling, and I dig my nails into my palms to make myself slow down. 'You don't have a job when you're in Euston, and there isn't anything about a partner—'

'I thought you said I didn't have a job?'

'What? Oh, sorry, not a work partner, but like a wife or whatever. There wasn't anything about children, either.'

'That's a shame.' Joe says this really quietly, like he's talking to himself. 'What else?'

'Well, you become a bit paranoid – thinking someone was trying to get into your flat and writing to people in parliament – and you were kind of . . . ' I search for the word, 'reclusive. But,' I hurry on, trying to make it sound better, 'you were friendly with one of the neighbours. He didn't know anything about . . . all of this . . . but he said you used to chat.' God, that sounds lame – and just thinking about what comes next is making my throat dry up. Plus, I realise I've switched tenses – from the present to the past – which I'm guessing gives Joe a bit of a clue that he's not alive any more.

'How do you know this?' Joe's tone is calm and remote, like none of this is anything to do with him.

'It was in the paper.' I open my mouth again, but nothing else comes out.

'Because I died.' It isn't a question.

'Yes.' It's barely a whisper.

'In my early fifties.'

'I'm sorry, Joe.'

'That's not so bad.' This surprises me – but maybe people didn't live so long back then. I'm really hoping he won't ask anything else, but . . .

'I committed suicide, didn't I?' His voice is flat, almost robotic.

'Yes.' I put a hand on his back, which feels solid and stiff, like he's already lifeless.

He doesn't look at me.

'How?'

'Sleeping pills.'

'Who found me?'

'The police. The neighbour – your friend – was worried about you.' I don't care what he asks, I'm not telling him the rest.

'Did I leave a note?'

'The paper didn't mention one. Just that there was a book and some papers in a wastepaper basket, partly burnt. They didn't know if you'd set fire to them on purpose, or if it was an accident from a cigarette – so you must have started smoking – but they also said the flat was kind of messy, so maybe those things weren't even meant to be in the bin.'

'I see.'

I daren't look at him, but out of the corner of my eye I can see a muscle move in his jaw. It's like he can hear what I'm not saying.

'When I found I'd brought *The Robe* back to my time, it was sort of burnt round the edges – and of course it had the papers in it, so I reckon you were right that you put the papers in there.'

'For all the good it did. Anything else?'

I try to swallow, but I can't. I feel as if I'm choking. I point to the blue knitted rabbit on Joe's pillow. 'That was beside you.'

Joe leans over, pulls the rabbit into his arms, then sits, hunched over, staring at the floor.

Chapter 58

I don't know how long we sit there, side by side. Joe doesn't move or speak for ages, and I don't think I *can* speak. I tilt my head up and blink a lot, trying to stop myself crying.

Finally, he looks up and says, 'I checked Dorothy's old room after you'd gone. That book was on the shelf. It looked fine, and the papers and photo weren't there – which is fair enough, if they hadn't been put there or didn't exist yet. But the book must still be in your home, as well. I don't understand how it can be in two places at once.'

I'm not surprised he doesn't want to discuss his death any more. No one would. It's too big to think about, too final and terrible and strange – and that's for me, so what it must feel like for Joe . . .

But this, we can talk about. 'Well, I'm not sure how it works, but I think it's the same as with the clock: objects can exist in both our times at the same time as long as they're meant to be there, if you see what I mean. And obviously stuff happened to the book in between being here now and being in my time, which is why it looked different. And I know it applies to people as well – or to one person, anyway.' I explain about Mr Smith and the two clocks, and about Jean and Robbie.

'That's . . .' Joe looks like he's having trouble taking it all in, which is hardly surprising. 'But he can't save his wife and child – so that means you can't save Annie . . . so that's that. Why didn't you tell me before?' He throws the rabbit down on the bed and turns away from me. 'We might as well give up – and you can bugger off home.'

'No!' I grab his shoulder. 'Listen to me, Joe. When I asked Mr Smith about that, he said it's different for me – for *us* – because I'm not like him. He was actually here – alive in 1955 – so he formed a part of what happened to Jean and Robbie, even though it wasn't his fault or anything. I wasn't, which means that I'm only a . . .' I stop, trying to think of how Mr Smith put it. 'A possibility. He said I'd gone back in time by accident – because you and I connected through the clock, which was kind of random – but he reckoned I'd kept on coming back after the first time because I wanted to help. And I *do* want to help, Joe . . . and a possibility means a *chance*.'

There's a long silence before he turns round to face me. 'There's hardly any time left. What if you just disappear again?'

'I don't think I will.'

'But you can't know that.'

'The clock broke.'

'So . . .' Joe looks confused. 'How did you get here at all?'

'Because I've got this.' I put my hand in my pocket.

The minute my fingers touch the oscillator, I realise there's something different. It's still the same shape – a small, hard cylinder, and slightly sticky, like before, but there's something attached to it.

A piece of paper?

Slowly and carefully, I pull the whole thing out of my pocket. It's an ordinary sheet of paper from a pad, with ruled lines, folded in half and sort of crackly and a bit stiff, like it got wet and dried out again.

'What is it?'

'OK . . . so this –' I point to the oscillator – 'is the bit of the clock that contains the quartz. The minute I touched it, I found myself back here – and it was in my pocket, so I reckon that as long as I'm holding it, or I've got it on me somewhere, I can stay. But this bit of paper . . . I've never seen it before. It definitely wasn't in my pocket, and it doesn't look to me like it's from now, so I *think* the reason it might be here is that it's stuck to the cylinder.'

'All right . . . ' Joe sounds like he's hardly daring to breathe. 'Can you unfold it?'

It takes me a while, because I have to keep one hand on the cylinder, just in case, and I don't want to tear the paper, but after some fumbling I manage to get it flat on my knee. It's covered in a frantic scrawl, done with pencil pressed down so hard that in a couple of places it's gone through the paper.

'The writing's like mine,' Joe says quietly, 'only . . . '

'Angry.' I don't look at him.

'Go on, read it.'

'OK.' I'm desperate to know what it says, but terrified at the same time. My hands are shaking so much I nearly drop the whole thing. 'Here goes.' It's quite hard to make out some of the words, so I'm slow, but I'm determined to get through it all.

'*Frank's in the Middlesex* ... What's the Middlesex?'

'Hospital in Fitzrovia. Well, that's where it is now, anyway.'

'Right. *Been so long, didn't know he was still alive but had ... letter. F dying, wanted to talk to me. Difficult to hear. At first ... sentimental – how much he loves us, etc. Said Dorothy found out it was Mrs Hewitt getting money off Mum. D said it was his fault, he must do something. He told her he'd fix it, then went to see Mum at A. Terrace on day of party in morning. Did not know about party but said no one saw him go in house. Mum ... frightened, asked him to leave. He wanted to talk to her about Mrs H but when ... neighbour came to door and they were on step ... chatting so he thought how to make it up to Mum. Said he'd asked her who coming so knew Mrs H would be there. Got ... poison from shed and put it in some sandwiches, with gloves. Crying, said he was trying to help but forgot it was fish paste we didn't like and put stuff in meat paste, just one plate – said chose meat paste not jam because you can mistake for ptomaine poisoning and nobody will know. Had remembered about shed from Dorothy saying Annie helped Charles clearing out. Said he ended up not discussing Mrs H with Mum because he thought he could solve the problem without telling her and she wanted him to go. When I said why didn't he tell police he started crying, saying it was terrible about Annie. All ... self-pity, kept saying he felt so ... guilty as if that makes it all right. Wanted me to feel sorry for him! Said he'd give my name to the hospital for who to contact when he died so I would make the ... arrangement. Said I want nothing to do with it, they can put him straight in the ... incinerator. Couldn't look at him. Tried speaking to the police but they don't want to know. Wrote to . . . Kenneth Baker but no proper reply just . . . standard letter. Nobody cares, they won't listen and it is too late . . . Oh, Joe, I'm so sorry . . .* '

'Just keep reading.'

'OK. Yes. Right . . . *I've had enough. No point talking to Dr Joffe, this is better. Joe Palmer, 13 November 1991.*'

Chapter 59

'*Ask you to forgive me* . . . I reckon that burnt piece of paper was from his letter to you. I suppose he must have tracked you down, and written it when he went into the hospital.'

'Bastard!' Vibrating with fury and frustration, Joe launches himself off the bed and starts pacing up and down the room again. 'Bastard, bastard, BASTARD!' He whirls round savagely and kicks the desk. 'Shit!'

I shove the quartz and the paper back in my pocket for safety. 'Joe, calm down!'

'Bastard!' He yanks the calendar off the wall and rips it in half.

'Keep your voice down.' I jump up and catch hold of him before he can do any more damage.

To my surprise, he sags against me, arms round my neck as if I'm the only thing keeping him upright. 'Oh, Millie . . .'

We stand together in the middle of the room, surrounded by torn paper, the red numbered days from the calendar jumbled around our feet.

No crying now. When Joe lets go of me and steps back, I see, for the first time, the expression of total defeat that I'd seen on the photo of him as a much older man – and that's a thousand times worse than tears. 'Come on, sit down. It's all right.'

'How?'

'It's a confession.'

'Yeah, wonderful.' Joe's tone is scornful. 'A confession we can't show anyone, because they'd just say we made it up. And Frank's supposed to be *dead*, remember?' He laughs, bitterly. 'You realise he made that confession to make himself feel better? Too late for any punishment, but he wanted to ease his conscience – and give himself a giant pat on the back for being honest, of course.'

I suddenly remember something Mum said about Dad, really clearly – *he had affairs then confessed to me like that made it OK because he was being honest*. That made me furious with Dad, and it's like even if I still love him, I don't respect him any more. Doesn't sound like Joe ever respected Frank, because why would he? And he was too young to remember him properly from before he went away to fight. And Frank didn't just hurt him: Joe's life was already destroyed by what happened, and then having to hear that and no one in authority being interested. Maybe he'd forgotten about Mr Brighouse by then – who, anyway, would either have been dead or long retired . . . No wonder he'd had enough.

Even though the law would say Frank only caused two deaths, in reality he'd killed Joe by speaking up just as he'd killed Annie by silence, and Rose by . . . well, just coming into her life.

'He thought I'd be grateful enough to fix up his funeral. *Unbelievable*. I hope he rots in hell.'

'He deserves to. If that's what happens. Do you think God exists, Joe?'

'He'd better! I can just hear Frank at the pearly gates, telling St Peter that he was,' Joe puts on a whiny voice, '"only trying to help". You have no idea how typical that is – having his great scheme to dig Mum out of a hole that he'd made in the first place, and then making such a mess of it that . . . that . . .' Joe shakes his head violently. 'You can bet he wasn't near as sorry about Dorothy and Kathleen as he was sorry for himself – and he's never given two hoots about Annie. You know that thing about Dorothy telling him Annie helped Dad – Charles – with the shed? That was because he never asked about her, not once – we had to remind him she existed.' His hands clench into fists. 'That's it! He thought she was . . . Because she's not . . . not like other people . . . He thought he could just . . . That it wouldn't matter what happened to her. Because – to him – she's less important. And he thought I'd think that, too.' He turns to me, his brown eyes dark with emotion. 'Dorothy and me, we've *never* thought that, not for a single second.'

'You don't have to convince me, Joe.'

'God . . .' Joe buries his face in his hands. 'I *hate* him.'

A big bit of me wants to put my arms round him and never let go, but we're running out of time, and we need to think. 'That was something *else* Rose had to keep secret,' I say. 'His visit on the day of the party.'

'I reckon it was Mrs Millichip who came to the door.'

'But Shirley wasn't hurt until—'

'Mr Millichip went into hospital the same day. I said, didn't I?'

'Oh, right. Yes, you did.'

'She'd probably just come back. Bet she was wondering why Mum didn't invite her in for a cup of tea.'

'Do you reckon she thought the "fancy man" was there?'

'Maybe. I knew she was interviewed by the police, because of being there in the evening ... Perhaps she even said something about Rose being a bit off earlier in the day, but they were so sure it was Annie – right from the start – that they didn't take any notice.'

'Does Frank usually come here?'

'No, never. I thought last night was the first time. But I suppose we can trust that piece of paper, can we? How do you think it got in your pocket?'

'Not sure ... But I think it might have been Skye.'

'Is that your dog?'

I can't help laughing. 'My dad's girlfriend.'

'*Girlfriend?*'

'My parents aren't together any more.'

'Oh.' Joe looks awkward. 'That must be ... difficult.'

'Well, I'm certainly not happy about it, but compared to *this*, it's nothing ... Also, I think it's probably not such a big deal if a marriage breaks up in my time. At least, not as far as the neighbours or society in general or whatever is concerned.'

'It does sound as if attitudes have changed a bit – some of the things you've said ... Still sad, though.' He puts his arm round me, and it's lovely because it just feels so normal. 'But why would it be her?'

'Because the book got wet – in my time, I mean – and she offered

344

to dry it for me. I suppose she must have used a hairdryer or something, and the endpaper came unstuck.'

'What's an endpaper?'

'It's the paper fixed on the inside of the cover – if the book has hard covers, I mean, not a paperback. Like . . .' I go over and pick up a book about planes from the row on Joe's desk, and open it at the back. 'See?'

'I didn't know that was called an endpaper.'

'I wouldn't, either, only my dad writes children's books and my mum does the pictures, so they talk about stuff like that.'

Joe looks impressed, then frowns. 'The endpaper's glued down onto the cover, though.'

'But you could remove it, then put your piece of paper there and put new paper over the top and just glue it round the edges. The endpapers in *The Robe* are just plain, so it wouldn't be hard to match. I mean, *I* couldn't do it – it'd just be a mess – but *you* could. Those aeroplanes you made.' I point at the delicate wooden models. 'Really intricate and fiddly – you're obviously brilliant at stuff like that.'

'I suppose I could do it.' Joe examines the endpaper. 'If the paper was only folded in two underneath, that would make it almost flat. Paranoia would make people hide things, I suppose.' I can't see his expression properly because he's still staring down at the book but I know he's imagining his future self, in the lonely ruin of his life.

I put my hand on his. 'Don't, Joe. There's still time.'

'Not much. And I still don't understand how my note is here, in your pocket.'

'Well, I reckon Skye found the paper when she was drying the book, and put it into my pocket for safekeeping. That must have happened at some point between when I discovered the oscillator was in there a few hours ago, and just now. It stuck to the oscillator because there'd been something sticky in there as well – I know because I felt it.'

'But how could she put it in your pocket when you're here?'

'I've got a feeling I'm there, as well. When I came before, I must have been asleep in my time, but now ...' It flashes through my mind that I might be unconscious, maybe even in hospital, in the present, but this is not the moment to go there. 'Even if I'm not wearing this –' I point to my hoodie – 'there, I'm wearing it *here*, so ... Anyway, the point is, we've got it.'

'But we've just agreed it's no use. Mr Brighouse told me he couldn't do anything unless there was new evidence, remember?'

'It's no use *on its own*. But it's given us something to aim for – and we know where to find Frank, don't we? So, I suggest the first thing we should do is go and show this –' I pat my pocket – 'to Mr Smith.' Joe looks uncertain. 'He's the only other person who's going to understand, and we'll have more credibility with an adult on our side.'

'Yeah ...' Joe takes a deep breath, like pulling himself together, and a flicker of a smile crosses his face. 'Better than nothing.'

'OK, then.' I take the scrap of paper with the address out of Rose's handbag, loop the bag over my arm to leave it by her bedroom door, and I'm about to set off when Joe puts a hand on my arm.

346

'I know this isn't necessarily ... I mean, it might not work, but ... You're the best, Millie.'

I don't know what to say. My skin tingles as Joe leans towards me and puts up his hand to touch my cheek. I move so our foreheads are touching. 'Did we already do this?'

'You vanished halfway through.' He strokes my cheek. 'I hate it when girls do that.'

'Yeah, must be a real nuisance.' I put my arms round his neck. 'Promise I won't do it again.'

Chapter 60

'. . . and you said you might be able to help.'

Mr Smith was standing behind the shop's long counter in his brown dust coat when we arrived, examining a cuckoo clock, but the minute we walked in, he went to the door and turned the sign to 'Closed'. I showed him Joe's note – keeping hold of the cylinder – and we explained everything.

He's silent for so long that I think he's working out how to tell us there's nothing we can do. Finally, he says, like he's talking to himself, 'He must have been a deserter . . .'

'Yes,' Joe says. 'From Tobruk, June 1942. The army thought he'd gone missing in battle but he just legged it home. So he's a coward on top of everything else.'

'Not necessarily,' says Mr Smith, mildly. I'm surprised – Mr Smith told me he'd fought in the war, so I thought he'd be really down on that. 'Whatever your father may have been like beforehand, war changes everyone. There are things that no one should be expected to endure. Look at it this way – who wouldn't be afraid of death? There may have been a few soldiers who weren't scared,

348

but that isn't normal. Giving up – getting out – it's just a way of protecting yourself.'

'*You* didn't,' I say.

'No, but I understand why someone would. And the older I get, the more I think what a terrible business war is – for everyone.'

I think of what Rose told Joe: *I couldn't see a future for any of us. I wasn't strong enough.* She'd had her own war to fight, hadn't she?

'He must have ended up in Cairo or Palestine,' Mr Smith says.

'I don't even know that much,' Joe tells him. 'He won't talk about the war at all, or how he got home.'

'I believe there were quite a few of them, living on their wits and stealing military supplies to sell.' Like Mr Hewitt. Joe and I exchange glances. 'There was an amnesty for deserters a couple of years ago, but from what you say he's still using a false name, which makes me think he might be involved in criminal activity ... Of course, this may get your mother into hot water—'

'That's been worrying me. I mean,' Joe adds, 'what if we can't save Annie and it just makes everything worse for Mum?'

'It's a risk,' says Mr Smith, 'although there are extenuating circumstances – for one thing, you father appears to have deserted her as well as the army ... And if we succeed ...'

Rose will soon be a widow for real. Unless ... 'Mr Smith?'

'Yes, my dear?'

'You don't think – once the police find out about the blackmail – that they might decide that *she* did it?'

'That is certainly a possibility.'

'Then—'

'Hold your horses, Joe. As I said, it is a possibility, although I feel they are more likely to decide that this might just be a ruse to save Annie. However, if we do nothing, there is no likelihood of saving her. And if we can get a confession from Mr Palmer . . . ' I'm about to interrupt, but Mr Smith holds up a hand. 'We will tell Mr Brighouse that he has contacted Joe because he has something to tell him about the deaths of Dorothy and Kathleen – which is, in a manner of speaking, the truth – but we think it ought to be said in the presence of a solicitor. Where is Mr Brighouse's office, Joe?'

'Holborn. Brighouse and Hawkins.'

'Not too far away, then. Good. We'll have to hope Mr Brighouse isn't busy, but I rather doubt he will be – and in any case, this will take priority. We can then ask him to meet us at the hotel in the Seven Sisters Road, and you can ask to see Mr Palmer.'

'What if he isn't there?'

'Given the circumstances, I doubt he'll have gone very far. So, if you'll excuse me, I'll make the call, and—'

'But how are we going to get him to confess? I mean, he'll just tell Joe to get lost, won't he?'

'He might . . . but that, my dear, is where *you* come in.'

Chapter 61

Joe and I wait while Mr Smith goes into the back room to make the phone call. How am I supposed to make Frank confess? It's like both of them are just assuming I'll come up with something, because I did before. But with Mrs Hewitt, the typewriter was right there, with paper in the roller thing – there's no reason to think there'll be one of those in Frank's hotel room. And the thing with the lever in the execution chamber scared Florey and the maintenance man, but Mr Rutherford just assumed it was a mechanical fault . . . So if I tip over a chair or break a vase or something, Frank could put it down to a draught or a freak accident.

Joe leans against the counter, tapping his foot and looking as nervous as I feel, until – after what feels like a lifetime – Mr Smith comes back. 'All set. When we arrive, we're to go straight in, and Mr Brighouse will follow.'

'So he was OK with it?' I ask.

'So far, yes. Believe me, he's no more happy about any of this than you are. Of course, professional etiquette prevents him voicing an opinion, but I got the impression he believes Annie to be

351

just as much an innocent victim in this as your other sisters, Joe, and he's very concerned about your mother.'

'He's a good sort. I always thought he was on our side.'

'He said he'd need to make some arrangements, and then he'll be along. You understand, though, there's no guarantee this is going to work. All we can do is try.'

We walk in silence to the Holloway Road, cross over, then go past some shops and a couple of pubs to the Court Hotel. It's part of a row of Victorian houses, all narrow and four storeys high, and looks as if it's slowly falling to pieces.

We stand in front of the shabby door, gazing up at the sign with its flaking paint and the rows of crumbling windowsills.

'We'll only get one shot at this.' Mr Smith looks at Joe. 'Be polite – friendly, if you can. Whatever happens, do *not* lose your temper. And remember, as far as we're concerned, Millie's not here.'

Joe's face is rigid, like a mask, but he nods. Mr Smith rings the bell, and we wait.

What am I going to do when we get inside? Joe grabs my hand and squeezes it hard enough to hurt. He's looking at me like he's sure I've got this, but my mind's a complete blank. I can't bear the thought of letting him down, but what if I mess it up? There's so much at stake.

By the time we hear the click-clack of high heels on tiles and a woman with bright orange hair in an elaborate updo opens the door, I'm sweating and the back of my neck and scalp are prickling. My heart is beating so loud I'm kind of amazed that no one else can hear it, but I'm guessing that Joe's, at least, is doing the same.

'Help you?' She's plump, with a too-tight dress and a doughy, pouchy face covered in thick make-up.

'We've come to see James Marshall.'

'Oh?' The eyes narrow. 'Who's asking?'

Mr Smith holds up his hand and I barely see he's got a couple of notes ready between his thumb and finger before the woman snatches them and stands back to let us in.

The place is grubby and smells of cigarettes – not surprising as there's an overflowing ashtray on the reception desk. The woman jerks her head at the beaded curtain at the end of the hall: 'Number twenty – up the top.'

No one says anything as we climb the stairs. I reckon the walls must be pretty thin, because we can hear people moving about and there's lounge music coming from somewhere. A woman calls out 'Don't worry, dear, see you later,' and slams a door. I catch a waft of body odour and sickly perfume as she clatters past us.

By the time we're standing outside Room 20, my heart's hammering so hard it's almost painful. I daren't even look at Joe, and telling myself that I'll be invisible to Frank doesn't make any difference. Mr Smith looks at us both, and nods his head like, 'Ready?'

We nod back. Mr Smith squares his shoulders and knocks on the door.

There are sounds from inside – a drawer closing, then footsteps – and then it opens.

I know who I'm going to see, but it's still a shock. Joe, but older and filled out – more lines on the handsome, angular face and under the dark eyes, some flecks of grey in the black hair. White shirt with the sleeves rolled up, dark grey suit trousers. And – I sniff – alcohol.

I can see why he'd want to self-medicate. If I were him, I'd want to be unconscious for the next twenty-four hours, at least.

Frank steps back quickly, surprise and then anger flickering across his face. There's a few seconds' silence as we stare at him, and he stares at us – or at Joe and Mr Smith.

'Hello.' Joe's voice is calm, almost friendly. I'm amazed – and really impressed – that he can do it.

Frank's jaw tightens. 'Who's your friend?'

'Someone I'd like you to meet. Mr Smith, Frank Palmer, Frank Palmer, Mr Smith.' Joe gives a little bow to each man, like he's a footman at a palace. 'Now that we've completed the introductions, perhaps we might come in?'

Joe's behaving like he's acting in a play, and I can tell that Frank doesn't know what to do. He doesn't want us to come in, but there's no obvious reason to shut the door on us. I'm betting that, for all her protective looks when we came to the door, Mrs Orange Updo hasn't got a clue who he really is, and the last thing Frank wants is to attract attention.

Anyone could tell from the outside that the Court is *not* a luxury hotel, but this room is kind of basic – bed, dressing table with a big mirror attached to it, armchair, and wash basin – and looks like it could do with a makeover, or at least a clean. It's tidy, though – nothing of Frank's to be seen apart from a suitcase, a folded newspaper, and a small glass of what looks like whisky on the bedside table. I look around for anything I can use to scare him, but there's nothing.

'Joe thought you'd appreciate the company – in the circumstances.' Mr Smith sounds calm, too, as if our visit is the most normal thing in the world. 'Why don't you take a seat?'

Frank closes the door but doesn't move. 'What's going on?'

Mr Smith sits down on the armchair and crosses his legs as if he's settling down for a cosy chat. 'I can see you're upset. That's only to be expected at such a difficult time. Perhaps it might be a good idea if we all had a drink, Joe? I don't see any other glasses, but we shan't let that worry us, shall we?' Joe stares at him as if he's been hypnotised. 'I think,' Mr Smith continues, 'that Mr Palmer may have put the whisky somewhere in there.' He gestures towards the dressing table. 'Why don't you have a look?'

'Of course.' Joe goes over to the dressing table and starts opening drawers.

Frank's on him in a second, and I'm sure he's going to slam the drawer shut on Joe's fingers, but he stops short. 'What do you think you're doing?'

Joe doesn't flinch, even though Frank is right in his face. 'Just getting us a drink, that's all.'

'You're not old enough.'

'Oh, now,' Mr Smith, who hasn't moved from the armchair, is talking in a 'favourite uncle' voice, 'I think we can make an exception today, don't you?' I can't imagine where he's going with this – apart from unsettling Frank, which is obviously a good thing – but Joe seems to be playing along, so . . .

'And here we are.' Joe holds up a bottle of Johnnie Walker. 'Something else, too.' With the other hand, he holds up a small metal tube. 'Overnight guest, Frank?'

'None of your business.' Frank's losing it. I'm guessing Joe's never spoken to him like this before. 'You put that back.'

'Don't think I will, if it's all the same to you.' Without warning, Joe tosses the lipstick towards me. It's so totally unexpected that I only just manage to catch it.

Frank staggers backwards and sits down on the bed, mouth open. 'What the—?'

Joe ignores him, and passes the whisky to Mr Smith, who takes the cap off and raises the bottle in the air. 'Absent friends,' he says. 'You going to raise a glass, Frank?'

But Frank's not listening. He's staring at me, or rather, at the lipstick, which is – as far as he's concerned – hovering in the air on its own. Behind him, Joe gestures at the dressing table mirror.

I uncap the case with a flourish, lean over, and start to write on the glass in big, uneven capital letters, red as blood.

IT'S DOROTHY

'Fuck!' I turn to see Frank scrambling backwards over the bed. He's trembling, eyes wide, staring at my message.

'Steady on, no need for bad language.' Mr Smith recrosses his legs, looking very comfortable in his armchair. 'Don't want to disturb the neighbours, do we?'

'Look!' screams Frank, pointing a shaking hand at the mirror.

'Not sure what we're supposed to be looking at, old chap. Can you see anything unusual, Joe?'

'No.' Joe sounds puzzled and makes a show of looking round the room. 'Nothing out of the ordinary here.'

I carry on writing.

I KNOW WHAT YOU DID

Frank looks as if his eyes are about to pop out of his head. 'You can't ... you can't ... ' He doesn't seem to be able to get any more words out.

'Can't what, old chap?' Mr Smith. 'Something upset you?'

Frank whirls round and makes a sideways lunge for the pillow. For a second, I can't think what he's doing, and then I realise.

There's a gun in his hand.

Chapter 62

All I see in front of me is the round black O of the barrel, and for a second I think he's pointing it at me, but of course it's the mirror. I dive to the side and flatten myself against the wall by the window. The logical voice in the back of my mind telling me he can't hurt me is being drowned out by a great big silent scream of terror, so that it's all I can do not to pee myself.

Frank's not so lucky – I can see a dark stain on the crotch of his trousers.

'I say, old man.'

Frank whirls round, shaking so much that the gun judders in his hand. Joe's behind the armchair now, but Mr Smith is still sitting there, calm as anything. In fact, he's smiling.

'Why? Why can't you see it?'

'We can't see anything because there's nothing to see. Do put that thing down, there's a good chap.'

Frank's breathing is heavy now, like he's been running, but he doesn't move. I crawl back to the dressing table, lean over, and write:

SAVE ANNIE

Now I need to get his attention. Mr Smith is talking again, in a normal voice. 'You know, it occurs to me that you're behaving like a man with a very guilty conscience.'

I need to get Frank's attention. There's a lamp on the dressing table, with a heavy china base. If I lean over as far as I can . . .

'That's never good, you know. If you tell us what's troubling you, we can—'

Crash. I lose my balance and fall forward as Frank whirls round. There's a split second's pause – guessing he sees the writing – and he shoots.

The noise is *colossal*. I bury my face in the dusty carpet as the mirror explodes into a million pieces.

For a minute, I can't hear anything, and it's like that moment in the cemetery, when time stopped. I turn my head and see the carpet in front of me sparkling with tiny bits of glass. A large triangular piece with a straight edge, that must be from the bottom of the mirror, is hanging in the air in front of the wooden drawers, frozen, like it's in a photograph.

Then the whole room seems to make a weird jerking movement, and everything starts up again. The piece of glass lands on the floor, shattering, and there's a scream from somewhere downstairs, and footsteps running.

I watch Frank drop the gun and back away from the dressing table, tripping over the corner of the bed and falling sideways, onto his knees. He's gabbling and sobbing at the same time, and I can hardly make out what he's saying. 'I swear to you, I meant to give myself up. I was going to. I can't . . . '

The gun's on the carpet, about a metre away from me. Frank, still pleading and ugly-crying, has twisted round to face Joe, and doesn't notice it slide away when I crawl forward, glass pricking my skin, and nudge it underneath the bed.

When I get to my feet, I can see the glitter of glass on the eider-down, and Mr Smith standing up, one hand firmly clamped round Joe's wrist, like somebody holding a dog back from a fight.

'Francis Palmer, did you kill Dorothy Walsh and Kathleen Driscoll?' Mr Smith's voice is cold and formal, like a judge.

'Yes! I'm sorry. I never meant it, I was just trying to help Rose. It wasn't my fault . . . ' More sobs, and a second later, there's a splin-tering noise and the door flies open, slamming back against the wall as an enormous police officer charges into the room, followed by a second – and, at a much slower pace, a tall, silver-haired man in a pinstripe suit.

Chapter 63

For a moment, I thought that Frank might try to make a run for it, but he didn't even look round for the gun – and in any case, the big policeman was basically sitting on him about a second later. The pinstriped man, who turned out to be Mr Brighouse, repeated Mr Smith's question, and when Frank said yes, the policemen arrested him right there.

People were standing at the doors of their rooms watching as we trooped down the stairs – the policemen first, with Frank in handcuffs, and us following. We didn't see Mrs Orange Updo again – I heard Mr Brighouse say afterwards that the police had threatened to charge her with allowing prostitutes to operate on the premises, so I guess she decided to stay out of the way.

They took Mr Smith and Joe to the station to make statements – I went along too, squashed in the back of the car – while Mr Brighouse went back to his office. He told us he'd have to 'petition for a stay of execution' on the grounds that there was new evidence, and we must hope that Frank's confession would be enough for the Home Secretary to order things to be delayed while the police investigated ... So not perfect, but a lot better than the alternative.

I wondered if Frank would be able to claim that he'd been tricked into making a confession, but Mr Smith told me that the law about what the police could and couldn't do was a lot different in the 1950s, and he thought it would be all right.

Joe gives his statement, then I wait with him in a little side room while Mr Smith gives his. He's relieved – it's like all the tension just drained out of him – but he looks wiped out, and I know how he feels. 'You know,' he says after a long silence, 'I can see why Dorothy thought she ought to tell Frank about the blackmail.'

'Do you think your mum told her who it was?'

'I don't know. Maybe.'

'Do you think they had a heart-to-heart – Rose told Dorothy it was Mrs Hewitt and Dorothy told her what Charles did?'

Joe shakes his head. 'I don't think that's how she found out. Dorothy'd always want to protect Mum – and Victor, and Kathleen.'

'Kieran said that. And I reckon Charles convinced her that what he did was her fault – for being so attractive or some crap like that, and that's how Rose would see it, too.'

'He might have done that. Twisted everything ...' Joe frowns. 'Kieran's who you mentioned before, isn't it? He was helping you. Was that your boyfriend?'

'Yeah. It was really helpful talking to him.' Funny, I don't feel awkward saying this now. Something's changed, and it's not just because I'm exhausted. Joe's still gorgeous, and the quartz is still in my pocket, but my spidey senses are telling me I might not be here much longer . . . and that's OK because, although I want to stay with Joe, my life is elsewhere and I have to go back to it.

Or that's what I need to keep telling myself. There are a lot of things I want to say, but I know it's best if I don't go there.

I wonder if Joe feels something like this, too, because he gives me a funny little smile, kind of regretful. 'He sounds like a good sort.'

'He is . . . ' I suddenly remember something I've wanted to ask him, but with so much else going on, it kept slipping out of my mind. 'You know when you first saw me, you thought I was a prisoner?'

'Well, you obviously weren't a warder, so . . . '

'It's OK, I get it – but what did you think I was in there *for*?'

Joe looks embarrassed. 'Well, I didn't know. I thought maybe you were . . . I don't know, shoplifting or something like that. A delinquent.'

'*Delinquent?*' I grin at him.

'Tearaway.' He grins back. 'Scoundrel. Scamp.'

'Ha! I forgive you. Are you going to tell Rose you know about Charles?'

'Yes. When this is over. We can live together – her and me and Annie.'

He sounds so matter-of-fact and confident that I don't want to spoil it, so I hold up my hand to show him I'm crossing my fingers. 'I hope it works out. All of it.'

'We'd never have got here without you, Millie. I meant what I said – you *are* the best.'

'You're not so bad yourself.'

'As long as I'm not like him.'

'Frank?'

'Or Charles.'

'No chance. You're a million times better than either of them. In fact,' I deepen my voice, trying to sound like him, 'you're a good sort.'

'Very funny.'

'True, though. You are.' I lean my head on his shoulder. 'You're the best, too.'

Joe moves back, then rests his palm against my cheek and looks into my eyes.

I love you, I want to say. *I love you in your time and my time and all the time.* But I don't.

'Millie . . .' I think Joe's about to say something else, but at that moment Mr Smith comes back with a police officer, who tells us we're free to go.

The sun is shining as we walk back towards Mr Smith's shop. It seems incredible that this massive important thing has just happened, but everything else has just gone on as usual. I'm looking around at the shops and the people and the traffic and thinking, how can they not know? It's unreal.

As we turn the corner into Holloway Road, three things happen at once. A little boy, tugging at his mother's hand, almost bumps into Joe, just as I spot Pell's wool shop on the other side of the road and the dress shop next to it, and Mr Smith stops dead and looks at his watch. Then I catch sight of a clock mounted on the wall above a jeweller's shop and the realisation makes me stop dead, too.

Jean and Robbie. It's about to happen.

'What's up?' Joe, who's carried on walking, comes back to us.

'It's today,' I tell him. 'Here. Any minute.'

'What is?'

'The accident,' I whisper. 'The bus. Across there.'

'You mean . . . ' Joe glances at Mr Smith, who's standing in the middle of the pavement like he's rooted to the spot. People are muttering, trying to get past.

When I nod, Joe says, 'You didn't tell me that.'

'Didn't I? Oh, God.' I clutch his arm. 'I can see her. Look, in the wool shop. She's wearing a red beret, and—'

Joe slaps my hand away and starts to run.

Time doesn't stop, but I do. I can't move. I stand there, paralysed, as Joe starts to cross the lanes of the busy main road, dodging first one car, then another and another. Drivers hoot and shout and then a bus comes from the opposite direction, too fast, and Mr Smith is shouting in my ear and people behind us are jostling . . .

And suddenly my legs are working again, and I sprint towards the crossing—

And trip on an uneven paving stone and fall flat on my face. As I scramble to my feet, I can see that Joe's still running and the bus is bearing down on him and—

A colossal bang. The world disintegrates into a jumble of

screams and flying glass and the red beret with the velvet bow and a thousand different coloured balls of wool and Robbie's fat little legs in grey school socks and Joe's face and Mr Smith looking at his watch and the mirror exploding and Frank on the floor yelling and the noose hanging in the semi-darkness and Mr Rutherford's hand on the lever and someone's breathing underneath the white hood, the material going in and out, in and out, in and out, as the chaplain says 'Our Father', and there's no more time left, no more time, no more—

Chapter 64

Somebody's calling my name. Soft, gentle. 'It's all right, Millie. You're safe, darling. It's all right . . .'

Voices. Bright light. White room. Narrow bed.

No, wait.

Not room, cubicle. Not bed, trolley. Rails on either side.

Hospital. But . . .

Mum and Dad. Together. Must be dreaming.

'What's the time?'

'Ten past three.' Dad's voice.

'In the morning.' Mum leans forward. She's got a suntan.

Of course – she's been in Greece.

'Where am I?'

'Hospital.'

'Why?'

'You just keeled over. You've been unconscious for nearly twenty-four hours.' Dad peers at me. 'You didn't bang your head or anything, did you?'

'No. I just felt a bit weird, and then . . . I'm not sure, really.'

Time gets really slippery after that. I drift away again, and then there's a doctor, asking me questions, and then some other people, and Mum and Dad again, or maybe somebody else and then Mum and Dad again, or . . .

Actually, I don't really know.

After a few days – I think – things get normal enough for me to go home with Mum. It's nice being back in my room again – more space, for one thing, and all my stuff.

Mum's friend Cathy came back from Greece with her, which is unexpected – but nice, because Mum's happier than I've seen her in a long time. The doctor said they couldn't find anything wrong with me, but I think Mum's a bit scared of me going weird again, because she's being a bit funny about me going out by myself. I *know* there's some stuff missing in my head – like, blank spaces that feel like they should contain something important – but only from last week, although I can remember being at Dad's and having arguments and watching films and even what we ate. And being in the vegan café with Kieran, although I don't think we're dating again, or he'd have messaged me . . . wouldn't he? That doesn't seem like it's the really important bit, though. There's something else.

It's been over a week now, and I'm pretty much back on track with schoolwork, which is good, plus I've seen Yaz and the others – who had a ton of questions I couldn't answer because I don't really know what happened.

Mum's just asked me if I've got any washing because she wants to make up a load – which reminds me that the clothes I was wearing when they took me to hospital came home in a plastic bag. When I search, I find it under the bed: a bunch of stuff, including – hurrah! – my favourite hoodie. Dad said I'd been out somewhere, came back saying I felt ill, and then passed out – but where? And what was I doing? Some of the clothes look like they've got mud on them. The doctor kept asking me if I'd 'taken something', but I heard him tell Dad they'd done tests and nothing came up, so I guess the answer's no.

I give Mum all of the clothes except the hoodie, which I want to wear even if it is a bit dirty, and tell her I'm going for a walk and she's not to worry because it's broad daylight and I'll be fine.

The weather's not that warm today – so the hoodie – but I just want to be by myself for a bit with no one fussing or asking me if I'm OK. I feel like if I go towards Dad's flat it might help, so I get on the bus and look out of the window, hoping that'll spark something off, but it doesn't make any difference. When we go past the vegan café, I wonder what Kieran and I talked about in there. Maybe I ought to message him and ask?

It's not such a terrible idea. Kieran's been having mental health issues, so he might understand. I don't feel like we had a row or anything, and it's not like I've got anything else to work with right now, so . . .

When I pull my phone out of my pocket, a scrap of paper flutters to the floor.

I pick it up and turn it over: Joe Palmer, 13 November 1991.

Joe Palmer.

Joe.

A sudden pain, like a shard of glass, in my chest.

I take a deep, jagged breath.

There's an explosion inside my head. Everything sort of rushes towards me at once, so that I actually duck in my seat, and then it's like an enormous jigsaw assembling itself into a picture, every piece at the same time, and I *know*.

OK, that happened.

Except, what about the end?

I check my phone for the photo I took of Joe's grave, but it isn't there.

Does that mean our plan worked? If it did, the Wikipedia entries will be different. I stare at my phone for a long time. Shall I?

My hands are shaking as I start to type Annie's name, but after only a few letters I stop. Even if I could bring myself to click on the link, I can't find out that way, like it's just some random fact. I need to *talk* to someone.

Only one person to ask – so long as he's still there – and we're just coming up to the right stop.

Chapter 65

I find the shop easily. It's a lot bigger, because they've taken over the two buildings on either side, and brightly painted, with cool furniture as well as clocks. The ceiling-high wooden cabinets are still there in the original bit, though, and the long wooden counter.

The man who bobs up from behind it must be in his fifties, and he's not wearing a brown dust coat, but a smart suit and thick-framed black glasses. 'Can I help you?'

'I'd like to speak to Mr Smith, please.'

'Here I am.' The man smiles and turns his hands palm up like, *Ta-da!* 'Fire away.'

'Oh, sorry, no. The person I'm looking for is ... well, quite a lot older.'

'OK.' He puts his head on one side and looks at me. 'Are you, by any chance, called Millie?'

I stare at him. 'Yes.'

'So you *do* exist!'

'Well, yeah, but ... how come you know my name?'

'He always told us – if Millie comes, send her straight to me. He

371

described you – quite well, actually – but to be honest, I always thought it was some weird joke.'

'When you say "always" . . . '

'Oh, as long as I can remember. Since before you were born, in fact. Don't worry, I shan't ask you to explain. If he wants to tell me, I'm sure he will.' He lifts up the flap at the end of the counter. 'Come on. It's through the door, up the stairs – mind out for the stairlift – and on your right.'

I find Mr Smith – much older, and hunched over, but I'd recognise him anywhere – sitting by the window in his wheelchair in a lovely room with clocks all over the walls. 'I thought it must be you, my dear. I hope you're all right, are you?'

'Well, I woke up in hospital, and then I couldn't remember anything for a bit – from 1955, I mean – but I'm OK now . . . Except, I don't know what happened.'

'No good having a story without the ending. Why don't you nip through there –' he gestures at a door – 'and make us a cup of tea, and then I'll tell you. You'll find everything ready.'

There's a tray on the kitchen table, with everything set out, including two cups. Guess he really has been expecting me, then.

'You were really brave,' I say, when we're drinking our tea. 'When we were in that room with Frank.'

'No more than you.'

'Yes more – he couldn't have hurt me with that gun, but you could have been killed.'

'What did I have to live for, back then? Jean and Robbie would have been killed by that bus before they'd had a chance to find out

372

what happened to me. Not caring isn't bravery, Millie. What Joe did – *that* was brave.'

'What happened? I mean, I saw him cross the road, but ...'

'He saved them, my dear. All of them – our daughter Jenny was born the following year, in January. She's a grandmother herself, now. That was Robbie's son you saw downstairs. He's been in charge since Robbie retired – that was about ten years ago, just after Jean died.'

'I'm sorry, Mr Smith.'

'Don't be, my dear. We had a wonderful life together, and she passed away very peacefully. Not everybody meets their right person, but as Jean said at the end, we were very lucky – I was hers, and she was mine.'

'And Annie? Was it all right?'

'Yes. A reprieve. Thanks to you, Frank made a full confession – and many people would say he got exactly what he deserved. Are you all right, my dear?'

'I ...' I shake my head, unable to collect my thoughts. I had been so focused on finding a way to save Annie that I hadn't really considered that the only way it would happen was for somebody else to be hanged. I'd thought about what the reality of that meant – what I'd seen in the execution chamber – only for her, and not for anybody else, so that what would happen to Frank, if he were found guilty, had been abstract, with no details. And *of course* I'm glad about Annie – *more* than glad – but ... 'Sorry, I don't know how to put it into words.'

'I think I understand something of what you're feeling, Millie.

The world is not a perfect place. Sometimes even right and wrong can be complicated – and that's no less true now than it was in 1955. But better, surely, that a guilty person was hanged than an innocent person, while the guilty one remained unpunished?'

'Yes, of course.' I stare into my teacup for a while, thinking about this. When I look up, Mr Smith is watching me.

I almost can't bear to ask. 'What about Joe?'

His face tells me the answer.

Chapter 66

'We've got a lovely day for it.' Robbie helps Mr Smith into the wheelchair and shuts the car door. 'I'll meet you at the flower stall once I've parked.'

'By the way,' I say, as I push Mr Smith through the cemetery gates, 'would you like the clock back? I mean, it's in pieces, but . . .'

'No. It's served its purpose.'

'What happened to yours?'

'For now, it's an ordinary clock. But I've told my family to take good care of it – maybe it'll help somebody else, some day.'

'They don't know, do they? About . . .'

'Only that a very brave young man saved Jean and Robbie.'

'He didn't seem surprised when you asked him to drive us up here.'

'We often come. Jean's here, after all – as I will be, in due course.'

'Joe . . . Was it quick?'

I stop pushing when Mr Smith twists round to look at me. 'Very quick. He shoved Jean and Robbie out of the way the second before the bus hit him. He was dead before I managed to get across the road.' He reaches out his hand. 'I am sorry, my dear. You and he made a good team.'

I can feel tears pricking the back of my eyes.

'In another life, perhaps . . . ' Stop, I think. Please don't say we'd be each other's right person.

'Yes. But not in this one.' I'm managing not to cry, but only just.

Mr Smith squeezes my hand. 'He'll never really leave you, you know. He'll always be a source of strength. And what happened – the wonderful thing you did – that will stay with you for ever.'

Five minutes later, Robbie comes back with several bunches of flowers, which Mr Smith holds while I push his wheelchair up the path. It's a bit stony and uneven, especially the last bit, but we manage OK, and Robbie goes off to fill his watering can.

The grave is in the same place, and the stone is the same size and shape, but now the inscription reads:

FRANCIS JOSEPH DRISCOLL
28.01.1938 – 12.06.1955

HE GAVE HIS LIFE
TO SAVE A MOTHER AND CHILD

I put my fingertips against the letters, hoping to feel something, but there's only cold, hard stone. I know that Joe wasn't – isn't – my right person in either of our worlds, but only in the 'now' of the midnight clock, which was as close as we could ever get to being real at the same time. *But*, I tell him silently, *I'll always love you.*

As I step back, I can feel the ache of loss in my heart – only now it's not sharp but blunt and dull, as if I've been feeling it for a long time and I'm used to it.

There's a gravestone beside Joe's which wasn't there before, with two names on it:

ALEXANDER MALCOLM BRIGHOUSE

20.08.1908 – 17.10.1994

ROSE ETHEL BRIGHOUSE

27.02.1913 – 15.04.1989

'So . . .' I sit down on the patch of grass beside Mr Smith's chair. 'Rose married *Mr Brighouse*?'

'She did. I think she found a measure of peace in the end, poor woman.'

'Joe would have been pleased,' I tell him. 'He liked Mr Brighouse. What happened to Charles?'

'Well, I don't know the whole story . . .' Mr Smith looks down at me, and I remember that we didn't tell him about Dorothy. 'But I've always suspected that there was an element of . . . well, let's call it natural justice – but in an entirely literal form. I don't know if Joe told you about the abattoir, did he?'

'Yes. Charles worked there.'

'He did indeed. About six months after Annie was freed, there was an accident. A gate was left open and some of the cows made a run for it. You can hardly blame the poor beasts, and of course the traffic panicked them ... It was all quite a mess, and a few of the people trying to round them up were badly injured – although Charles Driscoll was the only fatality.'

'Some might say it served him right.' The sharp voice makes me jump – I'd been concentrating so hard on what Mr Smith was saying that I hadn't heard anyone coming.

'Well, hello there.' I scramble to my feet as Mr Smith greets two elderly ladies, both carrying bunches of flowers. 'Shirley, this is Millie.' I nearly tell him we've already met, but she obviously doesn't recognise me, and I realise that in this new version of events, we probably haven't.

'Nice to meet you, dear.'

'We've come to see Joe and Mum,' says her companion, and I find myself staring at the round face, blue eyes and beaming smile of Annie Driscoll.

Chapter 67

'You visited me, didn't you?'

I open my mouth, but it's like I've been struck dumb. I feel Mr Smith's hand on my arm, like a warning, but still I can't think of anything to say.

Shirley's looking confused. 'What do you mean, Annie?'

'Oh, she did.' Annie's voice is firm and certain. 'Long time ago. Except . . .' she peers at me, 'now I can see you're far too young. Must have been someone who looked exactly like you.' She laughs. 'Don't mind me. I get confused sometimes.'

'That's OK. I'm Millie – nice to meet you.'

'And I'm Annie.' She looks delighted. 'It's nice to meet you, dear.' She leans towards me and adds, quietly, 'After all this time.'

Mr Smith told me on the way home that Annie moved in with Shirley at Aylmer Terrace after Rose and Mr Brighouse passed away, because Shirley's parents had died a couple of years earlier and she was lonely by herself.

Two weeks later, I still can't stop thinking about it all. Annie had seen me – or anyway she had a memory of me. It was like that moment with Helene Bone being cool with me knowing Joe even though he died before I was born: something being not true but not not true, either.

I know that life isn't a fairy tale, and that deserving a happy ending doesn't mean you'll get one, but all the same ... Annie seemed happy enough, telling me all about the different kinds of flowers, and how she and Shirley come every week to change them, then showing me how she liked to arrange them in the containers; and Mr Smith said he thought Rose had found 'a measure of peace' – which, given her life, was certainly better than nothing. And Mr and Mrs Smith had been happy – and, although I can never actually know this, maybe Joe dying like he did was a happy ending, in a way.

I think about him often. He could never be my right person, but I think what Mr Smith said was true, and he will always be a part of me, as long as I live.

Mum's shouting up the stairs, something about a parcel. That won't be a fairy tale, either, because she's not going to get back with Dad ... although I think there *might* be something going on between her and Cathy. Thinking about it, she always got *really* excited whenever Cathy came to stay, and they've always written to each other – real letters – as well as messaging and Zooming all the time. Plus, I've been wondering about what Cathy said on the phone, about it being 'complicated'. At the time, I thought she meant generally complicated, but now I think it might have been about her and Mum – especially as Mum told me it wasn't all

Dad's fault and how she was still figuring stuff out . . . Who knows? Perhaps she and Cathy are each other's right person.

I'm not sure that Skye is Dad's, but she is definitely OK. Actually, more than OK, because if it hadn't been for her, we'd never have known about Frank's confession – because it turns out I was right and she *did* put that note in my pocket. She didn't read the note because she reckoned it was private, so no explanation required, just a big hug. She said it was just as well she had put the note in my pocket, because when she was helping Dad pack up my stuff to bring back here, she couldn't find the book. She was really apologetic, but I said not to worry because *The Robe* had served its purpose – which is absolutely true.

I don't have the main bit of the note, either. It must have fallen out of my pocket, along with the cylinder, when I was picking myself up off the pavement just as the bus crashed.

I can't imagine what's waiting for me downstairs, because I never get parcels – unless I order something, and I haven't – and it's not my birthday.

'Here you go.' Mum waves a big jiffy bag at me from the kitchen table, where she and Cathy are chatting over coffee. 'Kieran's mum brought this round. She said that talking to you has made a huge difference to him. You didn't tell me he's not been well.'

'Didn't I?' I say, innocently. As far as Mum's concerned, me and Kieran are still a thing, because I didn't want to stress her out more than she already was by telling her how ill he was or how I didn't have a clue how to deal with it. 'I'm glad he's feeling better. Want to join us? You can tell me what's been going on with you and him.'

'Yeah . . . maybe later.'

'OK. Let's go somewhere for dinner – just the two of us – and we can have a proper chat. Catch!'

She's a hopeless shot and I only just manage to snag the thing before it hits a bunch of crockery on the dresser – but then I realise it wouldn't have done much damage, because it weighs almost nothing.

I take it up to my room and open it. There's a scribbled note inside.

Millie,

Went back to Aylmer Terrace and found this in the skip so I thought you should have it.

Hope you're OK now and everything worked out. I have more good days now and I'd like to know what happened so message me (but only if you want).

Kieran x

He must be feeling a bit better, or he wouldn't have done it – and he clearly did get interested, in spite of himself, which *has* to be a good sign. Maybe I'll get in touch . . .

I think I *do* want to.

But where's the thing he found? I shove my hand into the jiffy bag, which really is *waaay* too big for purpose, and scrabble around till I pull something out: an envelope that looks like it's been buried – which, if it comes from the garden at Aylmer Terrace, it probably has. Under the dirt, I can see an address and a stamp, scribbled over, and a shopping list, with my name written over it in heavy capital letters.

Looks like Joe's writing.

I suddenly remember him in the garden, huddled up by the coal bunker and clutching Rose's handbag, hiding from Charles and Mr Hewitt. Rose had saved old envelopes to write on, hadn't she? There was a small notepad with a leather cover and a tiny pencil attached to it in her bag, as well.

That's what's inside this envelope – five little pieces of paper, folded over. We'd argued, and I'd gone back into the house to follow Mrs Hewitt upstairs. I'm betting he wrote this then, in the light from the kitchen window, and ran down the garden in the dark to put it in the tin he'd hidden in the Anderson shelter, which is how it ended up in the skip.

Wherever Joe is, he isn't here. He's gone, and this is the last contact I shall ever have with him.

I take a deep breath, smooth out the pages, and read.

Millie,

I don't know what will happen. I don't know if you will disappear before I can tell you this, or if you will ever see this letter. But I know you tried your best to help me, and I want you to know, from my heart, that nobody in the world could have been a better friend.

Have a wonderful life.

With all my love for ever, Joe x

Acknowledgements

I am very grateful to Veronique Baxter, Sue Bonfatti, Katy Brigden, Nick Canty, Fraser Critchton, Tim Donnelly, Katya Ellis, Ella Garrett, Nick Green, Paddy Gregan, James Gurbutt, Mike Harpham, Sara Langham, Stephanie Melrose and Alice Watkin for their enthusiasm, advice, and support during the writing of this book.